Praise for *Jewel of Persi*[illegible]

“Few authors capture the heart and soul o[illegible] te, a master of mood and majesty whose epic tale[illegible] page to become people, passion and life lessons et[illegible] ous historical detail and vivid prose to flesh-and-blo[illegible] you almost see, hear and feel, the story of Queen Esther leaps from the pages of history in a manner that will leave you breathless. Easily one of the most haunting books I’ve read this year.”

Julie Lessman

Award-winning author of The Daughters of Boston and Winds of Changes series

“Roseanna White’s books always thrill and inspire. When I see one of her titles, I grab it right up, because she writes with such insight and depth. Combine excitement, romance, and multi-dimensional characters with her talent for weaving stories that inspire without being preachy, and you have a ‘Keeper’ on your hands!”

Loree Lough

Author of 77 award-winning novels, including those soon to be released in her Lone Star Legends and First Responders series.

“This is biblical fiction at its absolute best. Roseanna White writes fiction saturated with immense truths. You will love this intriguing story of tenderness and nobility, cutthroat suspense and fierce love. Woven throughout is a bottom line truth; God’s purposes will be fulfilled even in times of battle. A true keeper for every book collector! Don’t miss out!”

Sharlene MacLaren

Bestselling author of Little Hickman Creek, The Daughters of Jacob Kane, and in 2011, River of Hope

And several stand-alone contemporary novels.

Absolutely loved this book! A splendid recapturing of the story of Esther from a different point of view that keeps the reader wondering how it is going to work out. White has an ability to use the historical details to polish the story to a high sparkle, instead of making it dull. The story will keep the reader turning the pages to discover how this all works out in God's overarching plan of history for the Jewish people. Can't wait to see what is next from the pen of Roseanna White.

Golden Keyes Parsons

Author of the Darkness to Light trilogy

"In *Jewel of Persia*, Roseanna M. White engages her readers in a beautiful story of the power of love, the strength of friendship, and the faithfulness of our Lord. Ms. White has a remarkable way of whisking her readers back in time with believable characters and a rich, detailed setting. The twists of this plot will leave the reader breathless yet hungrily turning each page for more, and when the last sentence has been read, *Jewel of Persia* will remain in the heart of the biblical fiction fan."

Jen Stephens
Author of *The Heart's Journey Home*

"This is the familiar story of Esther but recounted in a fresh, new way. Author Roseanna M. White dishes up quite a love story filled with intrigue and danger, told from a perspective that's fictional yet entirely believable. . . . If biblical fiction is your passion, *Jewel of Persia* is a book you won't want to miss."

Michelle Griep
Author of *Gallimore* and *Undercurrent*

"*Jewel of Persia* took my breath away! Roseanna White is an amazing storyteller, and as I read this brilliant story, the prose danced off the pages, breathing life into a host of characters. I fell in love with Kasia and Xerxes, and found myself cheering for them, *loving* them, despite their imperfections. Only a talented author like White could pull that off, and I am humbly impressed with her writing. This author *knows* the craft. I can't wait to read more from Roseanna White. She never disappoints."

Sandi Rog
Author of *The Master's Wall*

Jewel of Persia

Roseanna M. White

This is a work of fiction. All characters and events portrayed in this novel are either fictitious or used fictitiously.

JEWEL OF PERSIA

WhiteFire Publishing
13607 Bedford Rd NE
Cumberland, MD 21502

ISBN: 9780976544470

Cover model photo by Christian Agha Photography
Jewelry design by Vaphiadis Jewelery, Athens, Greece
(www.GreekJewelryShop.com)

Cover Design by Tekeme Studios (www.Tekeme.com)

To the jewels of my life, David, Xoë, and Rowyn.
And of course, my parents and sister, and their unfailing support.

Also, special thanks to Stephanie, Mary, Carole, Dina, and Sandi.
Invaluable critique partners ~ Precious friends.

Characters and Key Places

Abba (AB-buh) – see Kish

Amestris (uh-MESS-triss) – (historical) Queen of Persia, wife of Xerxes; a.k.a Vashti of the Book of Esther

Amytis (AM-i-tiss) – (historical) elder daughter of Xerxes and Amestris

Artabanas (art-uh-BAN-us) – (historical) younger brother of the late King Darius, uncle to Xerxes

Artaxerxes (art-uh-ZIRK-seez) – (historical) youngest son of Xerxes and Amestris; succeeded Xerxes

Artaynte (ar-TAIN-tuh) – (historical) daughter of Masistes

Artemisia (art-i-MEEZ-ee-uh) – (historical) female commander of several ships in Xerxes' army

Atossa (uh-TOSS-uh) – (historical) wife of the late King Darius, daughter of Cyrus the Great, mother of Xerxes

Bijan (bee-ZHAHN) – (fictional) Persian noble, member of the Immortals, friend of Zechariah

Chinara (chin-AR-uh) – (fictional) Xerxes' favorite daughter

Choaspes River (choe-AS-peez) – river that winds around Susa, renowned for its sweet waters

Cyrus (SY-rus) – (fictional) one of Xerxes' sons

Darius (DAR-ee-us) – (historical) grandson of King Darius, eldest son of Xerxes and Amestris

Demaratus (de-MARE-uh-tus) – (historical) exiled king of Sparta, Xerxes' advisor

Desma (DEZ-muh) – (fictional) Kasia's most trusted maidservant

Diona (dee-OH-nuh) – (fictional) one of Xerxes' concubines

Eglah (EGG-lah) – (fictional) one of Kasia's younger sisters

Esther (ESS-ter) – (historical) cousin and ward of Mordecai

Haman (HAY-muhn) – (historical) trusted official of Xerxes and (fictionally) best friend of Masistes

Hegai (HEG-eye) – (historical) a eunuch, the custodian in charge of the harem

Hystaspes (hih-STASS-peez) – (historical) second son of Xerxes and Amestris

Ima (EE-muh) – see Zillah (I)

Iona (ee-OH-nuh) – (fictional) one of Kasia's maidservants

Jasmine – (fictional) wife of Xerxes, friend of Kasia, mother of Chinara

Joshua – (fictional) Kasia's second eldest brother

Kasia (ka-SEE-uh) – (fictional) heroine; daughter of Kish and Zillah, sister of Zechariah, friend of Esther, and concubine to Xerxes

Keturah (keh-TUR-uh) – (fictional) Mordecai's late wife

Kish – (fictional) father of Kasia (called Abba by his children)

Lalasa (luh-LOSS-uh) – (fictional) one of Xerxes' concubines

Mardonius (mar-DOH-nee-us) – (historical) cousin of Xerxes, a commander of the army

Masistes (ma-SISS-teez) – (historical) younger full brother of Xerxes, son of Atossa and King Darius

Memucan (meh-MOO-cuhn) – (historical) one of Xerxes' counselors

Mordecai (MOR-de-KY)– (historical) cousin and guardian of Esther

Otanes (oh-TAY-neez) – (historical) head of the army, father of Amestris

Parsisa (par-SISS-uh) – (historical figure, fictional name) wife of Masistes, mother of Artaynte

Persepolis (per-SEH-poh-liss) – less mentioned but wealthiest of Persia's capital cities

Pythius (PITH-ee-us) – (historical) wealthiest man in Lydia, second only to Xerxes in the world

Rhodogune (ROH-doh-GOON-uh) – (historical) younger daughter of Xerxes and Amestris

Ruana (roo-AH-nuh) – (fictional) sister of Bijan

Sarai (sare-EYE) – (fictional) Kasia's youngest sister

Sardis (SAR-diss) – capital of Lydia, a province in the Persian empire

Susa (SOO-suh) – the most mentioned and most southerly of the four Persian capitals; a.k.a. Shushan

Theron (THER-uhn)– (fictional) Kasia's head eunuch and bodyguard

Xerxes (ZIRK-seez)– (historical) hero; King of Persia and Media

Zechariah (ZECK-uh-RY-uh)– (fictional) Kasia's eldest brother

Zethar (ZETH-are)– (historical) one of Xerxes' eunuchs and bodyguards

Zillah (I) (ZILL-uh)– (fictional) wife of Kish, mother of Kasia (called Ima by her children)

Zillah (II) (ZILL-uh)– (fictional) daughter of Kasia, granddaughter of above

Susa, Persia
The third year of the reign of Xerxes

The river called to Kasia before she saw it, the voice of its sweet waters promising a moment of unbridled sensation. Kasia cast a glance over her shoulder at her young friend. She ought not go. Abba forbade it—rarely enough to keep her away, but today she was not alone. Still. Esther was not opposed to adventure, once one overcame her initial reservation.

Kasia gripped her charge's hand and grinned. "Come. Let us bathe our feet."

Esther's creased forehead made her look far older than twelve. "We could get in trouble."

Kasia laughed and gave the small hand a tug. "That is half the fun. Oh, fret not, small one. My father is too busy to notice, and your cousin will not be back from the palace gates until evening."

"But the king's household is still here. It is unsafe."

"We will only be a moment." She wiggled her brows in the way that always made her young friend smile. "It will be fun. Perhaps we will even glimpse the house of women."

Esther's eyes brightened, and she let Kasia lead her another few steps. "Do you think Queen Amestris will be out? I have heard she is the most beautiful woman in all the world."

"Only until little Esther grows up." She tugged on a lock of the girl's deep brown hair and urged her on. The Choaspes gurgled up ahead, where it wound around Susa and gave it life.

Esther laughed and plucked a lily, tucked it behind Kasia's ear. "I will be blessed to have a quarter of your beauty, Kasia. Perhaps if I do, Zechariah will marry me."

"And then we shall be sisters at last." Kasia twirled Esther in a circle. A merry thought, though it was hard to imagine Zechariah settling down. He was two years her elder, but showed no signs of maturity at eighteen. If anyone could inspire it, though, it was sweet little Esther. Once she grew up, half the men in the Jewish population would probably bang at Mordecai's door . . . and probably a few of their Persian neighbors as well.

Esther joined her in her impromptu dance, then sighed happily. "I should very much like sisters and brothers. I am blessed that Cousin Mordecai took me in, but having him as a father provides no siblings."

Kasia smiled but knew she had better change the subject before Esther fell into memories of the parents she had lost. Though three years past, the tragedy could still pull the girl into a vortex of pain. "Any time you want to borrow one of mine, you are welcome. My ima certainly has her work cut out for her today, trying to keep a rein on them in weather so fair. I daresay much of the royal house will be out to enjoy it. Surely we can spot a few of them."

"And how will we know the queen? Will she be encrusted with jewels?"

Kasia laughed, even as guilt surged to life. She ought to get home and help her mother with the little ones. Soon. Five minutes and she would be on her way, back in ample time to check the bread and sweep the day's dirt from the floor. For now, she could spare a thought or two to the palace. "She will be decked out in the finest Persia has to offer, surely."

"Cousin Mordecai says that the king wears jewels in his beard at his feasts."

She had heard the same stories but widened her eyes with exaggerated shock for Esther's benefit. "In his beard? What if one were to fall into his soup?"

Their laughter blended into that of the river, and Kasia's pulse kicked up. The weather was warming again, and when the sweltering summer heats came, the king's entourage would leave. Kasia could not wait for the change in seasons. Her body may not tolerate it for long, but there was something intoxicating about feeling the sun's burning rays upon her head. She always volunteered to gather up the barley seeds they roasted on the roads in the summer, and not just to spare her mother the task. To feel it. To be nearly overwhelmed. To watch the world around her quiver in the rising heat and let herself sway with it.

Esther paused a fathom from the river's bank. "It will be freezing. The snows still cover the mountains."

Perfect. Kasia grinned and sat down to unfasten her shoes. "We will only step in for a moment."

Esther sat, too, and soon they tossed their shoes aside and helped each other up. They ran the six steps to the river, where icy water lapped at Kasia's toes. She shrieked. "Oh, it *is* cold! Why did I let you talk me into this?"

Esther laughed and pushed her another step into the water. "I? Ha! And you are supposed to be the responsible one, taking care of *me*."

"Responsibility begs to be escaped now and again." She waded out one more step, careful to lift her tunic above the water.

When Esther stepped in, she gasped and leapt back onto the bank. "You are mad, Kasia. Your feet will be ice all night."

A price worth paying for this freedom slicing through her. How could something that touched only one part affect her whole body? Her feet felt the prickles of a thousand needles that coursed like spears up her legs. A shiver sped along her spine, down her arms, and left her laughing. She turned to Esther, intending to tease her into joining her.

The levity died in her throat. Faster than she knew she could move, she jumped back onto the bank and put herself between Esther and the men that stood a stone's toss away, watching them.

"Kasia? What are you . . ." Esther trailed off, having apparently spotted the men. Fear sharpened the intake of her breath. "Your father will kill us."

"Hush." Kasia reached back with one arm to be sure her charge remained behind her. Her gaze stayed on the men. They each had a horse beside them, and gold roundels on their clothing. Bracelets, torcs, gems. A million things that shouted nobility and wealth.

A million things that meant trouble.

She dipped her head, gaze on the ground. Had she been alone, she would have grabbed her shoes and run, perhaps with some vague apology as she scurried off. But she could not risk it, not with Esther there too. What if the girl tripped? Or moved too slowly? Kasia could never leave her young friend exposed to two strangers.

One of the horses whinnied, fabric rustled, and footsteps thudded. Kasia tossed modesty to the wind and glanced up.

The taller of the two men moved forward. His were the more expensive clothes, the heavier gold. He had a dark, trim beard that did nothing to hide his grin. "My apologies for startling you. We should have continued on our way after we realized your cry was not for help, but I was intrigued. You often wade into the river swollen from mountain snows?"

Esther gripped Kasia's tunic and pulled her back a half step to whisper, "Kasia, just give your apologies so we can *go*."

Sage advice, except she doubted a man of import would take kindly to his questions going unanswered. She forced a small smile. "Not often, lord, no. I rarely have the time, and I should not have taken it today. My parents are expecting me home. If you will excuse me."

The man held out a hand. "Far be it from me to detain you, fair one. But it is not safe for a beautiful young woman and her sister to be out alone. Do you not know that the court is yet in Susa? What if some nobleman concerned only with his pleasure came across you?"

The words ought to have terrified her, given the sweep of his gaze. But then his tone . . . teasing, warm. A perfect match to that easy smile.

Her chin edged up. "I expect if such a man were to come upon me, he would try to charm me before accosting me. Then I would have ample time to convince him that his pleasure would be better pursued elsewhere."

He chuckled, took another step closer. "But on the off-chance that your wit would fail to persuade such a man—there are some very determined men in the king's company—I feel compelled to see you safely home."

"No! I mean . . . it is not far, we will be fine. I thank you but . . . ."

The man's eyes narrowed, his smile faltered. "You must be a Jew."

A logical deduction—her trepidation at being caught with a Persian man would not be shared by a woman of his own people.

Still. The tone of his voice when he said the word *Jew* was enough to make her shoulders roll back. As if they were less because they had been brought to this land as captives a century ago. As if they had not proven themselves over the years.

She narrowed her eyes right back. "Proudly." Not waiting for a reply, she spun away and grabbed Esther's hand.

"Kasia, our shoes."

"We shall grab them on the way by and put them on when we get back," she murmured.

A mild curse came from behind them, along with quick footsteps. "Come now, you must not walk home barefoot. Please, fair one, you need not fear me. Sit. Put on your shoes."

He reached the leather strips before they did, scooped them up, and held them out. The gleam of amusement still in his eyes belied the contrition on his face. He offered a crooked smile, his gaze never leaving Kasia's.

She had little choice. Esther's fingers still in hers, she reached out and took their shoes.

Esther pressed closer to her side and hissed, "Kasia."

The man's smile evened out. "That is your name? Kasia? Lovely."

"I will pass the compliment along to my parents." She would *not* ask him his. Certainly not. Instead, she handed off Esther's shoes to her with a nod of instruction.

Esther huffed but bent down to wrap the leather around her feet and secure it above her ankles. Kasia just stood there.

The man arched a brow. "I have no intentions of hoisting you over my shoulder the second your attention is elsewhere."

"And I would see you prove it with my own eyes."

He shook his head, smiling again, and backed up a few steps. "There. You can sit and put them on, and you will be able to see if I come any closer. Is that satisfactory?"

Though it felt like defeat to do so, it would have been petulant to refuse. She sat and swallowed back the bitter taste of capitulation. Glanced up at the man and found him watching her intently, his smile now an echo.

Who was he? Someone wealthy, obviously. Perhaps one of the king's officials, or even a relative. She guessed him to be in his mid-thirties, his dark mane of hair untouched by grey. He had a strong, straight nose, bright eyes. Features that marked him as noble as surely as the jewelry he wore.

But it was neither the proportions of his face nor his fine attire that made her fingers stumble with her shoes. It was the expression he wore. Intent and amused. Determined and intrigued.

He fingered one of the ornaments on his clothing, gaze on her. "Who is your father, lovely Kasia?"

She swallowed, wondering at the wisdom of answering. Surely he had no intentions of seeing her home now, of . . . of . . . what? What could possibly come of such a short encounter? It was curiosity that made him ask. It could be nothing more. "Kish, the son of Ben-Geber. He is a woodworker."

Esther made a disturbed squeak beside her, but Kasia ignored her.

The man's mouth turned up again. "Kish, the son of Ben-Geber. And I assume he is not inclined toward his daughter socializing with Persians? It is a prejudice I find odd. Are you not in *our* land? Have you not chosen to remain here, even after King Cyrus gave you freedom to leave? It seems very . . . ungrateful for you Jews to remain so aloof."

Kasia sighed and moved to her second shoe. "Perhaps. But it is an outlook hewn from the continued prejudice the Persians have against *us*."

"Some, perhaps." The man flicked a gaze his companion's way. "But most of us recognize that the Jews have become valuable members of the empire. Take Susa for example." He waved a hand toward the city. "It is such a pleasure to winter here largely because of the Jews who withstand the heat in the summer and keep the city running. We are not all blind to that."

She inclined her head in acknowledgment. "And some of *us* recognize the generosity of Xerxes, the king of kings, and his fathers before him, and are grateful for the opportunity to flourish here."

"But . . . ." He cocked his head, grinned. "Your father is not one of those?"

Kasia sighed and, finished with her shoes, stood. "My father has lived long under the heel of his Persian neighbors. Were it not for the size of our family, he would have returned to Israel long ago."

"Ah. Well, fair and generous Kasia, I thank you for taking the time to speak with me. Your wit and eloquence have brightened my day." He stepped closer, slowly and cautiously.

Esther shifted beside her, undoubtedly spooked by his nearness. But Kasia held her ground and tilted her head up to look into his face when he was but half an arm away. "And I thank you, sir, for your kind offer to see us home, even if I must decline."

"Hmm. A shame, that. I would have enjoyed continuing our conversation on the walk back to the city."

With her eyes locked on his, she was only vaguely aware of his movement before warm fingers took her hand. She jolted, as much from the sensation racing up her arm as from the shock of the gesture.

He lifted her hand and pressed his lips to her palm. Her breath tangled up in her chest. If her father saw this, he would kill her where she stood.

But what was the harm in a moment's flirtation with an alluring stranger? He would return to his ornate house and forget about her. She would go to her modest dwelling and remember this brief, amazing encounter forever.

A stolen moment. Nothing more.

His other hand appeared in her vision even as he arched a brow. "A gift for the beautiful Jewess."

That tangled breath nearly choked her when she saw the thick silver torc in his hand, lions' heads on each end. "Lord, I cannot—"

"I will it." He slid the bracelet onto her arm, under her sleeve until it reached a part of her arm thick enough to hold it up, past her elbow. Challenge lit his features. "If you do not want it, you may return it when next we meet."

"I . . ." She could think of nothing clever to say, no smooth words of refusal.

With an endearing smirk, he kissed her knuckles and then released her and strode away. Kasia may have stood there for the rest of time, staring blankly at where he had been, had Esther not gripped her arm and tugged.

"Kasia, what are you thinking? You cannot accept a gift from a Persian man! What will your father say?"

"Nothing pleasant." Blowing a loose strand of hair out of her face, Kasia let her sleeve settle over her arm. It covered all evidence of the unrequested silver. "He need not know."

"Kasia." Esther's torment wrinkled her forehead again. "What has gotten into you? Surely you are not . . . ?"

She glanced over to where the man mounted his horse and turned with one last look her way, topped with a wink. Blood rushed to her cheeks. "Perhaps I am. He is a fine man, is he not?"

Esther sighed, laughed a little. "He seemed it, yes. But your father will never allow you to marry a Persian. As soon as he decides between Ben-Hesed and Michael, you will become a fine Jewish wife to a fine Jewish man."

"Yes, I know." Her breath leaked out, washing some of the excitement of the last few minutes away with it. "It hardly matters. The loss of one bracelet will probably not bother him. He will consider it restitution for our dismay and think of it no more."

Esther lifted her brows. "But he said he would see you again."

"Do you really think a man of his station will bother himself over a Jewish girl whose father cannot afford a dowry?"

"I suppose not."

Kasia looped her elbow through Esther's. "Come, little one. We had better hurry home."

Esther renewed her smile. "You have quite the romantic story now. Someday, when you are an old married woman, you can pull out that torc and give it to your daughter along with a tale to set her heart to sighing."

Yes . . . someday.

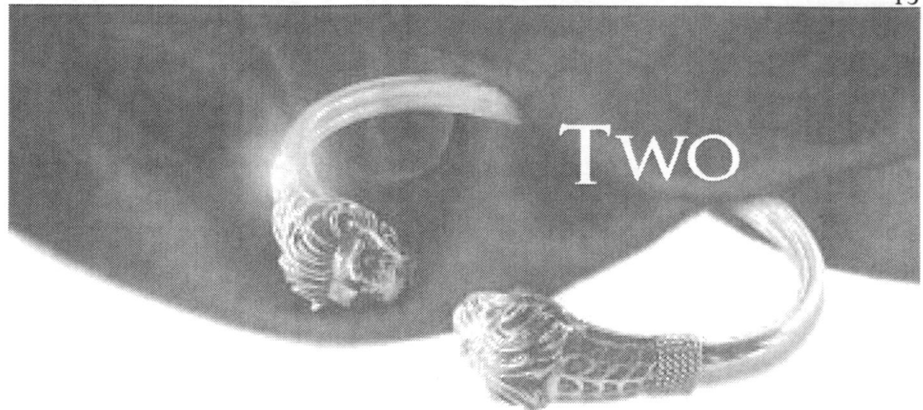

Two

Esther tore through her chest of belongings, tossing away each object to meet her hands. It had to be here. Somewhere, under something . . . she could not have lost her mother's silver bracelet. Impossible. She rarely wore it, only when she wanted to look pretty for Zechariah. The last time had been—

No. She rocked back on her heels and pressed a hand to her mouth. Three days ago, when she spent the day with Kasia. When they went to the river. She did not remember taking it off again that night.

There was no need to think the worst. It was probably at Kasia's house, that was all. Surely it had slipped off there, and not in the streets. Or, worse still, at the river.

"Esther?"

At her cousin's voice, Esther scooped up the mass of her belongings and shoved them back into the chest, dropping it shut just as Mordecai stuck his head into her small chamber. He was so tall he had to duck before entering, though otherwise his build was slight.

He smiled. "There you are. I am not needed at the palace today, so Kish and I are going in search of some wood for his next project. Would you like to spend the morning with Kasia?"

Relief settled on her shoulders. "I would like that, cousin. Thank you." She could ask Kasia if she had seen her bracelet, if perhaps her ima, Zillah, had found it . . . and if she had heard any more from the rich Persian. Unlikely, but worth a question.

She stood and followed her cousin through the house and out the front door. Mordecai drew in a deep breath of the fresh air, closing his hazel eyes as if to better savor it.

Esther smiled. She had never met him before her parents were killed, but in the three years since he took her in, she discovered him to be a man of depths that flowed down to his soul. Not often did he speak up in a crowd, never did he draw attention to himself. But he lived with a whole heart. He seemed to treasure each moment. Each breath of fresh air. Each bird song. It was no wonder he was the one chosen to represent the Jews at the palace. There was no man more respected in Susa.

She could not figure out why he never remarried after his wife died in childbirth five years ago, along with their babe. But at the same time, she was glad. Had he brought a new woman into the house, she may not have appreciated having to tend to a nearly-grown girl like Esther.

That was a selfish thought, she knew. Mordecai deserved the happiness a wife and children of his own would bring him. Besides, his heart was too large to necessitate pushing her aside once he had children of his flesh. He had told her more than once that she was like his daughter, and he meant it.

Just because she had lost one father did not mean she would lose this one.

He smiled down at her and took the first step onto the street. "You have grown again. We shall have to get you some more clothes. Perhaps Zillah and Kasia will help you with that next week."

"They are always happy to help."

Mordecai nodded, but his smile faded. It was so out of character for him that Esther stopped. "Cousin?"

He halted too, and drew out a smaller smile. "It is nothing. Only . . . Kish is still considering Ben-Hesed or Michael for your friend?"

"So far as I know. They are . . . cousin! Are you going to ask for her?"

"I . . ." Mordecai blushed—actually blushed. "She has grown into a lovely young woman. Beautiful, but so much more. Tender and caring, with a zeal for life. And she loves you. I know not if she could ever feel so warmly for me, though."

"How could she not?" Esther tucked her hand into Mordecai's elbow and gave him her brightest smile. "I doubt she has considered it, but I shall plant a few thoughts in her head."

Mordecai groaned, but it ended on a laugh. "I do not need my twelve-year-old daughter approaching a woman on my behalf. I will try to find a few moments to speak with her to see if she would welcome further attention from me. If so, then I will speak with Kish."

Dear, sweet Cousin Mordecai. The Lord had surely been watching over her when he led this man to her door after the accident.

Well, she would do what she could to help, no matter what he said. Surely Kasia would forget about any other man when she realized Mordecai was interested in making her his own. She had expressed admiration for him more than once. And to have her dearest friend under the same roof—it would be a perfect arrangement.

They walked the short distance to their friends' house in silence, but entered to the usual chaos of a large family. Kish bellowed instructions at Zechariah in the wood shop, and inside the family's space the little ones shrieked and giggled and dashed about.

Kasia's mother, Zillah, looked up and smiled. "Kasia is working on the bread, if you want to help her."

"Certainly." She turned first to Mordecai and leaned into him for a moment. "Have a good morning, cousin. When will you be back?"

"By the midday meal, I imagine. Have fun with Kasia and the little ones."

"I will." Smiling first at him, then at Zillah, she headed for the outdoor kitchen at the rear of the house. She found Kasia up to her elbows in bread dough. "Would you like some help?"

"Have I ever turned it down?" Her friend's grin made Esther sigh. Kasia was so beautiful. Her hair was thick, so dark and rich, her cheekbones pronounced to set off her large almond eyes, and her curves . . . .

Sometimes Esther despaired of ever growing up. It took so long. Here she was nearly thirteen, and she still had the figure of Kasia's eight-year-old sister, Eglah. Or worse, eleven-year-old Joshua. How would Zechariah ever come to love her if she looked like his little brother?

But Kasia—it was no wonder the Persian had been unable to take his eyes off her. No wonder Mordecai had set his heart on her. Esther grinned as she pulled a second bowl of dough forward. "You will never guess the conversation I just had."

Kasia lifted her brows. "Let me see. You told Mordecai how in love you are with Zechariah, and he promised to speak with Abba this morning to arrange for a betrothal."

She laughed and bumped her arm into Kasia's. "No, but a similar topic. Concerning *your* pending betrothal."

"Ah." Some of the brightness left Kasia's voice. "Not nearly so interesting. Michael stopped by last night, and it was all I could do to stay awake through his prattle. If Abba selects him as my husband, I shall sleep through the rest of my life. Though he is better than Ben-Hesed, and apparently my mysterious Persian will not be returning."

"As expected. But I have a feeling you need not resign yourself to Michael yet. There is another suitor lurking in the shadows."

"Oh?" Without so much as pausing in her kneading, Kasia lifted a dubious brow. "And who would that be?"

Esther rolled her lips together and plunged her hands into the dough. "Hmm. I really ought not say. He did imply I should refrain from interference."

Now Kasia halted and turned to face her. "What a tease! But no matter, there are few enough men you speak with. It must be . . . Abram the butcher."

Esther laughed. "You think I consider him a better choice than Michael? He is ancient."

"He is thirty-five." Kasia chuckled and got back to work. "Surely anyone younger than the king cannot be called old. It is probably against the law."

A snort slipped from her lips. "Perhaps. They do have some ridiculous laws. But it is someone much better than the butcher. More handsome, younger, and wealthier."

Kasia's hands stilled, and her eyes focused on the middle distance. "All that? I must say, I am both intrigued and at a loss. I can think of no one . . . at least . . . ." She turned her face to Esther, brows pulled together. "Surely not . . . ?"

Lips pressed together again, Esther wiggled her brows. She half expected Kasia to leap with excitement, giddy laughter on her lips. Instead, she went thoughtful and turned back to her bowl. Not the reaction Esther had expected. Perhaps she should have held her tongue. Oh, Mordecai would be mortified if she had ruined things.

Kasia shook her head. "I thought . . . he grieved so for Keturah. And it has been so long since her death, I assumed . . . ." Her gaze, sharp now, found Esther again. "You are certain? Serious? *He* is serious?"

Esther could only nod.

Kasia's eyes went wide. "I cannot grasp it. He is so . . . ."

"Yes. He is."

Kasia used her wrist to smooth back a stray lock. "And I am only . . . ."

"You are everything a man could want, Kasia." Esther drew her lower lip between her teeth as she regarded her friend. "He did not want me to say anything. He intends to speak to you himself before he approaches your father, to sound out your feelings. I wanted to . . . give you time to think about it, I suppose. I would hate to see either of you hurt."

Kasia drew in a long breath, looking at a loss for what to say. "You need not fear me hurting him, little one. If he is interested, there is nothing to think about. There is no better man in Susa, and I would be honored if . . . and Abba. He would be so proud."

Esther nodded, though she would have wished for a little more enthusiasm. Perhaps it was just eclipsed by surprise. "Do you love him, Kasia?"

Kasia's eyes came into focus on Esther's face. There was no gleam she would have called love, but there was something. Something sure, something calm. "I could very easily, if I let myself consider it. The very possibility of such a union—it is much more than I dared dream. I have so little to offer, and he is so well respected. Although . . . I have heard that he has a pesky daughter. On second thought, maybe I would not want to deal with the little—"

"Ha!" Esther rammed her side into her friend, and they both dissolved into laughter. Satisfied, she sighed. "Well then. Your Persian man has not come to your door, demanding to speak with your father?"

"Obviously not." Though Kasia rolled her eyes, Esther did not miss the hint of disappointment within them. Ah, well. Mordecai would banish it soon enough.

Esther leaned close. "What did you do with the torc?"

"I am still wearing it. I was afraid the girls would find it if I took it off."

"Oh! My mother's silver bracelet—I cannot find it, and the last time I wore it was when I came over the other day. Have you found it around your house?"

Kasia shook her head, concern saturating her face. "I will ask Ima, though. You do not think . . . ."

The very thought made tears sting her eyes. "I hope not. If I lost it at the river, I will never find it again."

"You could." Kasia leaned over to touch their arms together. "If Ima does not have it, I shall check at the river this afternoon. We will find it, little one. I promise."

Knowing Kasia would look for it eased the knot of anxiety inside—she could simply smile, and all of creation would jump to help her. A girl could not ask for a better friend, a better neighbor. She would be blessed indeed when Kasia married Mordecai.

Kasia fell to her knees, bent over until she was prostrate, and wished for some extra light. Granted, in the summer she appreciated the protection their roof afforded with its three-foot thickness, but at the moment the way it blocked the sun was more curse than blessing.

Her mother clucked behind her. "Kasia, what are you doing? Searching for dust?"

"No, for Esther's bracelet."

"You still have not found it?" Ima sighed. "Perhaps you ought to retrace your steps from the other day."

Kasia straightened and rubbed at her neck, sore from all the craning and stooping she had done that afternoon after Esther left. "I suppose I shall have to. Poor little Esther. It is the only thing she has left of her mother. I cannot bear the thought that she lost it."

Ima gave her a small smile and reached out to cup her cheek. "You are a sweet one, my Kasia. Go now, before darkness falls."

"Do you not need help with the meal?"

"I shall make do. It is for Esther's sake, after all."

Kasia smiled at her mother and turned to find four-year-old Sarai standing behind her, thumb in mouth. The wee one removed the finger long enough to ask, "What you looking for, Kas?"

She scooped up her little sister and gave her belly a tickle. "A silver bracelet that Esther dropped the other day."

Sarai's eyes went wide. "Silver? And round? Like this?" She traced a circle in the air.

Ima fisted her hands on her hips. "Have you seen it, Sarai?"

The child tucked her head into Kasia's neck. "I found it in the kitchen. It is safe and pretty. On my doll. It is a belt."

Ima lifted one dubious brow and reached for Sarai. "Come, little one, let us go get it. Kasia, would you stir the stew while I take care of this?"

"Of course." She turned and headed outside to the kitchen. Perhaps after the meal she would run the bracelet over to Esther to ease the girl's mind.

Although the trip would probably not ease *her* mind.

Kasia drew in a shaky breath as she passed the threshold into the moderate winter sun. Her friend's news from that morning still rocked her. How long had she known Mordecai? He had always lived in the house three doors away, in a modest part of town despite his wealth. She remembered when he wed Keturah, how happy he had seemed. She remembered the bliss on his face when he shared with Abba that a babe would join them soon.

She remembered the stark pain that etched age onto his countenance when Keturah and the babe died.

Though only eleven at the time, Kasia had wanted to wrap her arms around him and hold on until the pain went away. It had seemed as though nothing would ever ease his agony.

Until Esther. Esther had brought joy back to his eyes, a smile back to his lips.

They were lovely eyes, well-shaped lips. Mordecai was a handsome man, though she rarely stopped to consider it. It had seemed pointless. He had already found his perfect mate, had lost her. He would not marry again lightly. So if he spoke for her, then . . . .

He loved her. Unbelievable and amazing.

Shaking her head, Kasia grabbed the wooden spoon from its rest and stirred the stew in the large pot over the fire. She saw him more often than any man outside her family, but never had she detected a shift in his feelings. Esther would not have lied to her, though. If she said he intended to speak with her, then he would. Probably soon.

The thought brought her pulse up—until a different set of eyes came to mind. Silly. She shook her head again to dislodge the wayward picture. Mordecai was a far better man to pin her dreams on. He was everything she could possibly want in a husband. Handsome and strong, kind and caring, intelligent and wealthy. Jewish.

The Persian . . . he could not be more wrong for her. He was arrogant, aggressive, surely did not share her religious views. And gone. He had ridden off on his horse and would never enter her life again.

Not her waking life, anyway. Though he had certainly plagued her dreams the past few nights.

"Kasia."

She looked up at her father's voice. His firm, displeased voice. She rarely earned that tone, and hearing it now made her shoulders tense up. "Yes, Abba?"

He stood in the shop's rear door and glowered at her. "Get your mother and come here. Now."

When he gave her that particular look, dawdling was not an option. She flew towards the door even as she said, "Of course, Abba."

Thankfully, Ima was emerging from the girls' room as she entered. "Ima, Abba wants you and me to go to his shop. Now."

Ima's brows drew together. "What is it?"

"I know not, but he was very cross."

"Probably a problem with the Persians again." Ima loosed a sigh and set Esther's bracelet down. "I cannot think why he would need both of us, but I suppose we shall find out."

They moved together out the back door and into Abba's shop. The scent of cypress shavings greeted them first, and then the steady regard of three men.

Kasia froze just inside, halted by the weight of those gazes. Abba's, hard and demanding. A curious one from the man nearest him, a Persian in elegant clothes whom she had never seen before. And then the third . . . was he not the companion of the man she had met the other day?

Her knees nearly buckled. No wonder Abba looked so unhappy.

Ima slipped an arm around her and looked to Abba. "My husband, what is happening?"

He kept his harsh gaze on Kasia. "I think our daughter can best answer that question. Tell us, Kasia. How is it that the king has decided he will take you as a wife?"

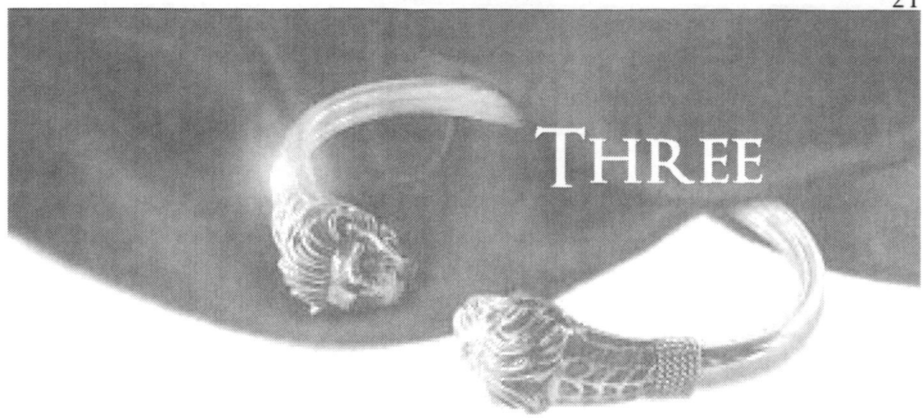

Three

Kasia stared at her father for a long moment, certain her confusion clouded her face. "The *king*? I do not understand."

Abba snorted. "Of course not. Had you any wit, you would have obeyed me when I told you *never* to speak to an unfamiliar Persian. And what do I find? You met two of them the other day and did not even see fit to mention it."

The torc on her arm scorched her flesh, and her mouth went dry. "Abba, it was unintentional. We simply . . . came across them. This man," she said with a gesture toward the somewhat-familiar Persian, "and his friend. The other offered to see us home, but I refused. That is all."

"That is all," Abba echoed. He folded his large arms across his chest. "And yet somehow that was enough to make it to the ear of Xerxes and intrigue him."

Oh, curse her over-active tongue! But why would the king care? He did not have a reputation for valuing eloquence in his wives. Obedience perhaps, but she obviously had work to do there. "Abba . . . ."

The familiar Persian stepped forward. "Allow me to introduce myself. I am Haman, trusted only below the princes themselves. And this should not come as a surprise—surely you are not blind to your daughter's extraordinary handsomeness."

The muscle in Abba's jaw ticked. "Her beauty is no business of the king's. She is a Jew."

"A Jew in his land." Haman's voice lost all hint of warmth. "Try to refuse him and you will learn how quickly the heel of Xerxes can crush. It seems to me you have too many mouths to feed to lose your livelihood over this."

A shadow moved around the corner. Zechariah. She gripped Ima's hand and prayed as she had never prayed before.

This could not be happening. It was not possible. Yes, she disobeyed her father by venturing to the river. Yes, she spoke to the Persian when he forbade it. But how had that turned into *this*? This was not what she had dreamed of the last few nights. She wanted nothing to do with Xerxes. The other man, perhaps, but even him . . . it had been a dream. Nothing more. Nothing that should have become such a nightmare.

Where was *her* Persian? Had he, too, told the king about her? Was he perhaps even one of the king's scouts, who deliberately searched the land for beautiful virgins to add to the harem? Had his interest been only on behalf of his king?

"Kasia." Ima managed to turn her name into a moan, a plea. "Tell them they have the wrong girl."

Her shoulders sagged. Perhaps they could have tried that argument if only strangers had arrived today, and before she admitted to meeting them, but now?

Haman smirked and strode over to them. Kasia battled the urge to recoil against her mother as he approached.

He reached out, gripped her wrist, and raised her arm until her sleeve fell back. The silver torc gleamed. "No mistaking *that*, is there?"

Her parents both gasped, and a shuffle came from her brother's hiding spot. Kasia let her eyes slide shut. She should have taken it off. Should have refused it to begin with, no matter how alluring the stranger's gaze. It had probably been nothing but a brand—something to prove she was chosen for the king.

She was a fool. And now she would have to pay the price for it.

When she opened her eyes, Abba's face was mottled red. "Is this how I raised you, Kasia? To play the harlot for a Persian dog?"

Haman spun around, jerked her with him. "Watch your tongue, swine."

Abba ignored Haman and glared at her. "You have shamed us all. Why would you accept such a mark from our oppressors? Do you think they give without asking something in return?"

Tears stung her eyes. "I am sorry, Abba. I tried to refuse it, but—"

"Enough of this." Haman released her arm and motioned the other man forward. "This is Hegai, the custodian of the women. He will instruct you on what you may bring to the palace. I suppose you have no dowry?"

Abba's fingers curled into his palm. "Even if she did, I would not give it to you. No daughter of mine weds a Persian, even Xerxes himself. Especially Xerxes himself."

Haman look unfazed. "Then I suppose you are officially one daughter less. This girl is coming with me. Fight me, and you will lose."

Abba looked like he might try anyway. Kasia ran to him and threw her arms around his waist. "I am sorry, Abba. I did not mean for this to happen."

"I know." His voice went soft and low, a mere murmur against her hair as his arms closed around her. "I know not what to do, daughter. I do not want to lose you, but how does a lowly Jewish man fight the king of kings?"

She buried her face in his chest. It smelled of wood and Abba. "You do not, or the family will suffer."

He held her tighter for a moment, then eased up again. "It will be like burying you, child. You will be in another world, another life. They will make you Persian. Strip you of your heritage."

"They cannot strip my soul of its love for Jehovah."

"They will try." He pulled away and touched his knuckle to her chin. "I will spare your siblings the truth of this. I am sorry to do it, sweet one, but it is better they think you in the bosom of Abraham than another wife to the tyrant."

A few tears splashed onto her cheeks. "You will tell them I am dead?"

"I see little choice."

"Abba!"

Ima bit back a sob. Kasia shook her head as a wash of numbness swept over her. Anger and pain, as cathartic as they would be, would change nothing. But perhaps logic could. "People will have seen them come in here. They will see me leave."

"I will tell them the Persians came inquiring on a price for carving. They have done so before, even if they rarely deign to give me their business."

Haman snorted. "I imagine if your daughter pleases the king, he will gladly have a few pieces commissioned."

Abba's nostrils flared. She was unsure what he thought about that suggestion, but it made her knees go weak. How, exactly, was a girl to please a king? "What of my leaving with them?"

"You will not." Abba straightened his spine, rolled back his shoulders, and stared down the Persians. "You will leave separately, head to the river where you met them before. "

Haman waved a hand as if such details were of no concern to him. "As you please. Hegai, instruct her on her possessions while I settle the contract."

The other man gave her a gentle smile. "You will receive new garments and jewelry, perfumes and oils. Bring only a few small items of sentimental value. With all respect to your father, you seem to have nothing else worthy to be seen in the king's household."

Kasia swallowed back her dismay. She would have nothing familiar, then. Nothing of home, since they never had enough money to spare for trinkets, and she had given all her childhood treasures to her sisters. "I . . . I can think of nothing to bring."

The sorrow in his eyes said he understood. "Very well. Eat with your family one last time, then go to the river. We will be waiting there."

She managed a nod, kept her back straight as the two men left. But the moment they were gone, her knees buckled and she fell to the floor. Ima's arms encircled her in the next second, Ima's tears mixed with hers.

This was not how she should have felt upon her betrothal. This was not the betrothal she should have had. Had she not been thinking just minutes before about marrying Mordecai? Now he would think her dead. And Esther . . . .

"Ima, please." She spoke in a whisper at her mother's ear. "Please tell Esther the truth. She should not have to face yet another death."

Ima's sobs hitched. "I dare not cross your father on this. I know how it will hurt her, but we will comfort each other."

There was nothing to do but nod. And wonder who would be there to comfort *her*.

Zechariah stood just inside the doorway, where the cool breezes brought by the rain could whisper over his skin. Behind him, the house was silent. No weeping, no mourning, no frantic prayers to a deaf God. No more pleas to the heavens that Kasia be returned to them.

His nostrils flared as he swallowed back anger and grief. They knew he had been listening. Still, they expected him to play along. To bid his favorite sister farewell as if she were only running an errand. To wonder with the others where she was when darkness fell and the rains came with it. To search the banks of the swollen river long into the night.

He had done what they expected. Had trudged back home with a solemn Mordecai a few hours earlier. Had held his tongue. But his heart—his heart cried out to Jehovah, "Why? Why did your creation help in this terrible ruse?"

He had thought, when he heard Abba's plan, that it would never be believed. But then the unexpected monsoon had rolled in, and it became all too possible that a girl could have fallen into the river and been carried away. Never to be found, never to be seen again.

That much, at least, was true. She might as well have been swallowed by the palace, never to emerge again. Except, of course, when the king's household left Susa and headed to its summer home at Persepolis. When would that be? Another month? A fortnight? Soon. They never stayed longer than half a year.

Zechariah folded his arms over his chest and watched the water drip from the roof. It seemed as though in a few minutes, Kasia would come stumbling from the room she shared with the other girls to get breakfast started. She would smile, joke about his secretive nightly training. He would tease her about her suitors.

It was her beauty that cursed her. He had known her face was exceptional—it was hard to miss when his friends stared constantly—but he had never thought she would gain the attention of the king. That did not happen in their neighborhood, to their community. It should not have happened to his sister. Why could the king not have given his attention to the women of his own country, who would be honored and pleased to become another of his concubines?

Light footfalls alerted him that he was no longer alone a moment before Esther's soft voice broke the stillness. "Any word?"

He turned, saw that her eyes were red and swollen, circled with dark shadows. She had stayed with the younger girls through the night but obviously had not slept much. Zechariah shook his head. "I cannot imagine there will be any, at this point."

Esther blinked rapidly. "How can you say that? Perhaps she took shelter with someone."

"They would have heard us searching." He sighed and pinched the bridge of his nose. These lies tasted like wormwood. Did the king realize he was chipping off another shard of this young girl's heart? As if he would care, even if he knew. "I am sorry, Esther. But Kasia is gone."

The shake of her head was violent, and the tears she had blinked away from her eyes ripped from her throat. "No. I cannot accept it. She is . . . she was . . . oh, Zechariah, it is all my fault! She never would have gone down to the river yesterday, but for me. She must have been looking for my bracelet."

"Esther, no." He raked a hand over his hair. How could Abba insist on this falsehood? Poor little Esther—she did not deserve such guilt. Kasia would have wanted her to know the truth. Even in her last moments with them . . . . "I'd forgotten—everyone must have. They found your bracelet yesterday. They mentioned it at dinner last night."

Though a measure of pain left her face, confusion replaced it instead of relief. "Then why would she have . . . ?"

Realization flushed her cheeks. Zechariah's tired mind took a long moment to make sense of that, until he realized Esther would have been with Kasia four days ago, when she had first met the Persians. And now she would think she could have prevented this had she told someone what happened.

Zechariah sighed and rested a hand on her shoulder. She was nothing but a wisp. Too delicate, surely, to carry such a burden. She would try. But perhaps she would let him shoulder part of it, if she realized it would not be a betrayal of Kasia's confidence.

He bent down so that he could meet her watery brown eyes. "She told me," he whispered. "About the men you two met the other day at the river. You are thinking of that, are you not? That she went back to that spot?"

How could a girl no more than a child look at him with a gaze so very old? "I know she did. She had been unable to put it from her mind, then I told her . . . you know Kasia. She would have gone back there to settle her thoughts."

Zechariah reached up to thumb away a stream of tears from her cheek. "What did you tell her?"

She pulled her lip between her teeth, eyes on his shoulder.

He drew in a long breath and straightened. "Tell me, Esther."

She would not appreciate the tone—it would remind her that he was a man, she a child, in spite of the shy smiles she gave him. He had done his best to ignore her attention in the past to keep from embarrassing her, but right now he would demand obedience along with her childish devotion. It was the only way to help her.

Her shoulders slumped, her gaze fell to the ground. "Mordecai was going to speak for her."

A curse very nearly slipped out. If only he had, a week ago. Then Kasia would have been too busy with wedding preparations to sneak off to the river, and the ill-fated meeting with the Persians would never have happened.

Zechariah scrubbed his hand over his face. "Let us not mention that to Abba, hmm? It would upset him all the more, to realize what could have been."

Her nod looked heavy, sad. "I am sorry, Zechariah. I should never have mentioned it to her. Then she would not have—"

"Shh." Unable to stand the sorrow emanating from her face, he pulled her against his chest and rested his chin on the top of her head. "This is not your fault, Esther. It was an accident. Kasia escaped to the river more frequently than you know, to think and relax in the few moments she could."

"But—"

"No buts. She went for a walk last night, nothing more. Got caught in the rain, slipped into the river. It is a tragedy, but it is not your fault."

A shudder ran through her.

He knew the feeling. "We have both lost a sister this day. The pain will not soon ebb, but we shall get each other through it. I will be a brother to you, as she had been your sister."

It may not be what she dreamed of right now, but it would suffice. It was all he could offer, especially if he convinced Abba to let him join the army that would soon set off for Greece. And even after the war, after she had grown . . . there could never be more.

Not with this secret between them.

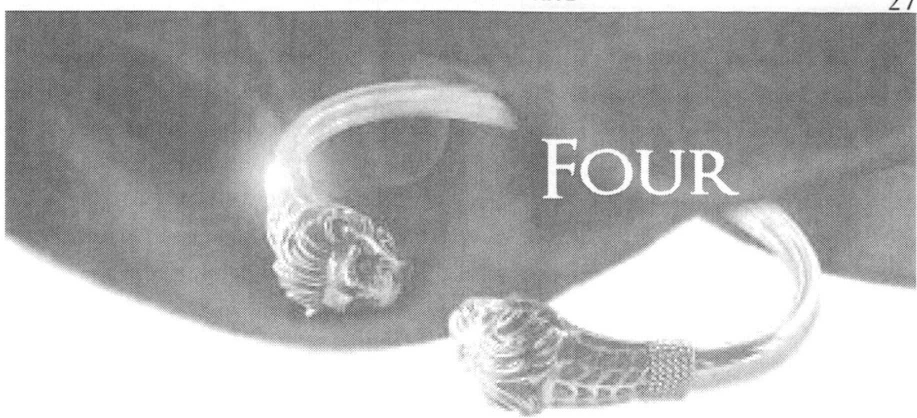

FOUR

Kasia blinked her eyes open and stared at the rich, unfamiliar surroundings. Brick walls with a mosaic of mythical animals. Red-polished lime floors covered with thick rugs. By the door two stone dogs stood sentry. Was it her imagination, or did they snarl at her?

She pushed herself up in the bed, softer by far than her pallet on the floor at home. Light from the low windows winked off ornaments of gold and silver. Everything mocked her, screamed that she did not belong.

The heavy wooden doors swung open, and Hegai strode in, a line of servants behind him. He smiled, but it did little to ease the ache inside.

"Awake, I see. Good. We have much to do, and not much time to do it in. If you could rise, Kasia, we need measurements for a new wardrobe. Then you must have your first treatments in oil of myrrh."

She swung her legs out of the bed and planted her feet on the floor, even as questions swirled through her mind. "I have heard about these preparations. They are a year in total, are they not?"

"Usually, yes." Hegai sighed and motioned a man forward. She assumed him to be a tailor, given the string he held up to her. "But not in your case. The king granted me a week, and I had to beg for that much."

She nearly fell back onto the bed. "A *week*? I . . . but . . . *why*?"

Hegai shrugged and motioned more servants to the bath sunken into the floor. "I do not presume to know the mind of the king. Perhaps it is because he anticipates leaving soon for his campaign against Greece and wishes to make you his wife beforehand."

The room rocked around her. "What did Haman tell him about me?"

"I know not, but he need only speak the truth to capture the king's attention." Though his gaze turned critical, she saw satisfaction within it.

Kasia forced herself to swallow. "Who was the other man? The one with Haman when they first saw me?"

He motioned more servants to the other side of the room, where they set out dish after dish of aromatic food. Her stomach knotted in protest. "I am not certain," he said. "Probably Masistes, the king's younger brother. He and Haman often ride together."

Masistes. She wanted to ask if she would ever have cause to meet him in the palace but did not dare. What was the point? She needed to purge her mind of thoughts of any other men. Michael, Mordecai, Masistes. Dwelling on any of them would only make her circumstances worse.

The door swung open again. She looked that way, expecting more servants, with more things that she would not know what to do with. But the first two who entered were empty-handed, and they stepped to each side of the doorway once through. Three more figures entered then. Servants on the ends, but in the middle glided a glimmering woman.

Hegai fell to his knee. "Queen Atossa. I did not expect you in the women's house today."

The queen mother? Kasia dropped to the floor along with the tailor, feeling blood warm her cheeks.

The queen's laugh sounded sweet and amused. "I could not resist a visit when I heard about the unusual circumstances of the newest addition. Rise, please."

Kasia waited for Hegai to obey before following suit. Careful to keep her chin at a respectful angle, she gave into curiosity and gazed at the matriarch of Persia. A daughter of Cyrus the Great, it was her influence that assured Xerxes would be king, rather than Darius's older son by another wife. The whisperers called Atossa all-powerful. What were the chances that she would be an ally?

The woman smiled. "Your name is Kasia, I hear. My son is very much intrigued by you."

She was unsure which son the queen mother referred to, but it seemed ill-advised to ask. "I am but your humble servant, my queen."

"Today, perhaps. But soon enough you will be a consort to the king of kings. You have been here only a few hours, my child, yet already you have friends and enemies. Learning who is who is more important than oil of myrrh." With a flick of her wrist, she sent servants scurrying out of her way so that she could float forward. When she paused, one of them pulled forward a chair, which she sat upon without so much as glancing behind to check its position.

The wrist motioned to her, and Kasia sank down onto the bed. She knew no chair had appeared behind her. "I am grateful for any advice the queen can give me."

Atossa acknowledged her with a minuscule nod. "Wine." As a servant dashed to the corner of the room, the queen folded her bejeweled hands in her lap. "You are a Jew, which accounts for some of your enemies. Haman in particular detests your people. Not surprising, since he is an Agagite."

Kasia's brows pulled down, but she pressed her lips together.

"You are wondering, then, why he encouraged the king to add you to his harem?" Atossa loosed a dry laugh. "He expects you to stumble, to displease my notoriously impulsive son, and so to provide the king with reason to punish your whole people."

The world fell upon her shoulders in a suffocating burden. Perhaps tonight she could slip out of the palace and disappear forever.

"In addition," Atossa continued, "your presence has already enraged Queen Amestris. She is a jealous woman, especially of young virgins half her age who have caught the eye of her husband. She is a queen—she understands that her husband's wealth is measured in sons and wives as well as gold. So long as she is certain *her* son will be the next king, she is docile enough. But his impatience where you are concerned has labeled you a threat. Tread lightly when around her, and avoid her whenever you may."

Much more easily done if she were nowhere near the palace. Egypt was a temperate place, was it not? Perhaps she could hitch a ride with a caravan.

"However." Here the queen paused and gave her a smile that seemed . . . motherly. Warm. Sincere. "You have friends as well. I am always pleased to welcome anyone who angers Amestris, as are most of the other wives. Keep your hand soft and your demands few, and the servants will respond well to you. Since you will see us more than anyone else in the palace once you leave the house of women and join the house of wives, those ought to be your priorities."

Kasia could only nod.

Atossa breathed a laugh. "All women new to the palace have questions. You may ask yours—you have no time to learn the answers on your own."

The servant who fetched the queen's wine handed a cup to Kasia as well. She took a sip, grateful for the time to gather her thoughts. So many of them swarmed that she barely knew where to begin. "I understand that I ought to make the queen mother and other wives my friends, where possible. But what of the king? Ought I not try to please him as well?"

The queen's smile went patronizing. "My child, that is a task no one woman can accomplish. He is eager to have you, and you may hold his attention for a while. A week, a month at the outmost. If you are lucky, you will produce a child, which guarantees another visit from the king. But there are always new virgins finishing their year of preparation. Discontented wives of absent nobles to seduce. The destruction of rival empires to plot."

"He sounds horrible." The moment the word slipped out, she slapped a hand over her mouth and prayed Jehovah would strike her dead here and now.

Atossa laughed. "Your opinion is not unexpected, given your upbringing. He is not horrible, child, he is . . . the king. His attention is by necessity fractured. He must be many things to many people. To his wives, he is at once the axis around which you turn and a star afar off in the night. Do what you can to please him, Kasia, or at least to keep from angering him. But know that whatever you find with him, it will be fleeting. That is the way of things. Life here, for all its polish and sparkle, is largely uneventful unless you fall into a scandal." She leaned forward, eyes gleaming. "Which I would not advise."

The advice seemed unnecessary—until Masistes' teasing gaze filled her mind's eye. "Noted. Duly. I shall . . . ." What? Resign herself to a life of nothingness? She was not so sure she could. But she would not dishonor her father, her husband, and her God by acting on silly dreams.

She would *not*. "I shall find contentment in my place."

"Then you will be better off than most of the wives." Atossa smiled again and then stood. "I shall let Hegai proceed. After you go to the king, I will pay you another visit."

Kasia jumped to her feet, though she had no idea how to say farewell to royalty. Would those lessons be poured upon her this week along with the oils and perfumes, or would she be let to blunder her way through? She suspected Haman and Amestris would be in favor of the blundering. Hopefully Hegai and Atossa's attention would save her.

Mordecai nodded to his manservant as he shut the door behind him. Esther sat in the same place she had when he left three hours earlier. Her fingers kept busy with the mending, but her expression was a hollow mask of pain.

That was how she looked when he first met her three years before, after her parents' deaths. He had hastened across the miles the moment the news reached him, but still she was alone for a month, with naught but a neighbor to watch her. His heart broke that day, when he beheld the small girl who looked ready to give up on life. It broke again now at the return of the dispassion.

"Daughter."

She looked up with the smile she always gave when he called her "daughter" instead of "cousin." But it was a dim echo of the smile that graced her features one short week ago.

Mordecai sighed. "We will be dining with Kish and his family tonight."

Esther's gaze fell again. "I am not hungry."

"I know." He crouched down beside her and urged her chin up with a finger. "But you must eat, dear one. If you waste away and leave me too, then how will I survive it? I need you, Esther. Kasia's family needs you. You were closer to her than any of them, and they are comforted by your presence."

Her face twisted in agony before she turned it away. "How can you be so calm about her loss? How can you go over there without it piercing you anew?"

A question he could not answer. Not honestly. How could he explain that the part of his soul that had blossomed as he watched Kasia, as he came to love her, did not accept this loss at all? It felt as though she were only on a journey. Visiting family in another province. Not here, but not *gone*. Not for good.

It was a delusion—he knew that. But when he cried out to the Lord his God, he felt a whisper of peace wash over him like the river flooding the plains. And the soil of his being was left fertile with hope.

Perhaps he was a fool to think she might return. But he was not enough of one to share that, to get another's hopes up where they could be dashed against the rocks of reality. Still, he could not escape the peace, the feeling that the young woman he loved so much was well.

To Esther he could only say, "I trust in Jehovah, my child. I find my sustenance in him."

"But he allowed this to happen. He sent the rains that *killed* her."

"Those rains fall on the just and the unjust alike. He allows much tragedy, or so it seems to us. But we cannot see the future, precious Esther. We do not know what greater tragedy may have come had this one been withheld. It is our part to have faith in his divine orchestration. To put our hand into his and keep our eyes open, so that we might see what small blessings blossom under our tears."

She turned her face back to him. He would not have said she looked convinced, but her eyes were no longer shuttered behind the dull pain. They blazed with an ache magnified by her tears. "What blessing can come of this, cousin? You have lost yet another woman you love. I have lost a dear friend, a sister, a would-be mother."

"Yes, we have. But there is another family of friends three doors down that has also lost a daughter, a sister, and one they loved far longer than we did. Who are we to withhold what comfort we can give them, because it hurts *us*? Is it not our part to ease their burden in whatever way we can?"

When she blinked, a drop of brine fell from each eye. "You are too good, my father. I cannot be like you."

"No?" He smoothed back a few stray hairs from her face and smiled. "Odd. In you I see a spirit far sweeter than mine has ever been. If you will turn over your injured heart to Jehovah, I think you will find far more strength at your disposal than I have."

Her lip quivered, making her look far younger than her twelve years. "How do I do that?"

"Pray, little one. Ask him to touch you, to speak to you. Ask him to bring clarity through the pain."

A frown creased her brow. "And that will work?"

"Jehovah will not keep his comfort from a contrite spirit. Seek him, and he will pour a balm over your soul."

Her nod was small. "I cannot fathom any good coming of Kasia's death . . . but I will look for some."

Not the total surrender to almighty Jehovah that he would have wished, but at least she would keep her heart open to the Lord's ministrations. Mordecai nodded and stood, held out his hand. "Come. We must go to our friends."

The pinched look eased away from her face as she put her hand in his. "Yes. Let us go to our friends."

Gossip sprinted through the palace, and it did not earn Kasia any friends. For a week, she endured hostile glances from the virgins nearly finished their year of preparation. She listened to their mutters and snickers as she walked by on her way from lesson to lesson. More than one "accidental" bump sent her into a table corner or statue.

She would go to the king tonight, and she would go with bruises on body and soul. She would go knowing the other soon-to-be wives hated her for receiving the best room, a higher daily allotment of oils and perfumes, the undivided attention of Hegai. And for being put ahead of them in the line of women awaiting their turn with the king of kings.

Gladly would she have traded places with any one of them. But instead here she stood in her chamber, listening to Hegai instruct her on her final minutes before meeting her husband.

"You may take anything you like with you," he said. "Most select their own dress and jewelry. Some take incense or gifts they make for the king. What do you wish?"

An escape? Kasia swallowed, though her throat felt dry and swollen. Perhaps some fatal disease would strike her down before she came face to face with Xerxes. One could hope.

Moistening her lips, she shook her head. "What do you recommend?"

Hegai smiled, even chuckled. "No one ever asks—they spend so long planning, they care little for what I have to say. But I offer my advice freely to you. Dress simply. Do not detract from your natural beauty with too many adornments. Take no gift, as you have had no time to make one with your hands and could otherwise give nothing the king has not first given you."

He held up a hand and twirled a finger. She spun in a circle so that he could see her from all angles. "The king was intrigued by stories of simple beauty, not riches. Go as *you*. Offer him what you are, who you are. I think he will find it pleasing."

Though she nodded, her hands trembled. She clasped them together. "Will you select my clothing for me?"

"I will." He moved to where the new garments rested, chose a few of the fine pieces—a sleeveless red sheath in the style of the Egyptians, topped with a robe of white linen so finely woven it was translucent. Servants helped her into them behind the screen, and then she emerged and turned again for the custodian's approval.

He nodded. "They suit you well. One necklace, I think, to showcase the fine column of your throat."

"And my torc." Perhaps that would prove a mistake, wearing the gift that reminded her of Masistes, who continued to haunt her dreams. Or perhaps the king would recognize what marked her as his, if that was its purpose.

"Of course." He handed her the silver with its two lions' heads, and while she fitted it onto her arm, he selected an intricately worked necklace for her.

When he turned her to face the mirror of polished bronze, Kasia held her breath. But the image was not so unfamiliar. Finer clothing, yes. And the wink of precious metals was new. But it was her face, unchanged. Her hair, if glossier and trimmed to have more motion in its length. She was still Kasia, daughter of Kish. But how would Kasia, daughter of Kish, fare as Kasia, wife of Xerxes?

The door opened, and seven servants entered. Hegai welcomed them with a nod and a smile. "Your escort. They will take you to the king's chambers and will remain your servants in the house of wives. The rest of your things will be taken over in the morning, once the king gives instruction on where you will stay."

She looked to the servants, but none met her gaze. She turned back to Hegai. "Is there anything else I should know?"

"More than I can tell you right now, and we are out of time." He smiled and approached her, rested his hands on her shoulders. "You will be all right, Kasia. Queen Atossa has promised to take you under her wing, and she will see that you learn all you must. For now, think only of the king, your husband."

Did he not realize that those thoughts made her stomach clench in terror?

He dropped his hands and stepped from between her and the door. "Go."

She knew not what else to do, so she obeyed. Strode forward with all the false confidence she could muster and took her place in the middle of the servants. They led the way out through the gardens, toward the king's palace. Twilight lit the path, and the fragrance of jasmine touched the air. Soothed her soul.

They moved through a small rear door, along a dark hallway, and finally into a chamber far larger than several of her neighbors' houses combined. The rich appointments did little to make the cavernous space feel more welcoming. At least it was empty of anyone but her own company.

One of the servants turned to her. "The king declared a week-long feast as plans are finalized for the war. Some nights he may return early, other nights when dawn streaks the sky. We will wait with you until he comes—is there anything you would like?"

She could be waiting here for hours? Kasia shook her head. "Thank you, but no."

The darkness of the room propelled her to the low windows, where the last streaks of sun were visible on the horizon. She sucked in a breath of appreciation when she beheld the vista from the king's window. The entire city of Susa stretched before her, awash in fire and shadow from the setting sun. There, far to the side, wended the river. There, the temple. That meant that her family's house was somewhere in that cluster of darkened silhouettes.

A pang of homesickness struck her in the chest. She had barely had time to miss them during waking hours these last days, but now thoughts of her family filled her. Ima would be putting the littlest ones into bed for the night, picking up the remnants of a busy day. Abba would be settling down to a few minutes of repose, talking with Zechariah about the project they would work on the next day. Zechariah would try to work in a few comments about joining the army, but Abba would put him off again, saying God's chosen people had no place fighting for their oppressors.

Did they miss her? Did they weep for her still?

A shaft of pain lanced through her, and her eyes slid shut. Hebrew words, usually spoken only at home, came to her lips. "Jehovah God, pour out your healing balm upon my precious sisters and brothers, upon my parents. Ease their grief and their pain. Help Zechariah release the anger I know he felt. And Esther . . . she must feel like yet another loved one has abandoned her. Help her to find a friend to sustain her, and to find comfort in comforting my family. Bless Mordecai for all his goodness and righteousness. Let him not suffer any more for my sake. He deserves better. He deserves the best you have to offer."

She paused, half expecting loneliness to swamp her. To feel isolated, cut off from God and her people alike as she had all week.

But her conscience resonated now within her. Her God was a living God. A present God. Even in the midst of captivity, when the remnant of his children called out to him, he answered. He was as close as a prayer. Had she but cried for him sooner, this week would not have passed so slowly, with such agonizing solitude.

So long as she kept her heart aligned with him, he would sustain her. No matter the back-biting, the sneers from the other women. No matter the disregard she knew to expect from her husband. Even here, she would remain a child of Jehovah.

A shift rippled through the servants, and the one nearest her whispered, "The king comes."

Even as the words were spoken, Kasia heard the door open. She drew in another long breath of peace and thanked Jehovah for stilling the tremble of fear in her limbs.

"Leave us."

The voice sent a different kind of tremble up her spine. It should not have surprised her that the king sounded so much like his brother, but she had not been braced for the similarity. It brought an image of that forbidden face to her mind, one that she struggled to push back down.

The shuffle of feet moved toward the door, and Kasia knew she must face her king. Her husband. As she turned, she wondered what other similarities she would find between this man and the one she had met at the river.

The king stood at the mid-point of the room, his eyes locked on her. Eyes that were filled with light. He had a nose straight and strong. A mouth quirked up into a half-smile.

Kasia let her eyes go round, let the last of the anxiety seep out. "You? *You* are the king?"

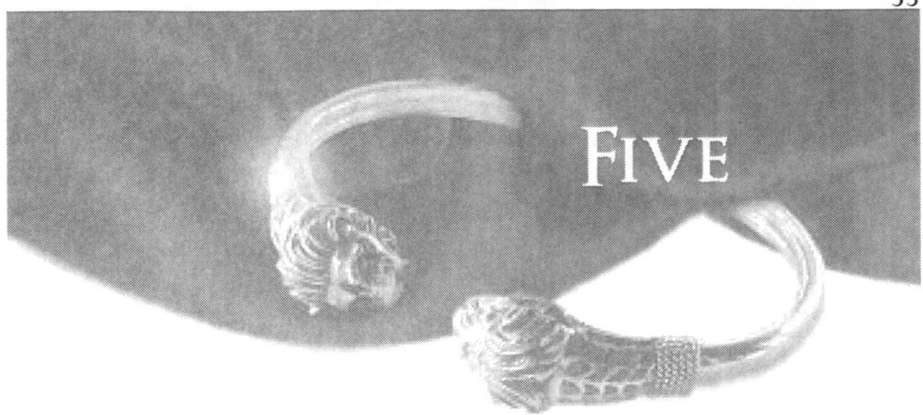

FIVE

Xerxes watched realization light Kasia's face and thoughts roll through her eyes. She was as beautiful as he remembered, the changes his custodian made enhancing what captured him from the start. He evened out his smile and took another step forward. "Haman did not tell you I was the one with him?"

She shook her head, eyes still wide. "He said nothing. And Hegai assumed it was your brother."

He chuckled—and determined to express his displeasure to Haman. "So you thought that I, as brother to the king, had . . . what? Told this brother of your extraordinary beauty and relinquished my interest to the crown?"

Kasia eased forward, her gaze on his face. "Something like that."

"You ascribe to me far too much selflessness. Even were I my brother, I would not have given you up. Not with the way you have been haunting my thoughts."

She kept moving toward him, albeit slowly. He caught the glimmer of a torc on her arm under the sheer fabric—the torc he had given her. Ah, yes. He had haunted her thoughts as well. She shook her head, sending glossy dark waves swaying. "I dreamt of you. But I did not realize it was you, the king . . . ."

And therein lay her greatest allure. He could not remember ever meeting someone who did not know who he was. But it was evident from their first exchange that she had no idea about his identity. Her interest was in him. The man, not the king. A distinction he did not realize he wanted until he saw the flame of desire in her eyes unrelated to his title or wealth.

He smiled at her and held out a hand. Her pace increased from hesitant to eager, though she stopped before him without touching him. In her eyes he saw the same battle waged ten days ago. Modesty against instinct, curiosity against restraint.

He rested his hand against her cheek and knew the passion would win. She would not understand it enough to curb it. "And what would you have done if I were my brother, and you met me again after becoming wife to the king?"

Her eyes slid shut. "I would have prayed to God for the strength to resist these things you make me feel."

Did she know how her words made desire curl up inside him? "And would your God have granted it?"

Her eyes opened again, and now they smiled along with her well-shaped lips. "He would have. My God values covenants—he would have helped me be faithful to my husband."

"Then let us be grateful I am your husband, so you may be faithful *without* resisting these things I make you feel." He returned her smile and then, unable to help himself, leaned down to brush his lips over hers.

His own reaction he knew and expected. The surge of blood through his veins, the headiness of indulgence. It was hers that interested him more. He felt the quaver that arched her back and lifted her up onto her toes. When he anchored her with an arm around her waist, she slid one of hers around his neck, rested the other against his chest. It was an invitation he had no desire to refuse—he deepened the kiss.

She responded with a sweet hesitancy underscored by fire and even made a noise of protest when he pulled away a moment later. He gazed into her eyes, clouded now, and smiled. "I knew my impatience was well placed. I would not have wanted to wait until after the war to see you again."

"I am glad you were insistent." She reached up to trace the contours of his face. Her expression reflected both confusion and contentment. "I could not understand why you were, though. Even realizing who you are . . . Hegai said it was my beauty, but you have wives already more beautiful. And some of the virgins awaiting their turn with you—they are stunning."

A laugh slipped out. "I must say, none of my wives have ever sung the others' praises." He kissed her again, softly. "Perhaps, were you simply standing there among them, I would not call you the most beautiful. But I knew the first moment I saw you that I must have you. You, above anyone else."

She stroked her fingers over his beard. "Why?"

"Why?" He caught her hand, kissed it. "Because when I followed the sound of your cry and saw you in that river, there was utter rapture on your face. As if you had given yourself totally to the sensation of cold water, as if that single moment were enough to live for. I want you to feel that for me, to give yourself to me that fully. Will you do that, lovely Kasia?"

She smiled when he said her name as he had at the river. "I will. I cannot do otherwise."

Just as he hoped. "Then when you spotted me, you leapt back onto the bank to protect your sister. You made each decision in the next few moments based upon what would benefit her and keep her safe. I want you to be so devoted, so dedicated to me. Will you promise that, lovely Kasia?"

Her smile went luminous. "I will. Even were you not *you*, I would pledge such loyalty to my husband. But because you *are* you . . . that much and more."

Just as he wanted. "When you spoke of your father, in spite of disagreeing with some of his principles love shone in your eyes. I want you to love me as thoroughly as your husband. As a man, rather than a king. Will you give me that as well, lovely Kasia?"

She lifted her brows. "That kind of love requires time, tending, a full, open heart. But given how much I feel for you already, after so short an acquaintance . . . I think it safe to promise I will. Shall I let you know when I do?"

Ah, how quickly he had come to treasure that amused smile of hers. "Please. Do you want to know the final thing that sealed your fate?"

She looped her arms around his neck. He would not have expected such ease already, but he would not argue. "Of course."

"You said you were a Jew proudly. I want you to be my wife as proudly, to serve me from your heart. Will you give such allegiance to both king and empire?"

Now her face hardened. Would she be surprised to know he was glad of that? Glad she stiffened in his arms? "Will I be your wife proudly? Yes. Will I take pride in what my husband accomplishes for his empire? Yes. But will I give you the same allegiance I give Jehovah? I cannot. You are my husband and king. But he is my God."

He slid a hand into her hair and urged her head back. "Good. I would have been disappointed if you promised to give up such a crucial part of yourself. And would not have believed you, which would have cast your other oaths in doubt."

She relaxed—until he pressed his mouth to her neck. Then her pulse kicked up, and her hands gripped the back of his robe, his hair. "So the king values honesty."

"The king hears lies all day. From you, lovely Kasia, I want only truth. For you, I want not to be the king. Call me Xerxes, my love."

"Xerxes." His name sounded like music on her tongue. And when she looked into his eyes, he knew that she offered all she was.

For the first time in his life, he held a treasure all his gold could not buy. But somehow he held it anyway.

He never intended to let go.

The moment Kasia awoke she became aware of the solid arms around her, the broad chest upon which her head rested. Contentment flooded her.

Xerxes shifted onto his side and held her close, leaned down to kiss her. His kisses were like strong wine the night before, lulling her into a realm between waking and sleep, where sensation was magnified. She wished it were still night so that she could lose herself again. But reality must return with the morning light. He would have to put back on his kingly robes and attend to the many guests in the palace, the business of managing an empire. She would have to get settled into her new home among the other wives.

He chuckled against her mouth. "What thought troubles you, my love? You tensed up."

"I am sorry." She summoned her smile again. "It is only that I hate the thought of leaving you."

His eyes sparkled, his lips turned up. "Perhaps the king should command the sun to reverse itself."

She chuckled and snuggled against him. "There are some things even the king of kings cannot do."

"Sad but true. We will be interrupted soon. And I see new worry in those captivating eyes. Tell me what it is so that I can erase it."

The stroke of his hand on her back made her smile. "I know not what to expect now."

"Ah. The drawback of cutting your preparation short." He kissed her nose. Her heart nearly burst at the sweetness of the gesture. "Well, my love, in a few moments the servants shall slip into the room to help us dress. Then I shall go back to strategizing my invasion of Greece, and you shall settle into your new rooms, which shall be second only to the queen's."

She blinked at how easily he spoke about going to war. "Are these rooms not occupied by another wife?"

Xerxes arched a brow. "The best ones are, yes."

"Could I not take an empty one somewhere?"

"Kasia." Though he chuckled, confusion shadowed his amusement. "It is how my favor is made known."

"I know, but . . . the exceptions made for me already have not settled well with the others. I am still uncomfortable in all this wealth . . . and I do not relish being moved with each new addition."

His gaze was both fond and wary. "You think you will be so easily displaced from my favor?"

"I was warned to expect it."

"You are so open." He chuckled and then paused, contemplation in his eyes. "It will not be understood—but then, I enjoy confusing everyone now and again. You may pick whatever room you want, lovely Kasia, and you may keep it as your own whenever we are in Susa. I will give the instruction as soon as the servants arrive. For now, give me a kiss to last me until I see you tonight."

"Tonight?" She knew her excitement saturated her voice—and knew it was probably unseemly. A wife of the king would be expected to graciously accept whatever was handed her, be it more attention or less.

But he looked pleased, so she cared not what was expected. "You shall indeed. Now—that kiss."

She gave it willingly, and sighed when the sound of the door opening intruded on her senses. Xerxes pressed one last kiss onto her lips and then pulled away. He rose without any inhibitions, and his servants leisurely draped a robe around him. There were far too many eyes present for Kasia to get up so easily, but her maidservants seemed to understand this. One of them approached with clothing and a small smile.

Kasia sat up, her back to the rest of the room, and reached for the tunic. Her motions halted when Xerxes demanded, "What is that?"

His voice sounded harsh, cold. Cloth clutched to her chest, she craned her head around. "Pardon?"

His gaze narrowed upon her side. "You have bruises, and they look only a few days old. What happened?"

"I bumped into some of the statuary." Hopefully her smile looked self-deprecating, nothing more. "I am sure my grace will improve as I grow used to my surroundings."

He planted his hands on his hips. "Tell me whose hand caused these bumps. I will see them punished."

"Not on my account, please. It is nothing. I have gotten worse by playing with my little brothers."

"You are too forgiving, Kasia. First you praise the others' beauty, now you defend their cruelty." He held her gaze for a long moment.

She begged him silently to relent. She could not bring trouble on the heads of those other women, whose resentment was perfectly understandable. But if she refused to give names if he asked for them directly, he would have no choice but to punish her.

Xerxes sighed, and his face relaxed. "As you wish, my love. But be assured the story of your forgiveness will reach the ears of whoever did this to you, so that they realize my displeasure is tempered only by your kindness." He flicked his gaze to one of the servants, who nodded.

"Thank you." She gave him a smile and slipped the provided garment over her head. Somehow she suspected it would take a lot more forgiveness than that to hew herself a place here.

He moved to tenderly cup her face and leaned down to kiss her. In spite of their audience, Kasia allowed herself to soak up all he poured into the touch. It would have to be enough to sustain her through the day.

A moment later he swept from the room, and with him went her breath. It sucked out in a sigh that left her deflated. The same maid who had smiled at her stepped close to her side. "Shall we show you to the house of wives, lady?"

Kasia shook herself and studied the servant. She was probably a few years older than Kasia, with features that looked European. "Certainly. What is your name?"

"Desma." She dipped her head.

"It is good to meet you, Desma. And the rest of you?"

The other four maidservants introduced themselves, and then the two eunuchs. Kasia suspected it would take a day or two to remember them. They fell into formation around her and moved forward, leaving her little choice but to go where they did.

An attempt not to gawk at the hallways they traveled proved futile. How did one man amass such wealth? Everywhere, gold and silver and bronze, the finest polished stone, the rarest wood.

As they turned a corner, she spotted a statue carved of fine cypress that she would have loved to stop and examine. The figure itself held no interest for her, but the grain was exquisite. Her father would have considered finding such a piece of wood a treasure in itself.

Her nostrils flared, and she inclined her heart to Jehovah. Prayed that he would bless her father, her mother, her siblings. Esther and Mordecai.

It took several minutes to reach the separate palace that Desma introduced as her new home. But as soon as they stepped inside, Kasia smiled. Children's laughter and squeals sounded, along with mothers' and nurses' admonitions. Her gaze settled on the courtyard, where a group of well-dressed women clustered with rhytons of wine in their hands and a banquet of fruit and bread on a table between them.

How long before she saw them as her equals? Would she ever?

Desma stepped closer to her side. "Shall I show you the available chambers, mistress?"

Kasia swallowed down the rising panic and directed the question toward God. A peace settled over her. "No. Take me to the meanest one."

Desma's spine straightened. "Mistress?"

"I have enemies enough here, Desma. I will not create more by putting myself above any of them."

"But you *are* above them, mistress. The king has never given any of his wives the choice of their chambers."

"Perhaps not. But since he has given it to me, it is my prerogative to choose the place most comfortable." She smiled, wondering if this girl realized that until a week ago, their situations were not so different. "I daresay even the vilest of these rooms will be far more luxurious than to what I am accustomed. In my father's house, I was fortunate to share a room with only my four sisters and not also with my five brothers."

The corner of Desma's mouth tugged up. "Ten of you? Your mother must be a woman of limitless patience."

"And limitless love." Who was helping her with the wee ones now? The twins were the next eldest girls, but they were too involved with their own thoughts. Ah well, they would have to step out of their private world. At least Eglah and Sarai were well behaved. The younger boys, though . . . they delighted in giving the girls grief.

Desma sighed. "Very well. This way."

They skirted the courtyard and moved down a hallway lined with doors. Desma stopped before a closed one at the end, and another of the maidservants—Leda, was it?—tugged the iron ring to open it. The taller of the eunuchs, Theron, entered first and took account of the chamber before nodding. The group broke their ranks so that she might enter.

It was a dim room, the only windows low and small. But the scent of flowers wafted in from them, and the appointments were blessedly simple.

Desma shook her head. "It is too close, surely. There is another—"

"No, it is perfect." She noted two other chambers connected to this one, probably intended for the servants or perhaps a child or two. Put together, it was as large as her father's house. "Perfect."

Though her surprise was colored with disbelief, Desma relented with a tilt of her head. "As you wish, mistress. We will have your belongings brought over."

Three of the maids scurried away, and the eunuchs took up position in the corners of the room. Kasia looked around, wondering how a wife was to pass her days when she had no household, no mending or cooking, and no babes.

"Well, this is most unusual."

At the vaguely familiar voice of Queen Atossa, Kasia spun back to the doorway. Xerxes' mother stood in all her regal splendor with a lifted brow and a crooked smile.

"Here you are in the lowliest chamber of the house of wives, yet my son assures me you are all he hoped and more."

When the queen mother took a step into the small room, her presence seemed to fill it so much Kasia felt she should kneel in deference. She allowed herself only to dip her head. "He gave me leave to choose my own rooms."

"And you chose this?"

"As you see."

Atossa shook her head, but her face reflected approval. "You are an odd girl, Kasia. And I have not seen the king smile so brightly since he was a boy. Come, share the meal with me and some of the other women I think you will like. We will introduce you to life here—and teach you how to avoid Amestris, though you will have to appear at her feast this week."

More relieved than excited, Kasia followed her new matriarch out the door.

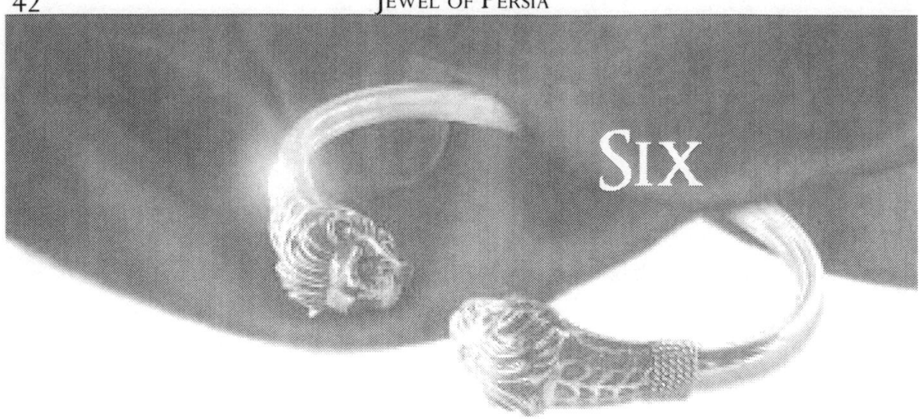

SIX

Xerxes settled onto his throne and scanned the courtroom. Even at such an early hour, it was filled with men chattering, arguing, laughing. Some in military regalia, others in the finery of private citizens. Still more in the rough garb of commoners come to seek help or counsel.

All signs of a busy, productive empire. And yet on this morning, the empire made his smile dim. This morning, he would prefer to forget he was king for a few more hours.

"My lord." His uncle appeared at his side, a telltale line in his forehead. Artabanus could out-worry any man in the kingdom—if Xerxes listened to his every concern, nothing would ever get done. The war was a perfect example—he had very nearly changed his mind about the campaign based on Artabanus's advice. Had it not been for that startling vision they shared two years ago . . . .

Even his uncle could not maintain his skepticism in the face of the god.

Xerxes greeted him with a smile. "What is it today, uncle?"

"Another stretch of canal has collapsed at Athos."

Xerxes stifled a groan. This was *not* how he wanted to spend his day. He would rather dwell on thoughts of his sweet Kasia and her excitement at another night in his arms. "Naturally. A plan we adopted to *avoid* problems, and it causes more. I wonder if sailing around the mountain could prove any more a travail than bypassing it. Repairs?"

"They are reinforcing the walls, I believe, but the collapse killed a great many workers."

Xerxes rested a knuckle against his lips and sighed. "Something must be done about these continual collapses. Has every group encountered it?"

"All but the Phoenicians."

"An exception worthy of note." Xerxes straightened and lifted a brow. "What are they doing differently than everyone else?"

Artabanus's mouth flopped open for a moment. "Well . . . I recall hearing something about how ridiculously wide their excavations were at the start—twice as wide as the rest of the canal. There was some grumbling about it."

Sometimes it felt as though the rest of the world were idiots. "Artabanus, there is a reason we put the Phoenicians and the Egyptians in charge of the bridge over the Hellespont. Their engineering acumen is unsurpassed. Has it occurred to no one that they made it wider to avoid these collapses?"

"I know not, my lord, I was only apprised of all this recently. But of course, you speak rightly. Should all adopt the model?"

"Where possible, unless it would take longer to widen it than to shore it up and finish. They must use discretion, if that is not asking too much." Perhaps he ought to have put Phoenician overseers in charge of this entire project too. He had instead opted to maintain autonomy between the different nations working on the canal, but what he gained in peace he lost in quality.

"I will make your wishes known."

"I trust you will. Mardonius!"

His cousin and oldest friend set his course for the throne. Artabanus stiffened but managed a polite greeting.

Mardonius offered him a taunting smile, then nodded with more sincerity to Xerxes. "The king is looking well this morning."

Xerxes chuckled. "For once I believe your flattery. Have you seen Haman yet?"

His friend shook his head. "He is probably riding with your brother, master."

"If you see them before I do, tell him to come to me at once."

"Certainly." With a courteous bow, Mardonius strode off.

Artabanus released a pent-up breath and muttered, "I maintain that such a wise king ought not surround himself with such injudicious advisers."

His lips wanted to twitch up. "Uncle, need I remind you that the advice you consider his greatest offense is the war you now believe in?"

"If a man advocates a wise course for the wrong reasons, it makes him not wise, my lord. Only lucky. It is obvious from our visions that the god wishes you to lead us against Greece. That does not mean the evil one will not try to turn your certain victory into defeat through the bad advice of fools."

"But even within the advice of fools is often hidden a pearl of wisdom. A wise man searches it out before dismissing the rest. And when a wise man has a wise uncle to help him discern those pearls . . . ."

His uncle's lips finally curved up. "Then blessings will follow, and soon enough you will rule all the world. You know my worries are only out of my devotion to you."

"Indeed. Go, write your missive to Mount Athos. I will speak with Darius for a moment."

"Ah, of course." Artabanus turned and offered a warm smile to the young man hurrying toward them. "Good morning, my prince."

Xerxes' eldest son stopped a step before the throne and grinned. "The same to you, uncle. Father, you look well this morning."

"So I am told." He drew in a deep breath and, as Artabanus said his farewells and disappeared into the crowd, measured his son. He did it often these days. The law said he must name his successor before he went on campaign, and though Darius was the logical choice, he needed to be sure.

At eighteen, he possessed a man's height. But his shoulders were just beginning to broaden; his strength was stored in muscles slight and wiry. His face was fine-featured with the beauty his mother was famous for, though thankfully he had avoided Amestris's temperament.

It felt like a mere week ago Darius had been nipping at his heels like a pup. Could he possibly be old enough to rule half the world, to be the king of kings? And yet when Xerxes was his age, he had married Amestris, just become a father, and was even then plotting how to convince his own father to name him king instead of his older brother.

Not to mention that though Darius was too young, his other sons were younger still. The only answer for it was to live a good while longer and give this man-child more time to mature.

A determination made doubly pleasurable given the company he would have waiting in his chamber whenever he willed it. Kasia could keep a man young while he waited for his sons to age.

Darius grinned anew. "Rumor says your excellent mood this morning is due to the latest addition to the harem. Is it true you rushed this girl through the preparations in only a week?"

Xerxes returned his grin. Perhaps his son was more man than he gave him credit for. "I hardly have time to waste, considering how soon I shall leave to inspect the gathering armies."

"Mother is in a snit about it." Darius chuckled. "Not that *that* is unusual."

Xerxes thanked the god again that his son shared his good humor. "You have seen her this morning? How is she feeling?"

"When I asked her that, she said 'large.' Which undoubtedly contributes to her snit. She droned on for a while about how she is ever expanding with another of your babes, and you are entertaining yourself with a wench young enough to be your daughter."

Xerxes rolled his eyes. "I shall pay her a visit and assure her she is yet the most beautiful woman in all Persia." If her vanity was not given its regular stroking, they would all pay for it.

"More beautiful than the new one then? She will be glad to hear it."

"There is no face lovelier than my queen's. But remember, my son, that there is more to a pleasing wife than her face." He arched a brow. "I suppose it is time to find you a wife of your own. Has anyone caught your eye?"

An odd expression flitted over Darius's face. "I . . . would rather wait until after the war. I have little desire to get attached to a woman only to leave her within a month or two."

He doubted it was so simple but saw no reason to press. "When we return triumphant, then. Ah, there are your uncle and Haman."

The two men drew near, looking merry. When they stopped beside Darius, Haman gave Xerxes a courteous bow. "Mardonius said the king wishes to speak to me. You saw your Jewess again last night, did you not?"

Xerxes folded his arms across his chest. "Yes, though she was unaware of the 'again' until I entered the room. Why did you not inform her I was the one she met before?"

"She did not recognize her own king?" Haman snorted. "I assumed she knew."

"Or wanted her to be in as much discomfort as possible? My friend, your distaste for her people is too consuming."

Haman looked none too concerned at the rebuke. "They are a race of slaves."

"As is your own. How grateful you should be, then, that your king is one who grants grace to the peoples he conquers. Hmm?"

"I am most grateful, master. It is the Jews who refuse to acknowledge your power and might."

Masistes laughed and slapped a hand to Haman's shoulder. "You will never convince him, my lord. And I must say, I too wonder how she could not recognize you."

"I daresay she did not expect the king to be riding with only one attendant—she would not have seen my eunuchs. And since Haman did not make it clear and Hegai had assumed it was *you* Haman rode with . . . ."

Haman attempted to fight back a grin. He failed. "Fascinating. Masistes, your brother's new wife thought herself in love with *you* and yet forced to marry another."

Darius shook his head. "What a terrible week she must have spent."

Haman rolled his eyes. "It serves the girl right for her shameless conduct."

"Shameless? She is shameless for trying to talk her way out of a situation she considered dangerous?" A familiar heat thrummed to life in Xerxes' chest, pushing him to his feet. "Whatever your opinion of her and her people, Haman, you will do well to remember that she is now my wife."

One thing must be said for Haman—he always knew when to back away before Xerxes' temper could flare too hot. "Of course, master. I am glad you have found some entertainment with the girl."

Masistes took a step away. "Well, I am intrigued. I say we visit the women, flatter the queen, and get a glimpse of my brother's newest paramour. What say you, my lord?"

Xerxes grinned and fell in beside his brother. "The queen could use some flattering. Let us go."

He had not paid a visit to the women's palace in several weeks, but he was not surprised to find the gardens flourishing, the adornments shining. The younger of his children ran about, darting this way and that, though the older ones were at their studies. He kept a close eye on all his sons' progress—some of them would be generals, others satraps, governors. All must learn to bear the burden of responsibility.

His gaze raked over the women that were out of their rooms. A few sat at looms, others stitched, some fastened gold decorations onto their clothing. Still more, Amestris among them, merely sat. Usually she made it a point to outdo the others and produce the loveliest garments for him, herself, and their four children. But she was not exactly a young woman anymore . . . perhaps carrying this child was harder on her than he knew, especially with the added stress of this week's feast. He ought to arrange a special gift for her. If he were lucky, it would deflect her irritation over "the wench young enough to be his daughter."

Kasia he saw nowhere. It took a moment for the expectant spike in his pulse to smooth back down to normal.

After pausing to greet each child and its mother he finally reached Amestris and gave her a smile. "There you are, my queen. The child in your womb must be blessed indeed, for you are lovelier today than ever."

Amestris turned her eyes up. They were a perfect almond shape, the color of a round of amber. But the only spark to light them these days was of irritation. Her temperament had worsened when she became queen. It seemed power fed her discontent.

Her smile, if insincere, was nonetheless stunning. "How kind of you to visit me. Unless it was another of your wives you came to see?"

Yes, there was that spark that could so quickly be fanned into a dangerous hatred. Xerxes grinned into it. "Naturally I must pay my respects to the group, but seeking you was my primary goal. Is it not so, Darius?"

His son smiled guilelessly. "The moment I told him you were not feeling well this morning, he hastened to see you."

She looked far from appeased. "The others are muttering about this Jewess. Why must the king shame us by adding a slave to our numbers? One the very age of his esteemed daughter?"

It was all he could do not to roll his eyes. His brides were always within a certain age group. Could he help that his eldest daughter was now of marrying age as well? "I assure you, Amestris, all I do is out of concern for you. Have you not made it clear I am to find my entertainment elsewhere when you are with child?" Or with a mild ache in her head. Or a sore toe. Or in a sour temper. Or sometimes, he suspected, if her hair would not lie just so. Between all her complaints, she would not receive him three hundred sixty of the three hundred sixty-five days a year.

Amestris settled her arms over the protruding round of her stomach and scowled. "Is she pretty?"

"Pretty enough. Not so beautiful as you." He leaned down and pressed a kiss to her cheek. "Is there anything I can do for you?"

The tension around her mouth softened. "I am ready to deliver this babe and present you with another son, that is all. This new girl—is she a full wife or a concubine?"

"Uh . . . ." He straightened and glanced to Haman.

Haman arched a brow. "Her father had no money for a dowry, master, so she received the lesser contract."

Amestris's lips turned up. "Very well. Enjoy her while she holds your attention. And see that she is cautioned to stay out of my way. I am in no mood for the airs of an upstart concubine who knows not her place."

"Of course." He stepped back, giving the others a chance to smother her with flattery. His eyes tracked over the courtyard again.

Hegai stood in the corner—if anyone knew where Kasia would be, it was the custodian. He moved toward him.

Hegai bent low in greeting. "My king. We are honored to welcome you this morning."

"Certainly. I was very pleased with Kasia. You did well with her."

The servant smiled, his eyes bright. "Thank you, master. The young lady was very open to my advice, so I took pleasure in sharing your preferences. She is a lovely girl. A disposition unlike any of your other wives."

"Indeed. Is she settling in well?"

Hegai's smile curled into a grin. "You may want to see for yourself. She is in the back garden."

Since his companions said their farewells to the queen, he motioned them to join him. "We will do that. She selected her room?"

"Yes, master." Humor laced his tone.

Xerxes lifted a brow. "Let me guess—the smallest, barest one she could find."

Hegai chuckled. "You know her well for so short an acquaintance."

Darius, Masistes, and Haman drew near, so Xerxes only nodded and led the way down the hall that would open into the rear gardens. He stopped them just inside the door.

Amidst the trumpeting blooms and trees stretching toward heaven, a gaggle of tots sat entranced around a cross-legged Kasia. Though the eldest of the children could not be more than four, they all held still, faces intent upon her. And she sang. Hebrew, but he needed no vocabulary lesson to understand the playful tone. Her voice clear and sweet, she moved her hands in a dance of movement. When she tapped each child on the nose in turn, a chorus of giggles broke out.

Finding a woman who had a way with children was no great thing. But finding one whose face betrayed total delight as she lifted her voice? One who laughed along with them as if there were no greater joy? He had never met another creature who mustered such passion for each moment of life.

His brother stepped close to his side. "Lovely. I can see why you were intrigued."

"Lovely, yes." Haman sounded nowhere near impressed. "But better suited for a nursemaid than a wife of the king of kings."

He shot his friend a glare. "She pleases me. Let that be that."

"I will speak not another word of her."

He glanced at his son to see whose side he would take up, and his breath bunched up in his chest. It was a look he knew well, that expression on Darius's countenance. Knew it by feel. The same intrigue he himself was given to, the very one that had overcome him upon *his* first sighting of Kasia.

No. He would not suffer his son mooning over her, risking scandal and bad blood. He would not allow himself to consider that Darius was far closer to her in age. He would not let himself wonder if she would get a glimpse of the pup at his side and realize that her husband was, as Amestris helpfully pointed out, old enough to be her father.

Curse it.

"Father!"

The happy squeal stole his thoughts back from that vortex, and he looked down in time to scoop up little Chinara, who was aimed at his knees. With a chuckle, he settled her on his hip. "And a good morning to you, little sweet. Have you run off from your mother again?"

The wee one offered him an impish grin and no apology. "That is Kasia. She told us a story about a shepherd boy who fought a giant, and he won! And then the boy grew up to be king, but his sons were bad, and their people would not listen, and so eventually your father's fathers carried them away." She clapped chubby hands to his cheeks. "I know not why that made them cry. I like it when you carry *me* away, Father."

He laughed and rewarded the mite's wit with a kiss upon her brow. Chinara always brightened his day. "Shall I carry you around all day with me? You can help me pass judgment and plot out our great war against Greece."

Her face gathered into a mask of consideration. "No. I shall listen to more of Kasia's songs. But perhaps tomorrow I will help you, Father."

"I will look forward to it." He placed her back on her feet and then made himself face reality. The exchange would have caught Kasia's attention. When he looked up, would he find her gaze had shifted and locked on Darius?

Her attention had indeed been snagged from the children. She had pulled her knees up, wrapped her arms around them. Her expression registered fascination, her eyes reflected what he would have called love, though she may apply the word more carefully than he. But she looked not at Darius. Nor at Masistes, at Haman, at any of the children. Her attention was his, and his alone.

Evening could not come fast enough.

Seven

Esther jerked up in her bed to fight the enemy holding her down. It took her a moment to realize her cover was tangled in her limbs, nothing more. Still, her heart thumped too fast, too hard, and dark images pounded her eyes.

There had been water everywhere. Pouring from the sky, surging from beneath. Wave upon wave beating her until she could not tell which way was up. Just as she thought her lungs would explode, Kasia's name had burst from her lips and the nightmare had vanished.

Only it had not. Kasia was still gone, lost to those waves. Had her last moments been like that? The burning, the confusion, the mad fight for salvation?

Esther tossed her cover aside and crawled out of her bed, desperate for fresh air. Exiting into the main room, she heard the soft snoring of the servants and silence from Mordecai's chamber. She held her breath and let herself out the front door.

The night washed cool and refreshing over her. She knew not where she intended to go, but her feet would not stand still. They took her down the street, stuck close to the houses, and paused at the end. A low wall stretched ahead. Over it she would find the Choaspes River.

Dare she?

Kasia would have. She would have cast a glance over her shoulder to be sure no one followed, then run off with a grin. She would have plunged into the water until it erased all her worries, then reemerged the better for it.

Until the night the waters did not relinquish her again.

With a shudder, Esther turned back toward home. She took a step, then stopped when the sound of metal clashing against metal reached her ears. Weapons? Out here? Curiosity underscored her alarm—she slid forward until she could see over the wall.

The moon, three-quarters full, shone down and bathed the earth with silver light that erased all color and left it shimmering. It gilded the two men, caught their spears and daggers arcing through the air.

Her breath caught when she recognized Zechariah, his face stony, his arms bulging as he parried off his attacker. She was set to release it in a scream when the attacker broke off. And laughed.

"Were it possible, I would swear you had been practicing on your own, Zech."

Zechariah relaxed his stance, but from where she stood in the shadows, his smile looked forced. "I have a few demons to battle."

"The Spartans themselves would tremble if they saw you tonight. Fight like that in the war, and the king will advance you quickly."

War? King? Esther pressed a hand to her lips. Surely he did not intend to join the army, to march against Greece. Surely she would not lose him, too.

Zechariah sighed. "Assuming I can convince my father to let me go. If he knew you were training me, Bijan . . . ."

"You are a man, Zechariah. Old enough to join the army without your father's permission."

Esther had the urge to lob a rock at this Bijan's skull for such a suggestion. Zechariah sighed again. "He just lost his eldest daughter. If I joined the king's forces, he would see it as losing his eldest son as well. I cannot do that to the family. I will not go without his blessing."

Yet the expression on Zechariah's face told her that though he may respect his father's word on the matter, he would also resent him for it.

Her poor Zechariah. Would he ever be content in the life he was given? To labor beside his father and take over the wood shop? Or would he forever yearn for more, for what he could not have?

Bijan snorted. "You are a better son than your father deserves. Did you see the way he sneered at me when I came into the shop last week? It is no wonder few other Persians make use of his skill."

Esther winced, but Zechariah chuckled. "He will never see that he is as judgmental of his Persian neighbors as they have been of him. I had better get back, Bijan, before I am missed. Same time tomorrow night?"

"I will be sure I am well rested so I might offer you more of a challenge." The Persian took the spear Zechariah proffered and, with a wave, trotted off down the river.

Before she could dash away, Zechariah turned. A start of recognition crossed his countenance, and he strode her way.

She pulled her spine up, rolled her shoulders back, and promised herself she would not cower.

"Esther." His voice, though low and harsh, sounded sweet to her ears. "What are you doing here?"

She tried to arch her brow in the same way Kasia would have. "I might ask you the same question."

The corner of his mouth tugged up, though he was quick to bite back the smile. "Ah, but I am not a slip of a girl out without chaperone."

"And yet I daresay my cousin would not be as angry at finding me here as your father would be you." She nodded to the spot where he had been training for a war not his own. "What are you doing, Zechariah? You know he will never allow you to go, so why torment yourself?"

He loosed a long breath and raked a hand over his hair. "I do not expect a girl-child to understand these things. Even Kasia did not, though she found it amusing."

Realizing Kasia had known and greeted it with good humor eased her heart. "So you will leave me to guess why? Is it that you do not enjoy your work in the wood shop? Are you seeking relief for the pain of Kasia's loss?"

He folded his arms over his chest and stared at her in the soft light of the moon. "Have you ever wanted something without reason, little Esther? As if it were part of your blood, part of your flesh, even though all logic tells you it cannot be?"

She took a moment to consider, then shook her head.

"I thought not. But can you imagine what it would feel like?" He let his arms drop to his sides and turned his face toward the moon. "I cannot shake the feeling that I was born for more than carving chairs and tables. The first time I took up a spear and shield, it was as though I could finally see through the veil always over my eyes, as if I glimpsed what my future could be." He looked her way again. "Have I shocked you?"

How could she be shocked when his tone conveyed such assurance? "The blood of warriors must still flow through you."

"Perhaps. And perhaps if there were a chance to fight *against* Persia rather than *for* it, Abba would not argue with my desire to take up arms." He sighed and studied her for a long moment. "Will you keep my secret, little Esther? If he found out I come here each night . . ."

"Of course." Her eyes tracked past him though, to where his training took place. One false move, one slip, and he could be wounded or killed. "Who is this Bijan? I did not recognize him."

"He does not live in this part of Susa—he is the son of a wealthy Persian, one who sought out the best to carve a chest for him, in spite of the fact that the best is Jewish. That is how we met. We began talking one day when Abba was out. He is one of the Immortals."

Esther blinked. One of the king's most elite fighters was training Zechariah? And found him so competent? "Oh."

"Mmm." He nodded toward the street behind her. "Come, let me deliver you home."

She turned when he touched her elbow and fell in beside him. Though her feet strolled sedately, her thoughts sprinted too fast. What if this hidden drive of Zechariah's ripped him away from her?

He stopped outside Mordecai's door and looked down at her. "I can trust you with this?"

Her chin edged up. "Need you ask?"

A quirk of his lips was her answer. "Good night, little one."

She slipped back inside, climbed into her bed. Now she would have even more images to plague her dreams. Kasia, swallowed by the river. And Zechariah, bitten by a spear.

If only she could survive without sleep.

All conversation ceased the moment Kasia stepped into the courtyard. She drew in a long breath, fastened a small smile onto her lips and made her way to an empty corner. The other wives began talking again, but their whispers were all pointed now.

"Presumptuous slave."

"I cannot believe the king is giving her such attention."

"He will tire of her soon."

"Did you see her room? And yet he calls her every night."

"Mistress." Desma kneeled at her knee, face pained. "Why do you suffer this? Put them in their place. However long it may last, you are the favorite of the king, and that gives you privileges."

Kasia shook her head and smiled when Leda arrived with a plate of food and a chalice of sweet watered wine. "But if I should fall from that favor, Desma, the impact will be all the harder if I exalt myself now."

Desma sighed. "Mistress, I served a favorite of the king before, but his esteem for you far outshines anything I have seen. Your heart is kind, your spirit bright. You deserve to take the honor your husband gives you."

Kasia cast her gaze over the courtyard and the assortment of women breakfasting. Some were old enough to be her mother and had been with Xerxes since he was an ambitious prince. Some were no older than she. All of the full wives had come from upstanding families, some were royalty in their own right. The concubines were of outstanding beauty.

Her maidservants had shared enough gossip with her over the past week of feasting that she knew who the king had once loved, who he never had any fondness for. Who to avoid at all costs, and who they thought would welcome her.

None had. Oh, some were nice when Atossa introduced her a week ago, especially when they saw her lowly chamber. But when she was called night after night, their warmth baked into a parched, dry chasm. Halfway through the week, she had given up attending the queen's nightly feasts. Why present herself only to be ignored or insulted?

How she missed Esther. Her sisters. Her chest banded at the thought of them. *A friendly face, Jehovah. Please, send me one friendly face.*

To Desma she sent a tight smile. "I feel unequal to the honor, my friend. If the king loves me, it is for no reason these women would recognize. I will be content if I can live quietly among them." So long as she could then spark to life in Xerxes' arms every evening. But what if he tired of her? What then would she have?

Her maid gave up. Kasia broke off a piece of bread and settled it on her tongue, but before she could swallow a shadow fell over her. Hegai crouched at her side. "Greetings, mistress."

Her heart knew relief. Every time Hegai spoke to her, it was to tell her that she would join the king again. "Good morning, Hegai."

"I come with tidings from the king. He must welcome another woman into the house of wives this night, but he wishes you to rest assured that he will see you again tomorrow."

Her joy froze in her chest, but she managed a smile. She had known this day would come. There were too many wives, too many brides that needed his attention. Still it hurt—how could it not? But she would not give the others the pleasure of seeing it. "Of course. If you speak to the king again, tell him I understand but will miss him keenly."

"Certainly. He also wishes you to have this."

From his upheld hand dangled a gleaming strand of white spheres that reflected the morning's light in an iridescent rainbow. She reached out a finger and touched one of them. "Beautiful. Are they pearls?"

Hegai chuckled and took the liberty of securing them around her neck. "They are. Have you never seen any before?"

She shook her head. "Not until I came here, and since then there have been so many jewels everywhere I cannot begin to guess which are which."

"I imagine my master will see that you learn them. He says these reminded him of the gleam of your flawless skin." Hegai grinned and straightened. "Wear them when he calls you tomorrow."

"I will. Thank you for delivering them. And I look forward to thanking my husband in person." She lifted a hand to touch the strand and felt heat stain her cheeks. Even before she looked away from the custodian, she felt the weight of many gazes upon her. Surely it was not strange for the king to send gifts to his wives—all these women wore jewels on throats, wrists, fingers, even fastened upon their clothing. Where would they get them, if not from Xerxes?

"Enjoy your day, mistress. I must prepare the new bride for her evening."

"Thank you again, Hegai." She sent him off with a smile—and wished he would stay a moment more between her and the rest of the wives.

Ah, well. After she ate, she would go to the back garden and entertain the young children for a while. They, at least, welcomed her.

As if summoned by her thoughts, two little hands appeared on her table. She knew those pudgy fingers well already, and was not surprised when they reached for a cluster of her grapes. "I believe you are to ask before taking another's food, little Chinara."

The girl grinned and popped a grape into her mouth. "May I have some grapes, Kasia?"

She tickled the wee one's tummy. Like Kasia's sister Sarai, Chinara giggled and pulled half away while her eyes begged for more sweet torture. Kasia chuckled. "And if I say no?"

Chinara pulled another grape from its stem and offered it to Kasia. "Why would you do that? You can always ask for more."

A far different outlook from the one she had grown up with. This child had no concept of want or waste, would never feel the pangs of hunger. Kasia smoothed back a lock of the girl's ebony hair and smiled. "I can indeed. And how is your mother this morning? Feeling better?"

"Recovered and apologetic."

The new voice brought Kasia's gaze up. This had to be Chinara's mother, one of the few wives she had yet to meet.

The woman grinned Chinara's grin and helped herself to the empty seat at Kasia's side. "Sorry if my little imp is bothering you. Keeping a rein on her is either impossible or I am a terrible mother."

Chinara hopped up on her mother's lap and snuggled in. "You are the best mother ever. And see, I told you Kasia is pretty, no matter what that mean old Sherene said."

The mother chuckled. "I had no doubts, little love." To Kasia she added, "I am Jasmine. You are obviously Kasia, and it is a pleasure to meet you. The others have complained of you so much I knew I would like you immediately."

Praise Jehovah, this woman would be a friend. Kasia smiled. "I fear they have spoken to me not at all, so I know little of you. But I look forward to remedying that, Jasmine. I find your daughter a delight."

Jasmine pressed a kiss to the imp's head. "She is that. Now." Her eyes, a strange gray like fog over the river, twinkled. "I saw Hegai give you the necklace. The king rarely has anything presented publicly. His gifts are usually given in private, so many women use their allowance to order jewelry they say is from him when we all know it is not. You will not have to stoop to that. He must love you immensely."

Contentment welled up. "I think he does. I hope so. No other man has ever made my heart awaken like this."

Chinara wiggled down and took off. Jasmine watched her as she dashed about. "You are blessed. I have found happiness thanks to Chinara, but if not for her . . . I angered the king by weeping the night we became man and wife, and he has never called me again. Perhaps he would have, to honor my father, had I not gotten with child and then been rendered barren from the birth."

"That is awful." Kasia reached out and covered the hand Jasmine had put on the table. "How do you smile so brightly?" And how could the same man who spoke to her heart ignore Jasmine's so completely?

Dimples flashed in Jasmine's full cheeks. "It is not so terrible. I feel no need to compete with the others—I am at the bottom of their hierarchy, and that is a secure place to be. They all like me well enough since I am no threat. But still the king treats me kindly, because he adores our daughter. It is sufficient."

"Yes, but . . . ." She flushed to a halt. Having only been married a week, she could not bring herself to ask if Jasmine did not miss the touch of a man, the roar of passion through her veins. That heady sensation of a long kiss.

Jasmine quirked a brow. "You enjoy his company. I have come to appreciate him in a friendly way, but there was no connection between us on that level. This is the best life I could hope for."

It struck her as sad, but Kasia nodded and let it go. "I have no desire to compete with the other wives. Perhaps you can help me avoid it."

Jasmine chuckled and rested her gaze on the pearls. "You can choose not to compete with them, my friend, but you cannot stop them from competing with you. But do not dismay. Soon enough they will get used to the attention the king pays you and realize that you can do them favors."

"Favors? I?" She laughed.

"Just wait. If you retain the favor I think you will, the others will come to you asking for advice, for extra portions, for a special word in the king's ear for their children."

Unfathomable. Right now it still felt as though her relationship with Xerxes existed in a plane separate from this one, unconnected to these other wives. As if a different Kasia came to life when the sun edged toward the horizon, one that could never show her face here lest she be judged.

Jasmine leapt to her feet with a heaving breath. "There she goes again. Forgive me, Kasia, I must run after her. Might I find you later?"

Kasia smiled as her new friend scampered off. "I will count on it."

EIGHT

In the corner of the room, two of Kasia's maidservants sat with their instruments while Desma sang. Kasia had taught them a few Hebrew psalms the day before, and she smiled now when Desma fumbled some of the unfamiliar words. It may not be perfect, but it did her heart good to hear David's lyrics.

Though her hands worked the loom, her mind and heart inclined toward Jehovah. *Thank you, Lord, for sending me Jasmine. Please help me to be a true friend to her and Chinara.*

The quick swell of joy crashed into concern. *But Esther, Jehovah God. Please care for her. Whom will she turn to when she needs womanly advice? Who will tease the sorrow from her eyes? I know she must be in such terrible pain . . . . Give my family and her cousin wisdom in what to say to her. Perhaps you could give Mordecai an assurance that all is well?*

She let the music minister to her spirit. All in all, a pleasant way to pass her afternoon and evening, since she need not prepare herself for Xerxes tonight. Never before in the chaos of her large family had she realized how precious these moments of quiet communion with the Lord could be. Floating on this golden sea, she could almost forget how sharply she already missed her husband.

But the night stretched long and empty before her. She tried not to think of which of the spiteful girls from the house of women would be in her husband's arms tonight. Such thoughts only made bile churn in her stomach. She breathed in a long breath. *Soothe my heart, Lord. I am but one of many wives, and I need your help to find peace with that lot. Please, help me to be content with Xerxes' affection, since I cannot have his whole devotion.*

"Now that is a wistful look on my lovely Kasia's face."

She jumped up, weaving forgotten. "Xerxes! What are you doing here?" Hardly caring about the answer, she rushed forward. Perhaps she must share him—but she need not let it soil the moments that were theirs.

Xerxes chuckled and opened his arms to receive her. "How could I stay away, knowing such a reception awaited me?" He caught her mouth with his for a long moment. "I missed you. I hoped to lure you out for a stroll through the gardens."

She tucked her arm into his. "Consider me lured."

He covered her hand with his as his gaze swept her room. That now-familiar quirk pulled up half his mouth. "What is this little hole you have chosen for yourself, my love?"

She pasted sternness onto her face. "Are you insulting my room, Xerxes?"

"I was unaware I even had such a small closet in the house of wives. And it is all but bare. Why have you not requisitioned more furnishings?"

She had not thought it bare, though another table would be useful. "I did not want to take anything away from another room."

"Then we shall have you some things fashioned. You know a woodworker, do you not?"

Her heart swelled. "I could have my father make me some things?"

Xerxes bent down to kiss her brow. "Of course. And if I am pleased with the pieces, I will order all the palace woodworking from him."

She turned to face him again and framed his face in her hands. "Do you realize what that would mean to my family? They would never want again, never have to wonder how to feed all the children—"

"Sweet Kasia." The precious contours of his face lifted in a smile under her hands. "I would do far more if I thought your father would accept it. Say the word, and I will gift them an entire city."

An image deserving of a laugh. "They would know not what to do with it. But honest work, recognition for talent—that is another thing altogether. Yes, I shall fill this room to the brim with my father's craftsmanship. How shall I get the order to him?"

"I will get instructions to your people. And speaking of gifts, I see the pearls suit you as well as I thought. You like them?"

She lifted a hand to the warm spheres resting against her throat. "How could I not? You could have given me wooden beads, Xerxes, and I would adore them."

Xerxes laughed and lifted the strand. "You would make them beautiful, but these suit you better. Now, shall we walk?"

With a smile, she let him lead her out of her room and into the rear gardens. "I am so glad you came to see me. I missed you already."

When he chuckled, his eyes gleamed brighter than day. Though she had known him so short a time, already she had each feature memorized. The darkest brown hair, untouched by gray, that framed his noble face. The broad stretch of his shoulders, the well-muscled chest she had fallen asleep on each night. Her blood surged at the thought.

"I missed you too. Shall I ignore the new addition and call you again tonight?" He spun her in a circle before settling against the trunk of a tree and pulling her to him.

The tease in his voice made her think him joking, but the insistence in his kiss made her wonder if perhaps he might, were she to ask. Longing welled up in her throat, but she pushed it down. It would have to be enough that he offered—were she to accept, it would lead to trouble. "Part of me wishes you would. But that would be a mistake."

"Would it?" He rested his forehead on hers. "By the god, Kasia, I am tempted. No other woman has ever consumed me so."

"And were you any other man, we could let it overcome us. But you are king, and you must tend to far more than me." She knotted her hands in his robe to anchor herself to him. "Why could you not be any other man?"

Her exaggerated wistfulness earned a smile. "Ah, but if I were, then I could not have made you mine. Your father would have refused any other Persian."

"Well then, you could have been born a Jewish man. That would solve everything." She grinned.

But when he loosed a laugh, something in it brought her shoulders up. "The god obviously knew better, sweet one."

"Mmm." She pulled away and held out a hand. Once he had enveloped it in his she meandered down a paths. "And I shall have to grow accustomed to sharing you."

"Does it make you jealous?" He sounded pleased by the idea.

She tilted her face up to the cleansing power of the sun. "Would you be jealous if I had other lovers?"

He growled low in his throat. "I would kill any who touched you. But it is different—you know it is."

"The world says it must be. But a heart is a heart, be it male or female. King or slave. Of course I am jealous, Xerxes. But I have been praying for peace about it. I have no desire to be consumed by envy and bitterness like . . . ." She pressed her lips together.

Xerxes laughed. "You have a point. I should not like to see you become like her either. You can at least rest in the knowledge that you are the one who holds my heart."

"Do I?" She swayed to a halt so she could turn to him. In his eyes blazed the truth of his words. Would it be enough? Enough to sustain a marriage like theirs? "I wonder that the king can afford to put his heart in anyone's hands."

He raised her hand to his lips. "It is a risk. It would be a greater one, I think, to deny this. Can I trust you with my heart, lovely Kasia?"

Such a great responsibility, yet it settled on her shoulders like the kiss of the sun. "Always. I will guard it with every ounce of life." She hesitated a moment. Perhaps it *would* be enough—if she met it rightly. "Logic tells me it is too soon, but my heart bids me tell you anyway. I love you, Xerxes."

His eyes slid shut. "You have found the perfect way to guarantee my thoughts are with you this night instead of my new bride. And tomorrow . . . ."

She lost herself for a long moment in his embrace, then pulled away when the sound of laughter reached them from another part of the garden. The breath she dragged in was as unsteady as her legs. "Is it tomorrow yet?"

Xerxes laughed and led her onward. "Soon enough. And how did you spend your today, my love?"

She felt her expression change from longing to excitement. "I made a friend. Chinara's mother, Jasmine. She has been unwell all this week, but she was about again today."

His brows drew together. "She is the first friend you have made?"

Kasia pressed her lips together. She had avoided mentioning how standoffish the others were, knowing it would displease him. "They are wary of anyone in your favor. Your mother and Jasmine both assure me this is normal."

The noise that came from his throat sounded unconvinced. "You must be careful, Kasia. The intrigues of a harem have been known to alter empires before."

There went her ease. "Intrigue?"

He grinned down at her. "Have you not heard that it was my mother who guaranteed I inherit, not the argument offered by the Spartan about being the first son born after he became king?"

Her lips twitched. "I may have heard mention of that theory, yes."

"It would be foolish to assume women have grown more passive in the last decade. Though few will cross Amestris when it comes to my favoring Darius as my heir, they will still squabble among themselves in an effort to secure lesser positions for their children."

A shiver skittered up her spine. Though Xerxes had usurped his brother's claim to the throne peaceably, she knew enough of history to realize it was more often achieved by assassination.

Xerxes stopped and measured her. "You are right that the others will be wary of you. You must never trust them too fully. When they see that my love for you does not fade, they may smile to your face, but they will also fear your children will take the positions they think meant for theirs."

A knot grew in her throat. "Jasmine?"

"The one safe friend, I should think." A corner of his mouth pulled up. "With no son to fight for and a daughter secure in my affections, she remains above the eternal plotting."

"Good." Her breath whooshed out. "I like her very much."

His eyes narrowed, as if thoughts crowded his mind. "You will do well to model her in one respect—keep your thoughts free of ambition. Much as my soul yearns for you, my reason must still consider the best of the empire. The offspring of a Jewess might go far, but no son we have together will ever be king. Know that now. I will not have you getting ideas in a few years that will endanger either our love or the security of my other children."

She pulled her hands free of his as fire seared her cheeks. "You lecture me about my non-existent ambitions for a son who may not ever exist? This, Xerxes, is why talk of love should be reserved for later in a relationship. If you knew me, you would never insult me with such a warning."

The blasted man looked amused. "I may have known you only a week, my love, but I am well acquainted with women in general. Though the weaker sex, they inevitably outdo men in conniving. At this moment, you are the epitome of humility and modesty. I would keep you that way—but once-sweet maidens often become ambitious shrews in the royal house."

She folded her arms over her chest. "I am duly advised. And let me assure you in turn, my husband, that I have no desire to see any child of mine on the throne. I will consider my life full if I can keep them far from intrigue and but live with your affection."

That one-sided pull of his mouth was as aggravating as it was alluring. "A lovely sentiment, but short-sighted. Much as it pains me to contemplate it, I will not live forever. Will you then be content to take the small portion your marriage contract entitles you to and retire to some obscure home? Would you not prefer your children have the means to care for you in your old age?"

"'Means' does not necessitate obscene wealth. But I will take your words to heart and be sure I never grow accustomed to these comforts."

Xerxes threw his head back in laughter and slid an arm around her shoulder. "You go to an extreme, dear one. Comfort you will always have. Luxury may not be as forthcoming, unless your sons provide it . . . or unless you curry the favor of my heir."

At the warning in that last part, she lifted her brows. "Is that another game your wives play? Seeking the good opinion of your sons?"

His lips thinned. "To varying—and sometimes dangerous—degrees. At least it has been so in past reigns. I once caught my elder brother in a compromising situation with one of our father's youngest wives. As I watch my son grow into a man, I can but hope he has the sense to avoid such traps." He arched a brow her way. "What think you? Did he strike you as sensible enough for that?"

She frowned at the sharp question in his gaze. "I have never met your son, my love."

Amusement replaced the inquisition. "Of course you have. Your first morning here, when we came to see you in the garden."

Searching her mind brought nothing but a vague recollection of the others who had been with him. "Really?"

"Indeed. Darius, my brother Masistes, and Haman were all there."

"I shall take your word for it." Lips twitching up, her anger faded. "I can recall only how my heart swelled when I saw you with Chinara. I care not what position our someday-children have in the empire—I just hope you love them like that."

"Ah, Kasia." He held her tight. "Never change."

She snuggled against him and let peace wash over her. "Only as you desire and the Lord wills."

He pulled away with a sigh and a glance toward the heavens. "I have guests to greet. Shall I walk you back to your pathetic little room?"

She laughed and slapped his chest lightly. "Go to your feast, Xerxes. I will linger here another moment."

After a warm kiss, he took a step away but then paused. "Have you explored the compound yet?"

The very thought had terrified her each time someone proposed it. She shook her head.

Xerxes smiled. "In the next few days, I will show you our winter home in its fullness."

She smiled and raised her arm in farewell. "I will look forward to it."

He strode away with all the confidence of a man who ruled half the world. Kasia smiled and shook her head. Her husband was so sure of himself he could mount an invasion of a continent . . . while she was so insecure she could not venture beyond this one building. Perhaps after he showed her around, it would not seem so overwhelming.

A frisson of unease washed over her, and she froze. She was not alone. Her eyes scanned the flowers and trees, the fountain pulsing with clear, sweet water. Her gaze snagged on the form of a woman. A woman whose stomach was round with child, whose face was hard as stone, whose eyes spewed unmitigated hatred.

Kasia gulped. “Good evening, my queen.”

Nine

Mordecai stood and stretched the soreness out of muscles left too long in one position. It had been a tiring day, full of complaints from his people. Tomorrow he would take them before the officials to work out what could easily be handled. What they could not solve he would take before the king three days hence.

He drew in a deep breath. With all of Persia preparing for war, it seemed that people forgot to respect what would be left behind. Thievery and vandalism were growing steadily, and the Jews suffered it more than anyone. Perhaps it would improve once the growing number of troops marched out to meet the rest of the army. He hoped so.

Turning away from the gates, he headed home, ready for a quiet meal with Esther. At the next corner, he put one foot onto his street and halted. His spirit weighed heavy within him, blurring his vision and stealing his breath. "Jehovah?" he whispered.

The crowds repelled him like the wrong end of a loadstone, pushing him back out of the street and in search of solitude. He had no idea where he was headed but gave his feet leave to take him where they and the Lord willed.

At the riverbank, he fell to his knees. Not until his forehead touched the ground did a measure of peace restore his breath. "What is it, Lord?"

Eyes bright and deep, lit with concern. Lips full and lush, their smile forced. Full, shining dark hair.

"Kasia." He squeezed his eyes shut and curled his fingers into his palms. "Does she live, Jehovah? Does she need your help?"

Panic surged up, urgent and insistent. He could waste no time on conjecture—questions would have to wait until later. "Jehovah God, cast your protection over her this moment. Let your heavenly warriors take up guard around her, warding off the workers of iniquity. Lend her your wisdom, that she might out-strike any serpent. Lend her your love, that she might remain gentle and uninjured by whatever travails befall her. Lend her your authority, that she might stand strong against whoever seeks to crush her."

A hot breeze whirled around him. Light edged the vision behind his closed eyes.

No relief, but rather more pressure. He clasped his hands over his bowed head and prayed whatever words came to his tongue, wondering if this was how his ancestor Hananiah had felt when tossed into the fiery furnace in Babylon.

He heard the beat of wings larger than any bird's fly over him.

Amestris stared down the new concubine and let her blood boil in her veins. What was it about this girl that had Xerxes so enthralled? She looked like no more than a peasant, ill suited for jewels and fine linen.

Her husband had dressed up peasants before. Amestris took no issue with the pearls on her throat, with the silver on her arm. Something else about this girl, though, set her teeth on edge.

She took a step toward the Jewess, then another. Were it not for the awkwardness of her babe-heavy stomach, she would have demonstrated what true grace was—something this base-born wench could never know.

The girl set her head in an angle of deferment, but her eyes . . . they did not seek the ground, carried no fear.

Amestris stopped a few feet away. "You have much to learn, concubine. Do you think you are special because of the way my husband looks at you?"

"I think I am nothing." Yet the humility was underscored by iron.

The boil of blood snapped and sizzled. "Were you not cautioned to stay away from me?"

Now the wench's brows lifted. Such insolence. "And so I have, my queen."

"You say from a step away."

"Where my husband left me. I feared it would be rude to leave without greeting when I saw you, but if you wish, I shall go at once." She lifted an arm and motioned toward the garden's entrance.

Amestris's gaze narrowed on the flash of silver on her biceps, and her hand whipped out to grab the girl's arm. "What is this?"

"I—"

"Silence." She tugged the wretch closer, shoved her sleeve out of the way, and hissed when she saw the twin lions' heads on the torc. "You dare to steal from the king? Next time, take something not given him by my hand. Did you think no one would recognize the gift I commissioned for his birthday feast? Stupid Jewess."

The girl's eyes flashed, but not with guilt or rebellion. She swallowed. "I did not realize it was a gift from your blessed hand, my queen. I will return it to the king the next time I see him."

A red haze drifted over Amestris's vision. He had given it to her, the faithless dolt, given *her* gift to this slave. She ought to have the girl's arm cut off to show them the price for such audacity. She ought to have a knife plunged through the harlot's heart for daring to steal the king's. She ought to—

The air heated, the red over her eyes blazed a white so hot Amestris gasped and dropped the girl's arm, stumbled back a step. When she blinked, her vision wavered. The Jewess stood as she had a moment before, but something had changed. Her shadow had lengthened to nearly half again what it was before, had broadened. It looked . . . masculine.

Demons. Amestris took another step back and snarled. "Enemy of Ahura Mazda! No servant of Angra Mainyu will live under my roof."

Through the girl's confusion shone the authority of the uncreated evil one. "I am a servant of none but Jehovah."

Amestris spat. "Call him what you may, slave. He is still the enemy of my god."

The wretch arched that insolent brow again. "That only speaks to the nature of whatever devil *you* serve."

Amestris rested a hand on the curve of her stomach. "You make a grave error by opposing me. You are nothing but a harlot with a flimsy contract, easily severed." She lunged forward, gripped her arm again, and tore the lion torc from her.

The girl grimaced and covered the rising welt of where the lion bit her. But she made no protest. Perhaps she recognized the fire of Ahura Mazda when she saw it blazing from an enemy's eyes.

Amestris stepped back again, her chest heaving. "Get out of my sight."

Her chin edged up instead of tucking to her chest. When her hand fell from her arm, Amestris gasped to see the welt had vanished already. The work of the demons, no doubt.

The fool offered a mocking smile. "As the queen wishes." She turned leisurely to the path that would lead to her pathetic closet.

Amestris's hand fisted around the torc. At least the harlot was taking her demon with her. She could almost glimpse it, the shimmer of an outline around the girl, taller and wider. It warped the light, made the image of the concubine waver.

The babe inside her leapt. Perhaps he, too, sensed the presence of their nemesis. She covered the bulge in her stomach with a firm hand. "Rest, blessed one. I will not let her near you."

Fury bubbled in her throat. How dare the king bring that creature here? She had always known he was an idiot, more concerned with his own pleasure than the good of his family. But this—this was too much.

She spun back toward the private entrance to her suite of rooms, paying no mind to the servants that surged around her. Not until she had gained her chamber and halted in the center of the room. Then she narrowed her gaze on one of her eunuchs. "You—bring Haman to me."

"Yes, mistress." He bowed and sprinted back out.

She looked down at the torc still clutched in her hand. With a curse, she hurled it against the wall. "Wine—now. And where is the fruit I requested? Would you beasts have this prince inside me starve while I await the start of the feast?"

Food and drink appeared on the table, but Amestris was not calm enough to eat. It would churn into wormwood in her stomach—she must see this taken care of first.

What would the god have her do? She could work to nullify any influence the girl had over Xerxes, but that would take time. Months, even years. Usually she was patient with such schemes, and confident enough in the knowledge that her husband's attention was fickle.

This one was different, though. She had seen it with her own eyes while they frolicked like adolescents in the garden. This was not his usual, short-lived affair. There was more to it.

The Jewess would not be so easily relegated to oblivion.

What then?

She paced from one end of her suite to the other, then beckoned her most trusted handmaiden to her.

The girl stepped close. "What may I get for you, mistress?"

"Hemlock. I want it put in that Jewess's food this very night—her girl will take a tray to her. Escape notice if possible, but bribe whomever you must if you are seen. When my husband discovers her dead, I will not have him realize it is on my order."

The maid dipped her head. "Shall I slip some into the room of another wife to cast suspicion her way?"

"Yes. Whichever was his favorite before this one." She waved the girl away and sat to await Haman. If anyone would be her ally in this plot against the Jewess, it would be him.

One of the maids slipped the torc onto the table, and Amestris tasted fury anew. Ah, well. Before the night was out, Xerxes would learn that betrayal cut both ways.

Kasia looked again over her shoulder. She could have sworn someone stood behind her, but each time she looked, she found nothing. Though this felt unthreatening, it must still be residual unease from her encounter with Amestris.

Remembering the queen brought a fresh chill to her spine. Had Amestris insulted her alone, Kasia would have accepted her opinions without complaint. But to attack her God?

She shook her head. The Persian Empire was renowned for its tolerance of other religions, had even encouraged her people more than once—Xerxes' grandfather releasing the Jews from captivity was a perfect example—but clashes were inevitable when monotheistic religions collided.

Amestris believed her Ahura Mazda was the one and true god. Kasia knew Jehovah owned that title. She had occasionally wondered if perhaps they were two different names for the same being, but the queen had succeeded in convincing her otherwise.

Her soul had recognized its enemy.

For an hour she sat at her loom and took up her weaving. For an hour she prayed for God's protection, for his presence to blanket the palace, for his strength to fill her. For an hour her fingers moved with confidence. But when her meal was brought in and she ceased her prayers, her hands shook.

The tray was silver, as were the bowls with her food. The rhyton of wine was rimmed in gold. The meat was covered in a sauce she could not name, the grain baked into a beautiful loaf, the fruit exotic, the wine sweet and strong.

All looked like sand.

"Is it not to your liking, mistress?" Desma asked with wrinkled brow. "I can send it back and get you something else."

And appear ungrateful. "No, it is fine." She sat, even reached for the wine.

Her stomach clenched, and she tasted bile. In front of her eyes dropped a hazy veil and on her spirit weighed a desperate need to commune with her Lord. She pushed away from the table and stumbled over to the multi-colored rug under one of the windows. Sinking to her knees was not enough, so she stretched prostrate on the ground.

"Mistress?" Voice alarmed, Desma dropped down beside her. "What is wrong? Do you need a physician? A magi?"

"No." Never in her life had her insides vibrated with this urgent need to pray. In her father's house, her faith had been relaxed and easy—here in the palace it seemed to demand every ounce of her being. Was this how it had been for the great prophet Daniel a century ago? For his friends Azariah and Mishael and Mordecai's ancestor Hananiah?

She was no prophet. But if spending her days in prayer was what Jehovah required in return for his presence, then she would lie on this rug indefinitely.

"Mistress?"

"I must fast and pray, Desma. There is no need for alarm, but I . . . I must. Please go see to your own meals now. I will need nothing further tonight."

After a moment of silence, feet shuffled out the door. But Desma sat on the corner of the rug, and Theron took up his protective stance against the wall.

The closest she would get to solitude. So be it.

Time washed away, all her senses focused on supplication. She saw only the ever-shifting lights behind her closed eyes, smelled only the sweet fragrance of prayers, heard only the whisper of the Spirit's wind.

She prayed for her husband. She prayed for herself. She prayed for the queen. She prayed for Esther and Mordecai, for her parents and siblings. She prayed for the children she may someday have. She prayed for Jasmine, for her servants, for the coming war.

Then her door opened and hurried feet pounded into her room. Leda fell to her knees before Desma. "The food—it was poisoned. The dog I fed a bite to has become paralyzed, his breathing slow and hard. Hemlock."

A chill danced over Kasia's back. She sat up and looked from one maid to the other.

Desma's mouth was agape. "How did you know, mistress?"

She shook her head.

Desma swallowed hard, her eyes wide. "Your God watches over you. If you would share him with your servant, I would learn to pray to him as well. For your sake."

Kasia nodded, even smiled. It would seem she had another true friend in the palace.

She dared not count her enemies.

Ten

Darius cuffed his brother on the side of the head with a laugh. "Hystaspes, you make me late. Go bother Mother."

The ten-year-old lunged at him with a mighty roar. "I am a lion! You must fight me off, Darius. What if you get attacked by a lion on your way to Greece? They have them in one of the mountain passes, you know. My tutor told me of them today."

Hence why he had been fending off these lion attacks all afternoon. Yesterday it had been bears. What would come tomorrow? Crocodiles? He flipped the boy off his back, careful to help him land gently. "There, lion, you are defeated. Now stay that way. Father wants me at the feast."

Hystaspes scowled and rested his elbows on his knees. "It is unfair. Why do you get to meet all the dignitaries while I am expected to eat in the nursery? I am a man too."

Darius arched a brow. "Amytis and Rhodogune would miss you."

The boy made a face. "Girls are so dull."

Darius laughed and tousled Hystaspes' hair. "If you were a man, you would not think so."

The boy wrapped his arms around Darius's legs and held on tight. "Take me with you. I will hide under a rug if I must, but please do not send me back to Mother. She was raving to Haman about some Jewess and will be in a sour temper all evening, then leave for her feast. And I do not *want* to go to the nursery!"

Darius's heart tripped at the mention of the new concubine, but he pushed her image away. "Then go find some of our other brothers to play with. What of Parham?"

"He got in trouble, and his mother told him he may not play this evening. Please?"

Darius sent his eyes to the dimming skies. "You can come with me as far as the hall, but then it is up to you to stay out of the way and hidden from Father's eyes."

The boy leapt off with a whoop of victory. "Yes! Thank you, Darius. I will be invisible as a specter, I promise."

Darius straightened his brightly colored tunic and gave his brother a light push, just for the point of it. "Hurry. Hopefully the new guests will still be presenting their gifts, and I will not have missed anything important."

With Hystaspes dogging his heels, Darius sped to the ceremonial palace where the new guests would be received. At least he was not the only late arrival—Haman rushed up the steps ahead of them.

Darius looked down at his brother. "Why was mother talking to Haman about the Jewess? Did you hear anything?"

Hystaspes shrugged. "They stopped when I came in."

"Hmm." He jogged up the endless stone steps and passed through the first of the columns when he realized his brother had stopped. "Hystaspes!"

The boy stood with head craned back. "I have never noticed before that those are griffins up there. Have you ever seen a griffin, Darius? In the wild, I mean?"

His tutor obviously needed to work a little harder. "They are mythical, you blockhead. Are you coming or not?"

"Coming, coming."

Darius led the way into the great reception hall. Its ceilings soared high overhead, precious stones embedded within the cedar. The black marble columns gleamed and reflected the low light of the sun like a hundred mirrors. Under his feet stretched a carpet as long as the hall, its pattern an intricate mosaic of every color. He motioned his little brother into the shadows and took a moment to survey the gathering.

All around him his father's military commanders were gathered into tight groups. At the front of the chamber the throne dominated on its step. Father still sat, scepter in hand, and smiled down at the visitors before him. One carried a huge gold bowl, another a length of rolled textile.

Excellent—they had not adjourned to the enclosed garden yet. He skirted the room until he had made his way to the front where several of his uncles waited.

"Ah, Darius, there you are." Artabanus smiled and motioned him to his side. "A bit late, are you not?"

"I was waylaid by a ferocious lion."

His father's uncle loosed a rich laugh. "Was the lion named Hystaspes?"

"How did you guess?" Darius looked toward the back of the hall but could not see his brother. Good.

An unmistakable shadow fell over him. "I am glad to see you emerged from the attack with your limbs intact, my son."

Since laughter coated his father's voice, Darius smiled up at him. "I wrestled the beast into submission with my bare hands."

"An able warrior indeed." Father nodded to one of his attendants, and a moment later a trumpet call rang out. All eyes on him, Xerxes raised his arms wide. "Welcome, noble guests and esteemed friends, to the final night of our feast. Let each man sit where he will and drink his fill—to the garden!"

A cheer went up. On most nights, no one could drink more than the king, and all was ordered at his command. He must be in a prime mood. Persia had Kasia the Jewess to thank, Darius suspected.

A sigh snuck past his lips as he followed his father to the garden. Xerxes was not just the king—he was the epitome of what a man should be. One of the tallest men at court, his figure was well hewn from years of military training. Though he passed most of his days on the throne, he could wield a spear or loose an arrow with the skill of any Immortal. He held his authority with a firm fist but a ready smile. He was fair, he was affable, and when his temper snapped, usually without much warning, he was as fearsome as the god.

Darius would be like that. A man of reputation, one who had earned respect through war and wise counsel. He would prove his bravery in battle, he would increase his strength through training.

Maybe then Artaynte would greet his advances with something other than laughter. She would realize that his being heir apparent was in fact *not* his only attribute, as she had accused a week ago. Those enticing lips would turn up in welcome instead of mockery. She would realize how blessed she was to have his heart.

If he asked his father for her, Xerxes would arrange a marriage with a snap of his finger. A better match could not be made—she was his cousin, her blood pure and strong. Masistes would be ecstatic to know his daughter would reign as queen someday. If Darius asked, she would have no choice but to wed him. She would be his.

But she would not be his. She would be like Darius's mother, the wife with all the honor but no affection for her husband. That was not the marriage he wanted.

Better first to earn her love. Right now she was but a girl who saw him as a boy, one she had known all her life. But once he returned a hero from Greece, that would change. She would see him differently, would come to love him. Then he would ask his father for her hand, and their marriage would be celebrated through the whole world.

Xerxes settled beside him with lifted brows. "I know that look. What lovely curves are you dreaming of, my son?"

Darius felt his face flush and cleared his throat. It took firm resolve to keep from darting his gaze to his uncle, who sat on a couch at his father's other side. "None worth mentioning. What of you? Is your pleasant mood thanks to that exquisite concubine we met the other day?"

The Jewess was a far safer subject than Artaynte, and thought of her had provided a welcome distraction over the past few days. Claiming such a creature was one of the benefits of being king. Concubines could be enjoyed and dismissed at will.

Strange though . . . that flash in his father's eyes spoke of involvement. Perhaps nothing was ever simple. "She pleases me well, yes."

Masistes laughed and picked up his rhyton of wine. "I imagine. Will you take her with you into Greece?"

Xerxes took a long drink from his gold cup. "I have not thought on which of my concubines will travel with me."

"My wife and daughter are already begging to go with us as far as Sardis." Masistes shrugged and chose a piece of meat. "I imagine it is safe enough for them to go that far. With your blessing of course, my lord."

Darius's father waved a dismissive hand. "As you wish, Masistes."

A bite of bread lodged in Darius's throat. It would take them over a year to meander to Sardis, gathering the army as they went, and then they would likely wait out the winter there. Time he thought he would spend *away* from Artaynte.

"What of the queen? Will she go into Lydia with us?"

"Doubtful." Xerxes surveyed the assembly. Darius looked over the garden too. The white and blue tapestries fluttered in the breeze as guests chose their couches of gold and silver. Slaves circled the room offering golden goblets of wine. It was a fine feast.

"It would be rather soon after her confinement," his uncle mused. "Parsisa will miss her, I am sure."

The words were right, but the tone of his voice made them all smile. It was no great secret that his aunt Parsisa did not get along with his mother. Most people did not get along with his mother.

Xerxes laughed outright. "Well, we must think of the health of her and the babe. I shall have to make do with concubines and send the wives to Persepolis where it is safe."

Masistes shook his head. "You agreed that Sardis would be safe enough."

"Safe enough for *your* wives. Not for mine." Xerxes winked and took another drink of his wine.

His uncle loosed a guffaw. "Which is to say, you would rather not be bothered with them. Understandable—your mind will be occupied with stratagem. And the Jewess, perhaps?"

Again, Darius saw a strange flash in his father's eyes. "Did I not just say I had not made up my mind?"

"But if rumor is to be trusted, you have seen no one else this week. Surely if she holds your attention so completely, you would not want to be parted from her. She must be an exceptional lover."

"Masistes. Enough." Temper colored the smile he turned on Darius. "What of you, my son? A man at war often needs a woman to soothe him. Will you choose a girl to take with you?"

A fine idea. He could find a slave so beautiful Artaynte would grow jealous, one who fawned over him instead of pointing out his shortcomings. "I may, at that. One with a fire to match what I saw in your Kasia. Does she have sisters?"

His father looked none too amused at the joke. "Four of them, but the next eldest, twins, are only twelve."

Masistes arched his brows. "You know the ages of her sisters? Planning to add them to your harem after they age a bit, too? A wise idea. If one is pleasing, then three—"

"Masistes! Shall I define 'enough' for you?" With a motion of a single finger, Xerxes ordered his cup refilled. "Her sisters will be left alone. And while we are leaving things alone, no more talk of Kasia. If you wish a companion but not a wife, my son, look not among the Jews."

Darius grinned. "A shame. If yours is typical, they are a people worth looking twice at."

His father threw back the entire horn of wine in one long series of gulps.

Artabanus leaned close to Darius's ear. "You will do well not to mention her again, my prince."

Darius's good humor turned into a frown. "It is a compliment of his taste."

"Can you not see the light of jealousy in his eyes? This one is special to him. If you praise her, he will think you intend a seduction."

"Absurd."

"Not so much. It has been done before and will no doubt be done again." The old man's gray brows drew low over his eyes. "My council is ignored more often than not, but in this you ought to heed me."

He looked back at his father. His shoulders were rigid, his jaw set, and his third cup of wine in his hands. Artabanus was right. The Jewess had dug deep into his being already. No wonder, then, that Mother despised her. He turned to Artabanus. "If ever I mention her again out of turn, I give you permission to whip me."

Artabanus smothered a chuckle. "To avoid such punishment, you will do well to school your thoughts as well as your tongue."

He focused on his plate but made no other response. He would grant that speaking of the girl did not settle well with his father, but even the king of kings could not read thoughts. It would do no harm to let his mind wander over the image of her curves, of the passion that filled her. He had no desire to steal one of his father's wives, only to distract himself from the critical cousin that was far too beautiful for his peace of mind. There was no danger in that.

"Darius!"

He looked up and smiled at the second eldest of his father's sons, his half-brother Cyrus. At the motion of his hand, Darius turned to Xerxes. "Do you mind if I go join Cyrus for a while, Father?"

"What, you prefer the company of the young princes to the old?" Father grinned and waved his hand. "Go, go. Enjoy yourself. Soon enough you will be on campaign where the luxuries will not be so abundant."

He smiled in return and stood. Still, he heard Artabanus's low, "Might I remind the king that he must name his heir before we set out? The time draws nigh."

His father's sigh sounded impatient. "I plan to make my official announcement in a few days. Not that my choice will be any great surprise to anyone."

Darius could not help himself—he glanced at Xerxes, who offered him a crooked smile and a lift of his cup. Blood surged through him and gave him wings.

He would be king someday. He had much to learn from his father, would not wish Xerxes' days to be cut short. But someday. Persia would be his throne, the rest of the world his footstool. He would be Darius II, king of kings, king of nations.

"Why are you grinning like a fool?"

Darius lowered himself to the couch beside his brother. "Father promised to announce me as his successor in a few days' time."

Cyrus raised his cup. "Excellent. Better you than me—primarily because if Father dared to name someone else, your mother would see the someone else did not live long enough to claim the title."

He chuckled, though his brother may be right. Mother had not earned her reputation through bluster. "Better to live as a satrap than die as an heir?"

"Here, here." Cyrus looked past him and smiled. "There are Milad and Bijan."

They joined their friends, laughed and joked, ate and drank. Darius could not have repeated anything they said, though. His mind was too busy painting himself a brilliant future. He would continue the expansion of the palaces at Persepolis. Authorize improvements here at Susa. Conquer the world, if there were anything left to conquer after his father took his vengeance on Athens.

When darkness had fallen and the moon risen high, Bijan passed off his rhyton. "I have to be going. A wonderful evening, as usual. Give your father my compliments."

Cyrus smirked. "Have you a tryst to rush off to, Bijan? The night is young, and you did not even finish your first cup."

Bijan offered a tight smile. "I need a clear mind. I am off to train."

"You have already achieved a place in the Immortals." Darius lifted his brows. "Why train extra now?"

"Because I would live past our first battle." Obviously not interested in being swayed, Bijan bowed and backed away.

Cyrus rolled his eyes. "He is too serious about fighting."

"It is where his hope of advancement lies." Darius surveyed the crowd. Most were well on their way to drunk, or already there, and the laughter and talk proved it.

His gaze fell on a group of high-ranking officials and visitors around his father. When Xerxes signaled his seven eunuchs forward, Darius wandered that way as well.

The wine had done its job on the king. Darius heard his belt of laughter as he drew within earshot.

"I have still the most beautiful queen in the world, even when she *is* large with child," Xerxes said with a wide grin. "You shall see. Zethar, go to the queen's feast and tell her to come in her royal crown so that all the world might appreciate her unsurpassed beauty."

The eunuchs bowed and departed, but Darius's heart thudded. If her mood had not improved . . . . He heard the word fly over the room, watched as the men all came to attention. Darius groaned. "Why do I get the feeling Mother will not like this?"

Cyrus, beside him again, sighed. "Because much as your mother likes to create a spectacle, she does not enjoy being made one. Let us hope she is feeling the need to be admired."

By a collection of men set on judging her, when she already felt large and cumbersome with the babe inside her?

Unlikely.

Eleven

Amestris glared at the eunuchs that dared intrude on her feast. "The king wills *what?*"

The head slave cleared his throat and bowed. As if a meaningless show of respect could soothe the vibration of rage inside her. "He has been boasting of your unsurpassed beauty, my queen, and wishes you to grace his presence so that his esteemed guests might bask in the awe inspired by your countenance."

Her husband wanted her to parade her swollen body before his guests for the sake of his pride? If so much rested on the beauty of her face, then perhaps he should have spared it a thought when he gave that harlot the torc commissioned by Amestris's hand.

Her fingers curled into talons and dug into her couch. "No."

The eunuch blinked. "My queen?"

"Are you deaf, slave? I said *no*. The king has taken enough from me. He will not strip me of the last of my pride by forcing me before an assembly of men in my condition."

He straightened, his eyes narrowing. "Perhaps the queen would like to rethink publicly disobeying her husband the king?"

"Perhaps the king would like to rethink the way he treats his wife the queen." She grabbed the maidservant who she had charged with holding the symbol of his betrayal and ripped the torc from her. With a sneer, she slung it toward the eunuchs. "Give that to your king. Tell him I hope it keeps him warm at night, because neither I nor the Jewess will be."

"Mistress." Her maid sounded panicked. "The king will be furious."

She leaned back against her chaise again, though she could not convince her fingers to relax. "His fury is no match to mine."

Xerxes spied his seven eunuchs returning and frowned. There was no female in their midst. Was Amestris unwell? He ought to have made it clear she was only to come if she felt up to it . . . though it was rare she felt unequal to flaunting her beauty.

The wine's stupor dissipated when he saw the expression upon Zethar's face. Xerxes stood. "What is wrong? Is the queen in labor? Unwell?"

Zethar's jaw ticked. He extended his hand. "The queen sends you this, master."

Xerxes felt his forehead crease. He reached out and took the broken circle of silver. She sent him a gift by way of apology? It was a bit extravagant for that, what with the intricately fashioned lions' heads . . . .

The last of the wine cleared from his head, and Xerxes cursed. He stepped closer to Zethar, kept his voice low. "Did she send a message along with this?"

Zethar leaned forward. "One she delivered for all to hear. Forgive me, master, for bearing such a message . . . that she hoped it kept you warm at night, because neither she nor the Jewess would."

He cursed again and closed his hand around the torc. He had forgotten Amestris had given it to him. But how did she get it back? She must have taken it forcibly from Kasia . . . .

Xerxes charged for the garden's exit, not even slowing to order his brother and son not to follow. There was no time. Amestris's threat that she would not keep him warm at night did not concern him, but Kasia?

"Father!" Darius broke into a run, but Xerxes refused to slow. "What are you about? Please, do nothing rash against Mother. You know how she is, especially when so near her time. She must not feel well enough to—"

"You do not want to take her part right now, Darius." He held out an arm to keep him out of the way as he neared the corner.

Perhaps she only meant that she and Kasia had discovered together that he had given to one a gift purchased by the other, and that they were *both* angry with him. Perfectly reasonable, and that would be no cause for alarm.

Yet it did not sound like Kasia. Had she been distressed, instead of festering she would hunt him down and demand an explanation. Her anger may have been quick that afternoon, but so was her forgiveness.

No. Amestris had not been speaking of shared anger.

"Brother." Masistes panted in his effort to keep up. "I called for your legal advisors as we left the feast. They can counsel you on how to deal with the queen's disobedience. There is no need to race to confront her—"

"I will not confront her." He turned toward the house of wives. His servants sprinted ahead of him to open the massive doors. They barely managed a wide enough opening before Xerxes reached them and hurried through, sideways.

"Then where are we going? What was her message?"

He ignored Masistes and barreled down the hall. All of his wives must still be at the queen's feast, otherwise the commotion would have brought them to their doors. But he knew Kasia would not be with them.

Zethar must have realized where he was headed—he led the way to her rooms and opened the door. When Xerxes stepped inside, his heart lurched into his throat and choked him.

Kasia. His sweet Kasia lay stretched on the floor, undoubtedly felled by Amestris's wrath. Why had he not been alerted? No, her servants lay about the room too. Had she ordered them *all* slain?

His hands shook. His stomach clenched. His vision blurred. Then his spine went stiff and his chin came up. She would pay. She would pay for Kasia's life with her own and—

The figures on the floor shifted as the noise of his entrance hit them. All but Kasia. One of her wide-eyed servants leaned close to her, though, and said, "Mistress, the king."

She was well. Not dead, not injured. She leapt to her feet with that enthusiasm he loved and raced toward him.

He met her in the middle of the room and closed his arms around her. "My love. She sent me the torc. I thought—I feared—"

Shaking her head against his chest, Kasia hugged him tight. "I am unharmed."

"Not for lack of trying on the queen's part." One of the maidservants stepped forward, and her eyes burned with fury. "Her food was poisoned, master. Hemlock. Had she taken a sip, a bite . . . ."

Kasia pulled away enough to send her maid a mild glare. "We know not that it was on her order."

"Yes, we do." Xerxes' hand still shook as he lifted it to her cheek, but not with grief or fear now. With rage, pure and hot. "She has tried me enough. Her arrogance I can tolerate, but to disobey me in front of all the world because she is angry with me—to try to *kill* you! I will not suffer it. She will pay for this with her life."

"Father, no!" Darius rushed forward, his distress coating his face.

It put not so much as a dent in Xerxes' determination. The boy would be better off without his mother's poisonous influence.

Kasia shook her head and splayed a hand on his chest. "Xerxes, please. She is the mother of four of your children, will soon deliver another."

"Her execution can be stayed until after the birth, then."

"My love, no. Act in haste now and you will regret it forever."

He doubted that. "She tried to kill you."

"She was angry, as you are now. But my God was watching over me, and he kept me from tasting the poisoned food. No harm has been done. And though her reaction was wrong, her feeling was justified."

He tipped her chin up with a finger. "Do you rebuke me, woman?"

No fear entered her eyes, though he read respect within them. More than could ever be said for Amestris. "Punish me for it if you must—my life is worth far less than hers. I have no children to mourn me."

Darius stepped forward with a worried frown. "You would take on yourself the wrath intended for your enemy? It makes no sense."

She did not so much as glance at his son. "Forgiveness is not logical. But it heals the wounds left by bitterness and hatred."

Xerxes sighed and lifted her hand to kiss her fingers. "I cannot forgive her. She would have stolen you from me, solely because she knows how it would pierce. But this crime was against you, and no one outside this room knows of it. If you wish her mercy, then mercy she shall receive. For this. But she publically disobeyed me. If I ignore that offense, everyone will whisper that Xerxes is a weak man ruled by his women."

Zethar inclined his head. "And their wives, master, will remember that the queen greeted your servants with anger and defamed you before them all. They will use it as an excuse to act the same."

"Your advisers on the law are right outside," Masistes said. "Hear their counsel before you make your decision on a punishment."

Xerxes nodded at the eunuch nearest the door, who motioned his advisers into the room. The seven of them filed in, the men of soundest wisdom and highest birth below the princes. Most of them had advised his father before him.

Were any fond of their queen? Or had they been bitten by her temper at some point?

They all looked around the chamber as if wondering why they had been called to one of the lowliest rooms in the palace compound.

Kasia tensed in his arms. Xerxes released her and urged her behind him, knowing she would be more comfortable shielded. "My noble friends, your king has need of your wisdom. You were all at my feast—you know I called Queen Amestris to me, and you saw that my eunuchs returned without her. Had her refusal been due to her physical condition, I would have understood. But she refused from anger—which she made clear to everyone within earshot. Such impudence cannot go unpunished. What is an appropriate reaction?"

The men exchanged a few glances, a few whispers. And if he were not mistaken, a few smiles of glee.

Not fond of her, then. He had expected as much.

The eldest, Memucan, stepped forward. "How harsh does the king wish to be?"

He clenched his teeth, swallowed, and forced himself to relax. "The king would see her killed, were it not for the children we share and the one even now growing in her womb. For their sakes, and only for their sakes, do I wish to spare her life. There must be a punishment less than death but still severe."

Memucan looked to another of the advisers with raised brows. At the answering nod, he said, "The queen has indeed done a great wrong, not only against the king, but against all of Persia and Media. For when the queen disobeys her husband, why should any woman in the empire obey theirs?

"If it pleases the king, she could be deposed. Knowing the queen as we all do, that may be harsher than death to her. The king could send out a royal decree and let it be written in the law, that the queen is never again to enter the presence of the great Xerxes. Let her crown be given to one more deserving."

Xerxes' lips tugged up. Losing her power would indeed be worse than death to Amestris. Yet it would spare his children the grief of losing a mother.

"This pleases the king very much. Write up the decree this very hour, and at first light it shall be sent out to every province in its own language. Let the world know that Amestris is queen no more."

There would probably be dancing in many a street.

Memucan bowed. "It will be done as the king says. And in her place, who will you name? One of your other wives?"

"Father." Darius stepped near, a line of worry between his brows. "You can take away her crown, but her power will not be easily negated. Whomever you appointed in her place would be dead before she could feel the weight of the crown upon her head."

Xerxes smiled. "It is a wise son who knows his mother so well. Let it be enough for now that she is removed. Another queen can be named when we return triumphant from Greece. There is no rush—I have my heir already."

Memucan and the other six bowed out to prepare the proclamation. Darius drew in a long breath. "Thank you, Father, for sparing her. I know she is a hard woman to love, but she is my mother."

"I am not the one to thank. Letting her live will undoubtedly prove as troublesome as the canal at Mount Athos, as you yourself pointed out."

His son acknowledged that truth with a glance over Xerxes' shoulder. "I will use what influence I have with her to caution her against riling your anger any more."

"I suggest you go to her now and keep her from anything rash when my decision reaches her ear."

"Yes, Father." Darius sped from the room.

Xerxes looked to Masistes. "Brother, bid our guests good night. You may tell them I am busy seeing justice done for the queen's crime."

"It is my honor to carry out your will." Masistes left, too.

Xerxes turned back to Kasia. "My son is right about Amestris's response, and not only for whomever I name the next queen. She will know that my anger is kindled largely on your behalf and will blame you for this."

Kasia pressed her lips together. He read no fear in her eyes, only sorrow. "I am sorry to bring you such trouble."

"It is no fault of yours." He tugged her closer so that he could rest his cheek against her hair. "I will have her removed to Persepolis as soon as possible. In the meantime you must exercise the greatest caution."

"I will. But there is no need to fear, my love. Jehovah has delivered me from her schemes this day, and I feel peace in my spirit that he will continue to protect me." Her arms slipped around him.

He stroked his hand along the glossy locks that tumbled down her back. "Your God is responsible for your being spared?"

She hummed. "The moment Leda brought in my meal, I felt the most urgent need to pray. I decided to fast and turn my heart toward Jehovah. He saved me."

"And when I came in? I thought the lot of you slain. Were you praying more?"

"In thanks, and for the larger situation. And for the dog."

"The . . . ." He glanced around the room. One of the guard dogs lay on a fine rug in the corner, its breathing heavy. He assumed it was the unfortunate beast given some of her food. "You bother your God with concern for a dog?"

"I could not stand the thought of it dying in my stead. I think it will recover, though, it only had a bite."

Xerxes shook his head. "What a strange creature I have fallen in love with."

She stretched up and bestowed a sweet kiss upon his lips. "You ought to get to your new bride. She will be anxious."

Was there a more bizarre woman in the world? One more baffling? More perfect? He cradled her head and gazed deep into her eyes. "Given the events still unfolding, it would be fairer to see her first another night. I will send her my apologies and make sure the situation is explained."

"Xerxes . . . ."

He silenced her with a kiss. Then pulled off the torc he had slipped on and held it between them. "I believe this is yours."

She stared at it. "I cannot. It was a gift to you."

"And so I ought not to have given it away two weeks ago. I would have apologized for forgetting its source, had she approached me privately. Things have changed. It is yours." He slid it up her arm, as he had done at the river. Now, as then, desire filled her eyes. Desire that had nothing to do with the silver. "You will come with me, my love, lest treachery visit this room again. I will see with my own eyes that you remain safe until the viper is out of my house."

Kasia nodded and tucked herself against his side.

Why could the rest of the world not agree with his will so readily?

Twelve

Anger mixed with fear on Amestris's tongue when Darius stole to her side. His face spoke much, though his lips remained pressed together. Bile rose in her throat. "My son?"

Darius sat and silently took her hand. She had not seen him look so stricken since he received the news of his grandfather's death three years earlier. He turned his head toward the entrance to the hall. Amestris followed his gaze and sucked in a sharp breath when Memucan entered, flanked by the other six highest officials.

She gripped her son's hand. "What is this?"

"You must have known he would retaliate, Mother," Darius murmured. "You cannot disobey him before such an assembly and hope he will overlook it."

Her chin tilted up. "It is he who has done wrong."

When had her eldest son's gaze become capable of such hardness? "When one rules the world, one is never wrong. He is the king of kings."

Memucan held up his arms, and the chattering women fell silent. His eyes scanned the crowd before coming to a rest on her.

The pompous old man. She had never liked him, and she knew he took pleasure in whatever punishment he would now hand down. Amestris reclaimed her hand from Darius and folded her arms over her chest.

"A grave crime has been committed tonight." Memucan lowered his arms and glared at her. "You all bore witness to it. The king sent for Amestris, and she refused him with words bitter and angry. Such offense is not to be suffered in the courts of Xerxes. Let all the world know that each man will remain ruler of his household and this woman called Amestris is hereby stripped of her crown. She is never again to enter the presence of King Xerxes, and her position will be given to another. One more deserving."

Amestris rose, wondering that she did not explode into pieces, given the way she shook. "No." Her voice came out as no more than a murmur, weak and incredulous. "He cannot. He cannot do this to me."

The women, after years of currying her favor, of seeking her smile and fearing her wrath, looked at her with horror. On her behalf? No, they were horrified *by* her.

By *her*! She sucked in a breath, ready to spew venom at the first shrew who dared speak against her.

None did. With the silence of death, they all stood and, without so much as looking over their shoulders, strode from the room.

Her fingers curled into her palms. Never could these backbiters agree on anything, never could they work in harmony. Yet now, in her hour of need, they united against her?

She narrowed her gaze on the wife of her husband's brother. "Parsisa. Do you dare leave your queen's presence without permission? I have not dismissed this feast."

The woman stopped but did not turn around. She moved only her face to present her profile. "You are not my queen."

Amestris sputtered, lunged, but Darius caught her and held her captive. She shoved at him, cursed the sting of tears.

Crying was for the weak. For other women. Not for her.

"Mother—"

"He cannot do this to me. How could you let him do this, Darius?"

He set her back on her feet with a sigh, though he did not release her shoulders. "You are fortunate he did not order your death."

Her blood ran cold. "He would not dare, not with his babe in my stomach."

"An argument that only convinced him to stay your execution until after the birth." Looking weary, Darius dropped his hands. "You have the Jewess to thank for your life. It was her words, not mine, that convinced him to spare you."

"The Jewess?" Her voice sounded hollow to her own ears. The Jewess could not possibly still be alive. She had ordered enough hemlock in her meal to fell five, no matter which of the dishes she chose.

Darius lifted a brow. "Apparently she was more given to prayer than hunger this night. For which you ought to thank the god. Had your scheme succeeded, nothing would have averted Father's wrath. He would have killed you with his own hands, babe or no babe."

Amestris stumbled back and sank onto her couch. This was not the world she knew. It did not obey the rules she had mastered, did not track the path through the heavens she had planned for. "He has taken it all. My crown, my power, my friends."

Darius sat beside her. "It is not as bad as it seems, Mother. Father has promised to name me his successor in a few days' time. When I am king you will be the queen mother, whether you hold the title now or not."

She straightened, forced her gaze to focus on her son's face. "You are right. He cannot wrest from my hands the power I forged with them. He can take *his* authority. But not my own."

Why did Darius look saddened? He patted her hand, drew in a long breath. "You will rally. Just promise me, Mother, you will cause no more trouble. I know this concubine distresses you. I know you are angry. But if you try Father more, I fear nothing will keep him from ordering your execution. Please—for your children's sakes, control your temper."

She watched the face of this eldest son, glanced beyond him in time to see a smaller figure dart away. Hystaspes, undoubtedly spying as usual. He too, then, would have seen his mother's disgrace firsthand.

What choice did she have? Darius was right. Her day would come again, but not while Xerxes sat on the throne. She would have to be careful, sly as a serpent, until he could be removed. "Of course, my son. I promise. I will not try him again."

Not yet.

Zechariah tilted the chair so that the sun caught the engraving he had chiseled. Nearly perfect. Nearly. One more tap . . . . He positioned the chisel, reached for the hammer. Halted at the sound of heavy footsteps nearing the door.

Abba's grumble told him Persians entered the shop. Zechariah put down his tools and stood to intercept them before his father could scare them off. His smile wavered when he saw clothing peculiar to the palace servants. Had something happened to Kasia?

He cleared his throat. "Good morning. How might I help you?"

One of the men extended a tablet with cuneiform script. "An order from the palace of Xerxes. A table and two chairs. The table is to be engraved with lilies. One of the chairs ought to be of a height for a woman at a loom."

Zechariah took the tablet and glanced at the writing. Abba had made him learn cuneiform so that he would not have to. His eyes widened at the price promised for the pieces. "Certainly."

Abba stepped up behind him. "Tell them to leave." He spoke in low Hebrew.

Zechariah turned his head and answered in the same. "These are feminine pieces."

His father obviously understood his meaning. Abba faced the Persians. "May we know for whom they are intended? We would tailor our work to suit the recipient."

The servant smiled. "The king's favorite concubine. If possible, she would have them before the king's house leaves Susa in a fortnight."

Zechariah's breath hitched. His sister was a favorite of the king? An odd thought. Odder still to think that in a few weeks she would leave the only city they had ever known. Headed where? To the magnificent ceremonial capital of Persepolis? Or perhaps one of the other two capital cities? Pasargadae? Ecbatana?

So far from home. From family.

How unfair that Kasia, who never wanted anything but a house full of children, got to see the world while he was stuck here in Susa. He said quietly to his father, "It has to be her. Would you deny her something to remember us by, something carved by her father's hand?"

Abba sighed.

The second servant turned from examining some of their completed pieces and held out another tablet. "From the king—orders enough to keep you busy for several years. He wishes all new furnishings for his personal palace, both here and in Persepolis."

Abba stared at the tablet without taking it. "Why would the king commission so much when he has never seen my work?"

The servant arched a brow. "He sees it now, through me. I was authorized to offer this only if I approved."

"Take it," Zechariah urged in Hebrew. "Surely you know what this would mean."

Abba's nostrils flared. "It is a bribe, that is all."

The first servant lifted a brow. "You are mistaken."

Zechariah's mouth fell open at the Hebrew words. Was this man a Jew, then, or just well educated?

"It is a man wanting to please the wife he loves and help provide for her family. Is that not a noble thing for a son by marriage to do? Is it not in keeping with the Law?"

Abba blinked rapidly. "How would you know he loves her?"

The man smiled. "Her chief servant chose me to come here because I am a Jew. He told me many things about your daughter, so that I might answer your questions. He assures me none have ever seen the king show such favor as he has for her. And she, in turn, wishes you to know that though she misses you all, she is happy with her husband."

Abba loosed a blustery breath. "Why did you not deliver these messages to begin with, man, instead of acting as though you did not understand us and knew not who sent you?"

"I was cautioned that only a few members of the family knew the truth of the situation, and that I was not to speak of her identity to anyone who thought her dead." He shrugged an apology. "I only respect your decision for secrecy."

Abba grunted but took the second tablet. "We will have the first pieces done before they leave. Are you able to carry a message back?"

The servant nodded, and Zechariah lifted his brows. Abba had not mentioned Kasia as though she were alive until now. What would he say to her?

Abba reached up and rubbed a hand over his eyes. "Tell her we pray for her."

"I will. Good day to you both."

Zechariah watched the two men leave and turned to his father. "I am nearly done this chair for Bijan. I can get started on the table within the hour."

Abba put the tablet down and moved to the corner, where he kept his best wood. "You will have to work on all three of those pieces, my son."

"Will you start on the others already? These are more pressing." He had not asked for the tablet to be translated, though, so how would he even know what the king had requested?

"No. There is something else more pressing still." Abba lifted out a few lengths of cedar. A ghost of a smile haunted his mouth. "Something more special than a table or a chair. You can handle those, can you not?"

"Of course." He wanted to ask his father what the "more special" piece was, but he would wait and see. Abba had that closed-mouthed look about him.

Zechariah picked up the second tablet. His breath leaked out as he read item after item that the king wanted made, the details for each and the price he would pay.

Enough to keep them busy for years to come. Enough to feed the family long after they finished.

Enough to guarantee his father would never allow him to leave with the army. Even with two of them, it would be difficult to complete all this in the amount of time the king had designated.

Time for his brother Joshua to learn the trade. Zechariah had hinted all year that Abba ought to bring him to the shop, but he had been ignored—probably because his father knew well he only wanted to train a replacement.

Things had changed. The great Xerxes may take Kasia away to places unknown, but he had effectively shackled Zechariah to Susa. He would have to resign himself, would have to shoulder the responsibility without complaint.

He would focus on the blessing Kasia had sent them. He would rejoice in what this meant for his brothers, who would now have ample opportunity, for his sisters, who would now have dowries to ensure good marriages. He would be glad. He would.

If only his soul would not yearn for what could never be.

"Is that all?"

Mordecai glanced down at the scroll in his hands and nodded. "It is. Thank you, my king, for taking the time to share your wisdom with your servant. I will make your judgments known."

He rolled the parchment up again and bowed. Only twice a year did he go before the king to present the cases that could not be handled by lower officials—once when the royal house first arrived in Susa, and once before they left. This time he had wondered if the king would be distracted, given what had so recently transpired with the queen, but he had seen no difference in his behavior. Had he not heard the decree himself, he never would have guessed that this man had just deposed his first wife.

Who could understand the mind of a king?

Before he could turn away, Xerxes held out a staying hand. "Would you walk with me?"

Mordecai fought to keep his surprise from showing. "I . . . of course, my lord. I would be honored."

The king looked pleased as he nodded and stood. With a single motion he swept his royal robes behind him and descended the step. Mordecai could not recall ever seeing him on even ground, but Xerxes did not need the step to tower above the court. They were of a height—something Mordecai encountered rarely.

"I will not keep you long," the king said as he led the way through the hall, "but I could not pass up the opportunity to ask a few questions of a man obviously learned. You must be of strong faith, to be so esteemed by your people. Am I right?"

Mordecai nodded. "My faith in Jehovah has sustained me through many a trial, my king."

"And you are a descendant of Shadrach, who was friend to the great Belteshazzar. One of the three who emerged unsinged from the furnace."

"That is right." Mordecai glanced over his shoulder when he felt people crowding in. The king's guard—he ought to have realized.

"I confess I am bemused by your God. In some ways, he seems much like mine. Both your Jehovah and my Ahura Mazda are uncreated. Both are said to be the father of all things good. Correct?"

Mordecai smiled. "Largely. Jehovah is the father of *all* creation."

Xerxes, his hands clasped loosely behind his back, sent him an incredulous look. "And this is where Judaism ceases to make sense to me. How can you worship a deity from whom both good *and* evil flow?"

"I do not." How to explain? Mordecai inclined his heart to God and prayed for the right answers to come to his lips. "Jehovah is all things good, yes—all wisdom, all justice, all mercy. Which means he knows that worship offered only out of duty is meaningless, so he gave his creation choice. And surely the king knows that creation often chooses unwisely."

Xerxes chuckled and motioned toward the exit. They stepped into the blinding sunshine. Summer would be upon them soon, and while the grounds within the palace complex remained green with life from the irrigation canals, the rest of Susa glistened golden brown in the unrelenting rays.

"Humanity is unwise, indeed." The king descended the steps and headed toward a lush strip of garden. "But we do not claim Ahura Mazda is all-powerful. Our god could not take choice away, and men are often swayed by Angra Mainyu. Does your religion have an evil one?"

"Certainly. We call him Satan. But unlike your Angra Mainyu, Satan is a created being, one who chose to oppose Jehovah. He was once an angel—like your lesser immortals—but rebelled against God." He hesitated, but decided he might as well voice his question. "I have often wondered about the opposition of good and evil in Mazdayasna. According to your religion, Angra Mainyu is also uncreated. How, then, is he not the equal to your Ahura Mazda? How can you know good will triumph?"

Xerxes lifted his brows and gave him a lopsided smile. "Is that not why we call religion 'faith'? We trust—and we labor." The king sighed and cast his gaze out over the garden. "I have respect for your people, and for your Jehovah. Yet according to Jartosht, there is only one god—Ahura Mazda. All other deities are demons, servants of the evil one."

"And according to our prophets, there is only one God—Jehovah. The deities other nations serve are idols, lifeless and without power. Even your ancestors acknowledged that my God is a living God."

"I have read their words." Xerxes' brow knit. "I know the stories of the three thrown into the fire, of the great Belteshazzar and the den of lions. I know that while some kings of Babylon and Persia had no use for your God, others acknowledged the power demonstrated on behalf of the Jews."

The king paused in the shade of a wide-stretching hornbeam tree. "The law of Persia and Media cannot be altered, because tradition holds that the king is a god. The words of our most esteemed prophet say that none but Ahura Mazda should be worshiped. In order to keep peace and prosperity in our empire, we allow all to believe as they please. It is a difficult balance."

Mordecai focused his gaze on a delicate flower, pink and vibrant where there should have been only desert. "It is. In the history of my people, it is when they concern themselves with other gods and forget Jehovah that ill befalls the nation. We seem to remember him better when in exile."

A hint of a smile captured the king's mouth. "I have a Jewess in my house—she has been entertaining my children with many of the stories of your people, and they are always so delighted that they tell me about them whenever I visit." The smile faded, and Xerxes faced him again. "Many of you claim your Jehovah is a personal God, that he cares for his children and orders the universe. I cannot discount the evidence of him. Yet with my own eyes I have seen Ahura Mazda."

Mordecai straightened. His curiosity was piqued . . . and his soul seemed to stretch forward, waiting to see if it would recognize truth or lie. "Have you?"

"Two years ago." Xerxes motioned him on again, following a winding path through the garden. "I was new to the throne, and my friend and cousin Mardonius was adamant that I punish Greece for rising against my father. The only voice of disagreement was my father's brother, Artabanus. When he first spoke against me, I was furious."

The king smiled again, ruefully, and shook his head. "But when I retired that night, I realized his was the more measured argument, the sounder wisdom. I decided that the next morning, I would announce my change in plans. That night I dreamed." He halted, gazed across the fountain spurting clear water. "A tall man, fine of face, came to me and taunted me for turning away from greatness. Though something in me quivered at the dream, I determined not to be affected by such things. I followed through on my decision and announced the change of plans. The people rejoiced."

At that, Xerxes rolled his eyes. "Then the next night, he came again. I awoke so frightened that I ran to my uncle and demanded he dress in my robes and sleep in my bed so that he would have the same dream."

Mordecai could not resist a smile. "Did that work?"

"Oddly." Xerxes chuckled. "It was a plan that would not have made sense in the morning, but he humored me. When he slept, the same figure appeared to him, asking why he dared try to dissuade me from the course set out by the god. He lunged at Artabanus with red-hot pokers aimed at his eyes. My uncle awoke screaming—and of a changed heart. The god's will was clear. I announced yet another change of plans, and the people rejoiced."

Mordecai shook his head. "Fickle people—yet devoted to their king, and rightly so."

"And to their god." Xerxes sighed to a halt and faced him. "Hence my dilemma. I have seen proof of my god—and evidence of yours too. But only one can be the true god. I was hoping your insight would show me they are one and the same, but I am not certain. Could it be so?"

His spirit seemed to close up around him, giving him the strangest sensation of a wall thrown up. "I cannot think so, my king. I am no priest, nor a prophet like Daniel, whom you call Belteshazzar. I have not the wisdom of my ancestors. But this dream of yours . . . I cannot say if it is from your god, but it would not be from mine. This much I know. Though Jehovah may promise greatness, he does not encourage pride. And he would never lunge at a man with pokers."

Xerxes arched his brows. "But did he not wrestle with your forefather Jacob? Is that not how he earned the name Israel?"

"You are a well-learned man." Mordecai could not help but respect a ruler who knew so much about the least of his subjects. "I have seen many a father wrestle with his children. Never have I seen one try to put out their eyes."

"Well, Artabanus can be very trying." Grinning, Xerxes turned back toward the palace. "I thank you for speaking with me. I wish there were a happier way to resolve our beliefs, but alas. We shall have to be content with mutual respect and disagreement."

Something stirred within him, tickled its way up until words came from his mouth that Mordecai did not recognize as his own. "You will see the power of Jehovah yourself, my king."

Xerxes inclined his head, eyes dancing. "Let us hope you have a touch of the prophet after all, my friend. I should very much like to see more of your God. From what I have read, he puts on quite a show."

Mordecai said nothing more, but he had to wonder if this king would take such proof to heart any more than his ancestors had. They were all happy enough to acknowledge his God's power . . . but never did they call him theirs.

"My lord."

Xerxes paused and turned to Hegai. The custodian hurried toward him from the women's palace, concern etched on his face. All thoughts of slipping away for a quiet dinner in solitude fled. "What is it?"

"The women." Hegai panted to a halt and sketched a bow. "They are arguing. I would not usually bother the king with such things, but it is over the crown."

Xerxes sighed even as he headed for his wives. He should have realized this would come up. He ought to have spoken to them days ago, but he had more pressing concerns. Naming Darius as his heir yesterday. Making sure Amestris made no foolish attempts before her entourage departed Susa this morning.

Now, though, he must deal with the ambitions of the harem.

Raised female voices reached him long before Hegai showed him to the courtyard in the house of wives. He halted in the shadows rather than make his presence known.

One of his older wives hushed a younger with a matronly scowl. "You are all fools if you think this is anything but a warning to the rest of us. The next to wear the crown will be *his* choice, not a result of your plotting."

The younger sneered. Had he once thought her beautiful? She looked hateful and petty now. "You are so complacent only because you think *you* will be queen, Suri, now that you are the senior wife. But he already had one queen he cared nothing for, why would he appoint *you* now that she is gone?"

Xerxes winced. The ways of women still astounded him sometimes. They fought their battles in secret, using weapons that one could not defend against.

Give him spears on an open battlefield any day.

Suri shook her head as if dealing with an out-of-sorts daughter. "Well, if he chooses for love, you ought to give up all hope of the title. It would go to Kasia."

Xerxes swept his gaze over the crowd of women, wondering what Kasia would say to that. He found her nowhere in their numbers.

An explosion broke out, snippets of angry words bombarding him.

"He would not!"

"She is only a concubine!"

"That wretch?"

"Never!"

Movement from the opposite hallway caught his eye, and Kasia stepped into the courtyard. He folded his arms to await whatever she had to say. This might be the moment when hidden ambitions came to light.

But her face spoke of pain, and she shook her head as if in sorrow. "Why do you grow so angry over what we all know will never be?"

"Because in this moment, you are the favorite." He could not see which woman answered her. "And in this moment, Persia has no queen. Why would the king not name the one he loves?"

"The king does not love me," Kasia said softly. He straightened—did she doubt him? Then her lips pulled up. "Xerxes does."

Ah. He smiled.

Suri shook her head. "You say that as if there is a difference, child. Let me assure you there is none. Even when his older brother was the presumed heir, Xerxes did nothing not geared toward ruling someday. Take that away, and you would not be left with a man. You would be left with a corpse."

He never would have argued with the words, would have denied that they were an accusation rather than a compliment. Until Kasia.

Did the others recognize the secret truth in her smile? "I am sorry you think so. My point, though, is that if he favors me, it is not as a queen. I am only a concubine, raised in a poor family with more children than luxuries. I am ill-suited to the demands of the crown. More, I am a Jew. I confess it proudly, but we all know one of my people will never be given such power."

Murmurs of agreement sounded, though most made it sound as though they insulted her rather than granting the point she herself made.

She looked at several of the women in turn. "You seem to find new reasons to dislike me at every turn, but let this not be one of them. I will never rule over any of you."

That was as good a cue for him to enter as any. He stepped out into the sunlight. "None of you will ever rule over the others."

All the women turned his way, varying degrees of surprise and guilt on their faces.

He glared back. "You think I know nothing of women's ambitions? The older among you, with sons nearly men, would plot the assassination of my chosen heir so that your child might take his place. The younger among you would lord your new power over the older and make life miserable in my palace."

He slashed a hand through the air. "No. I have my heir—and no need of a queen. I have an army to gather, a war to win. Perhaps when I return, I will have the time to worry with this. If so, rest assured I will not pick from your numbers. I will bring in new wives, ones whose sons will not age until Darius has already learned the ways of ruling and is ready to take my place. And if I name a new queen, it will be one who treats you better than you treat one another." His gaze flicked to Kasia, then back to the women at large. "The next to mutter about this will find herself divorced and sent home in shame to her parents. Do I make myself clear?"

They were quick to duck their heads, seek the ground with their gazes. All modesty, all demureness, all obedience.

He trusted the lot of them about as much as a den of vipers.

Stepping out of the courtyard again, he nodded to Hegai. "Thank you for telling me what was underway. Were all but Kasia present when I got here?"

"Jasmine left when the grumbling began. I suspect she is the one who informed Kasia."

"Hmm." He folded his arms, tapped a finger against his elbow. He would speak to her, but not when any would think it of import.

The perfect excuse dashed through the courtyard as if summoned by his thoughts. "Father!"

He scooped up Chinara with a grin and gave her a hug. "I wondered where you were—I have been here two whole minutes with empty arms."

The girl giggled and snuggled close. "Mother would not let me out of the room until the shouting stopped."

And her mother now wove through the dispersing crowd, a flush on her round cheeks. "My apologies, my lord. She heard your voice . . . ."

"And I am thankful she did." He kissed his daughter's head and, when she wiggled for freedom, put her down. His voice he pitched low. "I will be leaving soon, Jasmine. I will need eyes and ears in the harem while I am gone. Can I trust you with that?"

Within those strange silver eyes he read everything he had hoped for—recognition, respect, obedience. She nodded. "I would be honored to serve you, my husband."

"Good." He smiled and nodded over her shoulder. "She is on the run again."

Jasmine scurried away, leaving him alone with his custodian. Solitude had lost its appeal, though. "Have Kasia come to my palace now, Hegai. I would share a meal with her."

THIRTEEN

Kasia ran her hand over the dog's head and scratched behind its ear. The beast leaned into her and smiled. Whoever would have thought a dog could smile? "You are a good pup, Zad. Soon enough you shall have your strength back completely."

Zad rewarded her encouragement with a lick and sprawled in the grass. Kasia grinned and patted his side. "My family never had a pet," she said to Desma.

A masculine voice replied, "It is not a pet—it is a guard dog. You will spoil him, lady."

Her shoulders stiffened as she looked up into the face of her husband's brother. She had seen him several times this week, but never without Xerxes present. Something about him always made her uneasy—perhaps embarrassment at having thought it Masistes she met at the river.

Or perhaps it was that predatory glint in his eyes.

Kasia forced a smile. "He deserves the spoiling after eating hemlock on my behalf."

Theron shifted into alert. Masistes sent a demeaning glare her eunuch's way that seemed to say, *Remember your place, slave*. "Are you looking forward to the journey this week, lady?"

Masistes had sought her out in the private garden of the women's palace to talk about travel? "It will be interesting to see more of my husband's empire, but I confess I shall miss Susa this summer."

And her family. Abba and Ima, her brothers and sisters. Esther and Mordecai. But that was a pain she kept cradled close to her chest, especially as concerned Esther. She had not mentioned her even to Xerxes, though she spoke of her family. Jehovah was the only one here who would understand how deeply she missed her young friend.

Masistes may have intended the curve of his lips to be a smile. It looked more like a sneer. "Nonsense—no one could miss Susa in the summer. It is unlivable."

"And yet I lived here quite happily through sixteen summers."

Masistes lowered himself to the ground beside her with a chuckle devoid of amusement. "Sixteen summers. Forgive me for saying so, but you are older than I would have thought. How is it that my brother found you before you wed another?

Such beauty rarely makes it to sixteen without a husband."

She swallowed against the trepidation rising in her throat. "God obviously saved me for the king. He must have known I could love no other like Xerxes."

He breathed an unconvinced laugh. "Or perhaps it is because, in spite of your alluring looks, your father could offer no dowry. I have sought out information on your family—your beginnings were humble indeed. I imagine you are grateful for the increase in means."

"Only because now I can help those who nurtured me so well, in spite of humble circumstances." She focused her gaze on the dog. Perhaps if she ignored him, Masistes would go away.

"Nine siblings." Masistes shook his head. "I have claim to more, of course, but not from the same mother. And my father was able to support us all."

Zad growled low in his throat. Kasia wished she could too. "My father supported us well."

"Your father provided only for your basest needs." His gaze swept down her and sent a chill up her spine. "What would happen to those siblings, I wonder, if something were to befall your father? And if your brother slipped into Bijan's blade?"

The dog's growling grew louder. Kasia soothed him with a stroke and glanced at Theron, whose hands were fisted at his side. He could make no move against a menace not physical, but she knew he waited for such an opportunity.

She looked back to Masistes. "Why do you threaten me? Do you hate me because I am a Jew, as Haman? Do you not like my closeness to your brother, as Amestris?"

"It is a strange closeness—one must wonder what he has found in you." He plucked a lily and twirled it in his fingers. "He calls you every night he can. Visits you during the day when he must see another that evening. And yet he cannot be as attached as he seems, since he is not taking you into Greece."

He was not? Kasia drew her lip between her teeth.

Masistes' half-smile had none of the charm of his brother's. "Perhaps he is getting his fill of you now, since once we leave Susa it will be years before we meet up with the royal house again. And my brother is not famous for his devotion to his wives. Once out of sight . . . ."

She blinked back hot tears. Their love was too strong to be put aside, too consuming to be forgotten even after a separation of years. Was it not? She would not be relegated to the ranks of all the other women so soon. Would she? "Why do you speak of these things?"

"I want you to be prepared." He leaned close. So close she could smell the wine on his breath. "There is no purpose in loving a king. His heart belongs to Persia. You are only a diversion, my dear, while he finalizes his preparations for the war. He will forget his feelings for you, and with his affection will go the support he is sending your family."

She turned her face away. "You know nothing of his heart."

"I have known my brother all but the first two of his thirty-six years. You, but a few weeks. Do you dare claim to see him more clearly than I?"

She did—she must. But she only pressed her lips together.

Masistes leaned closer still, though he was careful not to touch her. "You would do well to find a lover not so occupied with matters of state."

Her head snapped back around, eyes narrowed. "Is this your sorry attempt at a seduction? Let me assure you now, my lord, that I will remain faithful to my husband all my days—no matter what he does."

"On the contrary." His eyes flashed, dangerous as lightning. "The next night the king calls another, you will come out here and order your slaves inside. Or else the following morning you will be getting news of a few deaths in the family."

"I will not be extorted. I will tell Xerxes—"

"And cause a civil war?" Masistes straightened again. "Then you love him not as much as you say. You would still taste my wrath, and it is not so much less potent than the king's. Is your father's life not worth one night?"

A rustle came from behind, and panic seized her tongue. When Atossa stepped from behind a bush, she knew not if it was her salvation or her destruction.

The queen mother's gaze locked on her son. "I believe your question is better asked of *you*, Masistes. Would you risk all you have for one night with your brother's wife? When he found out, he would not strip you of your holdings as he did Amestris—he would kill you."

Masistes stood, though he looked none too concerned. "He would not find out, Mother."

Kasia took to her feet to keep from feeling so overpowered by the others.

Atossa shook her regal head. "You give him too little credit. Your brother knows what transpires in his house." Her gaze flicked to Kasia and softened. "You do well to refuse this arrogant pup. Forget he ever approached you, child, and fear not for your family. He will not raise his hand against them. You." She glared at her son. "Keep your distance from Kasia. And if anything happens to her family, rest assured Xerxes will know who to blame for it."

Masistes rolled his eyes and brushed the soil from his clothing. "As always, Mother, your favor is clear."

"If I did not love you, I would not have taken the time to warn you—I would have gone directly to your brother and let *him* deal with you. Do not question my heart. If it seems I favor him, it is because he is king and I must focus more on his goings-on."

Masistes turned away, as if all this were nothing to him. As if the threat that had her quivering inside was nothing but a game.

She would never learn to live with such intrigue. Never.

He even dared to smile. "He is king only because of an accident of birth. Had *I* been the firstborn of Darius after his ascension—"

"Then the god would have made a grave error." Teasing colored Atossa's tone. "You may have the same temper, but you lack the wisdom your brother has shown. Get you back to your own house, my foolish son. I will not have you disrupting your brother's anymore."

Masistes chuckled and bowed to his mother. "Good night, sweet matron." He turned to Kasia. "My apologies for upsetting you. Rest assured I will find my amusement elsewhere."

Kasia sagged when he strolled away. These people were baffling. How could they toy so easily with matters of the heart, tamper so readily with fidelity and trust? Was nothing sacred to them?

Atossa's hand settled on her shoulder. "I know it does not seem so to you, but this is nothing to concern yourself over. Masistes will not harm your family, and he will not approach you again. He was only intrigued, I think, because he heard you thought it him you met that first day."

Her brows drew together. "Xerxes told him that?"

"He was chastising Haman for not making the truth known to you, that is all." Atossa patted her shoulder, then withdrew her hand. "You are given much to prayer, I hear. Why do you not return to your chamber and spend some time in quiet contemplation? I am sure your God will grant you a return of peace."

Kasia nodded and sent a glance to her servants so they could stir themselves. Prayer was exactly what she needed. Perhaps Jehovah could help her better understand this world she would spend her life in.

Xerxes hummed a snippet of one of Chinara's songs and stepped into the silent sanctuary of his private palace. He was glad the feast was over. Soon enough the expedition would begin, but he would enjoy these last days of quiet.

The women had calmed down, praise the god. Their docility was undoubtedly a show, but it was a show he appreciated.

"My son, wait."

He paused and turned to greet his mother with a smile. It froze when he saw the furrow etched into her forehead. "What is it?"

She shook her head and indicated they should continue moving. He led her into his receiving chamber and motioned her onto one of the gilded couches. "Is something wrong?"

She sighed and sank to the cushion. "Will you take Kasia with you into Greece?"

Xerxes frowned and motioned a servant to the wine. "You concern yourself over which concubines I take?"

"In this case, yes. I know you are fond of her, Xerxes. Why would you not include her in your entourage?"

He accepted the golden rhyton put in his hands and took a long sip. The wine did nothing to settle the question in his mind. "I want to. The thought of being away from her so long . . . but there are no guarantees in war. There is always the chance an enemy could take us unaware. Or that the travel itself could harm her."

Mother lifted her brows. "And if you leave her here, she will be dead by the time you return. Amestris still has much power, my son, and much hatred for Kasia. You would have done better to have her executed."

"It would have been simpler. But her anger was justified." He paced to a window and looked out over the citadel. It gleamed bronze in the evening sun. All the past week he had been weighing the situation. "You recommend taking her?"

"Strongly, both for your peace of mind and her safety. Would even the war be enough to distract you from worrying over her if she were not with you?"

His lips pulled up. "Probably not. I have never loved like this, Mother."

"Understandable—I am fond of her myself. She is the first person I have ever met who is completely free of guile."

He chuckled and took another drink from his cup.

When he faced his mother again, she had a contemplative look on her face. "I believe this to be the wise choice, but you must be cautious. What attracts you will attract others, and women will be in short supply."

"I trust Kasia not to involve herself in an affair willingly, and any who attempt to force her will wish they are dead long before I grant such relief."

Mother leaned back, regarding him steadily. "Perhaps you ought to have made that clear before now, Xerxes. I just interrupted your brother in the garden trying to threaten her into a tryst."

"*What?*" Blood surged, thrummed, and awoke every fear. "I will kill him! I will—"

"Calm yourself." A small smile fluttered over her mouth. "She was admirable in her refusal, and he will not attempt it again."

"That is hardly the point." His fingers gripped the chalice so tightly it was a wonder the metal did not deform. "Does he think such behavior will go unpunished?"

"He thought such behavior would go unnoticed. But had I not overheard and stepped in at the time, I have no doubt Kasia would have run to you to seek your help. He threatened to have her father and brother killed."

He could squeeze no tighter on the cup so dashed it to the ground. "I would threaten his parent and brother in return, were they not you and I."

Mother chuckled. "All he did was make a foolish attempt for a charming girl. To his credit, when he saw there would be no success, he desisted immediately."

"Irrelevant. The fact that he would even try! Perhaps I ought to seduce *his* wife and see how *he* likes it."

Mother shook her head and stood. "When will you boys leave behind the follies of youth? Leave his wives alone and let this rest. I only told you because I did not want it to reach your ears from another source—one that would not temper your anger."

It would have, he was sure. Kasia's servants knew to pass along anything of relevance. He grunted and folded his arms over his chest. "I will not forget this."

She glided forward and stretched up to kiss his cheek. "You have larger concerns to occupy you right now. Be content in the knowledge that Kasia loves you. Good night, Xerxes."

He let her go but held his ground for a long moment. The blood still simmered. Was he surprised that Masistes wanted Kasia? No—his interest had been clear enough. But Masistes was always interested in every new female, and it had never led to an attempted seduction before.

No matter that his attempt had been foiled. It was unforgivable that he would try to steal the wife of his brother and king. Unforgivable that he attempt it by a threat against his beloved's family.

But he could not afford vengeance yet. Masistes had command over one of the largest parts of his army, was governor of a few vital cities. The war was more important than punishment for a failed mistake.

He would remember this, though. Only a fool would think he would forget.

And Kasia—she was not accustomed to these things, she would be upset. He spun around and found the door open already. Xerxes shook his head as he strode forward. "Am I so predictable?"

Zethar smiled. "If I could not predict you, I would be a poor servant indeed."

When he arrived at the minuscule room that was becoming as familiar to him as his own, he was not surprised to find Kasia lying on her rug. With a motion for silence, he crept in until he could hear the cadence of her murmurs.

She spoke in Hebrew, but he caught a few words he recognized. Ahasuerus, which he knew to be his own name in her tongue. His brother's name. And . . . . "Who is Vashti?"

Kasia started and sat up, a hand to her chest. "How can a man who travels with a whole slew of servants surprise me so frequently?"

He chuckled and sat on the edge of her bed. "I suspect it is because you give yourself so fully to your tasks. Vashti is . . . ?"

"It carries the same meaning as Amestris." She rocked back on her heels and then stood.

Xerxes grinned. "She would hate it. We all ought to make it a point to call her that."

"Xerxes." Though she chided him, she sat beside him and snuggled into his side.

When he slid an arm around her and held her like this, it was as if the rest of the world ceased to matter. If only it were so. "How can you pray for her? She would be the first to call herself your enemy."

"All the more reason to beseech Jehovah on her behalf." Her gaze fell to the shawl draped over him, her hands splaying against the fabric. "This is exquisite. Such detail in the weaving—I have far to go before my skill could match it."

Xerxes lifted the hem of his favorite garment. "Amestris began it when my father announced I would be his heir. I wore it the first time when the crown was put on my head. Perhaps I ought to put it away now, given—"

"No." Kasia traced one of the shapes with a light finger. "You ought to wear it still, as a reminder of a time when things were better between you. Of all she invested in you and your children." She smiled up at him from under the sweep of long, black lashes. "The present ought not negate the past."

Was it any wonder his brother desired her too? Her heart could not be matched. He drew in a long breath and cupped her cheek in one hand. "Mother told me what happened with Masistes. Are you all right?"

Her shoulders stiffened under his arm, but she only cuddled closer. "Your mother assures me it was nothing to be upset about."

"A neat avoidance of the question."

She sighed. "I do not understand how he could take such a thing so lightly. He threatened my family as if life meant nothing, insisted on adultery as though it were not a crime deserving of death, and then laughed it off as if the whole thing meant no more to him than what bowl they serve his dinner in."

A chuckle slipped out. "A bowl? Really?"

She sent him an exaggerated scowl. "Sometimes, my love, I think the more bowls one has to eat out of, the less one realizes that the important things in this world are not made of gold or silver."

Until he held her, he had not understood that. "Yet you now have limitless bowls."

"No, the bowls are yours." When she smiled at him like that, his heart melted like gold in a furnace. "All I can claim is you—and that is all I shall ever need."

"Ah, I love you, Kasia." He kissed her to be sure she believed him, then smiled upon pulling away. "I suppose it is a blessing that you have not all the trappings of most women. It will be easier for you to prepare to join me in Greece."

Those beautiful brown eyes went wide. "I will go? Your brother said—"

"I had not made up my mind. There are always dangers in war, and I want you safe above all. But as my mother pointed out, there are dangers at home as well. I would worry incessantly if you were not beside me."

She bounced, laughed, and threw her arms around his neck. "Thank you, my love. I would have missed you so much."

"Have you a preference on which other concubines come? I know not all have been kind to you . . . ."

Arms still linked around his neck, she made herself comfortable in his lap and leaned back to regard him. "You would let me choose?"

A corner of his mouth tugged up. "I would hear your opinion, anyway."

She puckered her mouth up and seemed to mentally tick off a list. "Lalasa and Diona have not been among the cruel ones."

"Kasia." He narrowed his eyes. "They are the only two I have spent any time with since you joined us. Do you name them because you think they could be your friends, or because you think they are *my* choices?"

"I think they could be my friends *because* they are your choices." She managed to look both sweet and mischievous. "Which of your wives do you suppose are cruelest to me? Those you have still paid attention to or those you have ignored?"

He sighed. "Lalasa and Diona, then."

Zethar drew his gaze with a lift of his arm. "Master, a delivery for the lady. Furniture."

"Oh!" Kasia jumped up as servants entered with their burdens.

Xerxes joined her and examined the pieces as they came in. The table took its place first. "Beautiful. Your father is talented."

"This is my brother's touch." She traced a finger over the design carved into the legs. "Little though he enjoys the work, he excels at it." She turned to the chairs and frowned, though Xerxes could not see why. They were magnificent too—his steward had done well to offer the full commission. "These are also by Zechariah."

Ah, that explained the frown. She would wonder if her father's refusal to put his hand to the job had some deeper meaning.

Then he spotted the chest. "That was not commissioned."

The servant bearing it smiled. "A gift, master, from the patriarch of the family."

That grabbed Kasia's attention from the chairs. She spun around, fingers pressed to her lips and tears flooding her eyes. "A gift?"

The servant placed the large box upon the floor with care. "He says he knew you would need something for your belongings when you travel. This way, you will always know his prayers go with you."

She knelt beside the chest, and Xerxes crouched beside her. The designs any eye could appreciate; the inscription was in Hebrew. *And the Lord went before them.*

One hand still on the wood, she turned her face into Xerxes' shoulder. She took a moment to regulate her breathing, then looked up at him. "Do they meet with your approval, my love?"

"I certainly hope so, given that I already commissioned enough to keep your father and brother busy for the next five years."

She blinked back tears that glistened like diamonds. "You did?"

"When we return, lovely Kasia, you will see the work of your father's hand everywhere you turn."

Droplets spilled over onto her flawless cheeks. "How is it that a poor Jewish girl ended up the wife of a man so generous? You cannot know how I love you."

Words more precious than all the gold and jewels in Persia.

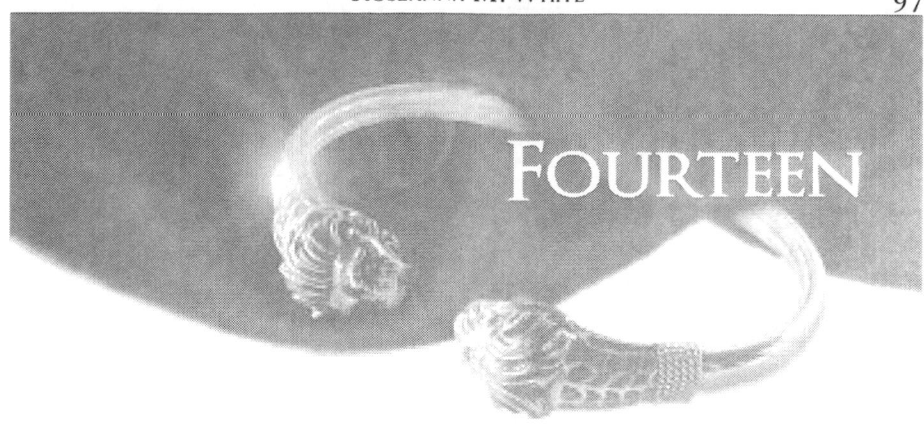

Fourteen

Outside Celaenae, Phrygia
Eighteen months later, in the fifth year of the reign of Xerxes

Kasia cuddled the babe close and pressed a kiss to his downy head. The tiny boy, only three months old, yawned and stretched one arm before nestling in. His complacency made her smile.

Zad stretched out beside her as she lounged against the cushions in her tent. All in all a peaceful place, this nomadic home of hers. Not that she would complain when they reached Sardis and she could enjoy the comfort of a bed again.

Desma crouched down to tickle the infant's foot. "Shall we play for you, mistress?"

"Please."

"Mistress." Theron stepped inside from his post at the exit, a frown on his brows. "Diona comes."

"Perhaps she forgot something?" Mindful of the baby, Kasia rolled onto her feet and stepped over the lazy dog.

The other concubine fluttered in, hands in the air. "He is raging again. I cannot abide it, Kasia, my nerves are too frayed." Diona lifted her copper curls from her forehead. "I could hear him bellowing from half a stade away."

Kasia chuckled and bounced the babe gently. "You know well our husband will not take his anger out on you."

"I know even better he will not take it out on *you*." Diona stretched out her arms. "Please? Will you go instead?"

With a sigh, Kasia relinquished her friend's son. "I thought you wanted a quiet night."

"Which I will obviously not get with our husband. This wee one has come by his screaming naturally."

She bit her lip to hold back a grin. "You know I never mind spending time with Xerxes, but he *did* call *you*."

Diona rolled her eyes, green as the hills of Phrygia. "Only because he thought you still unwell. Go, please. I shall be in your debt."

"Nonsense." When her maids stood, she motioned them back down. "Stay and rest. Theron will see me safely there."

"Oh, thank you." Diona walked out into the twilight with her, where slaves waited to see her back to the tent she shared with Lalasa and the three children they had between them.

Kasia raised her hand in farewell and took her place beside Theron. Xerxes' tent resided at the head of the procession that stretched for miles. Diona was right—his shouting was audible from a good distance, and his choice of words made Kasia shake her head. A few engineers scurried out as she drew near—the unlucky recipients of her husband's wrath. She entered as he tossed a frayed rope to the ground.

The other concubines always thought her mad for grinning at such a display. "Has the rope dared to offend the king of kings? Shall I stomp on it for you, for good measure?"

Xerxes spun around, and the light of anger in his eyes shifted to one of amusement. "Would you? The touch of your lovely foot may convince it to hold fast when it would like to break."

"Perhaps it would. It does seem the ground gets greener, the more I tread on it, undoubtedly due to the power of my lovely feet."

He laughed and gathered her into his arms. "Such phenomena has nothing to do with leaving the desert?"

"Nothing at all."

After one long kiss, he pulled away with narrowed eyes. "I sent for Diona."

"And scared her off with your bellowing." She poked a finger into his chest. "You will have all the world talking of your temper."

"I would not lose it so much if people were competent once in a while." He sighed, and the tension left his shoulders. "You are feeling better? You looked quite ill this morning."

"It passed."

"Excellent."

She drew in a deep breath. "Though I imagine it will return on the morrow."

For a moment he only stared at her. Then the fear-saturated sorrow overtook his countenance. "Not again."

"It will be all right." She rested her forearms against his torso and patted his chest. "I am already farther along than the other times. This one will hold."

Xerxes shook his head, his nostrils flaring. "You cannot know how it kills me to watch you go through this time and again, Kasia. The hope, the joy. The pain. I ought to be flayed for my part in it all—were I a stronger man, I would never touch you again."

He had threatened as much after the third miscarriage. "Shall I leave?"

When she feigned pulling away, he growled and held her captive. Just as she had known he would. "The damage is already done."

She smacked his arm. "A baby is not *damage*, Xerxes!"

"But the loss of one is."

Irritation tickled her chest, but it faded when she looked into his eyes. Each pain had struck him as acutely as it had her, if for different reasons. He could not understand the loss of hope—he was not a woman, and he had so many children already. But he grieved with her. He soothed each tear, held her through each dark night.

She brushed her hand over his cheek. "Why mourn for a child who is healthy and whole in my womb? Whatever the reason I could not carry beyond a few weeks before, this is different. It *is*."

"Let us pray so. I confess part of me hoped you would never conceive again. I know you long for a child of your own, but more than another son, I need *you*. And I fear that one of these miscarriages will take you along with our babe."

"At the risk of sounding treasonous, my love, I do not want a baby because you need ever-more sons. You can hardly keep count of the ones you have already. But *I* need a child."

He dropped his arms and spun away. It may have irritated her except that he turned back with a shawl and draped it over her arms. She had not even noticed her goosebumps.

Xerxes sent her a tight-lipped stare that always made others run for cover. "Why, then? Because of that ridiculous warning I issued your first week with me? That your future will be insecure without them? I promise you, Kasia, you will be taken care of. I will give you a city—ten cities to guarantee it."

"You are always so generous with your cities." She pulled the fabric up over her shoulders and breathed in the faint scent of myrrh. "It is not that. I need a little one to love."

Though he grumbled, he put his arm around her and led her to the lavish lounge area his servants set up each night. "Perhaps it will help that we will not be traveling much longer. You can grow large in Sardis while we wait out the winter."

"See? All will be well." She grinned and settled into her usual spot against a large pillow.

Xerxes sat beside her and nodded at his servants. They rolled up a corner of the tent and secured it.

Hills undulated into distant mountains, creating a vista strange and beautiful. As they marched, the golds and bronzes and coppers she knew gave way to waving amber grasses, trees large and green without the help of irrigation canals, and those mountains looming emerald before them. Beautiful . . . but still she missed Susa.

Xerxes tucked her to his side and rested his head against hers. Neither spoke. Not now, while they waited for the crimson streaks of sun to fade from the sky, for the rich shadows to drape over the mountains. They cuddled close and watched the heavens for the first prick of diamond light.

"There," he whispered in her ear, indicating a place she had looked at a minute earlier and found empty. Now a single point of brilliance shone.

Her lips pulled up. *Be with Esther, Lord Jehovah. Wherever she is, whatever she does, bless her. May she shine like the star after which she is called.*

As if he knew exactly when her silent prayer had ended, Xerxes motioned for the tent to be lowered into place, tilted back her head, and kissed her until the servants left them alone.

Xerxes could not withhold a smile when he looked down the hill behind him. His army stretched along the road as far as the eye could see. Had a greater force ever been assembled in all of mankind? If so, he had never heard of it. Surely there were more than a million soldiers—it took them over a week to march past any given point.

Celaenae was within sight, and a small group moved toward them on the road. When Masistes and Haman reined in beside him, he arched a brow. "Who is that, do you know?"

Masistes nodded. "That is why we searched you out. It is Pythius, the richest man in Lydia. I have been told his wealth is second in the world only to yours."

"Interesting." Why had he heard no mention of the man until now? "What does he want?"

Haman inclined his head. "To offer hospitality to you and your army."

Xerxes grinned. "Well then. Let us meet him. Wait—I will fetch Kasia first, so that she might rest in comfort the sooner."

"She looks unwell again today."

And when had Masistes seen her? Xerxes' fingers tightened on the reins. "She is with child."

"Again?" Masistes shook his head. "You test the god, brother. So many miscarriages cannot be good for a woman's body. If you want to preserve her life, you may have to be content with others to warm your bed."

A knot of fear cinched tight in his stomach. Did his brother think he had not considered that? His resolve hardened after each bout of pain and tears . . . but when she was in his arms, he forgot everything but the love surging through him. No one could ignite his passion like Kasia. When he could not touch her, it felt as though the sun had been snuffed out.

"She assures me that she is already farther along than she has made it before."

His brother looked unconvinced. "I just took Parsisa and Artaynte to her wagon. They have both spoken to me of their concern for her."

That at least explained how Masistes knew of her appearance today. "They cannot be more concerned than I. Ask them to pray."

"They have been, I am sure."

Together they turned toward the first wagon nestled within the safety of the Persian ranks. His, though everyone had come to think of it as hers. Which suited him nicely.

Ferocious barking issued from within. Xerxes grinned when both friend and brother held back with matching scowls.

Masistes shook his head. "You should have kept her from making a pet of that beast, my lord. It was a guard dog."

"And still is. Now he guards Kasia instead of the palace. Down, Zad."

A grey nose poked out of the wagon, and the dog acknowledged him with a happy loll of his tongue. Xerxes urged his horse alongside so he could scratch Zad behind the ears and look into the opening. Kasia offered a tight smile, but her face lacked color and her hand pressed against her stomach.

The knot rose to his throat, but he forced it back down. He refused to fear the child growing inside her would steal her from him before it drew its first breath. "Good news, my love. It seems there is a man headed our way to offer us his hospitality."

A measure of relief settled onto her countenance. "Wonderful. We are almost to Celaenae?"

"It will be visible when you crest the hill." He turned to address the driver. "Pull out of rank and come ahead with us. We will all meet this Pythius together."

"Yes, master."

After another smile aimed at Kasia, he urged his horse ahead of the wagon so that they might cut a swath through the surrounding army. A moment later he stood at the top of the hill yet again, where his personal entourage joined him. They would make an impressive picture as they moved down the hill—his commanders flanked him, his advisors and slaves formed rows behind, the wagon followed. Then the vast sea of soldiers, armed and ready to teach Greece what happened to those who opposed Persia.

When Xerxes lifted his hand, they started forward at a sedate, regal pace. The breeze picked up, and his standard snapped taut, then fluttered.

One man parted from the rest as they drew near. He looked the same age Xerxes' father would have been, with a mane of glistening silver hair and the broad shoulders of a warrior.

"This is Pythius?" He put his question to one of the advisers behind him.

"Yes, master. He is the one who sent your father Darius the gold plane-tree and vine."

He nodded and moved a step ahead of his companions. Pythius reined his horse to a halt and jumped down. By the time Xerxes reached him, he knelt with head bowed.

Xerxes' horse pranced. "Pythius of Lydia?"

"Your humble servant, my king."

His humble servant had a voice as deep and rich as the gold collar draping his neck. A man of means, indeed. "Rise. I hear you were a friend of my father's."

Pythius stood and looked up at him. "It was my great honor to know him, and it is with gratitude to the gods that I now welcome you. If it pleases you, my lord, I have a feast ready for you and your companions, and provisions for the whole of your army as they arrive."

"I accept with delight. Would you ride beside me into the city?"

"My servants shall lead the way." Pythius swung onto his horse and turned it around. "I have been awaiting your army with eagerness, as have my brothers and sons. I hope you have room in your numbers for those we would add to it."

The chuckle eased some of the tension in his chest. "There is always room for more, my friend."

A wide smile creased Pythius's face. "I have heard that some of you have wives and children with you. My wife wishes me to assure you that she has made preparations for them as well, both at Celaenae and Sardis."

"Excellent. We have been away from our homes for nearly eighteen months already, surveying and gathering the troops. I know they will all be grateful for the chance to rest in luxury once again."

"Of course." Pythius's dark eyes glinted with curiosity and excitement. "We have heard of your progress with the bridge, my lord—it is astounding. And the tales of the canal! I can barely fathom the amount of thought and preparation you, in your wisdom, have put into this expedition."

Xerxes nodded and breathed in deeply of the sweet air. "I have many wise advisers who have helped me ensure this conquest will be remembered for all time."

"I am proud to be one of the first to offer you assistance. Were I a few years younger, I would ask for a command." Pythius squared his shoulders, raised his chin, and met Xerxes' gaze. "Since I have not youth, I will offer what I *do* have. All that I possess, my king, I wish to give to you to fund this great war."

Xerxes knew his surprise must show on his face. "All that you possess? But my friend, it is my understanding you have much—and those who do are usually loath to part with it."

"It is true I am wealthy. But what is the purpose of riches, if one does not put them toward a good cause?" He shook his head. "I wish to finance the war. My slaves and farms make enough for me to live on, so all else I give to you. My treasury has four thousand silver talents and is only seven thousand gold Daric staters shy of four million. It is all yours."

Astounding. Given the size of his army and all that would be necessary to support them, Xerxes was prepared to demand what he may and take what he must as they traveled. But to have someone offer so much, freely? An auspicious start to his campaign.

"I have never met anyone so generous." He halted his horse and, when Pythius did the same, reached out to clasp his wrist. "Your hospitality I accept. And to show my gratitude, you may not only keep what you have in your treasury, I will give you the seven thousand staters you need to round it out to the full four million."

Pythius swallowed, and his nostrils flared. "You do me unspeakable honor, my king. I will serve you faithfully all the days of my life."

"And I will remember your generosity all the days of mine. See that you never change, Pythius, and I will hold you up as a shining example for the rest of mankind to imitate."

They started forward again, and Xerxes let his smile bloom full. The god intended greatness for them, and Xerxes intended to seize it. Whatever it took.

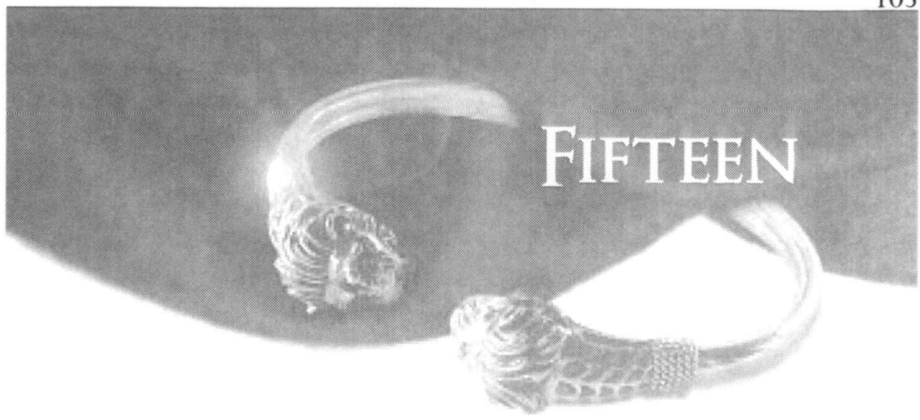

Fifteen

Susa, Persia

Zechariah eyed the gold of dawn and held up a hand. He had been here since morning was only a promise on the horizon, but soon all of Susa would rise. "Enough for this morning. I need to get home."

His three friends all released tired breaths and stretched.

Adam groaned. "You are more a slavedriver than Pharaoh of old. You fight as though the Greeks might visit our doors for revenge."

Zechariah smiled and strode to the river. The other three plodded along behind him, mumbling and groaning. Zechariah rolled his eyes. He worked them barely half as hard as Bijan had done him, before he left with the rest of the army eighteen months ago. They had no cause for complaint.

Though the other two said their farewells and started home, Adam dropped to his knees at the riverbank and plunged his head under the water. He brought it up again with a happy sigh. "Better. But if you see me not tomorrow, Zech, assume I have died in the meantime and leave me in peace."

Zechariah breathed a laugh and shoved his friend's shoulder. "You are the one who asked to learn, Adam."

"Because I feel myself growing fat as my father, doing nothing but sitting around the house all day pouring wax onto wooden tablets. I would rather be out chopping the wood. Collecting the wax. *Moving*."

"Yet when I make you move, you accuse me of killing you." He reached into the water and tossed a handful at his friend.

Adam splashed him back, but he grinned. "Because I have been growing fat as my father up until now. I am improving though, right? I had to tighten my belt the other day."

Zechariah poured cool water over his head and sloughed off the sweat. "If you were more concerned with how you handle your spear than how you look in your tunic, you would improve more quickly."

Adam grunted and wiped the drops from his face. "We are twenty now, Zech. Our fathers' businesses have grown since Persia went to war. Has it not occurred to you that we can afford to take wives soon? I would prefer my future bride not be disgusted when first we meet."

"I have not given much thought to a wife, no. I am—"

"Shh." Adam put a hand over Zechariah's face, though he covered his nose more than his mouth. Perhaps because his gaze was locked on something in the opposite direction. "Speaking of my future bride . . . if I believed in pagan gods, I would swear Cupid just struck me. Look. Have you ever seen such a beautiful woman?"

His friend fell in love at least once a week, but Zechariah would be the first to admit he had a good eye for female forms. He peered around him. And snorted. "Her? She is a child."

"Are you blind? She must be at least fourteen. Are not both the twins betrothed? They cannot be any older."

Zechariah looked down the river again, to where Esther stooped with a large clay jug. "You are right about that much. She is the same age as the twins."

"You know her?" Adam turned to her with large, round eyes. "Would you—"

"No, I am not going to introduce you."

"You need not scowl at me like that, Zech, my intentions are honorable."

"Your intentions are also as shifting as the wind." That, however, was not what made him scowl. How was it that Adam did not know who Esther was? He would know Mordecai, certainly—every Jew in Susa knew Mordecai. But Esther . . . had she closed herself off again, while he was busy with this latest project for the king?

Zechariah bit back a curse and splashed more water over himself. "Go home, Adam—and you had better be here an hour before dawn tomorrow, or I shall come drag you from your grave."

Adam stood up and sucked in what remained of his stomach. "Absolutely." His voice came out in a wheeze. "Tomorrow. See you then."

Zechariah watched him swagger off—veering to the right far more than necessary, though Esther did not look up from her task. He rolled his eyes and stood, then strode her way.

She glanced up with a start, though the caution in her expression gave way to welcome when she saw him. "I ought to have known it was you and your would-be soldiers out so early. Have you trained a new class of Immortals yet?"

He folded his arms over his chest. "What have you been doing, Esther?"

Her blink told him his tone had been too harsh, too accusing. "I am only getting water. Martha's back has been bothering her, so I offered to take on this task."

He scrubbed a hand over his face. "Not *now*. In general."

She still looked baffled. "Nothing out of the ordinary. Weaving, mending. Helping your sisters prepare for their weddings."

As any young woman should be doing . . . yet most young women had friends beyond the four girls that lived three doors down and emerged from their houses other than to fetch water for their servants. "Have you gone to the markets lately? Or across the city with my sisters and mother when they visit our cousins? Have you perhaps taken Mordecai his meals while he hears complaints at the palace gates?"

Enlightenment made her eyes dim. She turned back to her jug and dipped it in the river. "I am not overfond of crowds, you know that."

He took the heavy vessel from her while she stood. "You used to run off to the river at all hours. You went with Martha into the markets every chance you got."

Esther pushed to her feet and grabbed at the jug. "That was not me."

He held tight to the pottery. "If you insist upon reverting to this reclusiveness every time I get involved in a large project, I shall be forced to tell the king to find another to do his woodworking."

Disbelief sparkled in her eyes and emerged as a hint of a smile on her lips. "I think not."

"Esther." He released the vessel to her. If he tried to carry it, he would probably slosh out half its contents during the trip. She could balance it perfectly on her head without losing a single precious drop. "You worry me."

"Why? Because I prefer the quiet of my cousin's house to the bustle of the streets? Because I am content with the friends I have among your family?" She shook her head and set her water down. "That is ridiculous."

"Is it? My friend who just left had no idea who you were, though he lives on our street."

"And should I know all the unmarried young men in our neighborhood?"

He threw his hands into the air and faced away from the river. "Fine. But do not whine to me when your cousin eventually betroths you to a complete stranger. He will have no choice."

"He will not betroth me to a stranger." She lifted the jug to her head and started on the path toward home.

Zechariah sighed and fell in beside her. "I want the best for you, Esther. You are a sister to me."

"I am not your sister."

The quiet confidence in her tone made his jaw clench. They did not speak of her feelings for him. Never had they, and never did he wish to. Best to stick to the subject at hand. "Do you remember when you first came to Mordecai's house?"

When she drew in a breath, it sounded resigned. "Of course I do."

"You were such a sorrowful little thing. Any mention of your parents sent you into silence and solitude, even years later. Kasia once told me she lured you into adventure so you would not think of sad things so much. And it worked. Before she left us, you had become bright and vibrant, just like her. Do you remember that? The way you would laugh together, finish each other's sentences?"

"She understood me." She halted and looked up at him. Her eyes had always struck him as old beyond her years. Lately they had become ageless. Why had Jehovah forced her through so much? "But that was *her* vibrancy you saw, Zechariah, not mine. Kasia was the flame—I was but a mirror that reflected it."

"You are wrong." Had she truly been his sister, he would have pulled her close and squeezed the grief out of her. But she was right—she was not his sister. If he did that, she would take from it something he did not intend. "When you came to Mordecai, he changed your name to Esther because you brought the light back into his life."

Again her lips curled into that perfect, reserved smile. "A star, yes. One point of light, so dim in the heavens. What is a star next to the silver light of the moon?"

"A perfect complement. And when the moon hides her face, the star shines all the brighter."

Her eyes shimmered with tears. "You are a poet as well as an artist, Zechariah. Yet you would rather paint a battlefield with the blood of your enemies. Surely you can understand how I struggle with what is expected of me as well."

His heart beat a sympathetic cadence against his ribs. "All that is expected is that you be who we know you are inside."

"No. You expect me to be Kasia. But I cannot, much as I wish it otherwise. I cannot be that bright. I cannot be your sister."

How had he ended up in this quagmire? No matter what he argued, she would either feel the burden of unreasonable expectations or take from it a hopeless hope. He sighed. "No one thinks you must be Kasia—we only want you to be the Esther you were with her."

She looked at him for a long moment and then turned and walked away. Even then, he swore he felt the penetration of her gaze. Those eyes of hers said much. She might as well have demanded, "If you want me to be a mirror again, why do you refuse to provide the flame?"

He could not. So he turned back to the river and thrust his head under. Water gushed cool over him, providing a welcome crush of meaningless noise. When he emerged and slicked his hair away from his face, he could almost pretend the conversation with Esther had never happened.

His parents had long ago discovered his morning sport but had agreed to let him continue, so long as he was home in time to start the day. He entered the house to the smells of newly baked bread. Abba already sat with a wooden bowl of food before him, and he looked up with a smile. "There you are. Did you want to make the deliveries today, or should I send Joshua? We must clear some of the finished pieces out so we have room to begin that bed your friend's sister commissioned. Though why she insists it be fashioned from a single piece of wood . . . ."

"Apparently she is a fan of Homer's *Odyssey* and always wanted a bed like Penelope and Odysseus had." Zechariah grabbed a hunk of bread. "I will do the deliveries. Joshua is still working on that set of griffins, and you know how he gets if we distract him."

Abba chuckled. "True. I shall help you load everything up as soon as you eat."

The promise of a trip through Susa was enough to make him hurry through his meal. Zechariah and Abba filled their cart with finished pieces and hitched it to the donkey.

He smiled as he headed for the home of the absent Bijan. The reason came to the door with her usual coy grin. "Good morning, Zechariah. Have you heard about my betrothal?"

Zechariah jumped from the cart with a snort of a laugh. "Certainly—when your bridegroom came to our shop with your order for a monstrosity of a bed. What are you trying to do, Ruana, kill me?"

Mischief carved dimples into her cheeks as she stepped into the street. "Only with jealousy."

He chuckled. "I cannot believe you found a man willing to indulge your spending habit. Does he realize you will empty his treasury within the year?"

"I have little fear of that. He has been well compensated for his service in Egypt." She peered over the side of the cart, one hand twirling a lock of hair. "Lovely, Zech. Shall I show you where I want them?"

"Mmm." He hefted the first of the decorative screens and followed her inside. As usual, her mother was nowhere in sight.

She led him inside their massive house and toward the back, where her personal chamber took up the corner. As she walked, her hips swayed—exaggerated, he suspected, for his benefit. "We have heard from Bijan," she said over her shoulder. "They have reached Celaenae and will soon be heading to Sardis to await spring and the completion of the bridge and canal. He is anxious for action."

"I imagine so. All this time in preparation, and the war itself will probably last only a year. Greece cannot put up much of a fight." He entered her room, where his craftsmanship showed in nearly all her furniture. When her brother and father left, she had taken it upon herself to keep up the constant stream of new pieces. "The corner?"

"Yes." She made a humming sound when he set it down. "You are a handsome one, Zechariah. If you were not a Jew, perhaps I would be betrothed to *you*."

Zechariah laughed and turned to face her. Her beauty lay in generous curves, a well-proportioned face, and lustrous hair. Her allure lay in the easy flirtation without expectation. "Jehovah's wisdom prevails then, for my purse could never support you."

"You do have a point." Her perfect teeth gleamed as she grinned. "Just the one other piece, right?"

He nodded, and they headed back out together. "When is the wedding?"

"As soon as you get that bed finished." She wiggled her brows. "Will you procrastinate to spare yourself the thought of me in it with another man?"

"More like rush to finish so that I can resign myself the faster to the inevitable." He slapped a hand to his chest. "Though surely my heart shall break in two."

Her laugh rang out. "Get the other screen, you cruel man. I can at least enjoy the flex of your arms, even if your sarcasm crushes me."

He pulled it out of the cart and strode inside again. She followed, silent as he entered her chamber and positioned the screen beside its match. He turned back around. "Do you need anything else before I leave?"

"Just one thing." Her arms fell to her sides as she walked toward him, then lifted and settled on his chest.

His breath hitched. What if she felt the quickened beat of his heart under her hands?

Her eyes were dark with intensity. "I may not see you again before my wedding. So this is my last chance."

Her intent was clear, even before she lifted her mouth and shuttered her eyes. Zechariah closed his arms around her waist. The linen of her chiton was fine and soft, but it was the curve of her back that sent messages of awareness from hand to mind. He touched his lips to hers.

The kiss deepened, though he could not have said who shifted, who invited. When he pulled away, it was with a sigh. "You are a dangerous woman, Ruana."

"And here I thought you above flattery." After running her hands over his chest, she stepped away. "I imagine you need to get back. You have a bed to carve."

"That I do." He left. And knew that now he would indeed be tormented every time he set to work.

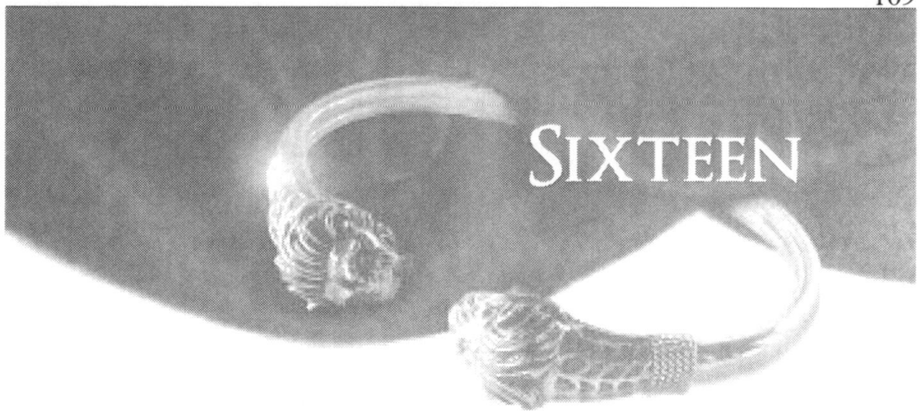

Sixteen

Celaenae, Phrygia

"I swear he is trying to torture me."

Kasia pressed her lips together against a smile. Not that Artaynte would have noticed it—the girl's gaze was locked on the other side of the garden, where Darius stood in the shadows with a local wench. Kasia looped her arm through her friend's. "I have no doubt of it. He always checks to make sure you are watching before going off with one of his . . . women."

A woebegone sigh eased from Artaynte's full lips. "Mother maintains he is trying to win my love. But the longer this goes on, the more I wonder if he is repaying me for all the harsh words I give him."

"I cannot say. I know him very little." All she knew was that the prince frequently studied his cousin when he thought no one noticed, and that Artaynte was miserable in her obedience to Parsisa. "I realize you must honor your mother, but why not talk to him of your feelings? It is silly to toy with each other like this."

Artyante sighed again and brushed her heavy, dark locks away from her shoulders. "She maintains that if one wants to hold the interest of a prince, one must make him think that interest hard-won."

Kasia looked again at the corner where Darius stood, nipping at the neck of the giggling girl. "When I met you, Artaynte, I thought you despised him. Begin to soften, otherwise he may grow so disheartened he will never speak for you."

"You may be right." A frown puckered Artaynte's forehead. She was a sweet girl, always eager to please. Too much so. "I will speak to Mother. Surely it is time to offer him some encouragement. I realize her wisdom in making certain he knew I did not seek an alliance based only on his heirdom, but he will never know I love him if I keep showing him such disdain."

Tempted to toss her hands to the heavens and shout "Thank you!" for that much of a breakthrough, Kasia contented herself with a smile. "I am sure your mother will agree."

Yet Artaynte's forehead did not smooth out. "What if she is right, though, and *his* interest is not deeply rooted enough to last? I do not want to be queen at the price of my heart. Look how that turned out for his mother. Better to trust the advice of mine—Father still loves her, so she must have done things right. She knows how to handle a prince."

Kasia pressed her lips together to keep from arguing the point of Masistes and Parsisa. Perhaps they *did* love each other. "Certainly she does. But Darius is not your father, nor are you your mother. Your love cannot be exactly like theirs."

"Why must matters of the heart be so complicated?" Artaynte pulled her gaze from Darius and turned to Kasia. "How do you keep the king's love, Kasia?"

She chuckled and scanned the garden in the hopes that he would be out. Her heart raced at the mere thought of catching sight of him, then slowed to normal when she did not. "I have no secret to share—I simply love him, and base all else on that. The opposite of your mother's advice."

"Hmm. It certainly works with your husband. How am I to know what would work best with his son?"

She could only shrug. "Shall I ask the king's opinion? He knows his son better than I do."

"No!" Horror made her friend's amber eyes go round and her cheeks flush scarlet. "Swear you will not!"

Kasia laughed and patted Artaynte's arm in reassurance. "I will do nothing to embarrass you, I promise." Her mirth died down when a familiar tug pulled taut inside, and another young man floated to the surface of her mind. "I have a brother the prince's age—Zechariah. He has been on my mind much these past few weeks."

As had Esther. She would be a woman now, of age to be married. Had they fallen in love, or had childhood affection vanished in the mists of time? For all she knew, they could have married other people, people she had never met. And what of the twins, of Joshua?

"When we return to Susa, you should ask the king to let you visit your family. I am certain he would approve."

Longing welled up, only to be eclipsed by reality. "He would. My father, on the other hand . . . ."

"Surely he will want to meet his grandchild."

Kasia smiled, appreciating that her friend spoke with certainty about the babe in her womb. Xerxes had refused to discuss it more this past week, as if doing so might prove a curse. But there was nothing wrong with this child. She could feel the difference. "Perhaps. And even if Abba will not allow the younger children to see me, he and Ima and Zechariah could come to the palace. I would love to feel my mother's arms around me again."

Artaynte's gaze tracked back to the prince. "What if he falls in love with one of these girls he charms so easily?"

She led her friend on a curve in the path, one that would take them out of view of the prince. "You have nothing to fear. He will not wed any of those girls."

"Not yet, since his first wife must be noble. But one could win his heart. What good will it do me to be his consort and queen if he has wasted himself on one of low birth?"

If Artaynte did not look so worried and oblivious, Kasia might have been offended. She smiled instead. "Yes, one must look out for those low-born wenches. Trouble-makers, every one."

Her friend flushed again. "Oh, Kasia, I did not mean—that is, *you* are not—the king is certainly not wasting himself . . . ."

Kasia laughed and bumped her shoulder into Artaynte's. "Rest easy, my friend, I know you meant no insult. But if I might make an observation, I think the fact that Darius avoids any young women of nobility speaks to his desire to wait for a particular one. And you are the one he watches."

Artaynte came to an abrupt halt and looked around. Mountains loomed ahead of them in breathtaking splendor, the Meander River winding close on their right. "We had better go back—Mother will be furious if I am late for the meal, and you know she hates us to go off alone."

Kasia sighed. They had no fewer than ten slaves trailing them, and they were still within the park adjoining the palace built by Cyrus. Getting back in time for the feast would be no great problem. But she had long ago discovered that Artaynte was no Esther—one could not lure her into adventure by dangling it before her nose long enough.

Which was a shame. The river gurgled by, all but begging for feet to be dipped in it. Far safer than the adventure bellowing from the jagged edge of the mountain ahead.

Male voices colored the air from nearby, and Artaynte's face melted into panic. "Someone comes. Let us hurry back before Mother—"

"You go ahead." Kasia smiled and released her arm. "It is my husband."

Rather than calming her, that pronouncement sent Artaynte flying away like a terrified bird. Kasia shook her head, exchanged a smile with Desma and Theron, and turned back to the path. From behind a hedge Xerxes and Pythius emerged, laughing.

Her chest squeezed tight. Of the millions of men surrounding them every hour of the day, none matched her husband. The noble bearing and strong, fine features, the authority draping his shoulders like a cloak . . . the good humor in his eyes. How did a love as great as this not consume her whole?

He looked her way, and his smile bloomed anew. He held out a beckoning hand. "Kasia, my love. I ought to have known you would be out—there is a river, after all, and undoubtedly some trouble to be found in it."

With a laugh, she rushed to Xerxes' side. "The Meander is far too calm here to lead me into trouble. Though it is alluring nonetheless."

Her husband slid an arm around her and dropped a kiss onto her head. "Hmm. Pythius, if I did not keep this woman surrounded by a crowd of diligent servants, she would be off climbing Mount Tmolus before I could stop her."

Pythius gave her a fatherly grin. "The more I know of you, lady, the more you remind me of my daughter."

She had already learned said daughter had died of fever a decade earlier. "The highest of compliments. And my husband, you must admit the mountain begs for an explorer's foot."

Xerxes ran a hand up her arm and gazed into her eyes. "Not yours, sweet one, given your condition."

Warmth bloomed inside. "Perhaps on our way home again, then. *You* can watch the babe for a day, and I shall go exploring."

Pythius laughed. "Where did you find this creature, my lord?"

Xerxes grinned. "In the river at Susa, crying in delight at the icy waters."

"Perhaps she is a nymph, then." Pythius nodded toward the Meander. "Our waters may not be icy today, nor sweet as the legendary Choaspes, but you should enjoy dipping your feet within, my dear. I shall go make sure tonight's feast is ready."

Pythius bowed and took his leave. Kasia turned to face Xerxes, grabbing his hands and tugging him toward the river. "What have you been doing today, O mighty king?"

He followed with a grin. "I just came from Otanes—we were discussing the likelihood of the city-states responding if we send out a demand for land and water again."

She still found it a bit odd that Amestris's father commanded the entire army and got on so well with Xerxes, but apparently Otanes was well aware of his daughter's difficulty—and grateful her life had been spared. Kasia nodded. "And you were headed to . . . ?"

"To Mardonius and Masistes, to get their opinions on the same."

"Ah." She laced their fingers together and glanced over her shoulder. The river's edge lay a leap away. "Have you time to bathe your feet with me?"

"No." He tugged her close and teased her mouth with his. "But I shall give it to you anyway."

She released his hands so that she could link her arms around his neck. "That is the type of spoiling I like."

"Shall I spoil you even more?" His lips traveled her jaw and nipped at her ear. "We could skip the feast."

"Not a chance, my love. I could not keep down breakfast or handle much lunch. I am famished."

He pulled away enough that she could see his peaceful smile. "Well, we certainly must not starve the little prince or princess you carry."

She arched a brow at him as he bent down to untie her shoes. "You speak of it."

Sighing, Xerxes unknotted the leather around her ankle and eased it from her foot. "Pythius assuaged some of my concerns. It seems his wife went through what you have in the beginning as well—but then she carried six healthy children and had easy, uneventful deliveries. He assured me I have every reason to believe this time will indeed be different."

Kasia planted her hands on her hips and sent him an exaggerated glare. "And you believe him, but you would not believe me?"

He gave her the crooked grin she could not resist and tickled the arch of her foot. "I trust experience before blind faith, yes. But when they agree, we can all be happy."

Another time, she may have jumped into the debate about experience and faith. But he tossed her other shoe aside and snatched her up with a playful roar, so she put it aside and squealed in laughter. It seemed the wise choice—even if that stretch of her soul said she would have to find a few minutes for quiet prayer before the feast tonight.

Haman nudged his friend on, deliberately keeping his gaze from the river where the king and his Jewess splashed like children. Masistes, on the other hand, halted again after a single step to study his brother. "I cannot fathom it, Haman. He has never been so dedicated to a single woman so long."

Haman sighed. "Must we have this conversation again?"

"He is more worried for her than the war. I suppose we must admit at this point that he genuinely loves her."

Haman snorted and frowned at Masistes. "Will that finally convince you to stop offering her your company? You will cause a civil war with your nonsense."

"Nonsense. She may have been upset by my ill-advised proposal in Susa, but she realizes my later whispers are no more than a jest."

Haman folded his arms across his chest. "Unless she were to accept, then you would undoubtedly forget you were joking. Sometimes I thank the god that I was not born in the palace. The lot of you have no more loyalty—"

"And you have no capacity for amusement. I know not why I tolerate you, Haman."

Haman smiled and jerked his head toward the path. "Because *someone* has to keep you in line. You are a fool, and we all know it. Parsisa is arguably the second most beautiful woman in Persia, but you are still set on seducing your brother's wives."

Masistes waved an unconcerned hand but fell in beside him. "Parsisa knows she has my eternal affection and admiration. She does not mind if I seek harmless entertainment elsewhere."

Haman glared at the two in the river. "That one is not harmless."

"A point I must grant, much as it pains me." Masistes released an exaggerated sigh. "Still, one must wonder what it is about her that has enthralled my brother . . . and long to figure it out for oneself."

"No, one must *not*." Haman shook his head and then looked beyond his friend. "There goes your daughter—were you not looking for her earlier?"

"Ah, yes. Do you mind?"

"Go." He waved Masistes off, then pressed his lips in a tight line. Given Artaynte's course, she had undoubtedly been with the Jewess.

A shadow seemed to pass before the sun. When he had encouraged Xerxes to take a concubine from among the Jews, he had not expected that she would do anything but irritate him after his initial lust was sated. Had he anticipated *this*, he would have urged the king to forget her.

How was he to know the wretch would earn the king's confidence, his heart? And not only the king's at this point—she had won the affection of Masistes' wife and daughter, of the other concubines. Darius still seemed beyond her reach, thank the god, but many of the other high officials greeted her with fondness whenever they saw her—usually on the arm of the king.

It did not bode well. Xerxes had already sent untold business to the Jewess's arrogant swine of a father—what else would she seduce him into doing for her people?

Amestris had been right to fear the wench's poisonous influence.

Haman headed for his quarters, sent his servants away, and pulled out a correspondence tablet. He opened the hinged wood and carefully peeled off the wax. A sharpened metal tool rested among his similar wooden ones, which he extracted for this task. It took twice as long to carve a message into the wood as it would into the wax, but Amestris must be apprised of this. She would send back a message similarly disguised, advising him on what she would have him do.

Once finished, he sealed the wax back onto the tablet and, with a wooden stylus, pressed a missive to his steward into it. Then he clapped the wooden form together, secured it, and called a servant to get it on its way. Given the series of outposts the Persian kings had set up for their official riders, it would be in Susa within two days.

Within the week, he would know what to do about this threat.

Seventeen

Susa, Persia

Esther breathed in the silent air with relief. Much as she enjoyed her visits with Kish and Zillah's brood, coming home brought blessed peace. Martha would be outside in the kitchen, and Jonah probably sat hunched over the accounts. Neither were much given to conversation; perhaps that was why Esther had grown so accustomed to uneventful, solitary days.

She paused when she spotted movement within Mordecai's chamber. He was on his prayer rug again, just returning to a sitting position. How long had he been there this time?

Knocking on the post by his door, she stuck in her head. "Do you need anything, cousin? A drink, some bread?"

Mordecai shook his head and stood. "Thank you, Esther, but no. I have not been here but an hour."

She could only nod. An hour in prayer seemed to her such a long time. Her cousin, though, sometimes spent a whole day on the floor beside his bed, moaning and muttering. He had been diligent about his prayers as long as she had known him, but these extended sessions did not begin until Kasia—

"Is there something I should pray for?" she asked to interrupt her own thoughts.

His smile was small but warm. "Perhaps. Zechariah weighed on my spirit today."

"Zechariah?" Her hand fell away from the post as she took a step back. "What about him?"

Mordecai chuckled and came her way. "The Lord gave me no specifics. Did you see him today?"

"Only a glimpse." She spun toward her room so she could deposit her basket of sewing supplies. "He has been hard at work on a bed this past week."

"For the palace?"

"Not this one. The sister of his Persian friend is also betrothed, and her bridegroom commissioned it."

Mordecai studied her. "It seems everyone is marrying this winter. Which reminds me that, though I would deny it, you are a child no longer. We should discuss your future soon, little one."

Her throat went dry. "Are you in a hurry for me to leave your house, cousin?"

He chuckled, as she had known he would. "I dread the thought."

"Then I would wait to marry." She strode to the table and poured herself a gulp of sweet watered wine to soothe her throat.

Mordecai's gaze did not relent. "Do you still favor Zechariah?"

Her fingers tightened around the cup. She nodded.

His lips curved up. "Perhaps that is why he was on my mind. If he is the husband you desire, I can speak with him and Kish to arrange it."

Her eyes slid shut. Would Zechariah refuse if their fathers both agreed to it? Probably not. He would not shame her like that. Would he? But even if he accepted, it would be only out of duty. "I would first have *him* realize I am not a child."

"I see." His voice came from a step away now, and his finger touched her chin. She opened her eyes to gaze into his—precious and familiar and confident. "He will realize soon, Esther. No man could remain blind to the amazing woman you have become."

"Thank you, my father." She gave him a swift hug and a fleeting smile. "I hope you are right. And perhaps I shall go pray for him now as well."

"I will call you when the meal is ready."

She headed to the sanctuary of her chamber and settled with a long exhalation onto her bed. Her prayers were probably a far cry from Mordecai's, but it helped to empty her heart and mind before her creator.

Eyes closed, she called Zechariah's face to mind. "Jehovah . . . ." What to pray? She could thank the Lord for crafting him so well. Those beautiful features, strong and confident. The form that had become so muscled over the last few years.

Her blood thrummed each time she spotted him. Yet he continued to look at her as though she were yet another sister. And why? Did he not have enough of those?

She squeezed her eyes tight against the sudden tears. No, he did not have enough sisters. He lacked one—and perhaps it made sense that he would expect her to replace Kasia. But oh, how she had longed to dash her jar of water to the ground last week and demand he accept her as she was, that he *love* her as she was. What would he have done if she had thrown herself into his arms and kissed him?

Her cheeks burned at the thought, and she cleared her throat. This terrible attempt at a prayer might earn her a divine thunderbolt. "I am sorry, Jehovah. You know my thoughts are not usually so scattered . . . ."

She sighed and buried her face in her pillow.

Why could Mordecai not have asked her to pray for the army again? They never caused her nearly so much trouble as that one would-be soldier three doors down.

Sardis, Lydia

"I cannot believe you have your own Spartan."

Xerxes chuckled and clapped a hand to Pythius's shoulder as they strolled along the outer wall of the palace. "I can introduce you to him, if you like. His name is Demaratus."

Pythius's brows hiked up his forehead. "The former king? I had heard he was exiled, of course, after advising his people to align themselves with your father. I did not realize he had found a home in your court."

Xerxes rested his gaze on where the once-ruler exercised outside the palace walls. Even now, years after Demaratus had left home and family, the man insisted on keeping himself in the physical condition required of all Spartan men. He still wore his hair long, he refused any adornments. Every morning he found a patch of solitude and put himself through paces to keep muscles firm and reflexes ready. He provided an example Xerxes intended to follow—sitting on a throne most of one's day was no excuse to succumb to sloth.

"I owe him much," Xerxes murmured. "It was his argument that convinced my father to appoint me his successor instead of my older brother. There are those who question his trustworthiness, but I have spoken to him at length. He still loves his nation as an ideal—but not its current people."

Pythius nodded, then frowned at something behind Xerxes. "Runners, my lord."

Xerxes spun around, and his breath caught. The runners' faces were etched with dread, and they had collected his brothers and cousins, Amestris's father and brother. They might as well have come screaming, "We have bad news!"

He was in no mood for bad news. Not now, when all they had to do was wait for spring and march to victory. He felt his face turn to stone, muscle by muscle, and strode toward them. "What is it?"

The two runners dropped to their knees and bowed until foreheads touched marble. Though they then rose together, only one opened his mouth. "Forgive us, our king, for being the bearers of evil tidings."

His hand fisted. "You will not suffer for whatever news you bring. Tell me."

The messenger ducked his head. "It is the bridge over the Hellespont, my lord. It has collapsed."

"Collapsed?" His vision narrowed, all the ambient noises faded to nothingness. "Collapsed *how*?"

The runner clasped his hands together but still shook visibly. "The straits had just been bridged, all was in place when . . . when a violent storm—"

Xerxes cursed and spun away, thrusting fingers through his hair. He pivoted back. "How bad?"

"It has been completely destroyed." The man dropped to his knees again, shoulders rolled forward in supplication.

"No." Four years of planning could not be obliterated in a single storm. He tasted the fear emanating off the messengers and spun away to keep from breaking his word and tossing them off the wall and down the rocky embankment of the mountain. They were not the ones to blame.

But someone was, and fury with them settled like blood on his tongue. He marched to the palace, knowing the rest would follow. "Unacceptable!" Perhaps he bellowed—he did not care. If his wrath could match nature's, then perhaps all would obey him instead of her. "What fools designed a bridge that could not withstand the storms the Hellespont is famous for? I will have their heads!"

"Master, the engineers are to blame for this. They—"

"Quiet, Mardonius." He sliced a hand through the air, tempted to ram it into his cousin's stomach. "Given that you are the one who had this brilliant idea to march against Greece, I ought to hold *you* accountable for this failure."

Mardonius scuttled to the rear of the group.

Masistes cleared his throat. "We will rebuild, my lord—"

"Of course we will rebuild." As he strode into the cavernous hall, Xerxes grabbed a towering golden pillar and sent it clanging across the floor. The ashes of burnt incense blew through the room. "But I do not have another four years to dedicate to this! How long before the men drink the river dry and descend on the land like a pestilence? We must be out of here by spring, or both the army and the country will suffer famine and drought."

"Surely a plan can be devised that will allow for quick rebuilding."

Xerxes spun on Otanes. Usually the man had more brains than his fool of a daughter, but apparently not today. "Do you not think we would have chosen such a plan to begin with, were there one?" He grabbed up a bowl of fruit and sent it flying. It made a satisfying twang when the metal struck stone. "I will give them three months. Three. We cannot afford more."

A cacophony of arguments sprang up from the men, which only made his vision haze. "If you must squawk like a bunch of birds, do it where I cannot hear you!"

Growling, he turned his back on them and fumed his way to a window. He *would* have his bridge in three months. He needed to get through Greece and burn Athens to the ground so that he might be in Susa again next year. They could not get stuck in Europe through a winter.

One year. He had one year to teach the arrogant collection of city-states who ruled the world, and he would not be stopped by an overblown rainstorm and the incompetence of slaves.

A cool touch kissed the burning on the back of his neck, and all the fury inside bunched into a knot. Then small, familiar hands rested on his elbows, and the knot unraveled into a mess of limp strands.

Kasia rested her forehead on his back. "What has happened, my love?"

He had no choice but to be soothed by the sweep of her hands up and then down his arms. "My bridge is destroyed. A storm. It is that blasted Hellespont, Kasia, it is set against me."

"The river?" He could hear the smile in her voice. "Yes, surely the river hates you, the spiteful thing. It must be offended that you would dare to bridge it. You ought to give it a few lashes to teach it a lesson."

Why could his mouth not keep from twitching up when she was near? "Scribe! Take down a message for those at the Hellespont. Their king orders them to give the river three-hundred lashes with a whip in punishment for its impudence."

"Xerxes!" Her whisper was both outraged and amused as she jumped around to face him. "You cannot—everyone will think you mad!"

He grinned and took her hands. "It will be cathartic. Besides, most of these nations think the river a god—they will only assume me supremely arrogant, not mad."

Her eyes sparkled with the amusement he so loved. "You *are* supremely arrogant. You are rearranging the face of the earth for this war—bridging rivers, digging canals, cleaving mountains in two. Already you claim every person in the empire as your slave—will you subjugate creation too?"

He chuckled and turned his face toward the scribe busily taking down his order. "Add that a pair of manacles should be thrown into the waters."

His name came out on a laughing groan this time, and she fell against his chest. Xerxes ran a hand up her back and into her mass of midnight hair.

Behind him, a throat cleared. "What of the engineers, master?"

He saw no reason to look at Mardonius or invite him any closer. "They will have to be executed."

Kasia stiffened and tilted her face up. "My husband . . . are men responsible for a storm?"

She at least kept her words so quiet no one else would hear them. He shook his head. "That area is known for its violent winds, my sweet. They should have taken that into account. The god's servants may have sent the weather, but it was human error that allowed it to wreak such havoc."

She nodded, but her eyes filled with tears. Ah, the emotions that went along with pregnancy—they were as tempestuous as the Hellespontine winds.

He tipped her chin up. "My authority is grounded in respect, admiration, and fear—failure must be met with punishment, or no one has incentive for success. It is either punish the thousands who worked on it or the few engineers at the head. Which is the kinder?"

"I know." She dashed at her eyes. "I am sorry—I cannot think why it upsets me so."

"I can." He kissed her forehead and set her away. "Worrying over it cannot be good for you and the babe, my love. Go back to your rooms and rest. I will not rage anymore, I promise." And now that he mentioned it . . . . "Why did you come in here, anyway?"

Kasia gave him a sheepish smile. "Pythius fetched me."

He chuckled and cupped her cheek. "A wise man, our Lydian friend. His loyalty proves to me that the god did indeed ordain this campaign. Which begs the question of why Ahura Mazda allowed this to happen without warning us."

Her smile was small and fleeting. "I will pray to Jehovah."

One of the coals inside fanned into a flame. "You pray to your Jehovah without ceasing, it seems—but he did not warn *you* of this either, did he? Yet you claim he and he alone controls the entire universe."

She jerked away with flooding eyes. "He may have formed the river and placed it in a pass that bears forth the winds. He may lift his hand and send out the rain to nourish the crops. But *you* are the one who chose to cross that river, knowing what storms may come."

The flame licked through the banked coals in his soul. "Do you dare to lay the blame for this at *my* feet?"

Anyone else would have cowered in fear, but not his Kasia. She only looked weary and far too pale. The flaming coals burned out quickly.

She shook her head. "I cast no blame. I only wish you would not dismiss Jehovah—or expect him to bend his creation around your will when you care nothing for his."

He caught her hand again and kissed her palm. "I respect your God, my love. I am sorry I spoke as I did."

Her gaze darted past him. "I am distracting you. And I am tired. I think I will not appear at the meal tonight, if you consent."

"Of course. I will dine with you in your chamber then. If you consent."

Her smile erased a few of the shadows under her eyes. "I would not dare deny the king of kings."

"Good." He kissed her hand again. "He gets testy when deprived of your company."

With the amusement alive in her eyes again, she took her leave. Xerxes allowed himself a steadying breath before turning to the men clustered just out of earshot. He beckoned them closer. "Have the engineers put to death and new ones appointed—and let it be known that they have three months to complete the project, or they will join their predecessors in the afterlife."

"Three months." Though he looked strained, Otanes nodded. "As you will, my king."

Masistes glanced at the scribe. "Will you really order the river lashed and manacled?"

Xerxes' lips tugged up at the corners. "Come up with some clever and demeaning words for them to shout while carrying out the punishment, Masistes."

"I?" Masistes flashed a wicked grin. "I have never had the pleasure of insulting a river before. It is brackish, is it not? Oh, this will be fun."

While his brother went off mumbling about bitter waters, Xerxes measured the remaining commanders. "I will not stay in Sardis beyond the winter. Three months—not a day more."

If that required rearranging the face of the earth still more, so be it.

EIGHTEEN

Sardis, Lydia
Three months later, in the sixth year of the reign of Xerxes

Darius hid the clench of his fists in the folds of his robe. "But Father—"

"I will not argue this again, Darius." Xerxes did not even spare him a glance. His attention was focused entirely upon the line of slaves with all his possessions. *His*. Not Darius's. "The whole point of naming a successor before I head to war is so that you can rule in my absence, and in the event that I am slain. It would rather defeat the purpose if you were slain along with me."

"Then why did you let me come at all? Why not leave me in Susa?"

His father sighed and finally turned to look at him. "You were eager to get out into the world, and I knew you would learn much in these years of preparation. Darius, I am entrusting my empire to you. Will you really gripe about ruling it from the comforts of Sardis?"

When put like that, Darius knew he could not argue. But still he wanted to. He had been counting the days until he was away from Artaynte, out in the fields where he could come into his own. How could he do that here, under her watchful eye? "I want to fight, Father. You are a skilled warrior—would you deny me the opportunity to be the same?"

"My skill came from controlled exercises—and a few forays before I was named the next king."

Darius felt his mouth twist. "Cyrus goes with you."

Xerxes let out a growl. "Cyrus's life is not worth as much as yours. You are my heir, Darius. *You*. If one of these bands of rebel Greeks wanted to cut me off at my knees, all they would have to do is get their hands on you."

"As if it would be so easy. Besides, if I were killed or captured, you would just name another in my place."

From where had *that* fear sprung?

Xerxes tossed up a hand and spun away. "I chose you for many reasons, Darius.

Though for the life of me I cannot remember them at this moment."

"That is easy." A grin won possession of his lips. "Had you named anyone else, Mother would have had him killed."

His father snorted a laugh and faced him again, arms akimbo. The amusement in his eyes shifted into something stronger, warmer. "I am proud of you, Darius. You have grown into an admirable man, otherwise I would not be so willing to leave you here as liaison between me and the rest of the empire. I would have given anything for such an honor when I was your age."

Darius nodded and decided to focus on that satisfaction rather than the niggling discontent. Was the control of an empire not worth more than the love of one woman?

Lately his father made him wonder. Sometimes Darius was unsure Persia still ranked at the top of Xerxes' priorities. It seemed that title had been given to the curvaceous Kasia. Part of him thought such dedication ridiculous—yet another part longed for Artaynte to look at him the way the Jewess did her husband.

Smiling it away, Darius embraced his father and nodded to the week-long stretch of army ranks. "Go tend your war, Father. I will keep the rest of the empire in working order—you will not be disappointed."

"I know." With a playful clap to the side of Darius's head, Xerxes stepped away. "I will be in touch. Do not get too attached to the authority, my son—I will ask it back from you when I have added Greece to our dominion."

Darius chuckled and lifted a hand in farewell. His smile faded as soon as the king was out of sight. No more dreams of becoming a war hero, then. Would ruling well be enough to earn the respect of Artaynte . . . or would he have to give up dreams of her as well?

"Mistress, we must go. The king wants to depart within the hour."

Kasia blinked and let her eyes refocus on the familiar pattern of her rug. She had been in prayer for a good while, but the pressure around her heart had not eased. If anything, it felt tighter than when she arose that morning. She tried to sit and winced at the pain in her back. Zad whimpered beside her and licked her in the face. With a halfhearted chuckle, she pushed him away. "Would you help me up, Desma?"

Desma put an arm around her, clucking her tongue. "You should not bend over so long in your condition. I am sure Jehovah would understand if you prayed in a chair."

Kasia let her maid haul her up. "No doubt he would. But I cannot concentrate so well when I am comfortable. I doze off." She spread a hand over the small mound of her stomach. "The fault of this wee one, I suspect."

"Better sleepiness than nausea." Desma grinned and roll up the rug.

She looked around at her chamber, devoid of everything but the furniture it had held upon her arrival here three months ago. "Where did the others go?"

"To prepare the wagon for you, mistress. Artaynte stopped in, to say farewell—she said she would wait for you outside."

Pain laced the pressure inside. When they started on this journey nearly two years ago, she never would have guessed she would become such good friends with the other women. Was it only because of proximity, or had they truly accepted her? Either way, she would miss Artaynte and Parsisa.

Either way, she would not miss them like she did Esther.

Theron filled the doorway and greeted her with a smile. "You have emerged from your prayerful stupor, I see. If you are ready then, mistress?"

Kasia smiled and followed her eunuch out the door, the dog bounding ahead of them. When she stepped into the warm sunshine, she fought the urge to turn and run back inside.

"There you are!" Artaynte rushed forward and wrapped her arms around her. "It will be torture watching Darius with his string of lovers with only Mother to talk to. If I thought I had a chance, I would beg the king to leave you here."

Kasia gave the girl a long hug. "I would be a surly, sour friend indeed if forced away from my husband." She grinned and tugged on a lock of Artaynte's hair. "You will understand that soon enough."

With a huff of disbelief, Artaynte pulled away. "We shall see."

Zad let out a string of low barks and growls and took off toward the wagon. Odd behavior for him—he usually stuck close to her side. Kasia looked to her servants. "Go see what he is about, would you, Theron? And Desma, put the last of the things in the wagon, please."

Theron frowned. "The dog will be fine. We will wait for you."

She sent a pointed glance to the seven servants lingering near Artaynte. "I think I will be well enough protected for five minutes, Theron. And I promise I shall not budge from this spot until you return for me."

"Why do you allow such impudence?" Artaynte whispered as Theron and Desma sauntered away, both scowling. "Simply command them."

"Speaking of commanding." Kasia nodded to where Parsisa beckoned her daughter. "You are needed, it seems."

"Will you not say farewell to Mother?"

"She stopped in earlier." She wiggled her fingers in Parsisa's direction and pulled Artaynte in for one more hug. "I will pray for you daily."

"I shall need it. Be safe and well. I look forward to meeting your son when you return." Sighing, Artaynte pulled away. "Stay with her," she said to one of her eunuchs.

The moment her friend left, unease crowded her mind and heart. Something was wrong, something that seemed to saturate the very air. Yet the sky was a promising, cloudless blue, and the morning sun gleamed bright and warm in the heavens.

All was as it should be, was it not? The bridge had been rebuilt. The canal was finished. The army swarmed in an orderly mass, ready to march onward to Abydus.

Not for the first time since she joined the royal family, she craved solitude like a drowning man craved air. She kept her gaze cool as she turned it on Artaynte's eunuch. "Go to your mistress. My own slaves return even now."

The slave offered no protest, no response at all other than obedience.

Her hands shook as she slid to the waist-high wall beside her. Before her the taunting pinnacle of Mount Tmolus rose up in one direction. The mountainside tumbled into the Hermus valley and the city of Sardis in the other.

Inside, warning bells clashed and clamored. "What is it, Jehovah? Why does such dread fill me?"

Her vision trembled and shook, and she swore the metallic scent of blood filled her nostrils. Moans echoed in her ears, and she had to grip the wall to keep her balance. "Jehovah?"

Without me is defeat.

Her throat closed off. She could but move her lips. "Without you? Do you not come with us?"

What part has righteousness with unrighteousness? And what part has holiness with evil?

Evil? She would grant that the Persian court did not seek the righteousness her God espoused, and she had prayed herself through the feeling of an enemy crouching behind her several times. But the Lord had always been with her. Going before her, as her father had promised he would. Why should now be any different?

"Lord . . . ."

Look up.

She knew even before she obeyed that she would rather squeeze her eyes shut tight. Paralysis already seized her limbs, her heart thundered a silent cry. Her gaze settled on the ground directly across from her, where scrub bushes nestled in every rocky crag. She moved her eyes up, over the increasing rocks and boulders, until her gaze caught on the spur of the mountain.

Darkness whispered like fog over the tip, its tendrils extending out slowly, seeking. In it was a roiling, writhing life that sucked the breath from her lungs.

All she could manage was a croak. "Oh, dear Lord . . . ."

Susa, Persia

Amestris blinked to clear her vision. A small hand tugged on her elbow, and pleading brown eyes looked up at her. "Eat."

She spared a smile for her youngest, though she was in no mood for his disruption. "You are hungry, Artaxerxes?"

The toddler nodded, sending dark curls dancing over his forehead. He tugged again on her elbow and stuck out a lip.

Fondness warred with impatience. She scooped up her son as his frazzled nurse rushed in. Another day, Amestris would have punished her for letting the boy get away from her. Today she had no time for such things. "There you are. Take my son for his breakfast."

Artaxerxes' arms clamped around her neck. "No. Mother."

"Mother cannot leave right now." She kissed his brow and plied him off. "But we will go play in the garden later."

Though he pouted, the little prince let himself be swept up into the slave's arms and taken from the room. Amestris drew in a long breath. Much as she would love spending her morning with her children, she could not. Ahura Mazda would not allow it.

She closed her eyes again and focused once more on prayer. For the last few months, her thoughts had been troubled by Haman's message. She was confident in her advice to await an opportunity to rid the king of the Jewess and her influence. But the heaviness in her spirit told her time was running short.

A ferocious need had awakened her before dawn stained the sky. She had ordered all her servants, all the palace, all of Susa to pray. Everyone knew the king's army would leave Sardis on this day, the war officially begun. They were told to pray for victory.

Victory could not come as long as Xerxes was ruled by the Jewish witch. "Ahura Mazda, show us how to serve you in this. Use your servants to rid the empire of this poison. Let not another day pass without demonstrating your might. Let your presence overshadow the king so that he might recognize the enemy beside him. Let your presence overshadow them all."

Sardis, Lydia

Haman followed the invisible tug, let his feet go where they willed. There was still much to do before they set off for Abydus in half an hour's time, much he should attend to. But the pull on his spirit was too strong to ignore.

He found himself outside the palace. His gaze tracked to the solitary figure gripping the wall.

The Jewess. All alone.

Purpose surged through him. One push, that was all it would take to send her over the wall and to her death on the rocks below. But he took only a step before a distant bark broke through the fog in his mind. He saw the dog nowhere, but still fear battled his determination. She was not truly alone, surely. One of her guards always lingered nearby, as well as that snarling beast. He could not . . . he dare not . . . .

He closed his eyes. "My god, if this is what you would have me do, you must help me. Send one of your servants to fill me with your might."

One second, he felt only his own wavering resolve. In the next, he jerked, gasped, and knew he was not alone in the shell of his body. His arms, when he lifted them, felt doubly strong. His legs, when he stepped, seemed to shake the very earth. His eyes, when they focused on the Jewess, sent an arrow of pure hatred straight to his heart.

Enemy of the god! He felt his lips peel back, felt his soul vibrate in expectation with each thundering footfall.

The god must have stopped her ears, for she did not seem to hear him coming. Her fingers gripped the stone until her knuckles went white. Perhaps her soul recognized damnation yawning before her.

No hesitation now. His arms came up, his muscles coiled, ready to pounce. A blood-curdling cry spilled from his lips as he lunged.

And a single refrain echoed through his mind—*Let your presence overshadow us!*

NINETEEN

The earth rushed up to attack her. Stones hurled themselves at her, branches stretched for a chance to scratch and gouge. Kasia's ears still rang with the yell of doom—a second cry tangled with it, one of agonizing fear. Hers.

The world spun, a confused mass of soil and sky, rock and tree. She tried to pull arms and legs up to protect her abdomen, but the cruel ground tugged them loose again.

With stillness came a sickening crack in her head. The crags and crevices of the boulder underneath her dug into tender flesh. She tried to take a breath—it seared her chest like fire.

And like smoke, darkness surged over the sky.

Was this death? This slinking, slithering blackness that descended from above until all light was blotted out? Did her vision dim, or the heavens themselves?

She wanted to lift her arms, to settle her hands on the precious life within her womb, but the heavy limbs would not obey her. Everything wavered, winked.

"No." She struggled to sit up but could only lie there and watch the darkness come. "Jehovah—"

The muscles in her abdomen fisted, screamed. Tears blurred the edges of the darkness. "Jehovah, save me."

A streak of blinding white pierced the blackened sky.

Had he gone blind? Half wondering if he dreamed, Xerxes spun around. Blackness, everywhere. "Zethar!"

"Here, master." His servant's usually-strong voice shook. "What manner of devil is this? The sun shone brightly a moment ago—the sky was cloudless."

Xerxes took a deep breath so his heart would quit its frantic galloping. "Clouds cannot cause darkness like this, nor can an eclipse."

"I will call the magi."

"Torches first, man. We must see." He knew Zethar would obey but could not make out his retreating form in the darkness.

He closed his eyes against the lack of vision and listened. There, the sound of his servant's familiar stride, moving away. There, animals whinnying and braying, snarling and growling. Was that Zad, barking as if a demon were on his tail?

"Father? What is this?"

Xerxes opened his eyes but did not see Darius. "I do not know, my son."

"My lord." Artabanas's voice, from nearby.

"Here, uncle."

A hand found his arm. "Ah. My lord, does this feel familiar to you?"

Realization jolted through him like lightning. He had indeed felt this before, this sense of overwhelm. Only then, in the deepest heart of night, it had not seemed so odd. "The dream."

"The dream." His uncle's voice dripped fervency. "This is the work of Ahura Mazda."

Yes. No. "Why would the god cover the land in darkness on the very day we set out for *his* war?"

"Who am I to say? We must call the magi."

"Zethar is doing so now." A flicker of flame appeared from around a corner, illuminating the face of another slave. "Good, light. Let us go calm the troops."

They located most of the high command with ease—or rather, the high command found them, drawn by the light of their torch. Within minutes, other points of flame appeared on the mountain and down into the valley.

The magi approached with heads bent together. These were the wisest men in Persia, the ones most skilled in things beyond human reckoning. They were the ones who understood the motions of the heavens, who could interpret the manifestation of things divine. But could even they understand this?

His uncle stepped forward to greet them. "Men of wisdom, what explanation do you have for your king?"

The magi exchanged a few more whispers before the most wizened among them bowed and stepped forward. "There is no question, my lord and master—this is a portent of your coming victory."

Xerxes gritted his teeth. "My victory is foretold by the obliteration of all light from a morning sky?"

"Of course, my king. Is it not common knowledge that Greece is represented by the sun, and Persia the night? The fact that night has overcome day on the very morning you begin your campaign is a sure sign that Persia shall also overcome Greece."

Xerxes spun and strode a few steps from his companions. He knew he looked out over the valley, but its details remained shrouded. The sun should be inching its way toward mid-morning. Instead the world was dark as the night of the new moon.

His soul wrestled with itself. How could something so fearsome be an omen of good things? Yet it resonated in that deepest cavity of his being, where memories of his encounter with the god lived.

The magi must be right. It was the only explanation—the god had led him to this, had insisted it was the only path to greatness. Victory was guaranteed. This was simply

Ahura Mazda's way of making it known to all the world.

He turned back around and surveyed his most trusted men. Then frowned. "Where is Pythius?"

Susa, Persia

Mordecai stood from his bench at the gate and searched the palace grounds nearest him. Few were out and about on this fine morning. Strange. Stranger still was the band of tension around his torso.

When a servant hurried by, Mordecai halted him. "My friend! Where is everyone today?"

The servant bobbed his head. "Praying, on orders of the queen. The king marches to Abydus today. All have been ordered to remain in their homes and pray for him."

When had people begun calling Amestris the queen again? Mordecai swallowed and nodded. "Thank you. I will head home, then."

He only went a few steps before he knew home was not where he needed to be. The river. He needed to go to the river.

As he reached the banks, a flash of white light streaked before his eyes, blinding him. He fell to his knees even as vision returned. "Jehovah? Is it Kasia again?"

He heard her scream somewhere inside his mind and doubled over when his skull seemed to crack in two and his abdomen rip apart. Gasping, he sprawled onto the ground. "Jehovah God, please—save her! Send your angels, Lord, to save your daughter."

He squeezed his eyes shut against the scalding tears and the unnatural pain. Logically, he knew there was no wound in his head, no cramp in his stomach. That did not stop the sensation of life collapsing.

He shut out the panic and prayed.

Sardis, Lydia

Pythius took another step after Zad in the darkness, sliding farther down the mountain than he had intended. His arms flailed. Certain he would fall, he tensed, ready for the impact.

His feet caught firm ground again, and his balance equalized. "Zad?"

The dog barked from just ahead, and Pythius followed the sound. Never in his life had he felt urgency like this. Never in his life had terror seized his heart as when darkness fell upon his city.

"Zad?"

A whoof sounded beside him, and a wet nose nudged his hand. Pythius patted the dog's head and followed him onward. As best as he could tell, they traveled down the mountain a bit more, then around an outcropping.

It was not so dark on this little knoll. Twilight instead of midnight. And the non-darkness seemed to circle a wide, flat rock with an odd lump on top.

Realization knocked the air from his lungs. "No. By the gods, no! Kasia!"

Zad bounded ahead of him and settled on the rock beside his mistress, whimpering and licking her face. Pythius swallowed back bile when the dog's muzzle came away red. "Kasia?"

She groaned and turned her head, but her eyes did not open. Pythius crossed into the circle of near-light and paused, shuddering. Within this twilight ark, his soul brightened along with his vision, the weight of the darkness lifted. He knelt beside her and took her hand. "Can you hear me, Kasia? It is Pythius. I am here to help you."

Her fingers gripped his as her whole body convulsed, knees and neck both straining toward her center. Pythius's nostrils flared. "No, my daughter. Do not deliver your babe yet, please. He is not ready, and neither are you."

A low, faint keen sounded in her throat. A perfect match to the teardrop that tracked down her temple.

His soul yearned to cry out but knew not which god to beseech. Athena, the guardian of his city? Hera, goddess of women? Or should he take his plea directly to Zeus?

Zad leapt up and flew past him with a round of barks. Pythius pressed his lips together and leaned over the prone woman to get a better idea of her injuries. Myriad scrapes and bruises covered her, but the seeping, dark stains under her head and trunk dismayed him most.

"Mistress? Mistress!"

Pythius turned and saw her two most trusted slaves running their way. "She is badly injured—and in labor, I think. I found her only a minute ago."

The eunuch reached them first and dropped to his knees on the rock. He inspected each limb, the back of her head, and held large hands over her stomach when another convulsion ripped through her. He looked with tight lips at the maid who had settled beside Pythius. "Pray, Desma."

The girl's eyes slid shut, pushing tears onto her cheeks. "Jehovah, God of my mistress, please. I know not what treachery has befallen us this day, what evil blocks your light from the sky. But I know that Kasia is your true and loyal servant. Spare her, Jehovah, please. Stop the bleeding, heal the injuries. Lord, Lord!" The girl cried out and buried her head against Kasia's side. She continued in a Greek dialect Pythius did not understand.

He did not need to. He gripped Kasia's hand tighter and whispered, "Jehovah." Of course. She was a Jewess, and hers was the God who held back the shadows from her now. "Jehovah. Save her."

The eunuch eased Kasia up a few inches and then lowered her limp form back down. "Should we move her?"

Zad barked from behind them, and they all looked his way. The dog whined and turned toward the way they'd come from, tail wagging.

"I assume that is our answer. He led us all to her—perhaps he sees what we cannot."

Pythius looked from one servant to the other, and they both nodded.

Desma sprang up. "I will prepare her chamber. Master Pythius—if you could find the king?"

"Of course."

The maidservant scampered over to Zad, and they soon disappeared into the blanket of darkness. Pythius cringed at the thought of stepping back into it, but there was no choice. They must get her to her room.

Theron gathered Kasia into his arms, and Pythius swore at the sight of her hair caked in blood. "We have no time to lose."

He expected the second step to take them outside the oasis of twilight—instead, it moved with them, beating back the shadows as they slid up the hill. He knew it was Kasia the half-light cradled. And when they reached the solid ground of the palace, Pythius had to step out of it and go in search of the king.

The darkness slid oily and suffocating over him. He turned back to Theron and Kasia. "Do you know what this is?"

Perhaps he was a fool to ask a slave for truth. But the eunuch offered a tight smile. "Ahura Mazda, I think. Each time we have felt this, our mistress bids us pray to Jehovah."

"And it works?"

Theron nodded. "It is the only reason she has survived this long in the palace."

"Then I will call upon him. Perhaps he will hear the supplication of a desperate Lydian, if the prayers are on behalf of his daughter."

"He will." The eunuch grimaced when Kasia tensed in his arms. "Another contraction. I must get her to her bed."

"Of course, go." Pythius drew in a resolute breath and turned to face down the darkness. He knew little of Jehovah, but one thing he was sure of—if this blackness came from the god of his king, he wanted no part of Mazdayasna.

He tried to call to mind his own gods, but their images looked like ash. He needed no more smoke and vapors, no more stone and marble. He needed light. And so far as he had seen today, only the God of Kasia offered it. His soul calling out for Jehovah, he went in search of the king.

Xerxes sprinted down the hall, not slowing until the doors to Kasia's chamber opened before him. He had been two miles away by the time Pythius found him, and the horse he had grabbed went lame halfway back—he ran the rest of the way.

The sconces and lamps did little to penetrate the darkness. It was no wonder the commoners were upset—they did not fully understand the omen, nor the workings of the god. He was not so sure he did, either, but every step he took through the day-turned-night reminded him that fear of the god was where wisdom lay.

Once he stepped into Kasia's room, he halted and sucked in a much-needed breath. His frown did not ease. Something was different in here. The flames burned brighter, the air was not so thick.

The god was not here.

His gaze went to the bed, where Kasia lay unmoving under a sheet, then to the corner of the room, where Desma swiped at her cheeks and fussed with a mound of rags. "What is going on?" he demanded. "Pythius said she fell from the wall, that she was badly hurt. Tell me she lives."

"She lives." The maid sniffed and rested a hand on the rags. "The babe was stillborn. A son, master."

"No." The word ripped its way out of his chest, rending it in two, yet made no more than a whisper into the room. He stumbled over to Kasia and knelt beside her. Strips of white cloth bound her head, trapped her hair. Her skin looked a deathly, pale olive against it, marked with angry red slashes and mottled bruises. Pressure burned behind his eyes and nose. "Does she know? Has she been awake?"

Her other maid, Leda, blotted at a wound on Kasia's arm with a damp cloth. "No, master. She was semi-coherent while the pains were on her, enough to respond to them and push. She has not stirred since."

"Lovely Kasia." He wove his fingers through hers and reached with his other hand to caress an unblemished portion of her cheek. "Do not leave me, sweet one. I shall never forgive you if you do."

Her head shifted into his touch, and her lashes fluttered open. Though her lips formed his name, no sound came out.

Xerxes reached for a chalice nearby and urged some liquid into her mouth. "There you are, my love."

She looked at him out of haunted eyes. "Something is wrong," she murmured.

"Yes." He lifted her hand, kissed it. "But you are alive."

"The babe." He would have expected panic, not that bone-weary resignation. She drew in a long breath, wincing. "Was it a son or daughter?"

His voice would not work until he forced a swallow. "A son."

Her fingers tightened around his. She drew in a shaky breath. "Why am I alive?"

Surely that sound was his heart, shattering into a million pieces. "Oh, my love, please. I know it pains you, but do not give up on life."

Her free hand landed on his head and stroked through his hair. "That is not . . . I felt the afterlife opening before me, I saw a terrible darkness . . . ."

"That was not death—it was the promise of victory." He nodded to the open window that somehow held back the god. "It is only noon even now."

"There is no victory without Jehovah."

"Hmm?" He frowned down at her. "This has nothing to do with Jehovah, my love."

"That is my fear." Her eyes slid shut. "I want to hold him."

It took him a moment to realize she meant the babe—when he did, he shook his head. "No, Kasia, it will only hurt you more."

"Please, Xerxes."

"Madness." He touched his forehead to their joined hands, then stood and nodded to Desma. Denying her was impossible, but he could have no part in it. He wandered to the window and motioned Theron over.

"Master?"

Xerxes folded his arms over his chest. "I did not give Pythius time to explain—what happened?"

The eunuch blanched. "She was saying farewell to Artaynte, and the dog ran off. She asked me to fetch him and sent Desma to the wagon with her things—we protested, master, but she insisted she would be safe with Artaynte's servants. I went after Zad, but I had not found him before the darkness came upon us. I heard her scream, and Desma and I hurried back to where she had been but found no one on the wall. We heard Zad again, below us, so followed the sound. He led us to her."

Xerxes' jaw clenched. "She must have stumbled in the darkness and fallen over the wall."

"Presumably—but that does not explain everything. Why did no one shout when she fell? Was she alone?" Theron shook his head. "Something foul is at work here, master."

"It was an accident." Was it not?

He looked out the window again. How many times had he gazed out at the mountain from this very spot while Kasia puttered around her room? He knew the landscape—knew how sharp a fall it was from the wall. How unforgiving the steep, rocky ground would be.

It should have killed her, as surely as it killed their child.

From the bed came a choking sob that made his throat close in response. He nearly went to her but held himself in place. When the babe had been taken away, he would hold her close and soothe her tears. But he could not look at the child. Better to pretend it was like their others, faceless and unformed.

She should have done the same. It sounded as though her soul were being rent from her body with each cry. He spun around and motioned to Desma. "Take it away. Now."

"No!" Kasia strained up when the maid lifted the bundle from her arms, reaching, grasping.

Xerxes rushed to intercept her arms and force her back down. "I know you want him, my love, but you must let him go."

Her face twisted in agony, her body twisted away from his hold. He held tight anyway. "Stop." It was more plea than command. "Please, Kasia, I cannot lose you too."

Though her struggling ceased, she pushed herself up and into his arms rather than lying down as he had hoped she would. "I am well."

"Do not be absurd. I have rarely seen men survive such injuries."

"But . . . ." Confusion flitted through her eyes. "I feel no pain. Only in here." She splayed a hand over her heart.

Xerxes shook his head. "Perhaps that is eclipsing the physical, but your looks tell the true tale. You are badly hurt—and I know not what lies under this bandage."

Theron stepped up behind Kasia. His face also told the tale. "It is bad, master."

Kasia went lax against his chest. Terror snapped its jaws around him, especially when he looked down and saw perfect peace on her face. She could not die now—lack of pain did not indicate the end, did it?

She smiled. "My wounds will heal. I need only to rest in him." Her eyes eased shut.

He gripped her shoulder and barely kept himself from shaking her. "Kasia!"

She hummed and turned her face into him again. Her breathing came deep and even. He relaxed. She slept, that was all.

A knock sounded as Xerxes eased her onto her bed. Leda scurried over to open the door.

"My king." Masistes stood in the opening, all the high command behind him. "Pythius told us what happened. Does she live?"

"She does." He leaned down to kiss her softly, then stood and moved out into the hall. The expressions on the men's faces varied from concerned to incredulous. No doubt they had assumed the worst. He swallowed. "She delivered a stillborn son."

Masistes winced. "I am sorry, brother. I know how you hoped."

Xerxes cleared his throat and straightened his spine. "At least she has been spared."

Pythius shook his head. His eyes were bloodshot and his face haggard, his shoulders bent in defeat. "I hoped the labor would stop and they would both live. And knew not how either could survive such a fall."

"Do we know what caused it?" Haman shifted a bit from where he stood behind Masistes and Mardonius.

Xerxes shrugged. "We assume when the darkness descended, she tripped."

Haman frowned. "There have been no other reports of injuries, for all the confusion. Do you not find it odd that she is the one person out of millions to suffer from the darkness?"

"I . . . ." He had not. But Haman was right. Why would the god insulate the rest of the army but not her? "It makes no sense."

Haman gazed into the room. "It is not so dark there as everywhere else."

His blood seemed to chill, slow. "No. The god is not in there."

"Perhaps that is the explanation then." Haman said no more—just bowed and walked away.

Xerxes stared at the place where he had been and tried to block out the thoughts clamoring to the forefront of his mind. Tried to cling to the promise Ahura Mazda had given him, to the sign they had received today.

But then, the god had said victory and greatness lay before him. He had never said at what price it would come. What if victory was not given, but must be bought? Perhaps . . . perhaps his son was the sacrifice required of him.

Pythius stepped close to his side. "Will she make it, do you think?"

He glanced at the friend that had so quickly come to cherish her as a daughter. "I think so." If not, why would she have survived this long? Surely if the god required her, too, he would have taken her along with the babe.

And yet . . . she alone stolidly refused to give Ahura Mazda his dues. She alone lay in a circle of dawn's light when the night of the god covered the rest of them.

How long before the deity lost patience with her and swept her away from him too?

TWENTY

Susa, Persia

Esther dropped her basket, left the door swinging open behind her. There was no time to waste on such trivialities, not if Mordecai was as ill as Martha had said.

"Cousin? Cousin!"

She followed the low, excruciating cry to Mordecai's chamber and pushed the door open with a creak. A gasp caught in her throat when she saw him writhing on the floor. "Mordecai!"

He clutched at his head, muttered something unintelligible, and curled into a ball. Esther dropped down beside him. "You must tell me what hurts you, my father."

"Everything. Head."

He had never been prone to headaches, and the way he clutched at it . . . . "Let me see. Did you strike it?"

"Rock."

"Oh, dear Lord, let him be all right." She peeled his fingers away and probed gently at the back of his head. And frowned. There was no blood, no knot. Nothing to explain the level of pain he seemed to be in. "I cannot find an injury, Mordecai. Are you sure you struck it? Did you fall?"

"Cliff . . . ."

She rocked back on her heels. "Susa has no cliffs."

He groaned and rolled onto his side. Perhaps pain clouded his memory? Or he could be delirious. She touched her hand to his forehead. It was cool. "My father . . . ."

When she rested her fingers on his arm, he jerked it away with a whimper. She let her hand fall against her leg to keep it from shaking. "Does your arm hurt too?"

"Cut."

"It is not cut." Why did she even bother with the tight whisper? Her words obviously meant nothing to him. He felt *something*. She loosened her shoulders. "I will call a physician."

"No." He grabbed her wrist and finally opened his eyes. The irises, usually a hazel as clear as the most precious of gems, were murky and dark. "No. Not . . . my pain."

"Cousin, that makes no sense." She lifted his hand off her wrist and held it. "Tell me what to do."

He gritted his teeth and closed his eyes again. "Pray."

His answer to everything. Esther shook her head and squeezed his fingers. "How? For what?"

"That this is sufficient." He winced, writhed. "To save her."

She bit her lip to keep from asking what "her" she was supposed to pray salvation for—and why she ought to be concerned with whoever it was when her cousin lay writhing on the floor.

"Esther?" Zechariah's voice preceded his appearance in the doorway by only a second. He wore a deep frown. "Martha said you may need help . . . what has happened?"

Tears stung her eyes. "I cannot tell. He says he fell down a cliff, which is obviously not possible, and he has no visible wounds. But if I touch him, he screams. He is in terrible pain, Zechariah, whatever the cause."

This time when he moaned, Esther thought she made out "Kasia."

Zechariah gripped her by the elbows and lifted her up. "Go brew him something to help with the pain."

She could not convince her feet to move when he released her. She wanted to wrap her arms around him and beg him to tell her Mordecai was not mad. She settled for wrapping her arms around herself and whispering, "Is it possible he misses her so much that . . . ?"

Zechariah touched her cheek and offered a weak smile. "I cannot think so. Go, little one. He needs whatever relief we can find for him."

She nodded and obeyed, but busying her hands did nothing to still her rampant thoughts. The menial task did not calm the frantic beat of her heart.

She could not lose Mordecai. She could not. He was all the family she had, the only one left in the world who loved her. If he were snatched away by some invisible pain, something she could not even fight or treat . . . .

"Is it ready?"

She jumped, screeched, and nearly dropped the clay pot of brewed herbs. "Zech. I did not hear you."

He leaned into the door and studied her. "Whatever this is, it struck him at the river, where Kasia would have been. That is all he was saying."

"Oh. But . . . what *is* it?" She set the pot down before it could betray her shaking hands.

Zechariah sighed and shook his head. "He said he prayed to take the pain of another near death."

Her confusion doubled. "Since when does Jehovah allow such a thing?"

"I do not understand it either, Esther." He glanced over his shoulder, back into the house. "He swore he would be well, that he only needs time—and our prayers."

She stepped away from the heat of the fire and blew a hair from her face. "Who do we pray for? Him, or this unknown, dying person?"

"Both, I suppose."

Esther pressed her lips together. "Well. I shall take him his drink and then go pray." She picked up the pot, even took a step. Then the tears caught up with her. "Tell me he will not die. That though he somehow feels the pain of this stranger, he will not die her death."

"Oh, Esther." He took the pot from her and put it down, then pulled her to his chest. A stray wood shaving pressed into her cheek. She savored the feel—it meant Zechariah. "I am no priest or prophet, to tell you how Jehovah works. But I know Mordecai. He never would have asked for something that would take him from you."

She should pull away—instead, she clung tighter. "I know. I just—it is selfish of me, but I cannot . . . I do not want to be left alone again, Zechariah. He is all I have left."

Was that his lips against her hair? "That is not selfish, and you will not be left alone, even if something happened to Mordecai. You know my family loves you like one of its own."

Though she nodded, she had her doubts. His sisters would not miss her when they married and moved. His brothers had not teased her or joked with her since Kasia left them. Only Zechariah treated her as he always had—and he was the one person she wished would *not*.

She pulled away, eyes on the ground. "I must return to Mordecai. I . . . thank you, Zechariah."

"There is no need for thanks. We are friends, and that is what friends do."

"I know." Friends, always friends. He loved her no more than the rest of his family did. She picked up the pot and stepped past him.

Sardis, Lydia

The kiss of the sun had never felt so welcome—especially in contrast to the tears that fell like rain from Kasia's eyes. She swiped at them, but more took their place. Perhaps she ought not have asked where they had buried her babe. Seeing that freshly turned soil marked by an irregular stone did not help her say goodbye.

Xerxes' hand settled on her shoulder, and his thumb rubbed at the nape of her neck. "We must go, my love. Unless you have changed your mind and would like to rest a while longer—"

"No. I am ready." She did her best to smile in proof.

Her husband did not look convinced. "You cannot possibly be well enough for travel, Kasia. I saw the wound in your head last night. You ought to be . . . ."

"Dead." The word made her shudder, but she rolled back her shoulders. "I know. But you cannot deny what you saw this morning, can you?"

He pressed his lips together and trailed his fingers over her arm. The night before, a deep gash had marred her flesh and scored her muscle. When she awoke this morning, only the faintest of lines showed where it had been. Her whole body had felt saturated in light, as if she had slept under Susa's summer sun.

Xerxes shook his head. "It is unnatural."

"As was everything else that transpired yesterday." She looked to the wall where she had stood and watched the first tendrils of darkness slip over the mountaintop. Her memory ended there. Her eyes followed the path she must have fallen, over the wall and down the steep hill. Theron had pointed out the rough, flat rock they had found her on, the dual stains of blood dark and taunting. "Praise Jehovah for hearing my cry. First he saved me, then he healed me."

"Jehovah?" Xerxes snorted a laugh—the derision in it knotted her stomach. "Where was he when your son emerged lifeless and still?"

Eyes burning, she splayed a hand over the abdomen that should have been swollen instead of flat. "I know not why he spared me and not the babe, but he held me throughout it. Had he not . . . ."

"This would not have happened to begin with." He took his hand from her shoulder and rubbed it over his face. "Kasia, you must stop denying Ahura Mazda. I know in my soul that is what killed our son, what nearly killed you."

There might have been some truth to that—the evil would have stolen her life if God had not intervened. "I believe we addressed this the first night I came to you, Xerxes. Jehovah is my God. Did you not grant that is a crucial part of who I am?"

He huffed out a breath and started toward the wagon, pulling her along by her elbow. "That was before *this* happened. And that conversation was about whether you would serve *me*, not the god. I only ask you to admit what everyone else does this morning."

She pulled her arm free. "Everyone admits something terrible happened yesterday, and everyone puts their faith in *you* when you tell them it was a good omen. It is you they worship, Xerxes, not your god."

"Ridiculous."

"It is not. Do you not see everyone's fearful glances at the sky? Then they see you striding about with confidence, and they relax." She halted and grabbed at his tunic. "You are a man above men, my love, and they follow wherever you lead. That is why you must keep your feet on the path of righteousness. If Jehovah does not go with you, you will meet with defeat."

A thunderhead gathered in his eyes then melted into concern. "All the world will follow me except *you*. Why must you tempt the god, Kasia?"

She laced her fingers through his and squeezed. "I follow you in all things but this."

"You do not. Every time I order something you do not like, you turn those large eyes on me and plead until I relent." Though the words were teasing, his face was not. "I cannot relent on this—I have too much to lose."

"Xerxes . . . ."

He shook his head, and his eyes went hard. "I will not watch another babe be snatched from your womb, and I will not tempt the god to snatch you from me as well. It seems Ahura Mazda will not grant me both a child with you and victory. So until I have one, we will not pursue the other."

A gust of wind screamed up the valley and whipped around her. In spite of the weaving of their fingers, it felt as though she could not touch him, that no bridge could span the chasm yawning open at her feet. An ache pulsed in her empty womb. "You will deny me the rights of a wife?"

His throat bobbed as he swallowed. "I realize this is largely my fault. Perhaps the god is jealous of my love for you. Or perhaps he is displeased I allow such willfulness about Jehovah. Either way, I cannot risk your life anymore. Until we have our victory in hand, Kasia . . . ."

Her head spun as she stared into the nothingness below. "I just lost a son—now I lose a husband."

"You have not lost me." Yet the assurance was tinged with frustration. "We will still spend our days together."

When he got that particular glint of determination in his eye, arguing with him was useless. Neither could she agree. So she just held his gaze until he looked away and tugged her forward.

The ranks had taken up formation along the road again. Some of the commanders were already astride their horses, others milling about with last minute preparations. Kasia glanced at the palace to search for Artaynte and Parsisa—she had seen neither since their farewells yesterday.

"Pythius is waiting for us," Xerxes said.

He stood at the edge of the road, his stance stooped yet rigid. When they approached, his gaze swept over her and his eyes went wide. "I did not believe it when they told me you were up and about already, lady. But had I not seen you myself yesterday . . . ."

"I know." She gripped the hand he held out. "Thank you, my friend, for all you did to help. I would have died had Jehovah not sent you."

Xerxes growled under his breath and released her other hand.

Pythius squeezed her fingers. "I wish he would have sent me sooner, so that I could have caught you before you fell." He gave her a tired smile and let go of her hand, then turned to Xerxes. "My lord. You have become a true friend these last few months, and I am grateful for this chance to know you."

Her husband smiled, but it fell short of his eyes. "Likewise, Pythius. Your generosity to me and my troops will live on long after you. I only sorrow that now we must part."

"The army is no place for an old man like me." Pythius's mouth wobbled up into an anxious smile. "I would ask a favor, my lord."

"After all you have done for us? Anything."

Pythius squared his shoulders. "Thank you. As you know, all five of my sons are set to march with you. I would ask that you release the eldest from military service, so that he might care for me and his mother in our old age."

Kasia's breath caught. The request sounded reasonable to her, but obviously Xerxes disagreed. His fingers curled into his palm. "Why would you ask this? Victory is guaranteed."

"It is war. Even the side that wins will suffer losses—I fear my sons will be among them." His laugh sounded rusty and afraid. "Can you blame an old man for wanting one son left at home to carry on his name? You yourself leave your heir behind—"

"Which was well established before this." Xerxes' eyes flashed with fury. "I did not change my mind out of cowardice when the darkness fell from the sky."

A decade fell off Pythius's face when he lifted his chin. "Sometimes fear is a sign of wisdom. How you can stand before your men and claim the darkness was a good omen—"

"Do you dare speak against the god? It was a promise of victory!"

"The only promise I felt yesterday was when I escaped your god in the presence of Kasia's."

For a moment, Kasia feared Xerxes would strike him. "Curse you, Pythius! I expect doubt from the low-born rabble, but not from you. If I release your son, everyone will know you asked out of fear and will succumb to their own. Yet here you are, proclaiming your doubt of the god and asking the impossible."

"I only ask for one son."

She had seen her husband angry countless times. Furious, disappointed. But all his frustrations over incompetence, all the ranting and fuming he was famous for dimmed in comparison to what burned now in his eyes.

Betrayal, underscored by pain. It turned his eyes dark and feral and made his muscles quiver. "Zethar. Bring Pythius's eldest son."

Pythius said nothing as the eunuch headed for a group of nearby men. Did he taste fear, as she did? She tried to swallow it down and stepped closer to Xerxes when she would rather have stepped away. "What will you do?"

His arm felt tense as stone when she put her hand on it. His gaze stayed trained on Pythius. "I held you up before all the world. Announced that your generosity was a sign of the god's blessing."

Pythius sucked in a long breath. "I know."

"I take all my family with me, with no guarantees that any will come home again. Yet a slave asks for his son?"

Pythius shut his eyes.

Kasia did too, and rested her forehead against the unforgiving muscle of her husband's arm. Still, she heard the approaching footsteps and the curious greeting of Pythius's son.

A tremor coursed through Xerxes' arm and shook Kasia all the way to her soul. "Your king has already given one son in this effort." His voice emerged steady. "Now you will do the same. Zethar, have this man cut in two and staked to either side of the road. Let all the army see as they march past what happens to those who betray Persia."

"Xerxes, no." She wanted to scream it, wanted to throw herself in front of the condemned and beg for mercy. But she could find no breath, and the world spun when she tried to move. Yet again she felt herself falling. Maybe this time the jagged ground would swallow her whole.

An arm caught her around the middle—her stomach rebelled. Dry heaves wracked her long after Xerxes lowered her to a rest at his feet. When she opened her eyes, Pythius was on his knees, head bowed, and his son was being led silently away.

Xerxes crouched beside her, but she averted her face. "How could you do this?"

"Better they fear the wrath of their king than think they have lost the favor of their god." He forced her to a sitting position and studied her face. Fury still sparked in his eyes. It left little room for compassion. "You are unwell. If you would rather remain in Sardis, you may."

He stood and strode away, leaving her to sway upon the rocky soil. Her gaze tracked to that plot of newly turned ground. It must hold her heart as well as her son, for surely there was nothing left inside her.

Pythius staggered to his feet and moved to her, pulled her up. A sheen of moisture covered his eyes. "Why does seeking your God above his cost us our sons, Kasia?"

She could only shake her head.

"I should have known not to ask. I should have realized . . . ."

"How could you have anticipated that?"

Nostrils flaring, he patted her arm. "Go with him."

Why? Why go and be denied both her husband and her Lord? She looked toward the tiny grave again.

Pythius turned her face with a firm finger. "Your place is among the living, daughter. Go with your husband. You are his heart, and who knows what he might do without you by his side."

Her gaze swung to the wagon, where Xerxes stood, back to the world. Something twisted inside her. She gave Pythius a swift hug and left him.

Jehovah God, do not abandon us yet.

Her husband gripped the wooden side of the wagon with white knuckles. Slipping up behind him, she slid her arms around his waist—he felt like a statue.

He pulled in a labored breath. "You should stay. Your heart is too fragile for war."

"You are my heart, Xerxes."

He said nothing, but he turned his head so she could see his profile.

From ahead of them, blood-curdling screams pierced the air. She knew that within minutes, everyone would know about the king's order, the king's wrath.

Only she saw the single tear escape his eye.

Susa, Persia

Mordecai rubbed the back of his head. The pain had gone when the burden to pray eased, but the memory . . . . For a long moment he stared at the earthen ceiling. Did Kasia live, or were the injuries too extensive, even without the pain?

He closed his eyes and whispered his wonder to the Almighty. Peace washed over him, though that did little to answer his question. It could mean she was out of danger—or resting in the bosom of Abraham.

Either way, he had seen the power of the Lord yesterday. Glory be to God. "What should I pray for today, Jehovah?"

An answer formed in his mind, but before he could put words to it, a knock sounded. Esther stepped in, relief sweeping over her face. "Good morning, cousin. You look better."

"I am." He sat and dredged up a smile. "I am sorry I frightened you yesterday, little one."

She smiled, but it shook around the edges. "I am only glad to see you improved. The one you prayed for—she is . . . ?"

He sighed. "I know not. Either at peace or healed. Esther—I cannot thank you enough for tending me yesterday. I realize how strange it must have seemed to you, but it was necessary."

Her smile steadied. "Of that I have no doubt. Are you hungry?"

"In a moment. First, would you pray with me that Jehovah goes with the army? I have the feeling he is angry with them."

"Of course." She came in and sat on the floor beside him.

They joined hands, bowed heads. And prayed that the Lord would go before their friends and neighbors who marched with the king.

Twenty-One

Troy, Anatolia

Kasia bounced Lalasa's younger daughter upon her knee. The other two concubines sat on opposite sides of their shared tent, glaring at each other.

"You look like a sheep with you hair like that, Lalasa," Diona said.

Lalasa rolled her eyes. "Our husband likes it this way."

Diona scowled at the cloud of Lalasa's ebony hair as a maid wove gold strands through it. "You will not be called tonight anyway."

"Were you not complaining an hour ago about how often you must go to him? Though how you expect to get with child again otherwise . . . ." Lalasa lifted her chin and patted the small bump of her stomach.

Diona folded her arms over her chest. "At least I have a son."

"Ah yes, one screaming son. The king can barely tolerate him. I am amazed he can stand to be near *you*."

Kasia sighed and lifted a hand to pinch the bridge of her nose. She pressed a kiss to the little girl's head and placed her upon her feet, then stood.

The other concubines looked her way when she did. She gave them a tight-lipped smile. "I ought to prepare for the meal too. You both look beautiful."

Lalasa's expression shifted to regret. "Oh, Kasia, we did not mean to upset you. Stay, please. We will not speak of children—"

"It is not that." But her eyes darted to the three little ones. Diona's son had taken his first toddling steps yesterday. He would soon be chasing after Lalasa's daughters.

Diona shook her head. "Forgive us our bickering, Kasia. It is the only way we can express the frustration."

"She is right." Lalasa patted a dark hand to the pouf of her hair. "We could tell the king how difficult he has been to please since we left Sardis, but you are the only one who can get away with such impudence."

"And were we you, he would not be so difficult to please." Diona let out a gusty exhale. "It has been two months, you are surely healed. Perhaps we should just send her in our place one night, Lalasa, and force his hand. The whole world would thank us."

Kasia forced a smile but turned toward the tent flap. "I will see you both at the meal."

Her servants around her, she stepped out into the warm afternoon sunlight and let her gaze wander to the knoll nearby. The walls of the once-great Ilium protruded from the ground in some places, but in others nature prevailed.

"Mistress? Where are you going?"

She ignored Theron and wandered up the hill. Only once she stood in the middle of a broken square did she halt. Directly before her stretched stone upon stone of a wall, but it tumbled into oblivion a few feet in either direction.

Had this been a room in Priam's palace? The hall where he ruled, perhaps, or the bedchamber where Paris had held Helen as his captive lover? Had the Spartan queen seen the masses of Greek warriors swarming the shores and wished she could put a halt to the war that stretched from year into decade? Did she miss Menelaus, her lawful husband? Or did she go willingly with the Trojan prince who had stolen her from her home?

Kasia drifted toward the tallest stretch of the wall, high as her shoulder. The Greeks had done an excellent job of razing the city—and where they stopped, time and weather had taken over. So little remained to tell the tale of a nation. She lifted a hand and rested it on the warm top of the stone, rough and dry, then trailed it over the shadow-cooled side.

Jehovah God, let me not crumble and slip silently into eternity. Let me not be destroyed and forgotten. Preserve me, Lord.

So often these past two months she had felt like an echo. She spent her days being lulled into a daze by the rocking of her wagon. The sounds of countless marching feet and stomping hooves, of men shouting and laughing, became no more than meaningless rumbles. Her mind circled from observation to vain longing to prayer and back again.

A river, drunk nearly dry by the army.

Her baby, under the earth.

Esther. *Dear Lord, be with her.*

Xerxes, beside her in the wagon. A kiss, a smile . . . then his attention would shift to a commander.

Her baby, who should have been growing large and cumbersome inside her.

Abba and Ima. *Dear Lord, bless them.*

The rumble of thunder in the distance—or was it the wagon, hitting a rocky patch of terrain?

A vision of a newborn, hair dark and damp, mouth open and squalling for milk.

Zechariah. *Dear Lord, draw him to you.*

Night on the horizon, looming lonely and cold.

The feel of arms around her, lips upon her—a dream, only a dream.

The empty future. *Dear Lord, go with me.*

"Mistress, get down. Please."

She glanced at Desma's pleading face. The stone of the wall was warm under her legs, a stray twig from an ambitious vine pricked her hand. She did not recall climbing up, but she dared not admit that. They would force her back to the unrelenting solitude of her tent. Instead she smiled. "It is sturdy enough."

Theron shook his head. "I hear someone approaching. We must go."

She did not want to go. Out here the sun could wash over her. In her tent lurked only shadows that promised a lifetime of the same.

No, not a lifetime. A year, then they would be back in Susa. Xerxes would have his victory, and so he would no longer fear touching her. She would be his wife again, she would feel the blood rush through her veins once more. She would awake from this stupor. She would feel. She would live.

What a vague hope. She sighed and looked in the direction of the voices. Just as likely, this drifting would create a vast sea between them. They would not be able to reach each other, to touch each other. Love would be but a memory. So brief. So taunting.

Dear Lord, let it not be so.

His laugh rang out, and a moment later Xerxes emerged from behind a piece of wall a stade away. One thing, at least, had not changed. Her heart still galloped every time she saw him. Love and hope still fought against the fog when he looked her way.

Like he did now. She imagined he smiled, though she could not tell from here. Perhaps he did not even know it was she—she probably appeared no more than a wisp atop the wall. Still, he came her way, his strides lengthening until he drew away from his companions.

Yes, he smiled, and the gleam in his eye almost convinced her that life was as it should be. "How did I know, when I saw the lovely figure of a woman atop a dangerously decrepit wall, that it would be you?"

Her lips curved in response to the tease in his voice. "You are a man of wisdom, my love."

"And you a woman of predictable daring." He stretched his arms up to grip her waist and swung her down to the ground.

She expected him to release her and step away, as he did when helping her from the wagon. But his arms came around her, and he pulled her close. His lips claimed hers—not in the perfunctory kiss that had become normal, but hungrily, deeply.

Oh, how she wanted him back. To tangle in his arms, to lose herself in his kiss. How she wished he would whisk her away, ignoring all the men waiting for his advice. She wanted her husband. She wanted Xerxes.

All he had given her since Sardis was the king.

He broke the kiss and rested his forehead on hers like he used to do. "I have kept you confined to your wagon too long. I miss catching you on the brink of danger."

"If this is my reward, I must find a few more walls to climb. Or perhaps I can swim across the Hellespont. Scale a mountain."

He chuckled and kissed her again, then tucked her to his side and drew her along as he returned to his companions. "Are you enjoying Troy, my love?"

She hummed. They had been in the region for several days, moving slowly and listening each night to a portion of the famous *Iliad*. This morning Xerxes insisted they all travel to the site of the citadel, so that he might see where Priam ruled. "It has certainly sparked my imagination."

"I know. I keep looking out expecting to see Agamemnon's forces on the beaches, their triremes moored behind them."

She relished the feel of laughter tickling her throat. "I was thinking more of Helen. Do you think she loved Paris, or did she miss Menelaus?"

"What a girlish, romantic question." He dug his fingers into her side, and she obliged him by squealing.

"Well, a decade-long war was fought over this woman—"

"Over the theft of her," he corrected with a lopsided grin. "It could have as easily been over Odysseus's faithful dog, had he been stolen."

She let out the expected sound of protest and raised her chin. "Here I had been siding with Menelaus, thinking how sorely he must miss his wife, to go to such effort to get her back. Perhaps I ought to cheer on Paris instead. He obviously loved her enough to steal her."

"It need not be love that motivated him either—it could have been the desire to possess the most beautiful woman in the world."

His grin said he jested, so she smiled back. But the fog crept close again.

"We shall hear the end this evening. Perhaps Homer will address the question of love for you, sweet one. Although if I recall, it is more about desecrating remains and the choice between long life or a glorious death . . . ."

The concerns of men. Kasia pinned her smile in place by sheer force of will and looked out over the ruins. "I look forward to the minstrel's song. He is a talented musician."

"The best." They paused beside a perfectly preserved well. Xerxes peered down into it. "And the story inspires a man to live tall and die proud."

A soldier Kasia did not recognize stepped forward. "We ought to offer libations, my lord, to the heroes who fell here. The magi could prepare suitable sacrifices to honor them."

A shadow slithered through the fog. The arch of Xerxes' brow looked far too amenable. "Not a bad idea. It would be a fitting end to the telling of the tale."

"Xerxes." She kept her voice low, but her heart thundered in her chest. "Will your god not be angry if you offer libations to the deities of the very people you march against?"

Because she knew hers would be.

His arm fell away from her waist. "Of course not. We would only be honoring the fighting men."

It would be a mistake. She knew it, but his face told her that he would not hear a warning—that he already read it in her eyes and dismissed it.

His mouth had gone tight, his eyes sharp, his message clear. She was to hold her tongue. If she mentioned Jehovah here, in this company, she would be punished.

She swallowed and nodded. "As you will. I need to return to the camp and make myself ready for the meal." She needed to pray.

He undoubtedly knew her real intent. Otherwise his "Of course" would have sounded more gracious.

Though she turned to leave, her feet would not budge. She drew in a steadying breath and met Xerxes' hard gaze. "I love you," she whispered.

His face relaxed, his smile reemerged. He lifted her hand and kissed it. "And I you."

A few minutes later she was in her tent, on her rug, consumed by what Theron called her prayerful stupor. It was better than the fog. It could beat back the shadows.

When she opened her eyes again, the land was draped in twilight. "Mistress, you must rise. You are nearly late for the feast."

She pulled herself to a seat as Desma knelt beside her with a hairbrush. "Mistress, please—you must pull yourself out of this. You drift like a cloud from day to day, place to place. Only in your prayers do you show any intensity. I cannot think Jehovah wills you live like this."

If not, he would have to show her how to grasp hold of life again, because this was the best she could do. She dug up a smile for her friend. "I am all right."

"You are not." Desma blinked back tears that stung Kasia's conscience as surely as they did her friend's eyes. "You have lost a babe—you deserve to grieve. But Jehovah preserved your life for a reason, and it is not so you can give up now."

"I have not given up. I just . . . I cannot . . . ."

Desma sighed and made quick work of the brushing. "I know. Come, Leda has a fresh chiton and your jewelry."

It took only a moment to slip into the soft, draping fabric, to secure the ropes of gold around her waist and throat. It took only a few minutes more to hurry across the camp to the tent that housed the feast.

She paused just inside it and looked around. The women usually gathered in a corner, but since arriving in Troy they had interspersed throughout, so that they might hear the singing of the epic with their husbands. She had enjoyed leaning close to Xerxes, pretending he would not send her away as soon as the minstrel concluded for the night.

She spotted him flanked by Lalasa and Diona—both bejeweled and looking smug. Odd. Lately, if one was satisfied the other was annoyed.

Xerxes did not look at either of them. He was saying something to one of Diona's maids, something that made the girl simper and laugh. Then he took her hand and pressed a lingering kiss to her palm.

Her heart gave one thud, then seemed to stop. It should not distress her. She should not care if the king dallied with one of the slaves—it was his right. And obviously had Diona's approval.

But the fog came rushing in, forcing her back a step.

He had three concubines with him. Dozens of wives at home. Must he seek entertainment outside the marriage bonds? Did he think this girl could please him when those who knew him well could not?

Angry tears burned at her eyes, and she spun back to her tent. Perhaps this was how the other wives felt when they saw the new additions to the harem. Perhaps they wondered why he always needed more women, younger and prettier, when he had *them* already.

After that first week, she had never minded the other wives. Through her prayers she saw that they went to him in the pursuit of holy union and lawful heirs, not an evening's recreation.

No, that was unfair. This was not about the morality—masters had a right to their slaves, even in the Law. She had learned not to be jealous of the other wives because she had always known he loved her best. She was the one he called most. The one he always wanted. The one that he never tired of.

An assurance she had no longer.

She did not want to be consumed so by jealousy. Madness lay down that road, or bitter hatred. This feeling spiraling through her was the abyss from which intrigue sprang. Slander, maligning . . . even murder. She would not succumb. She would *not*.

Back inside the sanctuary of her tent, she tore the necklace from her neck and tossed it into her trunk. She squeezed her eyes shut when the smack of gold on wood reminded her of Xerxes' tempers.

He was a man of passions, strong and shifting. She loved him for it, even as she hated this newest manifestation.

Desma positioned the gold more carefully and frowned. "What has upset you, mistress? Shall we tell the king you are unwell?"

"Let him wonder." As soon as the words escaped, she winced. "I sound like Amestris."

"Never." Desma grinned, though she sobered quickly. "What has upset you?"

Had she not seen the exchange in the tent, or did it not strike her as out of the ordinary? "Does the king often entertain himself with his wives' maidservants?"

Realization lit her friend's eyes. "I should have warned you. Leda overheard the plan while you were praying. Lalasa and Diona are tired and frustrated and have decided to give your husband their maidservants, so that they might share the burden."

Burden? She sank to the ground and wrapped her arms around her knees. What she would not give to share that burden again, to take her portion and theirs. "I see."

"Mistress." Leda crouched down beside her. "It is his love for you that makes him refuse his desire for you, which has led to this. Be comforted. You still have his heart."

She nodded and pulled in a long breath. "Thank you. Please tell him I am not feeling well."

She would miss hearing the end of the epic tonight, but she would rather wonder about that than watch Xerxes watch Diona's slave. Besides, if he went through with sacrifices as planned, she had no desire to be there.

No good could come of it.

Xerxes jolted up, the cry still raw in his throat. Already the nightmare sprinted away, too fleet of foot for him to pin down any one image. But the unease lingered—worse, grew stronger with each beat of blood through his veins. Something was wrong.

The woman beside him whimpered and thrashed, nearly smacking him. He jerked away with a curse. "Wake up, woman. It is only a dream."

The wench screamed, sobbed. Xerxes grabbed his tunic and pulled it over his head as he stood. More screams pierced the air than what came from Diona's girl.

"Master?" Zethar's voice shook as he entered. Xerxes blinked at the influx of torchlight. "You are needed. Everyone—it is as if demons chase them all in their sleep."

Yes, that was what it had felt like. Some devil bearing down on him, teeth gnashing, talons flashing . . . he gave his head a fierce shake to dislodge the image. "It sounds like a massacre."

"It started all at once. Those of us awake looked around for some enemy, but there is none."

His breath came faster than he would have liked as he strode from the tent. The cries surrounded him, loud as a storm with an undertone of whimpers. It was as though Fear had taken form and slunk among them.

His other eunuchs staggered over to them. He nodded a greeting. "Wake everyone you can and have them do the same with their neighbors. It is better when out of the clutches of the nightmare."

He took off at a run for Kasia's tent. This did not feel like the god, not exactly. Perhaps the screams sounded like his uncle's had when he awoke from the dream Ahura Mazda had sent, but Xerxes had never felt him like this.

Still, what if it were from him? What if, yet again, his wrath focused on Kasia? If he lost her now, after the torture of staying away from her—

Zethar's breath shuddered beside him. "I fear for my mother, master. What if something like this has struck Persia? She has no one, no one to comfort her."

"My son!" came a shout from his right. "Spare my son, god!"

Xerxes halted, listened. From every direction came cries of names and relations, occasionally an object. The ones dearest to each heart? The things they most feared for?

He surged forward again, and reached Kasia's tent within a few strides. Light spilled out when Zethar pulled the flap open for him.

He knew not what he expected. To find her in agony and near death was his worst fear. At the least, she ought to be crying out like everyone else. He admitted the possibility that she would have already taken to her prayer rug and would be beseeching her God for whatever she thought Jehovah could do.

He did not expect this. Kasia sat in the center of her tent on a mound of pillows, singing to a collection of at least twenty children. His own he spotted immediately. A few of the others he recognized as belonging to the concubines of his brothers and cousins.

"What in Hades is going on here?"

Theron bowed and stepped near. "They started coming an hour ago, tugging nurses along with them." He motioned to the servants sleeping against the outer wall.

Peacefully. "Mistress had been praying ever since the sacrifices. She stopped seconds before the first ones entered—your three, master. She welcomed them as if she had been expecting them and started singing to them. The rest arrived soon after."

The sacrifices. Of course. Ahura Madza had been displeased, had sent the spirit of fear to show them what they could expect without his blessing.

Yet . . . that did nothing to explain how Kasia managed an oasis of peace.

Twenty-Two

Susa, Persia

Zechariah craned his head around, though he still could not take in all the splendor. "You were right, Ruana, even you could not damage his treasury. This house . . . ."

Ruana graced him with her usual coy grin. "It is beautiful, is it not? The king rewarded Asho generously for the service in Egypt that injured his leg." She motioned him down a corridor. "My room is this way. I considered bringing the table you crafted for me before, but it was far too small."

"Too small?" He chuckled and followed her into the cavernous room at the end of the hall. When he stepped inside, his eyebrows rose. "Yes, I suppose it would have been. How do you not get lost in here?"

"I like space to move around." She twirled in proof. "My husband assures me his home in Persepolis is even grander, but I do not regret that we will remain in Susa this summer. I will enjoy putting my touch on this house."

His gaze drifted to the bed behind her. The masterpiece had taken him, his father, and Joshua months to perfect. How they maneuvered it into the room he could not say. "You are pleased with the bedframe?"

"It is the most amazing thing I have ever seen." Her dimples flashed. "Were you terribly tormented while making it?"

He laughed, but a few images sprang up before his eyes. "Terribly—I could neither eat nor sleep. I became a mere ghost of a man."

"I am glad to hear it." She chuckled and settled her fingers on his arm. It took monumental effort to ignore the heat that seared his flesh. "The table will go right over here, if you would like to measure the space."

He nodded and hoped he looked nonchalant as he moved away. Never would he admit that she had been in his thoughts nearly as much as he joked. But night after night she had inspired dreams that he had beaten from his mind in the morning with relentless training.

Adam and the rest probably hated him by now.

News of her marriage reached him a fortnight ago, at which point he tried to clamp down on his errant thoughts.

His sleeping mind had not received the message.

He held up his string to the place she indicated and marked down the measurements on the wax tablet he had brought with him. "Have you heard from Bijan recently?"

"Mmm. We just received their congratulations and well wishes. They were at Troy and would soon be moving on to Abydus to cross the Hellespont. Bijan asked that I give you his greetings."

"Send him mine when next you write him." He pressed another note into the tablet and glanced her way. She leaned against a post of the bed, studying him.

His throat went dry. Perhaps it was her husband's preference that she wear linen so fine it settled over each curve like a lover's hand. He had undoubtedly been the one to provide the bejeweled belt that revealed her figure and the glistening gems in her hair. A vision for her husband to enjoy—not for Zechariah.

He forced a smile. "You look at home here, Ruana. I am glad your dreams have come true."

Something flickered in her eyes. Something dark and dissatisfied, something that spoke of illusions shattered. Something that should not have made his pulse quicken.

Her smile looked as forced as his. "Most of them, anyway." She sank onto the mattress and patted the place beside her. "Come see how well your creation turned out."

"I ought not." Far too dangerous. "I would probably get wood shavings all over it."

Was it his imagination, or did her lips quiver? "I do not care."

He did. Should. Tried to. "Ruana . . . ."

She stood again, glided his way. The flicker in her eyes returned and kindled into a flame. "I need you, Zech."

The whisper lit a million fantasies that threatened to burn him alive. He tried to force them away, yet his rebellious hand reached for her even as he lips obediently said, "You have a husband to meet your needs now."

Tears welled up in her eyes as she wove her fingers through his. "Do I? It seems to me I have one far more concerned with his own pleasures. He told me to pursue mine wherever I may."

Sympathetic anger laced through the desire. How could her husband dismiss her so quickly? How could he not appreciate the beauty and wit, the passion and tease? "If that is true, then he is the greatest of fools. Yet he seemed so excited to be marrying you."

Never in the years he had known her had Zechariah ever seen such cynicism in her eyes. "Oh, yes. I am everything he wanted in a wife. Unfortunately, he wanted less than I assumed." She reached up to trail her knuckles over his cheek.

Lord help him. How was he to fight this? Abba would tell him to turn and walk away before the Persian witch could destroy him. Mordecai would advise him to pray.

What did Abba know? He had fallen for a proper Jewish girl, had made her a proper Jewish wife. And Mordecai—Mordecai could pray for the impossible, could pray even for a woman he had been told was dead. Their realities were not his.

He drew in a shuddering breath. "We cannot . . . you are married."

"He does not care."

He buried a hand in her hair, making jewels rain to the floor. He would leave. He would. After one kiss. Just one, to show her she was desirable, no matter what her husband said.

Abydus, Mysia

Xerxes stepped upon the white dais that had been built into the hill for him and drew in a deep breath. At his feet swarmed the mass of his army. Ahead of him stretched the wide mouth of the Hellespont where it emptied into the Aegean, completely covered by his triremes. And across the river, the hard-won bridge.

Nearly seven hundred ships, penteconters and triremes, were lashed together, aligned with the currents to take the strain off the cables. They had laid down wooden sleepers between the ships, covered them in brush, and finally smoothed it all out with soil. Earthen walls had been built up on each side, so that the animals would feel as though they walked across land.

A victory. He sat upon the throne his slaves had carried up and rested his chin in his hand. He had ordered a race among his ships, games for the soldiers. They deserved the sport after marching so far and would need it before crossing into Europe over the next week.

Victory was certain with so many men . . . so why did Pythius's words haunt him? *Even the side that wins will suffer losses.*

He tried to pick out familiar faces in the swarm. Brothers. Cousins. Uncles. Sons. Friends. Trusted advisors. If all went well, they may never see battle. All of Greece could do as so many city-states already promised—welcome them, pay their tribute, and not raise a weapon.

Hopefully it would be so simple. He could march all the way to Athens and burn it to the ground, without a fight. But if someone dared oppose them, there would be battles. And where battles, then death.

The war had barely begun, and already the losses weighed on him. Some had fallen to disease, to animal attacks, even to lightning strikes. His unborn son had been taken by the god's wrath. Pythius's son by Xerxes'.

How much more blood would be on his hands by the time the war concluded? Yet if they did not die in battle, it only meant they would succumb to the ravages of time.

"When I left you half an hour ago, you had declared yourself the happiest man in history," his uncle said as he labored over to him. "And now here you are with moisture in your eyes. What disturbs the king?"

He smiled at Artabanas and motioned at his people. "Look at them, uncle. So many men, all with dreams and desires, with family and lovers. Yet not one will be alive in a hundred years."

"That is not the worst of it." Artabanas settled himself onto the edge of the dais. "Sadder still is that at some point each one would rather be dead than alive. We are so overwhelmed by tragedy that life seems long, no matter how few years we have. The god barely grants us a taste of how sweet life *could* be."

"Mmm." He had his taste, and she sat in his wagon even now, watching the ships race by. But her eyes had been so empty lately. Did she wish she were in the grave with their son? By the god, he hoped not. "There is much good too. Just look at what we have achieved, uncle."

Artabanas surveyed the Hellespont and sighed. "It is a great force, my lord."

Xerxes leaned into the side of his throne so that he could better watch his uncle's lined face. Each wrinkle had been etched by concern—some well-earned, others needless. "Yet you were against this campaign at the start."

"Sometimes I wonder even now." The old man met his gaze only briefly, then looked at the fleet again. "I know what the god promised. We felt him in the darkness. Yet still the fear that came upon us at Troy lingers in my heart."

"It is groundless. Look around you. Is there anything lacking in my fleet? In the land army?"

Artabanas twisted the frazzled end of his silver beard. "No sane man could find anything lacking in the numbers. But that is precisely where my fears rest, nephew. What harbor will we find large enough for all your ships? If a storm comes upon us, what will keep them safe?"

Xerxes shifted again but could find no comfort on his throne.

Artabanas motioned to the great flock of foot soldiers. "And the land itself will be the enemy of the army. I know you have put up as many provisions as you could, but the deeper we go into the Europe, the harder it will be to access them. The earth cannot support us, and we have already drunk one river dry."

Xerxes stood and crossed his arms over his chest. "No prizes are won by those who sit and contemplate all that could go wrong. Yes, there are risks. With risk comes the greatest reward. Besides, it is not as though we are invading a collection of nomads. There will be farms as we go."

"Which the men will descend upon like insects."

Xerxes growled and tossed a hand in the air. "Your advice is never anything but caution and fear. What would you have me do, sit at home in Persia and let the empire stagnate? If a king took such council, there would *be* no empire."

Artabanas sighed again. "I know you would have me worry about nothing, but I cannot help it. You have put so much trust in so many people—and not all of them are deserving."

"Oh, is that so? And who, O wise uncle, have I mistrusted? Do enlighten me."

His words must have been tinged with red—Artabanas paled and cleared his throat. "I have never thought Mardonius the wisest choice for a commander—"

"He is skilled in strategy."

His uncle inclined his head. "And I wish you had not given so much control to Haman—"

"My brother's dearest friend." He paced to the edge of the dais and spun back. "Any other wisdom?"

Artabanas pressed his lips together. "The Ionians . . . ."

"A whole people now?" He kicked at a loose pebble and sent it skittering down the hill. "Where there is no trouble to be found, you create it. Do you think, with Greece on the horizon, this could possibly help?"

His uncle shrank back. "You asked, my lord."

"I did not expect a whole new list of nay-saying. Though I should have, it is all you ever offer."

"That is not—"

"Enough!" He sliced a hand through the air and stomped back to his throne. "Go back to Susa, Artabanas."

"My lord—"

"*Now*. I do not need your doubt befouling the entire campaign."

The old fool stood, straightened his spine, and rolled back his shoulders. And looked not so old, nor such a fool. "I will go. I will go and leave you to your rash advisors who flatter your vanity and push you into folly. And you will regret it when they lead you straight to disaster."

Xerxes' fingers clamped down on the armrest. He gritted his teeth together. "Get you gone, old man, before I dishonor the memory of my father by saying what is on my mind."

Artabanas spun and strode down the hill.

Too late. The day lay in ruins at Xerxes' feet.

Kasia glanced up at Zethar as they walked. "Is he terribly angry?"

"Brooding." The eunuch sighed. "Angry brooding."

Her heart thudded. Not since the news of the first bridge's collapse had she been called upon to soothe an enraged Xerxes. With all that happened since then, she was not so sure she would still be able to. "Has no one else spoken with him?"

"He will not let any in, not after Mardonius came and praised his wisdom in sending Artabanas home."

The corner of her mouth pulled up. "Being told he was right angered him more?"

Zethar smiled too. "You know the king."

Yes, she did. Even now. Still, she breathed a silent prayer as they neared her husband's tent. When they stopped, Zethar reached for the flap and motioned her inside.

An empty bowl hit the wall a foot to her right even as Xerxes shouted, "How many times must I say *no one is to come in*, Zethar?"

She must be mad—she had missed this. "Only once more—I am his last resort."

"Kasia." He spun to her with surprise on his face. "Which side will you take, then? That I should not have dishonored my uncle by sending him home, or that I never should have let him come at all?"

She entered his tent for the first time in months. In here was no fog. No shadow. She moved to him and rested her arms on his chest, her eyes closing in bliss. "You miss him already?"

A beat of silence, then a breath of a laugh as his arms closed around her. "It will not be the same without his anxious frowns. Which seemed like a good thing at the time—but now who will check me?"

She opened her eyes again and grinned. "Shall I take a seat on your council? The one beside Artemisia, perhaps, so that the females can bolster one another."

He chuckled and ran a hand slowly, gloriously up her back. "She bought her seat with five ships and a tyranny. What do you bring to give your advice credence?"

"Your heart." It nearly came out as a question, but she forced her tone to hold steady.

He rewarded her with a smile that knit together a few pieces of her being. "An unfair advantage against the rest of my advisors—I am afraid I cannot let you use that in matters of war. You ought to have let me give you a few cities. You could have rallied men from them and earned a command."

"Ah, missed opportunities." She snuggled against him. At least she was not missing this one, had not let her fear keep her from coming with Zethar.

He hummed into her hair and danced his fingertips down her back again. Were she a feline, she would have purred. "I have barely seen you since we left Troy," he murmured.

"You have been avoiding me—not once did you come ride with me." She looked into his face and saw a struggle, quickly resolved.

He sighed. "I was still confounded by that fear that swept through my army—and why in the world every child within a mile came to you before it struck."

Only the ones young and innocent enough to hear the whisper of Jehovah, but old enough to guide their nurses. She smiled at the memory of rapt little faces.

He tugged on a piece of her hair. "You have been avoiding me as well. Not once have you shared a meal with me."

It was her turn to sigh. "I did not want to watch."

His brows drew together. "Watch what?"

"You charming Lalasa's and Diona's servants."

He put his hands on her shoulders and set her back a few inches. "You are jealous of slaves? When you never were of the other wives?"

Her gaze fell to the heavy chain of gold around his neck. "I know. Perhaps it is because I knew I would share you with your other wives. I did not realize . . . ." She bit her lip and shook her head. "And I never *had* to be jealous before. Before, I was your favorite."

"Lovely Kasia." He cupped her face, lifting it up. She blinked away tears. It had been so long since he had called her that. "The slaves are nothing—I accept them only out of kindness to the concubines, who apparently weary of my demands." A smile teased his mouth. "I have been too hard on them. I want them to be you, and they never are."

She could be her, if only he would let her. "I am sorry I have avoided you, my love."

"As I am. No more, hmm? Otherwise I may send some other unfortunate relation home in disgrace, until I am left with only my own wisdom."

She smiled. And when he lowered his head, she strained up to meet him, curled her arms around him. The heat of the kiss fused their lips together and brought life pounding through her again—the glory of it gave her wings.

All too soon he broke away with a moan. "You ought to go."

"No." She held him tighter and trailed her lips down his jaw. "Let me stay. Please, Xerxes. I cannot go on like this. Let me stay. Let me live tonight."

"Kasia . . . ."

She pressed closer and nipped at his ear. "Do you not know how I have missed you?"

"Until these last few days, we were beside each other half the day." The insistence was weak.

"But there was always someone else on your other side." She ran her nose down his neck. "I have missed touching you."

His heart galloped against his chest. "You have touched me."

"Not like this. It has been like that first week after we met—I have dreamt of you every night, but awakened to realize I could not have you."

His hands settled on her hips. "You will drive me to insanity, woman."

"Fair enough—I will go with you." She pressed a kiss to the hollow of his throat.

"Kasia." The impatient twitch of his fingers promised pleasure, but his face still showed an unresolved will. "I know you want a child—"

"It is not about a child." She met his gaze so he could see that in her eyes, then kissed his lips softly. "It is about you. I want *you*, Xerxes, nothing more."

"It is not that simple."

"Why not?" She forced her fingers to relax so that she might sweep them over his broad shoulders, down his chest, around his back. If she had to use every weapon of the senses to prevail, then so be it. She could not spend another night with nothing but dreams of him for company. "If you want no risk of a child, then just hold me. Let me kiss you."

The passion was there, smoldering in his eyes. "Kissing you is never enough, my love."

"But ignoring me is?"

There—capitulation. "Ignoring you has been torture. The less I have you, the more I want you."

Anticipation shot up her spine. "What, then?"

His mouth quirked up into the grin she loved, even as he swept her into his arms. "I suppose I shall have to show you."

TWENTY-THREE

Xerxes awakened slowly, reluctant to relinquish the perfect dream. A warm body nestled behind him, but when consciousness got hold of him, he would no longer be able to fool himself into thinking it Kasia.

His eyes flew open, his senses went on alert. Curse and praise battled for a place on his tongue—he was a fool all right, one who ought to wish it a dream. Who knew what penalty the god would exact for this, but so help him . . . he rolled over, his breath catching in his throat. Hopefully the god would credit him for trying.

A smile won dominion of his mouth as he settled in again, his ear against Kasia's chest so he could hear the patient rhythm of her heart. Last night it had raced, swifter than any ship in the fleet.

He trailed a hand up her leg and tried to focus his mind on the coming day rather than the night past. There was much to do. Deliver the planned speech to his command, asking for their total dedication before they crossed into Europe. Then the first of them would put foot to bridge.

Kasia's fingers feathered through his hair, and her breath hitched, released. "Am I dreaming again?"

He chuckled and propped himself up. Her eyes were clear and bright again, her smile at the ready. He leaned over to kiss her. "I never meant to hurt you, my love. I only want to protect you."

She turned onto her side and draped an arm around him. "Will you try to banish me again?"

"I never banished you." He smiled at the arch of her brows. "Fine, call it what you like. And no. I cannot. Not anymore."

"Good. Because if you tried it, I would sneak in and kiss any objections away."

"I am surprised you did not try it before."

The shadows flickered through her eyes again, and he silently cursed himself. She rested her head against his arm and pulled in a long breath. "What of your fears?"

"They are still valid." He sighed and traced his fingers over her back. "I sent my uncle home for letting fears rule him. I may be a hot-headed fool, but I try not to be a hypocrite."

"Good." She moistened her lips and met his gaze again. "I dreamt of a child last night. A little girl, born when we get back to Susa."

He may turn into Artabanas yet—fear iced through him, threatening to paralyze. He swallowed it down. "Such dreams are expected, my love. The wishes of your heart, combined with the day's events. Nothing more."

Her eyes shuttered and her muscles tensed. "My dreams are not allowed to mean anything, though you have mustered millions based on yours?"

He sighed. "I have never heard of a dream prophesying a girl-child."

"Of course not." She pulled away and sat up, each movement an angry jerk. "History only records such things if the child goes on to greatness, and women matter little."

"Kasia—"

"You read the history of men. Women hear different tales, ones passed down from mother to daughter. I would not be the first to dream of a female child that is new in the womb." She looked around and grabbed her chiton. "Perhaps Jehovah sends the dreams when he knows his daughters need encouragement."

His jaw tightened, but he forced it open. "Look at me."

It took her several moments to obey.

Xerxes drew in a long breath. "You find comfort in your Jehovah, and in spite of your claims last night, you obviously desire a baby. I can stop neither, though both could anger *my* god."

"I am not afraid of—"

He held up a hand. "If you want to take your place beside me again, you will obey me in this. I cannot keep you from praying. I cannot stop a child from growing inside you, not as long as I keep you in my bed. But you will speak of neither. I will not tempt the god."

She pulled the garment over her head. "Why do you cling to faith in a god you think you can fool with silence?"

He stood too. "I will have your word on this, Kasia."

Her gaze focused on nothing, her chest heaved. Would she refuse? Had those claims of needing only him last night been a ploy to get back into his bed for the sake of a child?

Her shoulders sagged, and she turned into his chest. "You will have my silence. But both Jehovah and a growing child speak for themselves."

"I will deal with that if it arises."

She tilted up a face filled with challenge. "When."

Infuriating woman. How had he ever mistaken her for compliant?

And why did he love her more today than ever before?

Doriscus Fortress, Thrace

Kasia rolled over but could not find the heat she sought. Refusing to open her eyes just yet, she reached out . . . and found nothing but pillows. With a sigh, she gave in and looked for her husband. "Xerxes, what in the world are you doing?"

He was already dressed and stood in the middle of the chamber, an assortment of tablets on the table before him. He smiled at her over his shoulder. "Just reviewing the numbers."

A chuckle tickled her throat. "I doubt they have changed since yesterday. Come back to bed."

"I cannot rest, I am too eager to be on our way." He turned back to the table, mumbling, "One million, seven hundred thousand men. Amazing."

She rolled her eyes, but a smile tugged at her mouth. "Do not forget the twelve hundred seven triremes." She sat up and stretched, knowing she could not sleep with him counting in the lamplight. A shame—it was their last night in the bed she had enjoyed this week.

"Oh, I have not forgotten. You know, adding together the men in the fleet and those on land, it is well over two million. If we were to count all the servants and support peoples as well . . . surely it would be more than five."

She suspected some of the numbers had been inflated, but she would not be the one to tell him so. Slipping her garment on, she stood—and immediately regretted it. The flip of her stomach rivaled the acrobats that had performed for them last night. "Oh."

Xerxes spun to face her, frowning. "Are you ill?"

Frustration churned along with the nausea. "It is nothing." Nothing he would let her speak of. He would storm out if she dared mention that sickness generally started at this point in a pregnancy.

"You barely touched your food last night, so perhaps you are only hungry. Zethar brought in fruit and bread if you would like some."

Suddenly aware of the yeasty scent of the fresh loaf, she dashed to the corner to retch into the waste pot.

Xerxes' silence pounded at her when she rose again. He stood like a statue, his face set in an expression of hard denial. Then he spun back to his tablets.

Well, if he was so bent on calculations, he could do this one and realize the symptoms were right on cue for her to have conceived at Abydus. He probably had already, otherwise he would be concerned rather than silent. How long would he ignore it? Did he not realize the fear could be better dealt with together?

It seemed she had only managed to secure half her marriage. He still would not talk to her about anything that mattered. Troops and surrenders, landscapes and acquaintances. Nothing more.

She wiped her mouth on a rag. In some ways, half a marriage was better than the echo she had had since Sardis. The fog stayed at a distance. But the shadows—the shadows seemed to creep a little closer each time she had to close her mouth on her faith.

Dear Jehovah, let not my heart cost me my soul.

Xerxes tossed a tablet down with a thwack. "Zethar! Rouse everyone, and let us get an early start. I tire of dawdling."

Kasia shook her head. It would take as long to wake everyone up as it would to let them rise on their own. But when the king issued a command . . . .

Her servants stumbled in, Desma still rubbing at her eyes. She narrowed them upon spotting Kasia. "You are pale. How do you feel this morning?"

"Nauseous." Kasia pressed her lips together when Xerxes flew from the chamber. "Which apparently displeases my husband."

"He fears for you." Desma guided her to a seat and pulled back her hair. "Your belongings are packed and ready to go."

Kasia shut her eyes while Desma worked her hair into a braid. The farther they traveled into Europe, the more she longed to go home. She missed the sun-baked land of her birth. The parents she had not seen in two years. The cacophony of siblings scrambling around her. She longed for the friend three doors down who would dream with her about impossibilities. She wanted to be surrounded one more time by others who knew Jehovah.

She loved her husband, even this fierce version that had ruled since his terrible god had gripped him. But she did not want to need him so much, did not want the fog to hover, ready to pounce if he turned his back on her again.

"Would you like to eat before we go, mistress?" Leda asked.

Kasia pressed a hand to her roiling stomach. "Perhaps you could bring something with us for later."

They left the king's chamber and made their way to the walls of the fortress, where dawn was only a blush on the eastern horizon. Kasia let her head fall back so she could look up at the canopy of dimming stars. She missed watching for the first evening star with Xerxes, but now every evening was a feast, gathered for months in advance by those with farms along their path. The best they could find for the king who declared them his subjects and took with him everything they set up.

In so many ways, her husband was the most sensitive of men. Yet he never seemed to notice the strain of the farmers whose livelihood his people consumed in an hour. He never looked over his shoulder to note the destruction they left in their wake.

At least he only demanded one meal a day from the landowners. Any more might prove the end of them.

She oversaw the transfer of her things and settled onto the seat of her wagon as morning spilled soft and golden onto the land. Zad stretched out on the bench beside her with a spoiled whoof and rested his head in her lap.

Kasia smiled and scratched behind his ears. A few minutes later the wagon rolled into its place in the procession, and she turned to her maids. "I recalled another Psalm yesterday, if you would like me to teach it to you."

They grinned and reached for their instruments. She was blessed indeed to have servants willing to learn of her faith, to pray with her and support her.

Even if no one else did.

Mid-morning brought Zethar to the wagon with a weary smile of greeting. "The king wishes to know if you feel well enough for company."

She grinned at the eunuch. "Which is to say, he does not wish to come if my nausea will force the truth upon him? Well, tell the king he may join me without risk to his blinders."

Zethar chuckled. "And you would *actually* have me say . . . ?"

"I feel much better and would love some company."

"That I will gladly deliver."

She exchanged a grin with her servants and urged Zad onto the floor. Leaning out the opening, she spotted Xerxes riding her way.

A cry from the side of the road grabbed her attention. It looked to be a peasant, a man gnarled and old. He called out, "Zeus! Zeus!"

Xerxes reined in his steed, his curiosity evident. "Why do you call to your god, old man?"

The native fell to his knees at the edge of the road, arms lifted. "Mighty Zeus, why do you parade about under the guise of a Persian and call yourself Xerxes? If you wish to destroy Greece, you had no need to bring all of mankind with you—you could have done it under your own power."

Xerxes tossed his head back in a roar of amusement. The old man looked baffled, but not offended. Still chuckling, Xerxes shook his head. "Where is your home?"

The man motioned toward a ramshackle hovel not far off the road. Xerxes pulled out a few rounds that glistened gold in the sun. "If I am Zeus, then these must have been fired in the kilns of Hephaistos—perhaps that will increase their value."

He tossed the handful of darics at the man, who scooped them up as if they were indeed manna from heaven. "Bless you, mighty Zeus, for hearing the prayers of a poor husbandman!"

Xerxes chuckled again and urged his horse alongside the wagon. Kasia shook her head. "Greetings, Zeus. I would offer you hospitality, but I already promised a seat to my husband."

"Since when does Zeus care about such bonds?" He swung from horse to wagon in one smooth movement and pulled her close to nibble on her neck. "Mmm, mortal flesh. Much softer than what can be found on the goddesses at Olympus."

"You are terrible," she said on a laugh, squirming away from the tickle of his beard. Wishing every moment might be like this.

He caught her lips and held them captive for a long moment. When he pulled away, his smile looked content. "I have asked the Spartan to join us."

She had met Demaratus several times, always briefly. "Any reason?"

"He is the only man I trust with experience in a Greek military. I would put a few questions to him."

"I have heard only a little about his people. Is it true all the men wear their hair long, as he does?"

Xerxes smiled. "Indeed. They hold that long hair makes a handsome man more beautiful and an ugly man fiercer. What do you think, having seen Demaratus? Is there truth in that?"

"In order to judge, I would have to see *you* with long hair, my love, and decide if it could possibly increase your handsomeness." She grinned and wove her fingers through his. "Otherwise I only look at men and think, 'He is nothing compared to Xerxes.'"

"The answer of a woman either madly in love or smart enough to flatter her jealous husband." He chuckled and lifted their joined hands, kissed a knuckle. "I have also heard they all exercise nude the morning of a battle, so that their enemies see their fitness, their fierceness, and are stricken with awe and terror."

She could not tamp down a grin. "And shall I witness that for you, as well, so that I can lend you my opinion on its effectiveness?"

Zethar cut off his bark of laughter by leaning in to say, "The Spartan, master."

Xerxes winked at her and murmured, "You will pay for that one later, my sweet. Now scoot over, if you will."

She obliged, and Xerxes slid with her so that the once-king of the Lacedaemonians could vault up and take the spot on the end.

Demaratus greeted them with a respectful nod. "Good morning, my lord. Lady."

"Demaratus." Xerxes shifted a bit so that he was facing his guest. "I have a question for you, if you would offer me your advice."

Demaratus's brows lifted slightly. "Of course. What is it the king wishes to know?"

"About the Greeks. Tell me, will any of them stand their ground against me? It seems to me all the armies would have to unite to have any chance against my forces, which is unprecedented. I would hear your opinion."

One of the Spartan's brows edged higher than the other. "Would you have a truthful answer, my lord, or a comforting one?"

Xerxes grinned. "Comfort avails little on the battlefield. Speak honestly, my friend—you will be no worse off for it, even if it displeases me."

"Very well. The Greeks are an admirable people, hewn by intelligence and law, which alone have fended off poverty and despotism." Demaratus paused and tilted his head. "But I need only speak of the Spartans to answer your question. There is nothing you could ever say to them, my lord, to keep them from taking up arms against you. The Spartans will fight, even if no other state does."

Xerxes folded his arms. "Yet it is a small state, your Lacedaemon."

"True. There may only be a thousand fighting men, possibly fewer. But they will fight."

Something tightened in Kasia's chest, though she knew not what it was. Something that wanted to believe such determination was possible, even as she hoped no one would really challenge her husband.

Xerxes laughed. "You speak madness, my friend. What reasonable person would pit himself against ten enemies, much less a thousand to his one? Especially where each man is free and so has no leader?"

Demaratus smiled, but it was hard and a little sad. "I knew my answer would not endear me to you, but with all respect, my lord, you cannot understand our souls. You are the only free man in all your empire—everyone else, even your own brothers, are your slaves. They must obey you or be killed. Your rule is founded on authority and obedience."

She could well imagine Xerxes' glower. "That is what *rule* is founded on, Demaratus, not just mine."

"In a tyranny, yes. And you, my lord, wield it with wisdom. But when you march against a people suckled on freedom since birth, you cannot expect them to bow to slavery when once they were free to decide for themselves."

Xerxes waved a hand. "Illusion. A man may think his decisions free, but everyone has a master."

"And for the Spartans it is one unchanging law—one must never turn tail and run from a battle, no matter how many men one fights. One wins, or one dies trying. They fear this law, even more than your men fear you—and it makes them free. It makes them rise early in the morning to keep themselves strong, it makes them strive to be the best. Not for riches or to avoid punishment, but for respect and honor. You have heard the saying, I am sure—a man is freer in Sparta than anywhere else in the world."

Xerxes' shoulders relaxed again. "Your helots might disagree."

Demaratus chuckled. "Let us say, then, a *free* man is freer in Sparta than anywhere. And a slave, more a slave. We are an extreme people, born of an extreme land."

Kasia leaned back and drew in a long, silent breath. That kind of freedom . . . he was right that no one in Persia could know it. Her husband spoke law and held the power of life and death in his hands. She trusted him—but before she knew him? In her father's house, the law of Persia was obeyed only out of fear of reprisal.

Yet such freedom made sense to her, made her soul take note. She knew what it was to serve a law that made one better, that one obeyed out of holy fear.

Love the Lord your God with all your soul, with all your mind, with all your strength.

Often enough she had rebelled against first her father and now her husband—which rarely worked to her advantage. But the Law . . . it taught her how to grasp freedom of the soul through her love of Jehovah.

Xerxes said, "It is difficult to believe such a life could be sustained."

The Spartan nodded. "Our small size is what allows it. Sparta is largely cut off from the rest of the world. Our coinage was made deliberately heavy and awkward so that it would fade from use, and we trade with few. Where your nation survives by the expansion of empire, ours survives by isolation and unification. Even our women have daily exercises to keep them in peak physical form—they are too precious to be risked in battle, but their participation in the ritual is crucial to our way of life. Spartans are warriors. It is the condition of our soul. The Lacedaemonians will hold true to that, even against you."

"I still find it difficult to believe an entire race would choose to fight when loss is certain—but we shall see." His smile was audible in his voice. "Thank you for speaking with me so forthrightly, Demaratus. I will think on what you said."

Kasia sighed. As would she.

TWENTY-FOUR

Susa, Persia

Esther paused at the end of the street to pull in a fortifying breath. The palace lay before her, only a minute's walk away. Her cousin would be at the gate. Just beyond this street. Around one corner.

She lifted her chin and repositioned the basket on her arm. Today marked her fifteenth year. It seemed fitting that she evaluate who she had become, where she stood in life. But she had seen no crossroads, not if she continued on her current path.

So then, she must make one.

If Zechariah wanted a woman who went out into town more, then she would take her cousin a cake. If she must shine like a star to gain his notice, then she would douse herself in gold dust.

She planted her foot on the street . . . and sighed.

Did she really expect Zechariah to tumble into love just because she walked to the palace? She may now be fifteen, but that was the dream of a child.

"Are you lost, beautiful one?"

Esther jumped and turned to where a man leaned against the post of his door. He swept a lazy gaze over her. Perhaps some would have called the glint in his eyes appreciation—it sent a chill of warning up her spine.

She forced a swallow and a polite smile. "No, I am not lost. Only headed for the palace."

After a glance at the walls looming ahead, he sent her a smile he probably meant to be charming. "Indecisive then. Visiting someone you would rather not see?"

"Not at all."

He pushed off the post and stepped into the street. His stance carried no overt threat, but his eyes made her want to run the other direction.

He quirked a brow. "I am heading that way myself. I would be honored to deliver such a beautiful young woman safely to her destination. You are going to see . . . your husband, who serves at the palace? Perhaps I would know him—I serve there as well."

"I . . . ." What could she say? To admit she had no husband would not help her. But he would catch her in a lie. She pasted on another smile. "Thank you, but I must run home to fetch something I forgot."

"It *is* a fine morning for a stroll about the city." He stepped to her side and had the audacity to grip her elbow. "Allow me to escort you. I would meet your father, since your eyes say you have no husband."

Why would the man not leave her alone? She tried to tug her elbow free. "That is not necessary."

He would not release her. "Your father is at war, perhaps, and you cannot invite me home? Your mother then."

"You presume too much. Now unhand me."

He laughed, as if honestly thinking she jested. "And give up all chances of learning more about you? I would never forgive myself. I intend no harm, lovely one, only a few more moments to bask in your beauty."

A tingle brushed her neck a second before a shadow fell over her. "The young lady has made her wishes known."

Zechariah. Relief washed through her even as she wondered what he was doing on this street, with no delivery cart and in finer clothes than usual.

The Persian tugged her a little closer. "I saw her first, friend."

Zechariah's lips turned up in a cold, hard smile. He reached out, palm up. "Shall I see you home, Esther?"

She put her fingers into his. "I would appreciate it."

The other man relinquished her elbow with an exaggerated sigh—and a glint of resentment in his eye. "I see. Well, a man cannot be blamed for trying when he comes across such astounding beauty."

Zechariah made a noise that crossed doubt with threat and tucked her hand into his elbow. Hopefully he did not notice the way her fingers trembled. "Come, dear one," he said. "Let us go home."

The Persian said nothing, but she did not miss the way he measured Zechariah's height and form before spinning back into his house. Would he have challenged him had Zechariah not looked so strong?

This was ridiculous. She had never so much as seen the man before—what made him think he had any claim to her, any right to stake one?

Zechariah led her quickly around the corner. "What are you doing here without escort?"

And what made *this* man think he had a right to judge her, when *he* was the one who had told her to take her cousin a meal? She jerked her hand free and stormed ahead of him. "It is a perfectly respectable area, and I can hardly expect Martha or Jonah to leave their tasks because of my whim."

He caught up to her in a single stride. "You could have brought Eglah. She may be no bigger than you, but there is strength to be found in numbers."

Esther halted and spun on him. "I should not need a companion to walk a reputable street in the light of day, especially in a year when so few men are in Susa. Tell me,

Zechariah, why do those who remain think they can have their way on everything?"

He looked at her as if she had sprouted a tree from her ears. "That is surely not aimed at me—all I did was rescue you. Which, I might add, you have not thanked me for."

"I would not have been here to need rescuing had *you* not told me to get out of the house more."

Now he looked amused, the infuriating man. "You say you are in my debt for my perfect timing? Nonsense. I am only glad I could help."

"Why did I even listen to you? You are as much a fool as that Persian, thinking your will ought to make a thing so." She marched toward home again.

Zechariah chuckled and kept pace. "I too am glad we could resolve it so easily, by my mere presence. Though I would not have minded smashing his face in, in defense of my—"

"If you call me your sister again, I will smash *your* face in."

He laughed and pulled her to a halt. "I was going to say 'friend.' Esther, this is unlike you."

She focused her gaze on the house beyond his shoulder. "Nothing ever works as I think it should."

"Such is life. Do you think mine is what I thought it should be?"

For a moment, she just stared at him. "Because you are not a soldier? Yes, Zechariah, you are so cursed. You have a successful business. Talent and skill with both wood and weapons. A slew of friends who look up to you, female eyes on you everywhere you go. However can you get through the day?"

"Sarcasm." He tilted his head and blinked at her. "Do I know you?"

The fight went out of her, and her shoulders slumped. "I wonder that sometimes too."

"Esther." He touched her cheek to bid her look at him—something he had done often enough over the years. This time when she met his gaze, she could almost convince herself she saw awareness in his eyes. Almost. "One over-aggressive dolt should not ruin your special day. Take it as affirmation of the beautiful young woman you have become."

She attempted a smile—he did, after all, remember it was her birthday—but it fizzled out quickly. "It is not only that, though it is a perfect example. When he approached me, I had no clever words to save myself. Why can I not be like Kasia? You ought to have heard her that day the Persian man approached her, right before her death. She was witty and smart. She was fearless, while I cowered behind her."

His thumb brushed over her cheek and set her heart to hammering. "You were a child, Esther, and Kasia . . . she was too reckless for her own good. It is better to escape quietly where you may."

"Her recklessness earned her admiration and respect, and the man let her go—with a romantic story no less. My cowering did not help with escape at all."

"You did not cower."

"Sometimes I feel as though I live my life in fear, Zech. You would not understand that." She turned away, fearful even now that she would see distaste in his eyes, and started for home again. "Always afraid those I love will leave me. That I will not be what I ought. That when the days of my life are fulfilled, I will have no story to tell."

"Esther—"

"Kasia may have died too soon, but still she *lived*. She had suitors eager to marry her even though she had no dowry. She had a stranger who fell a little in love with her after one interaction."

"And she had fears." Zechariah leapt into her path. "She feared letting you down. She feared not being able to show you that life could be full, even with loss shadowing you. I imagine when she was being carried away, she feared how devastated *you* would be."

She sucked in a breath only to heave it out again. Unbidden, memories crashed through her. Kasia, outside in the kitchen that last day, joking about suitors. Kasia, searching her house for Esther's bracelet. Kasia, so full of life and love for others.

Kish, face ashen as rain poured over him, with the news that Kasia had sneaked off to the river and had not returned. The panic, the fear, the tears that rivaled the monsoon.

Zechariah the next morning, telling her to face reality. Holding her, drying her tears, fetching the silver bracelet for her. As if that mattered after losing the only true friend she had ever known.

His fingers encircled her wrist now, as if the same images flashed before his eyes. "You never wear your mother's bracelet anymore."

"It was broken," she said, gaze on his hand. It practically swallowed her wrist, and the skin was work-roughened. Nails chipped, cuticles uneven. Scratches marred his knuckles. Strong hands, honest hands. Oh, for them to hold her every day. "That was why it fell off."

"So get it repaired." His voice was a low thrum, like the creak of wood warming in the sun.

"Then it would not be the same bracelet my mother gave me." And she would remember that last day, full of hope and fear, every time she put it on.

He put a hand against her cheek, again urging her face up. She wanted to resist, knowing he would see how much she loved him, how much she wanted what he refused to give. But she looked up—and forgot how to breathe. His eyes had never gleamed so intensely for her before, he had never gazed at her like this, then glanced at her mouth. Surely he did not mean to kiss her—it must only be her overwrought imagination, so desperate for his attention. He had made his feelings—or lack of them—clear many a time.

But they could change. He could realize she had grown up. Surely it was possible that this one thing might go right for her.

He swallowed, then released her and took a step back.

And that, she supposed, was the answer to that.

Zechariah mentally cursed himself and took another step back for good measure. Still he was unsure what had happened. Memories had crowded him, and her pain, so sharp even after two years, had pierced him through. But never before had that made her seem like anything but a sister.

It was not *her*. It could not be her—it was only that his mind had already been on dangerous matters, his senses already heightened. That was all.

He cleared his throat and fought the urge to sprint away. "Come, we should hurry. I am late."

Her brows drew together, and she lifted her hands to clutch her elbows. Her basket swayed. "What were you even doing here, Zech? You are not dressed for work."

He bit back an angry defense and smiled. "I have a few measurements to take. Since there will be no labor involved, I thought I ought not drag shavings with me."

Her casual nod said she saw no reason to question him. But the caution in her eyes said she had noted the shift in his behavior.

Jehovah have mercy, if he were not careful he could destroy her along with himself. Why had no one ever warned him that giving in to one sin would tempt him to others? He did not want to think of Esther like that. He would not. No matter how soft her skin, no matter how forcefully it struck him right now that her face was absolutely flawless.

He would *not*.

She looked away. "I can get myself home without incident from here."

A responsible friend would disagree and insist on seeing her home. But then, a responsible friend would not be every bit the threat to her that the stranger had been. Given his thoughts at the moment, she would be safer without his company. "Very well. I will see you at the festivities tonight." Hopefully his grin looked as unconcerned and teasing as ever. "I have been working on your gift for months."

Her usual sweet smile curled her lips up, and she glanced at his face before turning away. "Have a good day. And Zechariah—thank you. For stepping in with the Persian."

He only trusted himself to nod, then he turned and hurried past the street he had found her on, to the next. Onward to the house that had become far too familiar and the back entrance that soured his stomach every time he used it.

But the moment he stepped into the chamber, shame lost its footing. Ruana sat on her bed waiting for him. "There you are—I expected you a bit sooner."

He pulled his tunic over his head. "I ran into a friend who needed help."

"Always the hero. Now it is my turn to be saved—from my longings. I have missed you."

"It has only been a week." But he pulled off his shoes and hurried to the bed.

Best to lose himself quickly, before he could think too much on how unheroic he felt.

TWENTY-FIVE

Malis, Trachis

Xerxes paced to the end of the tent, then back again. His every muscle hardened and tensed, his blood ran hot. He glanced at the scout he had sent out five days ago then at Demaratus, who still sat with infuriating surety.

Arrogance, nothing but arrogance. Three hundred men. Three *hundred* men stood before the walls in the pass they called Thermopylae, refusing to budge. He spun on the scout. "Tell me again what you saw."

The man moistened his lips. "The Lacedaemonians stood along the wall, their weapons and armor at their feet. They exercised nude, then brushed their hair."

"Brushed their hair." Xerxes glared at Demaratus.

The Spartan smiled. "If they are going to die, they want to look their best."

"And die they shall, if they do not move from the pass. I have given them four days."

Damaratus sighed and his smile faded. "I warned you that the Spartans would fight. But once you get through them, you will encounter no other resistance."

Why, then, did they even bother? There was no question that they would be killed. "So be it. Send out the Medes and Cissians—and bring any prisoners back to me alive."

"There will be no prisoners."

Xerxes ignored him and left the shade of the tent. The summer sun beat down, but with less intensity than his men were accustomed to. To them it would be like the finest of spring days. And this battle would be little more than an exercise.

Three hundred men. Absurd. "Zethar, have my throne set up on the hill so I can watch the battle."

"Yes, master." His eunuch turned halfway, then paused. "Will the king still be dining with Kasia this morning?"

He looked at the hill that would give him the best viewpoint, at the troops that would have to be put in formation and marched to the pass. There was time. "I suppose."

Her presence might soothe the building anticipation. Then again, it could just as easily do the opposite. The round of her stomach was hard to ignore these days. And the more frustrated she got with him for refusing to acknowledge it, the more frustrated he got with her for not seeing why he needed to.

They had already lost four hundred ships in the Hellespontine winds, crucial supply vessels among them. The Egyptians' camels had been hunted by lions in the pass near the canal at Mount Athos. Fifteen more ships had been captured by the Greeks. He must ensure as few other losses as possible.

Yet when he ducked into her tent she was, as always, on the floor in prayer. "Kasia, get up. I have no time for this today—the Medes and Cissians even now prepare to march on the pass."

She rose immediately—but the shadow in her eyes said his tone grated. Well, that was only fair. Her continual insistence on praying to a God that cared nothing for his campaign grated on him.

Then she smiled, and he sighed. Perhaps the trouble lay not with her God—perhaps it lay in the fact that not one among his people was as faithful to Ahura Mazda as she to Jehovah. He opened his arms to her and gave her a kiss of greeting.

When the babe in her stomach nudged him, he pulled away and frowned into Kasia's grin. How far along was she now? She was larger than she had gotten with their son, and never had he felt the boy's movement like this.

Everyone knew she carried his babe, but none spoke of it since he refused to. He could see the strain of that in her eyes. Still, he could not regret it. Not if it saved her.

"There is to be a battle, then?" She turned to where her servants had set out a meal for them and sat on her favorite cushion.

"It is inevitable. We must have access to the pass."

Her hum sounded sad. "They will all be killed. That too is inevitable, but it is a shame. They are a noble people."

He sat beside her, gaze locked on her profile. Something in her expression . . . . "Tell me you do not empathize with these arrogant rebels."

She turned peaceful eyes on him. "Can I not admire them for their dedication to their law, for their pursuit of honor? Seeing the line of them in front of that wall . . . it helps me understand the spirit of my eldest brother."

He tore off a piece of bread with more force than necessary. "Your brother would stand against my army?"

"My brother would have been part of your army had our father allowed it. I never understood what drove Zechariah to learn to fight. I never imagined what our forefathers must have felt when surrounded by the Babylonian army. I do now."

"Oh, that is right." He tossed the bread back down without tasting it. "Your father raised you to think I am a cruel oppressor, so obviously you take the side of the rebels."

She paused with her cup halfway to her mouth. "I may understand why they resist you, but I do not take their side."

Xerxes studied the angle of her chin, the gleam of her eyes, the straightness of her spine. "You actually believed all that nonsense Demaratus spouted about free men? You think it logical for them to fight to the death rather than preserving their lives by bowing to me?"

"Logical? No." She put her chalice down again. "But I think it faithful to what they believe."

He raised his wine to her in a mock salute. "Well, you are the expert on faith."

Her jaw clenched, she swallowed. Then she gave her usual grin. "Thank you for admitting it."

Xerxes sighed. She did not want to tease him out of his mood today, but still she tried. He ought to let himself be teased. "Forgive me, my love. I apparently have a bit of Darius in me—it pains me to see a battle on the horizon and know I must observe from a distance."

She slid closer to him and nestled into his side. "I did not mean to make you think I would wish the Spartans success. I may admire their bravery, but that falls far short of how proud I am of all you have accomplished."

"I know." Or at least, he ought not waste time debating it. "Let us eat."

They did so in relative silence, and afterward his gaze fell on her stomach again. A small bump twitched the fabric of her chiton. He reached out to cover the movement with his hand before he could think better of it. The babe kicked again.

Kasia let out a contented sigh but otherwise said nothing. Xerxes' eyes slid shut. Perhaps silence was enough. There had been no problems, no threats from an angry god. Either Ahura Mazda did not care about a girl-child, or he was appeased by how little attention Xerxes had given it—or perhaps how little she had spoken of Jehovah lately. One or all approaches was working.

Still. He could afford no risks today. "Sweet one, I need you to promise me something."

"What is it?"

He opened his eyes and studied her. In some moments the beauty of her face still struck him, sucked the breath from his lungs. But most of the time he saw *her*, rather than her features. The passion that ignited his own. The love that lit her eyes whenever she looked his way. She was the only one of his wives who truly loved him, the man. But today he needed her to obey her king.

"I appreciate the effort you have put into obeying me recently, Kasia. I expect you to do the same today. My men will face danger, and I know your instinct is to pray to your God. You must not."

He had no word for the look in her eyes. Fear mixed with sorrow. Anger colored by dread. "Xerxes. That is like asking me not to think, not to breathe."

"At least keep off your rug. If you must pray, let no one know you do it."

Her lips pressed together. Rebellion brewed in her eyes. "I do not pray in public anyway, only the privacy of my tent."

"The god can still see you."

The babe nudged his hand again, no doubt in response to Kasia's agitation. She drew in a long breath. "You would forbid me from seeking Jehovah entirely, if you could."

"Kasia." He drew his hand away. "What care of Jehovah's is this war? It belongs to the god."

"It is Jehovah's concern because *you* are Jehovah's concern. You are the caretaker of his chosen."

He shook his head and stood. "Your Jehovah has never spoken to me. Ahura Mazda has. And he has promised victory—by your own admission, your God led his chosen people to defeat."

She stood too. "Only because we had wandered from the faith."

"Then he can have no good in mind for me, as Persia is less faithful to him than Israel was."

Her lips quirked up. "More so than the Greeks, though—you have faithful Jews in your company."

He sighed. "I have made myself clear, and you will obey. No obvious prayers to your God."

She folded her arms over her chest, resting them on the mound of her stomach. "No *obvious* prayers."

"I would prefer, if you must pray about the battle, you pray to Ahura Mazda."

At that, she only blinked. He pressed a kiss to her forehead and strode for the throne his servants had set on the hill.

Better to focus on the fight he could win.

Persepolis, Persia

Amestris halted at the garden's entrance, her eyes not seeing the lush vegetation before her. Her ears did not hear the squeals of Artaxerxes or the impatient reply of her younger daughter, Rhodogune. Her soul—her soul felt the touch of the god.

He had visited her often since the king's ridiculous attempt to depose her. A whisper to let her know when to act. An image of a pointed finger in her mind to show her which direction to go. He had helped her gather the strands of power into her hands, to braid them into a sturdy rope.

She did not need the king to be the queen. She could hang her enemies without his help. But still the god bade her pray for her estranged husband, that he would remain faithful to Ahura Mazda.

News from Haman was encouraging. His attempt on the Jewess's life may have failed—the witch must have a powerful demon watching over her, perhaps even Angra Mainyu himself—but at least the child had been stillborn. And according to Haman, relations between Xerxes and the Jewess had been strained ever since. It was only a matter of time before the scales fell from the king's eyes.

My god, let it be soon. Let him see that she is your enemy, and so the enemy of Persia. Hold tight to him, Ahura Mazda. Do not let him go.

"Excuse me, my queen."

She focused on the servant bowing low before her. "What?"

"The jewelry you commissioned has arrived. Shall I set it up in your chamber?"

"Yes, yes. Go." She shook her head and stepped into the garden, only to stop again when she saw the look of accusation Hystaspes wore on his faces. "Why do you scowl?"

Her son shifted a bit, and finally Hystaspes shook his head. "Why do you allow them to call you the queen again, Mother?"

She lifted a brow that should have put the twelve-year-old in his place. Yet he only straightened his shoulders. She put a hand on her hip. "I see no one else with the title."

Hystaspes moistened his lips. "Father will be very angry."

"I do not see him here, either. Besides, he always repents of his rash behavior. He may not be able to change the law he made, but he will either find a way around it or let everyone quietly ignore it. It is his way."

Her son looked none too sure, and his doubt chafed. While he studied and played with blunted spears, she made the connections that would become his career. She burned incense and prayed blessings upon him. Any success he found would be thanks to her.

And if he stood against her, he would fail.

She narrowed her eyes on him. "Hear me well. A king might make the law, but everyone knows power is held within the harem. I will not kindle the king's wrath—but neither will I step aside while all I have worked for is undone. If you want security when you grow up, obey me now. I may have no crown, but I am still the queen."

She stormed past him before he could argue and went to find little Artaxerxes. He, at least, would not question her.

Malis, Trachis

Kasia stood on the hill, hidden from Xerxes' view though her eyes were locked on the same scene his were. She should have stayed in her tent, but she could not. Her spirit would not rest until she could see the battle boiling in the pass.

So this was war. Proud uniforms bloodied and ripped, sharpened weapons slashing and piercing. Cries of horror and rage, of pride and fear. Men trampled by their brethren, some falling into the sea at the bottom of the cliff. This was what her brother had yearned for?

She forced down bile and curled her fingers to her palm. Her soul stretched outward, upward, and she had to lock her knees to keep them from bending. *Lord Jehovah, rally your servants in Persia. Let them take to their knees where I cannot, that all our voices might be as one and provide a beacon for your angels.*

The Spartans had chosen their stand too well. In the narrow valley pass, number mattered little. Only a few of the vast sea of Medes and Cissians could surge forward, and they were met with unimaginable ferocity.

She winced when yet more of her husband's men staggered and fell. Was there no way to get around the Spartans' longer spears?

Even as she wondered, the Lacedaemonians spun as a unit and fled back toward the walls erected in the narrowest part of the pass. Her heart lurched, her hand lifted to her throat. It could not be so easy, they had no reason to flee. She had not spotted a single Spartan falling. Perhaps the numbers of their enemies had intimidated them?

No, it made no sense. No sense at all.

The Medes pursued, their victorious cry echoing down to her ears. They gained on their prey, drew closer and closer—

The Spartans pivoted and crouched, spears parallel to the ground. Xerxes sprang from his seat with a heart-wrenching curse as his front line ran straight into the unforgiving points.

Kasia winced but could not look away. A few spears flew from the hands of the Medes and found their targets. She counted three fallen Spartans. Three of the three hundred who once again loosed a terrifying scream and came at the Medes.

Her husband cursed again and shoved agitated fingers through his hair. "All these troops—where are the *men*?" He pointed a finger at one of his commanders. "Take in the Immortals."

Her jaw quivered. Could even the most elite fighting men gain any ground against this particular foe? Or would they fall as quickly as the Medes and Cissians?

The commander dashed away, and moments later the Immortals, already in formation, marched on the pass.

Her eyes slid shut. If Zechariah had managed to join the army, he likely would have been an Immortal. He was that skilled—she had snuck away a few times to watch him train with Bijan.

Bijan. He was marching toward death even now. Her brother's one Persian friend. She had never known him much, but now fear for him burrowed into her heart. She had to pray. The desperate need weighed her down, shook her knees.

"Kasia? What in Hades are you doing out here?"

She blinked Xerxes into focus. "My brother has a friend who is an Immortal. Bijan."

Her husband frowned. "The son of Navid? He is a friend of Darius and Cyrus as well. One of the most capable warriors I have seen. You need not fret for him, sweet one."

Not fret? Had he not been watching the same battle she had?

He came to her, cupped her face, kissed her brow. "Go back to your tent. This is no place for you."

Her servants tugged her away before she could protest, but it mattered not. Images of spears and shields, of daggers and swords still flashed before her eyes. Fear for her brother's friend, the only Immortal she knew, pounded with her pulse.

Jehovah-Jirah, take care of him. Jehovah-Raffa, keep him whole. Jehovah-Nissi, be a banner before him. If ever my brother showed him the Truth of you, let it burrow deep today. Let him feel your strength.

Desma got her to her makeshift bed before Kasia's strength abandoned her legs and banded around her heart. She curled up against the pillows, squeezed her eyes shut tight, and prayed.

TWENTY-SIX

Susa, Persia

Mordecai jolted from his pillow, eyes darting from left to right in search of the light that had pulled him from his dreams. He saw no indication of it now.

He did not need to. He jumped up. "Esther! Martha, Jonah!"

His cousin and the servants all stumbled into the main room a few moments later. "Jonah, go rouse any faithful Jews you can find. Tell them our friends with the army need our prayers, to gather here. Martha, we will need refreshment. Esther—go convince Kish and his family to come. He will resist, it being about the king's war, but they must. Zechariah especially. He has a friend in the Immortals, does he not?"

Eyes round, Esther jerked a nod. "Bijan."

"He must pray for Bijan. Go."

The three of them darted away. Mordecai dropped to his knees.

Within the hour, his humble abode filled to bursting with friends and neighbors, on their knees beseeching God. Jehovah would use their prayers to fuel his servants, to strengthen their might against the enemies'.

Zechariah settled beside him with a pained expression. "Bijan?"

Mordecai could only shake his head. "I know only that we must pray for him and his companions."

Zechariah swallowed and darted a gaze at Esther. Even through the veil of prayer, Mordecai saw a new complexity in that look. The young man's nostrils flared. "I have not prayed much these past months. I cannot think Jehovah would hear me now."

Mordecai gripped his shoulder. "Make your heart right with God, my son, and stay on your knees. There are bigger things at stake tonight."

Zechariah covered his face with his hands and touched his head to the floor.

Mordecai closed his eyes again and welcomed the Spirit into their midst.

Malis, Trachis

Xerxes stared at the darkened pass, exhausted but unable to sleep. Two days. Two days of death and defeat. He had thought for sure the Spartans would be too tired to fight well today, that his fresh troops would take advantage of that and find victory quickly.

He dared not consider how many of his men were dead tonight because of that misjudgment.

"Master, you will want to hear this."

He spun to see Mardonius with a stranger dressed in Greek attire. "Will I? Does he have some secret to defeating these cursed Lacedaemonians?"

The man stepped forward with a bow. "I am Ephialtes, master, and I have exactly that. This area is known well to us Malians—there is another way through the mountains, around the pass. I could show it to your men, and they could sneak up behind the Spartans. It is a more open space, and you could surround them easily."

Xerxes sat down for the first time in hours and stared at the man. Could he not have offered this two days ago? "Our numbers would have their natural advantage."

Mardonius smiled. "Exactly. Tomorrow could see a far different battle."

He surged to his feet again. "Have Hydarnes lead the Immortals where this Malian shows them, tonight." He spun to Zethar. "Everyone who remains behind must pray. I want each and every idle person beseeching Ahura Mazda for victory."

Ephialtes inclined his head. "You ought to plan for the frontal attack to launch tomorrow no later than mid-morning—all will be in position, and you can strike them from both sides."

Yes. "You will be well rewarded for this information if it leads to victory."

"It will." The Malian bowed. "I will guide your men myself."

He nodded and dismissed them.

This time tomorrow he would be celebrating. He knew it in his soul.

The Greeks fought with nails and teeth after their spears were broken and their swords fallen into the sea. Kasia watched from her hiding place, ignoring the continual prodding of her servants to return to her tent. She had spent the entire second day of the battle in there, trying to look as though she were not praying.

Now she felt the prayers of her people covering the pass. Peace had settled over her with the first breath of dawn, and she swore she had seen streaks of light brighter than the sun. Given that all had been commanded to pray, she had taken to her knees in the first hours of the morning. But when the battle began, her feet propelled her outside again.

From the start, it was different. Today the Spartans came farther down the mountain, into a wider area where the fighting was fiercer than ever before. Her husband's men were driven forward with whips, stragglers trampled.

Four times the Greeks managed to push back the Persians, but then the Immortals came in from behind. Surely the Spartans knew they were finished—yet the knowing only increased their fervor.

A hail of missiles blotted out her vision of the Greeks, but occasionally she caught glimpses of them, fighting even with spears in their chests. And then, hours after the enemies first stormed together, came the silent knell of death.

A soldier sprinted to Xerxes' throne. Kasia peeked between the leaves of her hiding spot to see him kneel before her husband. "Victory is ours, my lord."

"How many of our men died today?"

"We have not counted. But my lord . . . two of your brothers fell. Abrocomes and Hyperanthes."

Xerxes cursed, and Kasia nearly abandoned her position to go comfort him. But no, she must wait. He would not appreciate his men seeing a woman embrace him in his grief. He would want them to see him do just what he did—stand up, square his shoulders, and lift his chin.

"They died with honor and will be memorialized as heroes."

"Yes, master."

When her husband was distracted, she dashed away from the hill, back to her tent. Perhaps Xerxes was right, that she should not have filled her mind with such terrible images. So why did she not regret it?

She settled on her prayer rug and focused her gaze on the pattern without seeing it. Had her people fought so bravely when Babylon surrounded them? Probably not. At that point, they would have been fighting only for their lives, not for their beliefs. But as always, Jehovah had preserved a remnant.

As part of that remnant, she now knew what one *should* look like when battling the enemy of one's soul. The Spartans served their law, battled to the death for the right to live free. Even in loss, they won. Would her husband recognize that? Would he grant them the honorable memory they deserved?

Would he grant her the right to live for Jehovah, or would she spend the rest of her life afraid to kneel in prayer lest her husband rebuke her?

Her eyes slid closed. *Have I failed you, Jehovah? I have sought you so often, with dedication. Yet when my husband forbids me to pray, what am I to do? I want to obey him, honor him. Yet I am to love you above all. Help me strike the balance, Lord.*

And thank you for rallying your people to pray when I could not. I could feel them, could see the affect they had. Thank you for the faithful remnant you have preserved. Thank you for—

"Mistress?" Zethar's voice broke through her thoughts. "The king has lost two of his brothers. He has retired to his tent and could use your comfort."

Thank you for my husband, for a man I can love so much. Help me to help him and still honor you.

She let Desma assist her onto her feet and looked to Zethar. "Of course."

He lifted his brows, studied her. Then grinned and shook his head. "You were watching again, or you would have asked me for details. I suggest you not let the king know that, mistress."

"You are very wise, Zethar." She returned his smile and followed him out into the afternoon sunlight. "Is the king not rejoicing over his victory?"

"Before the people, yes, but the losses weigh heavily on him. He needed a few moments to indulge the grief, but he will not stay inside long. He will recover the faster with you beside him."

Her eyes tracked again to Thermopylae. The dead littered the ground like the leaves had in Sardis. Persians and Greeks draped over one another, enemies embracing in death.

So many of her husband's men dead, not by Spartan spears, but by their own people's impatience. By the whip of their commanders, by the feet of the soldiers behind them, by brothers shoving them off the cliff. Most of them had not fought for a cause, but by compulsion. The Persians had nothing at stake.

The same could not be said for their king. He had invested more than money and time in this war. He had poured his heart into it.

When she entered his tent, she found him leaning against a table, shoulders rolled forward. She rushed to him and wrapped her arms around his waist. "Zethar told me of your brothers."

A shudder stole through him. "They were good men, Kasia. Brave men."

"I know."

"Why does victory always come at such a steep price? Pythius was right." He pinched the bridge of his nose. "I have dispatched his two eldest sons back to Sardis to care for him."

She pressed her lips to his arm. "He will appreciate the gesture."

"Will he? Sending these two home will not give him back his firstborn."

Tears stung her eyes. "No. Nothing can ever replace the ones we lose. But that only makes us value more the ones who remain."

With a long sigh, he turned and wrapped his arms around her. "So many men died these last three days. There were moments I thought my ranks would be cut in half."

And though he would have mourned it, still he would have sent them in. She sighed too. "Praise God it did not come to that."

"Mm." He pulled back enough to smile at her. "I wanted to thank you, Kasia. I heard you prayed along with the others. I did not think I would ever see the day when you would bend your knee to Ahura Mazda."

A chill swept through her. "Xerxes . . . I did not pray to Ahura Mazda."

The pleasure leaked out of his expression. "I told you not to pray to Jehovah."

"You told me not to *obviously* pray to Jehovah. I did not kneel until everyone else did. But my love, you know very well I cannot pray to your god."

He spun away and tossed his hands in the air. "Will nothing convince you? Is it not enough that we claimed victory so soon after everyone beseeched the god?"

"I . . . ." She should keep quiet. But something welled up inside, a fountain of determination. She would cling to her beliefs as fiercely as the Spartans had. "Yours was not the only god beseeched. I prayed the faithful Jews would pound the throne of heaven, and I felt the presence of the heavenly warriors this morning. Did you see

Ahura Mazda?"

When he turned to her again, his eyes sparked. "What I see is a woman who refuses to obey her husband. A woman who puts her stubborn faith above everything."

"What else would you have me do, Xerxes?" She spread her hands, palms up. "I have no house, I have no child. I have no loom in my wagon, I cannot read. The other women prefer each other—when with them, I always feel removed. Shall I just sleep the day away, waiting for you to carve out a few moments for me? Shall I remain in the fog I lived in after Sardis?"

He sloshed some wine into a chalice. "It is your clinging to Jehovah that keeps you removed, Kasia. Look at you. Two years with me, yet still you wear the simplest of garments, rarely any jewelry."

She settled a hand over the lions' head torc, the one piece she never took off. "You have never complained of my appearance before."

"I do not care about your clothes, they just point to the larger issue. You *deliberately* remain apart. Always the Jewess. Never the Persian."

Odd . . . had her father not feared the opposite? She could still hear his low plea. *They will make you Persian. Strip you of your heritage.* "Because I *am* a Jewess, which you knew after our first conversation. You told me never to change."

He tossed the wine down his throat and slammed the cup onto the table. "And yet you have. If anything, you have become *more* Jewish since coming to me. You spend hours—*hours*—in prayer each day. I cannot have a conversation with you without your blasted Jehovah coming up."

She gripped her arm to keep her hand from shaking. "I have not so much as mentioned him in months. I have held my tongue about my God, I have held my tongue about my babe. What else do you want me to do, Xerxes?"

"I want you to trust my wisdom for once."

No, he wanted her to give up Jehovah. The races he ruled may be granted the right to worship as they willed, but not her. Not his wife.

She shook her head. "If I did what you asked, I would become like every other woman in your harem. Is that what you want? You want me to lose the very things that make me who I am, who you love?"

His oath stained the air. "You would not lose yourself if—"

"I *would*. I know I would. It is only through prayer that I keep myself from jealousy and conflict."

"You do not have to give up prayer, just give up praying to the wrong deity."

She stared at him, knowing her incredulity was on her face. "Why would I switch my allegiance? Yours is not a god who advocates humility, which is where I find my peace. Yours is not a god who sheds light on my soul with wisdom and law, but one who sends darkness. Yours, by your own admission, tried to kill me."

Xerxes growled and stomped a few paces away. "Because you opposed him."

She was there again, fingers gripping the waist-high stone. The valley tumbled before her, the spur of the mountain loomed nearby. Fingers of darkness crept over it, and in it she saw life. Evil, destructive life. A roar of fury, force from behind.

Kasia gasped and clutched at her throat, blinking to rid her eyes of the images before the hillside could attack her again. "Someone pushed me."

"You fell." His voice was flat, empty. "It was a tragedy, but you will not blame it on another."

But she could feel hands, large and powerful, against her back. She could smell spice and man. She could hear the thud of footsteps. But all she could see was the glow of inhuman eyes in the surging darkness, so terrifying she had forgotten to pray for protection. "No. I was gripping the wall already, I could not have run into it. Someone pushed me."

"And you bring this up *now?*"

"I just remembered."

"Convenient." His doubt sliced through her, much as his hand slashed the air. "I will hear no more of this."

Shadows seemed to slink in again now, always in her periphery. "You think I lie?"

He folded his arms over his chest. "Why not? You lied when you promised you would not bow your knee to Jehovah. You lied when you said you would not speak of certain things. You lied, for that matter, when you said at Abydus it was only I you wanted, that you cared not about getting with child again."

She staggered back a step, not sure what was shadow and what was tears. "That was not a lie. Yes, I want a child. But it was not only the loss of our son that consumed me those months, Xerxes, it was the loss of *you*. I would have been content to get you back, even if I had never conceived again."

"Yet you disobey me at every turn, insisting you know better than the wisest men in my empire. Do you know what your problem is, Kasia?" He jabbed a finger at her, and though he still stood several feet away, she felt the poke in her soul. "You trust your illogical, blind faith above evidence and reason."

Her tears dried up, her hands fisted. "And *your* problem is that you cannot abide anyone or anything not bending to your will."

His nostrils flared. "You are nothing but a Jew."

"And you are nothing but a king." She spun for the exit, not sure her arrow had hit its mark until she heard the crash of metal striking wood.

He cursed and threw something else. "Do not walk away from me, Kasia. If you leave this tent, you will never step foot in it again."

She pivoted back around, tired of relenting every time he made a demand that threatened her soul. "Will you banish me again? Go ahead. This time I will not waste any suffering on it, I will not fade away for needing you."

"You want banished?" He released a breath of dry laughter. "Have it your way. Zethar! See that Kasia's things are packed and loaded. At first light, she will return to Sardis."

The ground rocked and sank in on itself. She was uncertain how she remained upright with nothing solid beneath her. "Sardis? Why not send me all the way back to Susa, like you did your uncle when he dared to speak against you?"

He lifted a condescending brow. "So you can run away and be hidden by the other Jews? I think not. Sardis, where you will wait until I have finished my campaign. I will decide then what to do with you."

What to do with her? Fire consumed her, burning her eyes and her soul behind them.

"And Kasia—you will *not* pray to Jehovah for me or my army. I do not need anything from the God of slaves."

He did not want blessing, did not want God to go before him? "As you will, *master*." She pulled the torc from her arm and dropped it to the dirt as she left.

Twenty-Seven

Haman staggered through the retreating night, rubbing a hand over his eyes. An hour or two remained before dawn, but when the king called . . . .

He blinked against the lamplight when one of Xerxes' eunuchs ushered him in. "My lord, you called for me?"

The king did not look up. He sat on his throne and toyed with a broken circle of silver. "Have you heard I ordered Kasia back to Sardis?"

His heart danced at the reminder. "Everyone has heard, my lord." Most assumed it was out of concern for the babe she obviously carried, but the coin he had pressed into a certain palm revealed they fought. Finally the witch went too far and got the punishment she deserved.

"I want you to accompany her."

"I—what?"

Xerxes looked up. Shadows circled eyes dark with exhaustion . . . and something more Haman did not care to name. "I need someone I trust to go with her, to keep his eyes and ears open until I can make it back."

Ah. A spy against her then. "I would be honored to watch her for you."

"She is not the one I would have you watch." The king's eyes slid shut. "I trust her. But I do not trust others with her—I have seen the way the men look at her."

Haman swallowed his distaste. "Certainly, my king, but how much a danger could this be now, when . . . her figure has changed so much?"

One corner of Xerxes' mouth pulled up. "The danger is still there. You are the one man I trust not to fall in love with her."

"There is certainly no fear of *that*."

Xerxes chuckled. "Exactly. But she is more than another Jew to me, Haman."

Perhaps it was too much to hope that love would turn to hate through one argument. But distance would help. The chains of influence she had over the king would loosen—and Haman suspected he could further that in Sardis. "Of course, my lord. I accept this task gladly."

The king nodded, but his eyes had narrowed. "If anything happens to her, you will be held responsible."

So then, no second attempt at the wall. Haman smiled. "Obviously, my lord."

"Very good. Go ready yourself. I have ordered a hundred Immortals to accompany her to Sardis and then catch back up with us. They will see you safely there."

Haman bowed and took his leave. This twist of fate was unexpected, but he would harness it. What favor the king still held her in would not last long now.

Mist from the sea blurred the world, rendering it unreal and cool. Kasia moved woodenly to the wagon. Her belongings were inside, except for the jewels she deliberately left behind.

The pearls he had said were like her skin.

The diamonds that dimmed in comparison to the gleam of her eye.

The jet that put him in mind of her hair.

The jasper, no redder than her lips.

They were worth no more than his empty promises. If he was going to take back what mattered, he could keep what did not.

She jerked to a halt when the mist shifted enough for her to make out the clothing of the guard that would escort her to Sardis. "Immortals?" Spinning to Theron, she frowned. "Why would he send Immortals with us? Surely he does not think me so big a threat."

Zethar emerged from the cloud to stand beside Theron. "The opposite, mistress. He wants to be sure you arrive safe and well." He leaned closer and whispered, "You surely realize he already regrets his command."

She snorted and pulled her cloak tighter to ward off the mist. "He always regrets what he does in anger. That never keeps him from doing it, nor does it ever change his mind."

Zethar stepped nearer and held out his hand.

She looked at the torc he offered, at the plea in his eyes. No sympathy stirred within the cavity of her chest. Did Xerxes think he could undo it all so easily? "Tell the king that since I cannot have both, I would rather have my God than my husband."

"Mistress." Zethar's voice strained, begged.

She lifted her chin. "According to your master, I am no mistress. Only a slave."

"He did not mean it."

"It does not matter. He is the king—his word is law." Perhaps if the *man* had come to her . . . but instead he sent his servant to bear the burden of humility. Until he shouldered it himself, she wanted nothing to do with him.

Zethar's face crumpled. "You will break his heart."

"He is an expert at ignoring his heart. He will hardly notice." She spun away just in time to see three soldiers approach.

The eldest took a knee. "Greetings, lady. I am Fotius, and it is my honor and privilege to lead you back to Sardis. Please, advise me or one of my men if you need a slower pace than we set or wish to stop. We were given strict instructions to put your comfort and safety above all."

Was that supposed to touch her? She dredged up a smile. "Thank you. But I would like to reach Sardis as soon as possible."

"Certainly. I will be at the head of the company, my brother at the rear." He stood again and motioned to the man on his left, then indicated the remaining soldier. "Our most valiant warrior will remain at your side. This is—"

"Bijan, son of Navid." Of course. In his belated attempt to appease her, Xerxes would send her brother's friend.

Bijan frowned and met her gaze. "You know me, lady?"

She gave him a bare smile. "Only through my brother Zechariah."

"Kasia?" A thunderhead stole over his features as recognition lit his eyes. "Your family thinks you dead."

Perfect. Even her escort judged her lacking. "Zechariah and my mother know the truth. My father forbade them to speak it."

That seemed to restore his humor. "That does indeed sound like your father. The only man I know who would be ashamed that his daughter is wife to the king."

She granted that with a halfhearted breath of laughter and let Theron lift her into the wagon. As Zad bounded up behind her, the three Immortals left with nods. Bijan returned a few minutes later with his horse, and the entourage moved forward.

Kasia turned so she could see Bijan, who rode within reach of the wagon. "Have you heard anything lately from Susa?"

"Plenty," he said with a chuckle. "My sister squeezes as much gossip as possible onto one wax tablet. Your brothers and father have been very busy with work from the palace. Everyone assumes the king saw the things I ordered, though I now suspect that credit belongs to you."

She grinned, but it faded quickly. Would Xerxes cancel his orders with them after the war? "The king let me commission a few pieces, and his steward was impressed with the craftsmanship."

"Far more likely." He studied her for a long moment, his dark eyes sharp. "Not that I knew you well, but I grieved for Zech when he lost you. It never occurred to me you could be alive, much less the concubine of the king everyone speaks of."

Something thudded in her chest. Not her heart, surely—that was either absent or frozen. "Why would everyone speak of me?"

Bijan lifted a brow. "You are considered all but a goddess—the only creature in the world that can keep the king happy. When word spread that he was sending said creature to Sardis, a collective groan went out." Bijan glanced at her stomach. "I am surprised he did not send you back sooner, but I suppose he did not want to part with you."

A furry head nudged her hand, and she obliged Zad with a scratch behind his ears. Did Xerxes not want anyone to know he had sent her away in disgrace? That changed nothing.

She still knew.

Bijan cleared his throat. "I feel as though I should apologize. I think I said a few things over the years concerning the king's favorite concubine that I would not have, had I realized she was you."

She chuckled to cover her wince. "I suppose it is natural for people to be curious about any woman of interest to the king."

"That seems a poor excuse when I consider the thrashing your brother would give many of my friends here, had he heard the speculation."

Heat stung her cheeks. Time to nudge the subject elsewhere. "Ah yes, my brother against a band of Immortals. Would he have stood a chance?"

Bijan snorted. "More than. He is a better warrior than most of them. I am heralded as one of the best, and I know it is only because of the extra practice I got with Zech. He challenged me as few of these men ever have."

"Did you see battle?"

An odd expression settled on his face. "I did. The first day, and also yesterday. It was not what I expected."

"Worse?" She could not imagine facing down the Spartans.

"No." Brows knit, he drew in a breath. "When I faced the enemy, it was as if . . . as if another's arm steadied my own, as if someone breathed confidence and strength into me." He shook his head, dislodged the frown. "That must sound odd."

She pressed her lips into a close smile. "Actually, I prayed Jehovah would send his angels to do just that."

"You prayed to Jehovah for me?" Shock glazed his eyes, but under it she thought she detected recognition. "Why?"

"Because I felt the Spirit whispering that I should. Because you are my brother's friend."

He nodded and gazed ahead of them, silent. Content to leave him to his musings, Kasia settled back and patted Zad's side. There would be plenty of time to talk.

At the moment, she preferred to sit and not think.

Twenty-Eight

Susa, Persia

Zechariah soothed the plane over the wood. Sweat dripped from his brow, and he swiped at it with his forearm. His gaze went out the door, open to receive whatever sweltering winds might blow in.

His throat tightened when he saw Esther crouched in the street. She laughed at something Ima said and swept barley seeds from the hot road into a basket. He wanted her to glance his way. Wanted her to flash that perfect smile at him. Just to see if his heart would pound as it had every other time she looked at him lately.

Abba gave him a playful thump to the side of the head. "Watch yourself instead of her or you may slice off a finger."

Zechariah swallowed and checked to make sure no siblings lurked about. Joshua was out making deliveries, and the rest were in the house. "How does this happen, Abba? A few short months ago, I saw her as a sister. Now . . . ."

"It only takes one stray thought." His father grinned. "I knew your mother all my life, just as you have known Esther. I never expected to fall in love with her, but then one day I saw her, felt a bolt of attraction before I realized who she was, and I was doomed."

He laughed because Abba expected him to. "I feel doomed. So long I ignored her infatuation with me, and now I worry it is not as strong as this thing building inside."

This strange, stretching thing. It was not just attraction. That was far too simple a word for the complicated mess his feelings for Esther had become since that night they prayed at Mordecai's house.

There had been a seed of it before then, he would admit it. A seed planted when he rescued her from that over-zealous Persian. But *that* had been attraction. Since he put his heart right with Jehovah and refused to see Ruana again . . . .

Esther glanced his way, perhaps sensing his attention, and grinned. His heart hammered. "Doomed," Zechariah muttered. "Completely doomed."

His father chuckled. "Can I give you some advice?"

"Please." He smiled back at Esther then turned to Abba.

He found his gaze serious. "Take your time with her. She has loved you since she was a child and has been telling herself for years that you were not interested. While you could go to Mordecai today and arrange a betrothal, she would doubt your heart and think you did it because we pushed you. Woo her. Make it clear you love her before any arrangements are made."

When had Abba gotten so wise? "Good idea." He set down the plane and drew in a long breath. "Abba . . . I cannot marry her with secrets between us."

His father's hand stilled, awl poised over wood. "When you are the head of your own family, Zechariah, you may tell your wife what you please. But you will caution her not to speak of it here."

"Abba, it is ridiculous. Mordecai already knows she lives—Jehovah asks him frequently to pray for her." He had learned of that the day Mordecai writhed in pain he claimed was Kasia's. Keeping that from Esther had grated, even before the blossoming attraction took root.

His father's brows pulled down. "I did not know that. Even so, my decision holds."

"But Abba—"

"If you are serious about marriage, Zech, you ought to get started on an addition for your bride. We have the revenue now to expand the house."

Zechariah spun to look out the back door and into the open space behind it. Until his father's parents both passed on, they had all been crammed into their small house, as there had been no money for Abba to build extra rooms. But a space of their own . . . one with Esther puttering around inside, able to visit his family without being overwhelmed by them . . . .

Abba chuckled. "Go out, look around. We could get started next week."

He ought to finish here, but the allure was too great. Knowing he grinned like a fool, he strode outside.

He could build there, at a right angle to the main part of the house. Esther and Ima could share a kitchen, but they could make it bigger, add a second hearth. He would not put a door between the new and the old, not directly. But the kitchen would serve as a connection.

How large to make it? They had plenty of room, being on the outskirts of the city, but he needed to leave space for the rest of the boys to build too, as they married. Still, he wanted room enough that it would not be so cramped as his parents', no matter how many children Jehovah blessed them with.

"Zech? What are you doing out here?" Esther stepped out to the kitchen, where she set down her basket of roasted barley.

His lips tugged up. "Planning. Abba has decided it is time for me to begin the addition to the house. For my future family."

She paled, eyes flashing distress. "You . . . you are to marry?"

"Eventually." He sidled over to crowd her, under the guise of peeking into the basket. "First, though, I must win my bride."

Her breath came too fast, and a flush stole over her cheeks. Zechariah smiled and snatched a few heads of barley. What he really wanted to do was slip his arms around her waist and pull her close, take her lips with his . . . .

Her kiss would be innocent and sweet, with an undercurrent of eagerness. Those graceful arms would come about him, cling to him. Best of all, she would look at him with eyes brimming with love.

"Zech?" Her voice shook, her gaze filled with question more than love. A hopeful question.

He tossed the barley into his mouth and, after munching it, gave her a grin. "Would you like to take a walk along the river this evening, Esther?"

Her lips parted. She blinked. "I . . . I would love to. I will ask my cousin's permission when he gets home."

"Good." He trailed a finger through a lock of hair that escaped from her head covering.

She swallowed. "Zech . . . why?"

He chuckled and leaned down to kiss her forehead. How many times had he done that over the years? But never before had he so wanted to hover, to bend a little lower for another, more satisfying kiss.

Taking his time with her may be the wise choice, but it would not be the easy one.

He made himself back away, enjoying the flash of mixed longing and disappointment in her eyes. She wanted him to kiss her—perhaps had dreamed of it. And when finally he did, it would be worth the wait for both of them.

He smiled. "I need to get back to work. Thank you for helping Ima with the barley, Esther."

"I do not mind." She looked bemused, probably at his thanks for what she did all the time.

Good. That would ensure she thought of him as she went about her tasks, just as he would think of her. With a lifted hand in farewell, Zechariah went back to the wood shop.

Abba met him at the door. "I need you to handle a customer while I check on a piece of cypress. And tell him if he orders another monstrous bed, we will charge him twice what we did last time."

Bed? Zechariah's throat went dry as he scanned the shop. Ruana's husband stood in the corner, studying a mosaic. He had not seen the man since he first placed the order for the frame. Certainly not since . . . .

"Do not keep him waiting, Zech." Abba spun around and headed out the front of the shop.

Zechariah cleared his throat and prayed he was not about to breathe his last. "Good afternoon, Asho."

Asho looked up with a smile. No murderous intent gleamed in his eyes, but that may only mean he was subtle. "Zechariah, it is good to see you again."

"Likewise." He would rather have faced down a den of angry lions. "How can I help you today?"

Asho moved closer. Perhaps it was only to look at the chest his gaze latched on . . .

or perhaps he wanted to be within reach so he could throttle him. "Actually, my wife has a complaint about the last purchase she made."

Was that a dagger on the man's belt? "She has?"

"Mm." Asho sounded amused. Which made no sense at all. "That your brother delivered it instead of you."

"I . . . ." Zechariah frowned and leaned into the work bench at his back. "I was busy."

"Zechariah." Asho dropped his voice low and took another step toward him. Still, his eyes reflected only friendliness, perhaps even teasing. Could he possibly be as unconcerned as Ruana had claimed? "If you avoid her because you think I am upset by your . . . arrangement, let me assure you I have no problem, even though you are a Jew."

How was he supposed to greet that pronouncement? "That is not why I avoid her."

Asho's brows drew together. "Why then? Surely she pleased you, as often as you came."

Fire settled in his face. He had thought—what? That the husband was oblivious? He ought to have known better. The servants knew he was there, and they would be loyal to Asho before their new mistress. Not that he seemed to care, except to be upset on his wife's behalf now.

What was wrong with these people?

"That is not it either. I . . . it was wrong, Asho. I never should have—the laws of my people strictly forbid—"

"Nonsense." Asho brushed that away with a motion of his wrist. "She is very fond of you, and she has been distraught since you stopped coming. Please, will you not reconsider?"

And now her husband begged him to keep making love to his wife? "It is not nonsense. Besides, I hope to marry soon myself, and I will remain true to my bride."

Asho sighed. "She will be distressed at that news."

"Then perhaps her husband ought to comfort her."

The Persian lifted one superior brow. "I am afraid that is not the direction my tastes lie." He swept a gaze over Zechariah that made his skin crawl.

He stepped to the side, well away from Asho and that terrible glint in his eye. "Do you have any business today, or just this 'complaint' from your wife?"

Asho's eyes shuttered again, back to friendly ease. "A small chest, similar to that one. And deliver it yourself. I would see my wife smile again."

Zechariah said nothing as the man strode from the shop.

Sardis, Lydia

Darius frowned at the image out the window, where the band of Immortals set up camp for the night. A runner had arrived days ago alerting him to the pending arrival of Kasia and her guard, but that had not told him *why* his father's favorite wife had left his side. He had to wonder no longer when he glimpsed her an hour ago.

It seemed he would have yet another little brother or sister in a few months.

Obviously his father did not want to risk her health, but why had Xerxes not considered the memories that would hit her here? The moment her feet were on the rocky ground, she had looked toward that small grave, overgrown now with grass and the flowers Artaynte had transferred. Even from up here, Darius had seen Kasia's shoulders hunch, her head go down.

Footsteps sounded outside the throne room, and he stepped away from the window. It had taken her nearly an hour, but his newly arrived guest must finally be ready to present herself in greeting. He prepared a smile.

Kasia did not look up to see it, just stopped a goodly distance in front of him and dipped her knees in respect. "Thank you for receiving me, my prince."

"Of course. It is good to see you again. How is my father?"

Her jaw clenched. Interesting. "As he always is."

"Hmm." He glanced at the servants behind her, the court people milling about. "Are you feeling up to a walk? It will be good to speak with someone so recently with him."

She hesitated and flicked her gaze to his face. "As you wish."

He led her out to the walls, careful to head in the direction opposite from where she fell. With only their personal servants around them, she would hopefully feel comfortable answering his questions.

Although she looked far from comfortable. Her jaw was still tight, and she held her spine straight and rigid. He cleared his throat. "You must have left shortly after Thermopylae."

"The morning following your father's victory."

Should she not have called it "our" victory? Darius clasped his hands behind his back as they walked. "I suppose the battle convinced him it was not safe for you to remain, given your condition?"

She looked away, into the courts of the citadel. "I suppose you ought to know that the king has not acknowledged my condition, and everyone else has followed his lead."

He came to a halt, brows raised. "Why would he do that? Last time—"

"He is convinced last time ended as it did because his god despises me." She stopped a step ahead of him and turned to face him. "He seems to think if he pays it no attention, Ahura Mazda will not take his anger out on me."

That made a kind of sense, when one considered the timing of the stillbirth. He supposed. "All right, then. I shall follow his lead as well, before others. Though it is rather obvious." He paused, considered her. "Did he forbid you to speak of it as well?"

A tick in her jaw, then she nodded.

"Is that why you are angry with him?"

Tears flooded her eyes, but he did not regret the question. She shook her head. "That is not the only thing he forbade me mention. He also commanded me not speak of Jehovah."

"And you listened? I find that difficult to believe." For that matter, he was surprised his father had demanded such a thing. Much must have changed in the last six months.

"I obeyed more than I wanted to. But not enough to satisfy him." She swallowed and swung her gaze back up to his. "We argued. That is why he sent me back."

He could not stop the quirk of his mouth. "You surely realize he would have regretted it the day after you left."

"He regretted it before then. That changes nothing."

"True." He drew in a long breath. She looked tired, which could be due solely to travel and her condition, or it could be tied to the anger sparking in her eyes. "One thing I always remember you for is forgiving my mother so quickly after she tried to kill you. Will you not forgive my father for saying things he did not mean?"

The spark turned to a simmer in the brown of her irises. "It is easy to forgive those who mean nothing to you—there is no real hurt involved. Forgiving him, when he knew well what his words would do, when he knew all I had already given up for love of him . . . that will take energy I do not have right now."

Darius nodded and smiled. "Well, you may rest easy in Sardis and may speak of your Jehovah all you please."

She snorted and folded her arms over the bulge of her stomach. "May I?"

He lifted a brow.

She sighed. "I sought out Artaynte as soon as I arrived, but I was denied access to her. It seems her mother does not want her associating with an enemy of Ahura Mazda."

His spine snapped into alignment. "What? You were such good friends."

"Hence why I thought it odd when she did not visit after my fall. Apparently her mother forbade it then, too."

He frowned at the mountainside. "I am certain she will find you in some moment when her mother is absent." That was met with nothing but silence, which drew his attention back to her incredulous face. "What?"

She shook her head. "Do you know her so little? She never crosses her mother, even when Parsisa is not there to guarantee obedience."

Something knocked around inside, like a marble off stone. "I have barely spoken to her since we left Susa, so I suppose I know her little indeed. Is that, too, because of my aunt? Does she not approve of me?"

Kasia sighed and looked to the side, as if for an escape from the conversation. "Of course she approves of you."

The marble rolled to a rest in his throat. "Then Artaynte simply dislikes me."

"No." Her eyes slid closed. A breath huffed out as she opened them again. "Did you know that Parsisa kept your uncle guessing as to her true feelings for nearly five years before finally agreeing to marry him?"

"No, and I do not see what . . . ." He cut himself off with a curse and spun away, only to spin back again. "She toys with me? This is all a game to her?"

Kasia shook her head. "Far from it. It is of the utmost importance, hence why she is so careful to follow her mother's advice down to the last jot and tittle."

Was that hope fluttering from his stomach to his throat? It had been so long since he had felt any where Artaynte was concerned, he was not sure. "Then she cares for me?"

"I should not have gotten involved in this." She took a step back, hands up. "This is between you and Artaynte."

"Apparently it is between us and Parsisa."

A corner of her mouth tilted up. "Granted. And while I never much liked the advice Parsisa gives, it would seem I am not such an expert on things of love either, so I ought to keep myself out of it."

Darius chuckled. "Your current disagreement with my father has little to do with your approach to love—your feelings for each other have always been clear, which I greatly admire. I imagine when he returns and apologizes for his rash words, you will rush back into his arms."

Her lips smiled. Her eyes remained unconvinced.

He sighed. Nothing, it seemed, guaranteed a firm foundation for a marriage. Political arrangements held little affection and too much intrigue. Matches made for love disintegrated under the scorch of time and politics. How, then, could he ever hope to forge a lasting relationship with Artaynte?

Kasia stepped closer again, her expression soft. "I think the two of you will find your way. You care for each other, and there is no better match imaginable."

No, that was not hope fluttering. It was dread. "And if we married, she would sever her bonds of obedience to her mother and dedicate herself to me instead?" He shook his head and drew in a ragged breath. "I thought if I won her heart, it would be truly mine, and we would have what no one else in Persia seems to. But if she has cared for me all this time and denied it so completely because of her mother, how am I ever to trust her?"

Kasia speared him with a sharp gaze. "And how is she to trust *your* affection, when you spend each spare moment seducing every young maiden you can find? You have no call to be angry over games, my prince, when you play them yourself."

Why could Artaynte not speak her mind like this? At least then he would know where he stood with her. He grinned and held out his arm to guide Kasia back the way they had come. "I am duly chastised. And if I give up the maidens, do you think Artaynte will give up the disdain?"

She sighed and fell in beside him. "I cannot say. I hope so."

"Perhaps I will try it and see." And perhaps he would speak with Parsisa about her ridiculous decision to separate Artaynte and Kasia. How could his aunt think this lovely creature anything but a good influence on her daughter?

"I pray the two of you work things out." She paused just outside the door. "I nearly forgot—I promised to mention that Bijan was in the company that brought me here, and he would enjoy visiting with you if you have the time before he leaves."

"I shall seek him out, thank you." But he frowned. "You got to know him well enough on the journey to carry messages for him?"

"He and my brother were friends in Susa." She offered a small smile. "If you will excuse me, prince, I am rather tired."

"Of course." He did not follow her in, but turned back to the wall. How to digest what she had revealed about Artaynte? He could not pin down his feelings on the matter. He wanted to hope, wanted to think his dreams within reach . . . but they felt so ephemeral at this point.

He wanted her still. Of course he did. She was so beautiful, had such strong blood. She would make the perfect wife, the perfect queen. But did he love her still? Could he, given how little he apparently knew her? They had not spent much of their childhoods together, given that her father had his own province, not until the war-planning brought Masistes to Susa. He had never realized how completely under Parsisa's thumb she was.

It seemed, then, that he must decide if he wanted his aunt as his queen. Thinking Artaynte would stop listening to her once she was married was stupid and naive. There was the chance she would welcome the freedom from her mother, but he would not assume so. More likely was that Parsisa would always whisper in her ear, and then she would whisper in his.

One mother thinking she ruled the world from behind him was quite enough, thank you.

"Prince Darius."

He spun around and frowned. "Haman. What are you doing back in Sardis?"

Haman bowed. "Your father sent me, my prince, to keep an eye on the Jewess."

That explanation only deepened his frown. "Why would he do that?"

Though the man shrugged, his expression held no confusion. "He said that he did not trust her interactions with other men, and he knows I am above her charms."

By the god, that made no sense. He stepped to Haman's side and pitched his voice to a bare murmur. "Are you saying that my father doubts her fidelity?"

Haman's wide eyes carried no shock at the suggestion. "He did not say so. Of course, there is much he is not speaking of these days, when it comes to the Jewess."

"You refer to her condition?"

"It is curious." Haman sighed and shook his head. "Everyone knew the king had kept himself from her after her fall—his temper made it obvious. Then her figure began to change . . . of course, she was seen coming from the king's tent again, but one has to wonder which came first. Given that his temper never exactly improved, and he refuses still to acknowledge the child."

Ridiculous. She had offered an explanation for that . . . one that made a kind of sense. Perhaps not as much as this, but . . . she would not betray his father with another man.

Would she?

"It is a sad thing," Haman said, casting his gaze toward the mountain's spur. "To be expected, though, when a creature who won the king's attention by throwing herself at him is then denied his love. It is probably a flaw in her soul, this need to be in a man's bed."

No. Certainly she was passionate, but . . . . "That is nothing but conjecture, Haman. If the king thought such a thing had happened, he would have had her killed."

"Possibly. But he is still in love with her. It is not beyond reckoning that he would forgive her in part, but send her away from him to have the bastard child. Is it?"

He would not condemn her, even if it were true. Who had not had a dalliance at some point or another? True, it was unwise to engage in an affair when one's husband was jealous—and the king—but plenty had done it. It would make her only typical.

Which grated more than it should have. He did not want her to be typical. She had always seemed so much more, and he wanted one thing—just one—to be what it seemed.

He glanced toward the citadel as she passed before one of the windows. The child she carried was only obvious from the side. Otherwise one noticed only the rich cascade of her hair, the gleaming eyes, the mouth so quick to smile. The passion that imbued everything she did.

The passion that now radiated off her as anger. Would she be angry if she were guilty? He wanted to say no, but only because that, too, would make her typical. Just like his mother, furious because she was punished when she thought herself invincible.

Innumerable men would be willing to risk the king's wrath for her. Had one had success when she was lonely and cut off from her husband? If Xerxes thought so, then no wonder he sent Haman. Here she would be lonely and cut off once again.

Perhaps he ought to keep his eye on her as well.

TWENTY-NINE

Athens, Greece

Why did victory not feel sweeter?

Xerxes shifted the reins from one hand to the other and watched the smoke billow over the Acropolis. It rose in great black clouds, obscuring the sun and slinking shadows over the land.

Nothing felt right. Darkness underscored everything. They may have won at Thermopylae, but it had cost him thousands of men. He may have had the pleasure of ordering the fallen king of the Spartans beheaded, but it had only reminded him of Pythius's son and made him jolt awake in the middle of many a night, ashamed for dishonoring a valiant warrior.

Were Kasia here, she would have had some clever observation to put it all in perspective. Her smile would have lit up the dark places.

But she would have pressed her lips together and turned away from the sight of the burning temple. Not that she would ever defend the Greek gods, but she would see in it an echo of his ancestors burning the temple of hers. Why, she would ask, did a nation reportedly tolerant always try to destroy the seat of a conquered nation's beliefs? Why could they never respect the sacred?

Why, he wondered, did her disapproval haunt him even when she was not there to offer it?

He sighed and turned from the smoke. "We have a few Athenian exiles in our numbers, do we not? Have them brought to me."

Zethar nodded and strode away. Xerxes surveyed his troops, swarming over the city and destroying everything they touched. He had already dispatched a message of their victory to Artabanas. It would reach Sardis well before Susa. His son would rejoice, he knew.

What of his wife? Would she still be proud of what he accomplished, or would she turn her face and wish him ill, since he succeeded without the help of her God?

Pressure clamped around his chest. He covered the torc on his wrist, nostrils flaring at the feel of the familiar lion's head under his thumb. The metal was warm, solid.

He felt cold, vaporous.

Ahura Mazda had kept his promise. By the time they arrived in Athens, the Greeks had fled, all but a few priests in the temple gone in search of sanctuary. They'd had nothing to do but march in and set it to flame. Perhaps that was why the victory felt meaningless.

No. It was because when night descended and darkness wrapped around him, he felt only the presence of the god—and Ahura Mazda was not a pleasant bedfellow. Taunting, haunting dreams came nearly every night. Some only echoes of the ones that convinced him to embark on this campaign, others new and terrible. That same handsome face, laughing. *I have given you all I promised*, the god would say. *Where is your greatness, O King?*

Greatness? He could not say. When he surveyed his army, he saw only the hands splayed over emaciated stomachs, the demoralized faces of those who had watched brothers fall. Disease ran through the ranks. The fleet had suffered at the hands of the Greeks while the land army battled at Thermopylae.

He had lost his heart for this war. Or perhaps he had lost his heart entirely. Surely he toyed with madness to have such thoughts as he had entertained lately. Thoughts that he could go home now, while he still had some pride left. With Athens fallen, he had kept his promise to his father. He could return to Sardis, beg Kasia's forgiveness. Promise whatever he must to win her love again. She could worship her Jehovah all she pleased, before all of Persia if that was what she wanted. So long as she forgave him.

Zethar rode up, a band of Greeks behind him. "The Athenians, master."

Xerxes urged his horse around to face them. Though each had come to him of his own will, exiles for one reason or another, pain still creased their faces as they saw Athens smolder. He could understand that. "The god has given your city into my hands—but I am a gracious king, a respecter of those I conquer. Go, climb the Acropolis and make what sacrifices your faith requires."

One of the men dipped his head, but Xerxes still saw the tremor around his mouth. "Thank you, master. Words cannot express what that means to us."

He only nodded and pressed his heels into his horse's flank. Zethar took his place half a length behind. "Master . . . if you miss her so, call for her to return."

"No. As quickly as they traveled, she will be tired and worn. I will not force her on another journey—besides, the war cannot last much longer. Summer is giving way to winter, and I do not like the chill in the air."

Zethar sighed. "One of the maidservants caught up with me while I fetched the Athenians. Lalasa has given birth to another girl, and both are well."

Something should stir inside him. Something always had before, when he learned that another of his children entered the world. But the only image to flood his mind was of Kasia, her stomach round. He wanted to cover the bulge with his palm again and feel the child nudge him. He wanted to bend down and whisper to his unborn daughter that he loved her, that he was sorry for denying her very existence. He wanted to hold them both against him and close his eyes until the world shrank to just them.

Xerxes shook himself back to the present. "Send her my regards, and tell her I will visit this evening."

"Certainly. There is Mardonius."

His cousin must have succeeded in gathering all the officers and rulers of the people. Xerxes rolled his shoulders back and headed for him. "All is ready?"

Mardoinius inclined his head. "At your leisure, master."

They headed together to where the leaders, both military and political, sat in order of Xerxes' preference. He took his place on the dais between the kings of Tyre and Sidon. He sat higher than the rest—the king of kings, the king of Persia and Media, the king of the world.

The torc pressed into his wrist. He just wanted to be Xerxes again, just for a day, for a night. Xerxes, as he could only be with Kasia. Would she ever let him be so open with her again? If he laid his soul bare before her, would she still love him—or had he pushed her too far? She would forgive so much, so often, but not an offense against her God. He knew that, had always known that. Why had he pushed?

He motioned Mardonius to his side. "Go around the assembly, ask them each individually if they think we ought to meet the Greeks at sea to finish them off."

His cousin moved off. Xerxes sat back on his throne and pretended to listen to the chatter around him. Pretended to care. Pretended the war still mattered.

Mardonius returned an hour later, a smile upon his face. "We are all in agreement, master, that it is the best course of action to set our fleet against the Greeks."

Xerxes trailed a finger around the lip of his chalice. "Everyone?"

His cousin's smile faltered. "Well, there was one voice of dissent. Artemisia."

Hands still, Xerxes arched a brow. Artemisia had proven herself time and again—and he could not help but remember Kasia's teasing about joining his council and taking a seat beside the sole woman on it. "What does she advise?"

"She, ah . . . says you already have your victory, master, and that your fleet will be as inferior to the Greeks at sea as women are to men. Why risk another battle, when you have won Athens, and that was the whole point to the war? She advises that you hold your position on land here, or else march into the Peloppennese, because she has information saying the Greeks have no provisions on the island they have fled to, and you will starve them out soon enough. She further says that the best of men always have the worst of slaves, and since there is none better than you, it stands to reason that many of the nations supposedly your allies may turn on you in your moment of need."

"What did everyone else say to that?"

Mardonius's smile looked forced. "Her friends cautioned her to hold her tongue, fearful you would grow angry and have her executed. Her enemies encouraged her to speak, hoping you would grow angry and have her executed. All agree her advice is folly."

Xerxes snorted a laugh. "Truth be told, cousin, her advice echoes my own instincts. But I have such a large council for a reason, and I am willing to grant that when so many agree, they most likely have the right of it." He sighed and rested his palm against the arm of his throne. "Tell Artemisia that while I approve of her plan, the majority will dictate our course. We will meet them at sea."

Once they had complete victory, no one would blame him for going home.

Sardis, Lydia

A goldfinch sat on the bosom of a sunflower, alternately pecking at the seeds and letting out a warble of pleasure. Kasia pulled her knees as close to her chest as they would go and watched the bird stretch out its vivid yellow wings, only to find a more comfortable position and select another seed.

According to Darius, Artaynte had transplanted the flowers to the head of the little grave, had tended them all through the hot summer and made sure the plot was not overgrown. Kasia would love to thank her for the gesture, for the care it denoted.

Parsisa still would not allow it, even at the prince's prodding.

Alone again. Always alone in her husband's palace, among her husband's people. Without even her husband, now. Without the friends she had cultivated at the start of the campaign. The only one to ever speak to her was Darius, and he only did it out of pity for his father's once-favorite wife, she was sure.

No, she was not alone. She had Desma and Leda settled on either side of her even now, Theron guarding them from behind. Her other four servants carried out the tasks she assigned them inside, she knew. Zad stretched out beside her as always. Not alone. Not quite.

The dog lifted his head and let out a woof of greeting.

"Kasia! The prince said I would find you here."

She would have leapt to her feet, had leaping been possible with her stomach. Instead, she held out an arm for Desma to help her up and drew out a wide smile. "Pythius! I hoped you would visit soon, but the prince knew not where you were, to let you know I had returned."

The silver-maned man strode to her and gathered her in a tight hug as Zad danced a happy salutation. Tears pricked her eyes at the feel of strong, loving arms around her. Like Abba's arms, warm and solid. Oh, she missed her parents. Her siblings. Esther.

She cut her longings off there and pulled away to grin through her tears. "It is good to see you."

"Likewise." Pythius's smile had changed. Not so light and proud as it had been when they met. Now it was colored by the sorrow that had saturated them when last they were together. He looped her hand through the crook of his arm. "I am sorry it took so long for me to realize you were here. I did not even realize my sons were back."

She let him lead her away from the grave, in the direction of the gardens. "I sent messages to everyone I could think of, but none knew where to find you."

He chuckled—a low, ironic sound. "No, they would not have thought to look where I was. You might have though. Did you know, my daughter, that there is a Jewish temple here in Sardis?"

Her eyes went wide. "You were there?"

"I have spent most of the summer with a man named Timon, a Levitical priest whose family ended up here during the exile." He drew in a long breath and looked . . . peaceful. "I have been learning the Law of Moses, the Prophets. Studying so that I might convert to Judaism, and my wife with me."

Surely it thrilled her—it must, even though her numb heart registered no accelerated beating. "Pythius, that is wonderful."

He laughed again. "No one else thinks so. I cannot explain it to them, but I knew that day I found you on the mountainside that I needed your God in my life. I needed him to be *my* God. Whenever I am confused or doubt what I have learned at Timon's hand, I remember feeling him with you. And I know again he is a living God, and that his ways are best."

A Psalm crowded her mind at his words.

As the deer pants for the water brooks,
So my soul pants for you, O God.
My soul thirsts for God, for the living God.

His ways were best, yes, but so mysterious sometimes. So many days she sat by the sunflowers on her son's grave and wondered why the Lord had brought her here. Perhaps this was her answer. Perhaps all her suffering was worthwhile in the eyes of Jehovah because it brought this great man to faith.

Perhaps, when feeling returned to her heart one of these days, that would fight off the anger that had been glossed over with numbness.

"Kasia." Oh, how like Abba he sounded, able to make her name into a command to tell him what he wanted to know. "What has happened?"

My tears have been my food day and night,
While they continually say to me,
"Where is your God?"

She drifted to a halt and looked up at the spur of the mountain. Never could she do so without shivering at the memory of the shadows springing from it.

When I remember these things,
I pour out my soul within me.

"I am lost, Pythius, and I can find no star to guide me."

"You?" He patted her hand. "You are not lost, Kasia, though perhaps caught in an eclipse. You know where your direction lies."

Why are you cast down, O my soul?
And why are you disquieted within me?
Hope in God, for I shall yet praise him
For the help of his countenance.

She tried. She tried to pray as she had since she left home. How many hours did she spend in silence, banging at the gates of heaven? She prayed for her family, for Esther and Mordecai. She prayed for her heart to heal, she prayed for the strength to stand without Xerxes, to need him no longer.

I will say to God my Rock,

"Why have you forgotten me?

Why do I mourn because of the oppression of my enemies?"

It was hard to pray without praying for Xerxes, but so help her, she would *not* beseech Jehovah on his behalf. No more. He had named himself her enemy.

Pythius dipped his head down to look into her eyes. "Is it as bad as all that? So that you cannot even speak of it?"

She swung her head back and forth. "There is nothing left to speak of. He sent me here in dishonor, Pythius. He will not acknowledge our child, he forbade me mention Jehovah. My marriage is undone."

"It can be mended." He wiped a stray tear from her cheek with the pad of his thumb. "For months I writhed in agony, remembering my son and the king's terrible command. I hated him, Kasia. I would awake in the night consumed by it. And I would go to Timon the next day, demand of him why his all-powerful God did not avert these tragedies. Do you know what he told me?"

As with a breaking of my bones,

My enemies reproach me,

While they say to me all day long,

"Where is your God?"

"No," she whispered.

"He told me I could not love the Lord with all my heart if any of it was filled with hatred. I had to first forgive, then I could seek Jehovah and be filled with his understanding."

He, too, would tell her to forgive him? He, who had been stripped of his firstborn because of Xerxes' anger? "Perhaps that is the problem, Pythius. Perhaps I loved Xerxes too much, gave him what should have been Jehovah's."

"Oh, sweet daughter." He blinked, and in his eyes glistened the shards of a broken heart. "You belong to Jehovah completely. You know that. He led you to your husband, put you beside the king to be his heart where the burden of rule would forbid him to have one. Do you think Jehovah is finished with you, just because you fought with that stubborn man you love so much? Do you think he wills you not love your husband? You must not give up."

She curled her fingers into her palm. "What more can I do?"

"You can pray for him."

Why are you cast down, O my soul?

And why are you disquieted within me?

"He forbade it."

"And you will obey *that*? When you would challenge him on anything else?" Pythius shook his head and covered her fist with his strong fingers. "That is not the Kasia I know."

Hope in God;

For I shall yet praise him,

The help of my countenance and my God.

The wind whipped around her, blowing her hair into her face and drying her tears to a salty residue. The scent of the bronze fennel growing at the border of the palace garden teased her nose, the trill of a bird filled her ears.

Her soul—it rose as if pulled by a gentle, powerful hand, and as it tugged upward, her knees buckled.

Pythius fell to his knees beside her, his eyes closed and his lips parted. "He is back. Your God is back."

"It is the Spirit." Shivers chased one another down her spine, her arms.

Xerxes' face filled her vision. *Pray*.

Every muscle went tight. She would pray. *Dear Lord, be with Abba and Ima*.

The wind whipped the other direction, and something shook inside her. She could see her husband, smile fading into a frown—she squeezed her eyes shut against the image. *Be with Esther, Lord*.

In her mind's eye, Xerxes held out a hand, the lion torc gleaming on his wrist.

She staggered to her feet and spun away—but how to escape one's own heart? *Jehovah, please, not for him. Do you not remember what he said? Why should you hold him with your strong arm, when he will only deny its power?*

Her own words to him over the last six months echoed back at her. *Without him is defeat . . . you are Jehovah's concern. You are the caretaker of his chosen*.

But he had made his choice, had refused her God. She knew he would not bend his will to the Almighty, so why bother praying for him? He was too proud, too arrogant. Too determined to do everything by the strength of his own hand. *Let him*.

The wind swirled away, sucking her breath along with it. Then all was still, and she stood there like an empty vessel, useless and fragile.

Desma slipped an arm around her waist in support. "Mistress, what just happened? That is not how the Spirit usually visits you."

She could only shake her head.

Pythius appeared at her side, opened his mouth.

Before he could speak, Darius appeared from around a hedge, face stretched in a smile. "We have victory! My father has burned Athens to the ground."

Had there been anything left within her, it would have evaporated then. Without prayer, without anything from her, he had won. Now he would never be convinced that her God reigned over his.

Darius did not seem to notice her lack of response. With a joyous laugh, he twirled her around.

One rotation was enough to make her head swim. But at least lightheadedness was *something*. She chuckled and pushed away so he would put her back on her feet. "Enough enthusiasm, Darius. I get dizzy easily these days."

He laughed and put her down, eyes alight. "Forgive me. It is such good fortune though—the Athenians had fled their city like cowards, and Father marched in and took it without any resistance. We are feasting tonight! Bring your whole house, Pythius."

Pythius looked pained. "I thank you, my prince, but these old bones are weary. My sons will come, I am certain."

A feast, without her one friend. All the nobles in Sardis in one room, eyeing her with disdain even though they knew nothing of her argument with their king—thrilling. "Darius, I am exhausted too. I think I shall just—"

"Nonsense." Authority draped him, making him look so very like his father. Then it vanished behind a grin, and he reminded her instead of Zechariah. "Rest now, then dine with me, Kasia. There will be pomegranates."

He said that last in a singsong, earning a snort of laughter. She had not been able to get enough of the juicy red seeds since they ripened a week earlier. No one else outside her servants cared enough to notice—she supposed she owed him gratitude enough to show up at his meal. "Very well."

"Excellent." The prince turned away and all but danced back toward the palace. So confident he would get his way in everything.

She clamped down on her thoughts before reflecting on Darius could make her miss Xerxes—she would *not* need him anymore—and headed for her room with a bare farewell for Pythius.

She had a feast to prepare for.

Salamis, Greece

Xerxes looked out over the ships waiting to wage war the next day. They should have been anchored, but he glimpsed their sails unfurling, the white fabric catching the feeble moonlight. "Mardonius! What is going on?"

His cousin rushed toward him. "The slave of a Greek named Themosticles just came to us. He reports that the Greeks are in a frenzy and planning to retreat. His master is secretly on your side, and so he sent the advice that we should surround the island now, in the dark, and cut off the enemy. They are disunited—we can defeat them easily."

Trusting the word of a spy was always a risk—sometimes it yielded great reward, sometimes tragedy. Xerxes leaned back on his heels.

A flash of light caught his eye. He turned, expecting someone with a lamp to be nearby—but even as he swung his head, he sensed the shadows of night swallow up the flash.

He obviously needed more sleep. He shook it off and turned back to his cousin. What was the worst that could happen? They would fight, as they had planned to do tomorrow anyway.

Well, then. He nodded at Mardonius and turned back to his lonely tent. He would sleep—and hopefully dream of Kasia's arms around him. Tomorrow . . . he would worry about tomorrow when it got here.

THIRTY

Sardis, Lydia

Artaynte kept her pace sedate as she left the hall, forcing herself not to crane around and look at him again. Look at *them*. But she could not stop her hands from fisting in her garment, from twisting the linen until it was a web of wrinkles.

How could he? She had thought it nothing that afternoon, when she saw Darius lift Kasia high and spin her around. Excitement—understandable. Yes, she had heard the whispers that the prince spent more and more time with his father's wife—who had not? She had thought that nothing, had even been glad of it. Glad Kasia had someone to talk to.

Why had no whispers warned her that he was falling in love with her? He looked at her with the same desire he did all the other maidens that ended up in his bed, but not so simply. No, there was nothing simple about wanting the concubine of one's father, was there?

Nothing would come of it. Darius would surely not try to seduce her, and even if he did, Kasia would refuse him. But that was not the point. He could lose his heart to her. Since her arrival, he had paid attention to no other women. She had even heard he turned away his own slave girls. Could it be any clearer that he was in love?

Which left Artaynte exactly where she had been for years—in her mother's shadow, watching him give his beautiful smiles to someone else.

She turned down a corridor and rushed into a darkened alcove so she could cover her face with her hands and let the tears flow.

A hand landed on her shoulder. She jumped and spun, hand to her heart. When she saw it was only Haman, she let out a gust of breath. "You startled me."

Her father's dearest friend gave her a kind smile, as he always did. "You did not hear me over your tears. What distresses you, lady? I feel as though, in your father's absence, I must try to put it to rights."

Artaynte wiped at her cheeks. For as long as she could remember, Haman had been a close friend of her family, often traveling to their home in Bactra. But to tell him this?

She shook her head and gazed at the floor behind him.

Haman dipped his head into her line of sight. "I have daughters of my own, you know. And I believe the timbre of those particular cries denotes trouble with a man. Would I be correct to guess it is the prince you sigh over?"

Was she that transparent? Her sigh leaked out more like a groan. "It is hopeless."

"Nonsense. Everyone knows you are the logical choice for his first wife."

She blinked back fresh tears. "I want to be the one he loves."

"But you see the way he has been looking at the Jewess and worry." He nodded, no longer looking amused. "I confess his attention to her troubles me, as well. I hope he remains above her devious ways."

Her chin snapped up. "Devious—Kasia?"

He pressed his lips into a grim smile. "I pray the prince does not succumb to her so-called charms. I would hate to see her lead yet another of the king's trusted men into such a dangerous situation."

"Another?" She shook her head—but still a rock sunk into her stomach. "She loves her husband."

"Of course she does." Yet his tone said the opposite. "But surely you know how things work within the palace. There is love, and there are lovers."

The rock burrowed deep, made nausea churn. "Not always. My parents . . . ." The look in his eyes stopped her. She swallowed. "Surely they . . . ."

Haman sighed and patted her shoulder. "Your mother has protected you from this truth too long—it will only hurt you to realize the nature of princes once you are wed to one. Darius may very well choose to have an affair with the Jewess—and he would surely not be the first."

No. Not Kasia. She would never . . . not with Darius . . . not with anyone but the king, surely. Surely.

So why did her heart already ache as though she had seen her friend betraying her?

Salamis, Greece

Xerxes cursed, then cursed again for good measure. Artemisia had been right. *He* had been right—they should not have met the Greeks at sea. His quicker vessels had no advantage in these straits. The smaller, heavier ships of his enemy rammed them continually.

He watched Artemisia's trireme flee a band of Greeks only to find her way blocked by Persians. A moment later she turned, ramming the vessel by her side.

At least someone was learning from their enemy. "It would seem my women are becoming men, even as my men are becoming women."

But the others? Groans tripped over curses as he watched the battle play out. The problem was that the idiot sailors had not learned how to swim. Each time a ship sank, the men went down with it. The Greeks swam to shore, but his men? He did not want to count how many drowned before his eyes.

The longer the day dragged on, the worse it got. He sat, he paced, he watched, he turned away. And he knew. He knew as dusk crouched behind them that the Greeks had the upper hand. He knew it before he heard that his troops stationed on an island had been slaughtered. He knew it before darkness fell and the commanders gathered again.

Mardonius spoke the loudest. "We know their tactics now—we can regroup, and we will win. We have the manpower."

But what did it matter?

"We will never defeat them on the sea," Otanes said. "We should build a pass to the island, then march across and defeat them on land."

"I say set the rest of our forces toward the Peloponnese and let the Athenians starve on their island."

He did not even turn to see who came up with that one. He looked toward Artemisia. "What say you? You fought more like a man than the men around you today."

She inclined her head, a silver braid slipping over her shoulder. "My advice has not changed, my lord. You have the victory that matters. You burned Athens. Why concern yourself with anything else? If one of your slaves—" She motioned toward Mardonius. "—wishes to keep some soldiers here and fight in your stead, that would suffice. If he wins, the victory is yours. If he loses, the defeat is his."

Mardonius glared at her. "The woman's tone aside, the idea has merit. I would be honored to keep a select group of soldiers behind to fight for you."

His cousin must have been able to read in Xerxes' eyes that he was finished. Finished with the war, with the nights filled only with cloistering shadows. He needed Kasia.

Standing, Xerxes pulled his shawl around his shoulders—the one Amestris had woven, the one Kasia had complimented. What was it she had said when he mentioned putting it away? Something about remembering the good days.

He wanted their good days back. Would she forgive him? If he begged, if he fell to his knees before her? If he took back all he had said?

He did not know, and could only hope all these people before him could not see that their king stood in pieces.

"I will think on this overnight." He strode from the gathering and to the quiet of his tent.

Waving his servants away, he extinguished the lamp and settled onto his bed. No sooner did he close his eyes than the god appeared.

That handsome, leering face. "King of Persia," he said, voice echoing with disdain. "Will you curl up in defeat and slink away?"

Xerxes averted his face.

"You are a coward—you would have changed your mind about this war before it started had I not interfered."

"I wish I would have. Do you know how many men I have lost?"

The god sneered. "What are they to you? The mighty Xerxes has taken Athens and has all the world at his feet. Why concern yourself with the cost? Are you not the wealthiest man in the world? The ruler of all?"

He motioned outside. "Could you not see from your realm what happened today?"

"One lost battle does not mean a lost war." The god folded granite arms over his marble chest. "You are a soft, feeble ruler—I should have struck you down rather than raising you up. You will trade everything for that woman, when you know she is the enemy of your god."

Xerxes breathed an unamused laugh. "And why not? All you bring me are shadows and night, darkness and constriction. She brings light and freedom."

The god thundered, his rage filling every crevice of Xerxes' mind. A glowing iron appeared, its point a deadly red-white. Xerxes planted his feet and faced down his angry god.

"Turn from my will," the god seethed, "and I will smite you with all my wrath. Your war will be lost, your kingdom rent in two. Give your favor again to the Jewish whore and I will purge her entire people from the face of the earth. Choose carefully, O King. Your god or your lover."

The smothering darkness of Ahura Mazda or the soft light in Kasia's eyes? There was no choice, not really. He only wondered why he had tried so long to convince himself there was. "I would rather have her."

The roar from the god-man's mouth deafened him, and the poker loomed glowing before his eyes. "Then you will have neither! No longer will I send blessings your way, and you shall be undone by the women you think you rule. And the Jewess? I will destroy her."

"Jehovah will protect her." He may have doubted her God more than once, but he had always preserved her life.

"You dare to mention that name?" His very voice a flame, the god aimed the poker.

The dream held him captive. He could not lunge away, could not spin, could not raise his arms in defense. He could only stand there as the hot iron found his shoulder and scream when it seared his flesh.

He bolted up in his bed, hand covering the burn.

Zethar led all his eunuchs in at a run. "Master, what is it?"

Using the light from their lantern, he pulled down his tunic and looked at the front of his shoulder, where an angry circle of red defied logic. "Since when can dreams injure a man?"

Zethar crouched down and touched a finger to it, pulling away with a gasp. "It burns like fire."

Xerxes clenched his teeth. Was this the god he had lost Kasia for, one who attacked his followers, who hurt rather than healed? That was not the Ahura Mazda he had read about in the prophecies of Jartosht . . . but it seemed to be the one who had heard their prayers.

He tossed his cover aside and surged to his feet. "Gather the commanders again."

"They are still there, master. You have only been in here half an hour."

"Perfect." He strode out, back down the hill to where the officials indeed still sat together and talked. All heads turned toward him when he barreled into the assembly.

Xerxes looked from one trusted face to the next, and cared not a whit what any of them thought. Not anymore. "We go home."

"Master!"

He raised a hand to hush Mardonius. "My decision is made. The Greeks could decide at any moment to sail for the Hellespont and destroy our bridge. I for one do not intend to be trapped here after the harvest—the army would starve."

"But master, you cannot accept this defeat! After all, it is not about the planks of wood, but about men and horses, and we still outnumber the Greeks on that score."

"You want to take a land force into the Peloponnese, then do so, Mardonius. Choose whatever troops you want. I am going home."

Artemisia nodded. "It is the wisest course of action, my lord."

"You will lead the fleet back, Artemisia." He met her gaze through the night. "Take Cyrus and my other sons with you, and go to guard the bridge so that we might cross in safety."

Her head tilted up, silver hair glowing in the moonlight. "I am honored by your trust in me."

"You have earned it. Otanes, supervise the building of a causeway to make the Greeks think we are mounting another attack. While they focus on that, the fleet can slip away. By the time we march, the ships will be able to guarantee our delivery home, and the Greeks will not bother following them. Mardonius—"

"I will escort you out of Europe and winter in Thessaly with the men I select."

Xerxes nodded and then looked at each of his advisers in turn. None argued—none would dare. "So it is settled. We will be back in Susa in time for my birthday feast."

And back to Sardis within six weeks, back to Kasia's arms.

Assuming she would open them.

Susa, Persia

Esther had never heard such a joyous roar in the streets, such music and singing. She edged around a woman leaping and strewing myrtle. "What in the world?"

"Have you not heard?" A young man grabbed her by the hands and spun her with a laugh. "The king has taken Athens! Persia is victorious!"

He released her and scooped up another passerby to twirl. Esther shook her head and smiled. Fetching the spices Martha had asked for might not happen this morning, but the high spirits were contagious. She tucked her basket's handle into her elbow and contented herself with strolling through the market-turned-festival.

And why not rejoice? Each day brought a new treasure—a tender, secret smile from Zechariah, a hint from one of his parents that she would soon be one of them. She had been afraid to hope that first time he asked her on a walk, but now . . . how could she not?

He sought her out daily, sometimes for glorious hours at a time. They walked, they talked of future dreams, they reminisced and laughed. Each time he asked for her opinion on something to incorporate into his house, Esther's heart danced a quick step.

He had made no declaration for her yet, but she knew. He built their home, where she would someday live as his wife. His *wife*. She had not been so happy since Kasia lived.

She paused beside an unattended cart of pomegranates and wished her friend could share this time with her. Oh, the fun they would have! Laughing, planning, whispering.

Sisters at last.

Awareness kissed her neck, and she looked around, knowing Zechariah must be somewhere nearby. She knew not how she always sensed his presence, but … there—across the market, at the corner of a side street. He had an empty handcart with him and looked out over the dancing citizens with confounded amusement.

A female form spun into him, grabbed his hands, twirled him back into the street he had come from.

Esther chuckled and turned toward home. There would be no shopping today, and weaving through the crowd to find Zechariah would probably prove useless. But that was fine—she would have time with him tonight. Every night.

Yes, it was a day of rejoicing.

What a miserable day. Zechariah slathered another protective layer of clay onto the south-facing wall and wished there were a way to make the sun trace backwards, to undo what he had done. He had already asked forgiveness of Jehovah. He had snuck off to the temple and purchased a sin offering.

Still he felt dark inside, stained with the knowledge of what could happen if Esther found out.

Had he known he would run into Ruana that morning, he never would have left the shop. But she had rushed at him, smiling and laughing and dancing like every other half-crazed Persian in Susa. She had pulled him into a secluded alleyway, pulled his head down to hers before he could object.

He cut his thoughts off there, before he relived the shame of what followed. Yes, he had been overcome. But he would not allow it to happen again. He had not planned this tryst, and surely that counted for something.

"There you are." Esther slid from behind the wall and smiled. She looked so perfect, so beautiful. So innocent, so trusting.

No, the spontaneity counted for nothing. Not when it could hurt her. He was the lowest of men, and he did not deserve her love—but he craved it. Would do anything to keep it.

He smiled, praying it held no shadow of guilt. "Do you mind if I get some work done tonight rather than walking? I find myself eager to finish."

A blush caressed her cheek, and she bit back a smile. "I do not mind that at all."

"Good. I brought you a stool out." He motioned toward where it sat in a shaded spot nearby. "If you would still like to keep me company."

"Always."

Dear Lord, let it be so.

THIRTY-ONE

Sardis, Lydia

Kasia repositioned herself on the cushion and glanced at the prince. He still laughed, still held a cup of wine, still seemed inclined to continue the feast. Her eyelids felt weighted, and her back ached, but she could not leave until Darius either dismissed the gathering or granted her permission. She kept trying to get his attention to ask, but each time their eyes met, he only smiled before looking away.

Perhaps she ought to slip out as if attending to personal matters and then not return. Who would really care, anyway?

No one. The prince was the only one who ever spoke to her at these insufferable feasts he had been having all week, and he had company enough that he would not miss her. For the life of her, she could not understand why he insisted she come. She had nothing to offer this gathering.

She had nothing to offer anyone. There was nothing left of her. Even her prayers echoed dull and lusterless, never making it to heaven.

"You look unhappy." Darius settled beside her, grinning Xerxes' grin.

Smiling felt as foreign as the lush landscape around the citadel. "I tire easily these days." This was even worse than the shadows and fog—at least then her prayers had still come. Now . . . she had chosen Jehovah over Xerxes. So why did she end up with neither?

The prince frowned. "You ought to have said something."

"It is hardly worth complaining about." She turned her gaze on her plate. Darius had never seemed much like Xerxes when they were side by side, but now he reminded her of him with every expression.

"Kasia." There, that same teasing inflection his father would use. "Your well-being is more important than a dinner. Come, I will see you back to your quarters so you can rest."

"Oh, there is no need for you to leave your guests. My servants will—"

"Nonsense." He stood and held out a hand to help her up. "When Father returns, I intend to tell him I took the most excellent care of you."

"I doubt he will care." She did not mean to say it out loud, and the mutter was low—but the prince obviously heard her. His brows arched as he helped her to her feet.

He waited until they'd left the chamber before saying, "I find your thoughts surprising. You admitted my father regretted his anger before you even left Malis."

Her gaze followed the mosaics in the floor. Such bright colors, kept clean of scuffs and scratches by diligent servants. If only her life still shone so—if only another could scrub her heart clean. "He sent Zethar with an apology as I was leaving. I refused it."

"You were angry. Surely he will not hold that against you now."

She just snorted a dubious laugh.

Darius chuckled. "Perhaps with others the king is unbending and hard, but not with you. He has poured more favor upon your head than on any other ever before." He paused, dropped his gaze to her stomach. "The life within you is proof of that, is it not? I hear he had determined not to risk your health again, yet obviously you prevailed over his determination."

Why did he look at her like that, as though there were more to his words than their syllables? She forced a swallow. "It is hardly a victory when it cost me his trust. I came to him out of love, because I missed him—he accused me of doing it only to get with child again."

A stream of thoughts flashed through his eyes too quickly for her to keep up. She thought she spotted doubt, perhaps curiosity. But then only his usual friendliness shone out, and he ushered her down the corridor that would lead to her chamber. "That hurt you. And I am sure wondering if it were true hurt *him*. The question now, dear Kasia, is whether it cuts so deep because you love him still, or if it has snuffed out all affection."

It was hardly an appropriate line of conversation . . . yet fair enough, when one considered the way she had spoken to him of Artaynte. Kasia sighed. "I ought to fear what will become of me and my family if he sets his face against us. But I feel no fear. Yet I also feel no hope that things will improve. I feel . . . nothing. Nothing but anger—at him for the way he acted, and at myself for needing him so much that it came to this."

Contemplation settled on his face. "I cannot think you have reason to fear. Father is a fair man, especially given time to consider things."

His threat still echoed in her head. *I will decide then what to do with you*. A shudder tripped down her spine. "If he is fair, then the best I can hope for is a life of loneliness in the harem. In his eyes, I betrayed him, chose another over him."

Darius's eyes darkened. "In his eyes only, or in reality?"

The weight of the universe seemed to settle on her shoulders. Had she betrayed her husband? "He asked the impossible."

The prince halted and gripped her shoulders, jarring her a little to force her face up. "That is all you can say? I thought you loved him."

"I did!" She tried to focus on his eyes but could not—in them roiled and raged something that set loose the hounds of panic and fear. They nipped at her, their growls filled her ears until she wanted to spin and flee. Darius's fingers held her prisoner—

she pulled against him to no avail. "I loved him with all my heart, but he would have demanded my soul. I could not give him that, Darius, I could *not*."

His grip softened, his expression melted. He pulled her to his chest. "I am no one to judge you. I am sure you have regret enough without condemnation on top of it."

Kasia held herself stiff. His arms did not feel like Abba's or Pythius's, like Xerxes' or even Zechariah's. They felt strange, unnatural.

She pulled away with a shake of her head. "I cannot regret my daughter. Nor can I regret standing against him when he demanded I forsake my God."

Before she could work up the nerve to glance into his face for a reaction, a servant ran down the hall. "Master! I have just arrived from Athens, and I sought you out first."

Kasia's eyes slid shut. The runner's tone spoke of tragedy. How great? How many this time? What if Xerxes . . . no. Surely the Lord would not snatch her husband from her with this between them.

Would he?

"What is it?" Darius's voice was dread covered in urgency.

"Defeat, master, at Salamis, where we met the Greeks at sea."

"Defeat?"

The prince's echo bounced around inside her. She squeezed her eyes shut all the tighter, but still her heart thudded, pounded at her ribs. The babe within her gave a mighty kick.

Not Xerxes. Please, Lord, not Xerxes.

"The Greeks' ships were better suited for the area, smaller and capable of ramming us. We suffered great loss, many drowned. The king commanded a causeway built to make it look as though we prepare for a second attack, but he is coming home. The fleet has already set sail to guard the bridge, and the land army will have left this morning."

He is coming home. Praise Jehovah. Her eyes opened, though she looked only at the floor.

She felt Darius shake his head. "But how could this have happened? My father is an excellent commander, he surely would have seen the risks—"

"Our forces had received word from a spy, master, advising it. Everyone agreed it was the wisest course."

A quiver resonated inside. "When?"

The men both raised their brows. Kasia cleared her throat. "What day did he receive this advice?"

The slave frowned. "It would have been . . . five days ago."

The day they received word of the victory at Athens. The day the Spirit had come, had told her to pray for her husband.

The day she had refused.

"Oh, God." Her knees buckled. Theron leaped to catch her, and she gripped his welcome arm with shaking fingers. "Jehovah, forgive me. Forgive me, I should have listened."

Borrowing some of Theron's strength, she gained her feet again and stumbled her way down the hall, into her chamber. Desma scurried ahead of her to position her prayer mat under the window, facing Jerusalem.

Her knees struck hard, and she doubled over as much as her stomach would allow. "Lord, forgive me. You tried to warn me that my husband would need your wisdom, and I ignored you. My heart was so shadowed by anger that I did not care."

Colors shifted on her lids when she squeezed her eyes shut tight. "And yet, I had a right to my anger, did I not? He is so proud, so arrogant. He tramples the world and thinks it enough that he mourns those who get crushed."

Do you love him?

Her soul shook. Had she questioned that these past weeks? Had she spoken of it in the past tense minutes before? Yet the fear that seized her when she thought she might have lost him . . . . "Yes, Lord. You know I do."

Can you love him when your heart is black with anger?

Fresh tears burned at her eyes. "No. But he denied our child. He would have me deny you."

Your part is to choose whether you will love him, whether you will let my light shine through you. Leave it to me to provide the flame. Leave it to me to soften his heart to receive it.

A tongue of that flame flicked through her. How had she survived these weeks without its heat and light? Why had she not realized she could not both fight Xerxes over her God and then turn around and fight God over Xerxes? "Yes, Lord. I will. I *will* love him. Please, help me to forgive the hurts he has caused me. Forgive me for turning from the one you gave me to, for not listening to your Spirit."

For the first time since Thermopylae, she let the waves of longing crash over her, soak her being with the need to feel Xerxes' strong arms around her so that she would know he loved her. Know he would do all in his tremendous power to protect her.

Even if that meant hurting her.

She shuddered and curled her fingers into the fringes of the rug. Perhaps his logic was faulty, but he had only wanted her safe. In his eyes, her faith risked her life. He was wrong—but his heart had been right. He loved her.

Hopefully he still did. "Help us mend our marriage, Jehovah God. Strengthen our love and knit our hearts together. Shine through me."

Peace washed over her and eased the tension in her shoulders and back. Her daughter flipped within her.

Two years ago she would not have believed that love could be a choice, that it would ever need to be. Passion had made it easy to pledge her heart and to believe that would be enough to last forever. But the fire of first love was not its proof—its mettle could not be known until it had passed through the furnace of trial.

Hers would not burn up and fade to ash. Not so long as she had breath left for prayer.

Darius wandered the halls, sending even his servants away from him. He needed no company—his thoughts provided more than enough of that.

Defeat—unfathomable. How did an army so large, a fleet so vast, fall to the ragtag city-states? Would Persia really toss up her hands and let the Greeks have their victory?

No. Some would stay and fight, the runner had said, under Mardonius. But Father was finished. He would rejoin them at Sardis in another five or six weeks, and from there take his household home to Susa.

But *why*? Why spend four years preparing and then give it all over to a slave after nine short months on campaign? Why stand so firm at Thermopylae, burn Athens to the ground, then sound the retreat after one day of battle at sea?

A face filled his vision, and he suspected she was his answer. Kasia. His father would miss her. He could understand that. He could even understand why Xerxes would love her despite her infidelity. He still found it unbelievable that she had confessed to betraying him with another, but apparently Haman had been right.

And Father . . . did he not care? Had he decided to turn a blind eye? Was he willing to share her, so long as she also remained his?

Old fantasies roared to life. Was is possible she would accept him if he approached her?

He rounded a corner and collided with a petite, soft frame that let out a melodious cry of alarm. Grasping her elbows to steady her, recognition hit far more gently than it would have a month ago. "Artaynte. Are you all right?"

She tilted her head to look up at him. Dark hair cascaded back, wide eyes gleamed. Her rosebud lips parted. Small aspects that played into her staggering beauty. Yet his feet no longer faltered. His heart barely tripped.

Strange as it seemed, he missed the torment of loving her. Now . . . he wanted her, yes. And there was still no better choice for his future queen. But he had to wonder what, if anything, went on behind those lovely eyes. All he thought he knew of her was false, so what did that leave?

"Prince Darius." Her voice trembled. "The court just heard the news of the defeat. I was coming to see how you . . . that is, to make sure . . . ." She blinked, swallowed, and straightened. "You must be distressed. Is there anything I can do?"

He hated the cynicism that slicked through his veins. "Did your mother decide you should comfort me and let me think I had finally won your love and respect?"

Her eyes registered guilty shock before she dropped her gaze. "I know not what you mean. I was concerned for you, that is all."

"You need not worry for me. Not now." Her skin was warm and soft under his fingers, and he put the gentlest of pressure on her elbows to draw her a fraction nearer. "I have well learned how to handle disappointment—mostly at your hand."

She focused on his chin. "You never seemed terribly disappointed as you seduced every beautiful commoner you could find."

"You are jealous." He smirked, but it did not give him the pleasure he expected. "Surely you knew it was you I wanted. Had you quirked your little finger, I would have fallen at your feet."

She moistened her lips and darted a quick glance at his eyes. "Would have?"

He drew in a long breath. "In all likelihood, our fathers will arrange a match. You will be my queen, and I imagine we will find pleasure enough in each other's arms. But I do not intend to trust you with my heart, Artaynte. You would only ask your mother what you should do with it."

She winced, turned her face half away. "That is unfair."

"Is it? Either you have been acting on your mother's advice, my sweet, or you hate me."

"No. No, I . . . ." It looked to take considerable effort for her to meet his gaze and hold it. "Why can we not put the years behind us and start fresh? From this moment."

"What good would that do? You think I can forget that every word you spoke to me for the last five years was an insult?"

She lifted a shaking hand and rested it on his chest. Desire flared up, but he restrained it easily. She took a fortifying breath. "I want a relationship with you, Darius. I want the chance to get to know you honestly, so that we can come to love each other."

He released her elbow so that he might run his fingers through her hair and anchor her head where he wanted it. Leaning down, he hovered over her lips. "It is too late for that." He kissed her before she could argue, and wasted no time with a slow, gentle start. Better to let her see now what he wanted from her, what he would expect.

She would be his—but he would remain his own.

When he ended the kiss, he stepped away, around her. Smirked at the eunuch behind her who stood with clenched fists. Any other man he could defend her against, but not the next king. Darius could have tossed her to the ground, and it would have been death to the slave if he raised a hand to stop him.

But he would give her the honor her station—and her future station—deserved.

She spun to follow him, looking undone. "Darius, wait. Please."

He strode down the hall, toward his chamber.

Artaynte scurried to keep up. "Darius, just . . . just tell me you do not love her. Please."

His heart sputtered—not at her words, but at the fact that he knew exactly who she meant. What did it mean? That Kasia was so present in his thoughts even while he dealt with Artaynte? He could not be in love with his father's wife. It was one thing to consider a dalliance with her, but love . . . that would be dangerous.

Although on the other hand, perhaps only love could make it worth the risk.

He shook that off and focused on the pleading face beside him. "What business is it of yours?"

She looked about a finger-width from tears. "She is my friend."

"Is she? One would never know it." He opened the door to his room, stepped inside, and slammed it behind him.

He had had enough of that conversation.

Susa, Persia

Amestris crossed her arms and surveyed the masses of mourning Persians outside the walls. They rent their garments, wept, cried out in seeming agony. She shook her head at the theatrics and turned to her eunuch, newly returned from the city. "You would think we had been invaded. It is only one lost battle. Why do they carry on so?"

The slave bowed his head. "They fear for the king, mistress. News of the loss has reached them all, but no word on your husband."

She grunted and spun away from the wall. If only she were so lucky as to be widowed—but if anything had happened to Xerxes, the message of defeat would not have been so vague.

Ash drifted over the wall and made her sneeze. The idiot commoners were going too far to prove their distress. All over a man most of them had never seen but from a distance, that few had ever spoken to. If they knew him as she did, they would not be distraught.

The world would be a better place when her son ruled, and she through him.

Unease pounced onto her shoulders and drew her gaze toward the nearby gate. Her lips curled up when she spotted the Jew that represented his people. She could sense the demons that guarded him.

She hurried away, back toward the women's palace and her children. Perhaps one of the first things she ought to have Darius do when he took the crown was get rid of those troublesome Jews. She should not have to face the enemy of the god in her own home.

Sardis, Lydia

Darius watched her for a moment, then took stock of himself. For three weeks he had fought it, had tried to tell himself it was only a passing lust, that it was too great a risk. He had even tried to refocus his thoughts on Artaynte.

Nothing worked. Each time he saw Kasia, it hit him anew. He must have her—and he was running out of time. Father would be back in three more weeks, and finding opportunities to be together then could prove difficult.

Desire had never felt like this. Several of his lovers had gotten with child over the years, and seeing their rounded stomachs had always cooled his passion. Yet he never even remembered Kasia's condition unless she mentioned some symptom. With them, he had at once tried to be sensitive and yet cared little what they thought, what they wanted. With Kasia, he found himself craving her opinion, longing to hear her speak. Time and again he had sought her out, just to pass the time in conversation. He told himself he did it for her, to help her fend off loneliness.

He knew better.

She had been her old self these past weeks, the anger gone. Perhaps a sorrow lurked in her eyes, but she had been laughing again. Eyes bright. Passion for life pulling her taut as a bow ready to loose its arrow.

He was helpless against his longings.

The afternoon sun burned bright but lacked warmth, and Darius pulled his shawl higher. Kasia sat at her son's grave, beside the withering sunflowers. Pythius had passed an hour with her, but Darius had kept out of sight until the old man left again. He must make her his offer, but he would do it carefully. She would want no one to know.

Drawing in a long breath, Darius stepped away from the wall and forced confidence into his step. His nerves frayed and sizzled, as if he had never approached a woman before. But then, he had never tried to seduce one of his father's wives. Never had his heart been at stake.

She looked up at his approach and smiled. His pulse raced. Did she know what she did to him? She must. It was no great secret that she and his father enjoyed a passionate union, she was no stranger to the reactions of men.

He smiled back. "Good afternoon, Kasia. How are you feeling today?"

"Well." She reached out to have her maid help her to her feet. "And you, prince?"

He could only nod, his throat dry as she smoothed her garment over her hip. "Are you up for a walk?"

How could her eyes brighten even as her smile softened? "That sounds perfect. My legs were beginning to tingle."

Yes, surely she knew what she did to him. And if she did not mean to encourage him, she would not say such things. He darted a glance at the four servants surrounding her. "Alone, if you please? I have some things to discuss with you that are of the most sensitive nature."

She arched a brow even as her head eunuch stepped forward, with a muted, "Mistress, no."

Why did she suffer such impudence from her slaves? Yet she grinned at the beast. "Theron, it is only Darius, and we will not walk far. Stay within sight, if that will make you feel better."

Not exactly what Darius had hoped, but it would do. He offered his arm, and she set her hand lightly on the inside of his elbow. Once they were out of earshot of her slaves, he drew in a long breath. "You have seemed much happier these last few weeks."

One of those small, intoxicating smiles teased the corners of her lips. "I have put some things to rights within my soul."

"I am glad. Getting to know you has been very precious to me."

The smile bloomed full, and she cast him a warm glance. "To me as well. It is funny, Darius. In some ways you remind me of your father, and in others of Zechariah."

Who was Zechariah? He tried to remember if she had mentioned him before, but nothing came to mind. Was it . . . perhaps her lover? It would make sense if she had found a Jewish man in the ranks to comfort her when Father kept her at arm's length.

It hardly mattered. He chuckled because she expected it, and deliberately led her over a bumpy patch so that she would sway closer to his side. Ah, she smelled so fresh and feminine. "And you remind me of no one—there is no other woman in all of the empire quite like you."

Her laugh sounded dry. "I suspect you are right on that count."

"I am." He halted, the pulse pounding through him forbidding any longer delay. "Kasia, there is none to compare to you. I have always thought you one of the most exquisite creatures to be found. But since we have become friends . . . you have stolen my heart. I—"

"Stop." She pulled her hand from his arm and took a quick step away. Those spell-binding eyes shone with panic. Understandable. An affair with him would not be as simple as one with some random Jewish soldier. She shook her head. "You must not say such things, Darius. I am your father's wife and—"

"I love you." He closed the distance again.

She held up a hand. "No. No, you love Artaynte. You have loved her for years, you cannot just fall in love with another in the course of a month."

He caught her hand, pressed it to his chest. "I never knew her, she never let me. But you—you have always been so open, so honest. I have seen your heart, and I love you for it."

She tugged on her fingers. Were those tears burning her eyes? "Please do not say such things, Darius, I beg you. Let us forget this conversation—"

"Forget it? I cannot. I know you care for me—"

She blinked the tears away, and a hint of anger replaced them. Ah, such fire. How could he help but fall for her? No other woman would dare to give him a little push as she reclaimed her hand. "Care, yes, just as I care for my brothers. But I am in love with your father—your *father*, Darius—and you shame us all by even thinking such things."

"I realize he holds the greatest portion of your heart. But that did not stop you from finding your pleasure elsewhere before, so why should it now?"

Her palm connected with his cheek without warning. The sting was sharp—yet for some reason, it amused rather than angered him.

"How dare you!" She seethed, as if she had not already confessed to infidelity. Then she pivoted, tried to spin, but her foot caught on a rock.

Darius scooped her up before she could fall to the hard ground. And once he held her in his arms, what was he to do but dip his head and claim her lips?

Kasia morphed into a tigress and flailed her way out of his arms, her cheeks stained red. Yet when her dog charged up, she stopped him with a stern command.

Darius grinned. "Come, my sweet," he said in the voice that always worked on other girls. "Why pretend innocence when you have already confessed to betraying my father?"

The color drained from her face. "For my God, Darius. I chose Jehovah over him, not some other man. I would never go to another. Never."

Her eunuch arrived, seething, and Darius rolled his eyes. "Call off your beasts, Kasia. You know very well if either of them attacked me, it would be their deaths. You cannot want that."

Her jaw ticked. "Theron, take Zad back to Desma."

"Mistress—"

"Darius will not hurt me." She searched his eyes, as if not sure of her own words. "Would you?"

She might as well have pierced him with the slave's dagger. "How can you even ask? I love you."

"Stop saying that!" She raked her hair out of her eyes and watched the eunuch pull the dog away. "We will never be anything but friends."

"Why? Because of my father?" He edged closer, slowly. Yes, she retreated, but that was fine. She backed herself right up against the wall and then had nowhere to go. "You said yourself he will sentence you to anonymity in the harem. Is that what you want? A life devoid of passion?"

Her chin rose. "If that is what he decides, then so be it. Still I will love him and remain true."

"For how long?" He boxed her in, breathed in her scent. "I can bring you both excitement and steady adoration. Perhaps he will even turn a blind eye and—"

"This is absurd." Unable to move away, she straightened her spine. "How can you in good conscience make such an offer? I am even now carrying your sister!"

"It makes the timing perfect, really. There would be no consequences now. It would give us time to come up with a more permanent arrangement."

Her eyes flashed, and her hands landed on his chest. She intended to shove him away again, he knew, but he could not let her escape so easily. It would only take a kiss. One thorough, honest kiss. And she would be his.

Haman watched the prince tug the Jewess close, cover her mouth with his. She fought against him, but Darius seemed not to notice.

Artaynte did not seem to either. A cry of alarm whispered from her throat, and her hand covered her mouth. Eyes awash, she spun around. "Excuse me, Haman. I cannot—I must—" She dashed away.

Haman let her go. He did not want to see the girl hurt, but what good would it do to shelter her from Darius's nature? The prince would be just like his father and uncles, always wanting whatever lovely face he did not already own. And because he was the prince, the heir, he could take whomever he pleased.

Even the Jewess. She may fight, but her strength would fail. And her servants would not dare step in, or their lives would be forfeit. Darius would be her undoing. With any luck, she would get herself killed at his hand—but if not, it would be enough to ruin her forever in Xerxes' eyes. He would not want her when she had been in another's arms.

Indulging in one chuckle, Haman turned to retrace his steps through the garden.

Kasia kicked Darius in the shin and would have kneed him in the groin had he not released her. By the time Theron surged her way again, Darius stood a step away.

She poked a furious finger into his chest. "Touch me again, and the king will have to find himself another heir."

He had the audacity to grin. "And you wonder why I love you?"

Perhaps in another situation, she would have been amused at how like Xerxes he was. Not now. She stepped to the side of her servant and glared at the prince.

Darius sighed. "I will be here when you change your mind."

"I will not."

"We shall see." He touched his finger to his lips and ambled away.

Theron put a steadying arm around her. "Mistress?"

"I will be all right, Theron." Yet tears veiled her vision, and she sagged against him. She had just lost the one friend she had left in her husband's house.

Thirty-Three

Xerxes dug his heels into his horse's flanks. For forty-five long days he had kept his pace steady, knowing the world watched his retreat. He would not give the Greeks the satisfaction of thinking they chased him home—but his soul had strained toward Sardis. Now that it was within sight, he could curb himself no longer.

A horse approached from the city, and Xerxes smiled when he saw Haman upon it. He called out a greeting as his friend neared.

Haman fell in beside him. "Greetings, master. We have all been anxiously awaiting your return."

"All?" Did he dare hope? He had to. Yet fear shadowed him. "What of your charge?"

Haman shrugged. "Who can know the mind of a woman? She does not seem so angry lately, but then, your son may have cajoled her out of her temper."

His throat closed. "Darius?"

"Mm. Everyone else was wary of befriending an enemy of the god, but the prince took her under his wing. They have become . . . rather close." Something cold and wary sparked in Haman's eyes. "You may want to speak to them about that."

No. He trusted her. Even in her anger, she would not succumb to adultery—it went against everything her God advocated.

Although his son he was not so sure of.

He shook it off and urged his horse a little faster. "How is her health?"

"Well enough, I imagine. She spends most of her days out of doors, at the grave of her son." Haman lifted a brow. "If you ask me, such behavior denotes an unhealthy mental state."

Xerxes chuckled. "You just admitted you do not know her thoughts, so forgive me for ignoring your judgment on her mental state."

His friend sighed and looked over his shoulder. "Your brother is with you?"

"Directly behind. Go find him, I will ride ahead."

He focused on the looming walls of the citadel. Another minute and he would be there. Two months' separation over at last. If he had a god left to petition, he would have sent up a prayer that Kasia receive him.

Instead, he concentrated on closing the distance, then nudged his steed toward the grave. Hopefully she would be there. If not, he would take a moment to pay his respects to their son, then search her out inside.

The collection of figures he spotted was encouraging. Yes, it was Theron standing with folded arms beside the tree, so that must be Kasia sitting with her back to him.

She turned her head—his breath caught when he saw that beautiful profile. He swung off his horse.

Kasia pushed to her feet, and Xerxes swore his heart stopped. Would she flee? Turn her back on him again?

She rushed toward him, naked affection on her face. For the first time since the day of darkness, total peace blanketed his spirit. He ran forward. "Kasia."

"Xerxes." She flew into his arms, burying her face in his chest. "My love."

He could not hold her tight enough, could not take in all the sensations. The fragrance of her hair, the feel of her arms around his waist, of their babe nudging him in the stomach. He pressed a kiss to the top of her head. "My darling. Say you still love me. Say you forgive me."

She tilted her head back, and he lost himself in the simmering heat of her eyes. Though she did not smile, he knew her answer before she opened her mouth. "I love you always. I forgive you. And I pray you forgive me."

Unable to help himself, he pressed a gentle kiss to her lips. "You have done nothing wrong. I am the one who acted the arrogant fool, who lost sight of what mattered. I am so sorry, my love. The things I said, the things I asked of you—"

"And I am sorry." She pressed her lips together, tears welling in her eyes. "I obeyed you when I should not have. Jehovah bade me pray for you, and I refused."

He could barely force a swallow. That proved her anger more than anything else could have. "You despised me."

"I was angry." She focused her gaze on his chest, nostrils flaring. "I later learned that was the day the spy came to you, to convince you to attack the Greeks at sea. Perhaps if I had prayed, one of the Lord's messengers could have whispered a warning in your ear."

He saw again that flash of light, snuffed out by darkness. Was it possible? Had one of her Jehovah's angels tried to reach him, only to be stopped by Ahura Mazda's? Had it been her prayers all along that made the difference?

Resting his forehead on hers, Xerxes closed his eyes. "I will never again ask you not to pray to your God."

"And I would never again obey you, even if you did." A smile colored her words. Then her fingers fisted in his tunic. "It must have been awful, for you to give up the battle after one day."

He lifted his head so that he might meet her gaze. "All my advisors said I should have mounted another attack. But it ceased to matter. I only wanted you. Besides." He smiled and moved a hand to her stomach, where the babe continued to make her presence known. "Had I delayed much longer, we would not have been able to make it back to Susa before our daughter joins us. And that was your dream, was it not?"

The tears made her eyes glisten like sardonyx. "We still have two months before she is due."

"It will take us nearly one to get home, and I know you will be uncomfortable at the end of your time. I would have you resting at the palace for the last weeks."

She nestled against him, her lashes a black fan against her cheeks. "I have missed you so."

"Oh, Kasia." He cinched his arms around her and closed his eyes on the rest of the world. "You are the most important thing to me. The god was none too pleased—he came in a dream again, threatened to destroy you and all your people, to undo me through my wives if I chose you over him."

He opened his eyes again and found her gazing up at him, agape. "Yet you are here."

"I am here."

She swallowed. "Even though I chose Jehovah over you."

"Jehovah preserves your life, protects you, ministers to your soul." He shook his head and urged her to move to his side so they could meander toward the citadel. "My god works through darkness and fear. I have had enough of that. I want only you, and will trust that your Jehovah can fend off the anger of Ahura Mazda."

"He will." Her fingers wove through his, and she squeezed. "He could be your Jehovah too, you know. Then he could minister to your soul, protect you, preserve you."

If her ceasing to pray were the proof of her anger, this was surely the proof of her forgiveness. Xerxes lifted her hand, kissed her fingers. "I am no Jew, my love. It is enough that he bless you."

"Father!"

He looked up at the wall, where Darius waved to him with a smile. Xerxes lifted a hand in greeting. "I see you kept the empire in one piece while I was away."

His son laughed. "There has been little to do. I will update you at your leisure."

"Soon."

Darius nodded, cast a long glance over Kasia, and drew in a breath. Did his son not even have the sense to guard his gaze? "Well, I will leave you to your stroll."

Xerxes watched him stride away and then glanced down at his wife. Her eyes were focused straight ahead, and he had the distinct impression they had been throughout the exchange.

Best to get it over with—he would not be able to rest if he were wondering. "Haman said you and Darius became friends."

Her lips pressed together, pulled up. It was not a smile. "He was kind and attentive, but only out of pity. No one else has spoken to me since I arrived. Other than Pythius, of course, but he does not appear in public these days."

Pythius. "I am glad our Lydian friend has not extended his hatred of me to you."

"He does not hate you. Not any longer."

He appreciated the squeeze of her fingers, but that had not been the purpose of this conversation. "Good. And I am glad Darius welcomed you."

Did she hear the question behind the statement? Her brows arched. "I would have preferred to pass my days with Artaynte, had Parsisa not forbidden it."

He refused to be baited into discussing his brother's wife. Instead he stopped, put a finger under her chin. "I saw the way he looked at you, Kasia."

She sighed. "It is nothing. Perhaps a passing infatuation on his part, but he has long been in love with Artaynte."

"Artaynte?" He dropped his finger, brows creasing. "Why did he not say so? We could have arranged a marriage years ago."

"I believe he wanted to win her affection first. The irony being he had it all along."

"Well, time enough has been wasted, then. He needs to marry soon and start producing heirs. I will speak to Masistes before we leave Sardis in a fortnight."

And get his son wed as soon as they returned to Susa. Perhaps when he had the lovely Artaynte in his bed, he would not find the need to ogle Kasia.

He slipped the torc off his wrist and onto her arm, where it belonged.

Kasia left the feast with a smile on her face. Xerxes had kept her close to his side and frequently slipped an arm around her shoulders. For the first time in months, excitement overcame the exhaustion. She had her husband back. More, he had returned in a way she had not dared hope—contrite. Humble—or as humble as the king of kings knew how to be.

Light still infused her nerves. He had given her leave to worship Jehovah. He had cut his ties with his god. Perhaps . . . did she dare hope someday he would serve the Lord with her?

"It is good to see you happy again, mistress," Desma said from right behind her. "The sparkle is back in your eye."

Her lips pulled up even higher. "I never should have doubted what Jehovah could work."

Desma drew in a breath that sounded happy too. "I was glad to see the court speaking to you again tonight."

"Except Parsisa and Artaynte." Which pierced. And made guilt wiggle to life. She should not have mentioned Artaynte's and Darius's feelings to Xerxes, but it had seemed the only way to assure him the prince had no designs on her. Although perhaps she could have found another way had the prince *not* had designs on her. She could hardly admit that to Xerxes, though, unless she wanted to be a wedge between them.

She did not. And surely Darius would forget his supposed feelings for her when he had Artaynte.

"Ah, there she is."

Kasia froze, dread settling over her. Running into Masistes was never fun when Xerxes was not there—especially when he had a slur in his voice. She forced a swallow. "My lord. It is good to see you safely returned—your wife and children surely missed you."

"And I them." Yet as he swayed forward, thoughts of them seemed far from his mind. That lecherous glint was in his eyes. "Though not so much as my brother missed you. You changed the course of the war, my lovely. He should have kept you there so his heart was not torn. Although . . . ." He hiccuped, leered. "I suppose he did not want to watch you increase with another man's child."

Fire pulsed through her and made her tremble. "How dare you accuse me of something like that!"

Ice followed on the heels of the fire. He was not the first to make such an accusation. Did everyone think she had betrayed the king with another man? Did they all think he had sent her away because of *that*? Bile rose in her throat.

He chuckled and stumbled a step nearer. "You are a woman of passion, and he had ned . . . had niggle . . . had neglected you. I am only sorry I did not realize it so I could have offered my shoulder. And arms. And—"

"That is quite enough." She stepped back, happy to let Theron slide between her and the sot. "I have never been unfaithful."

Masistes loosed a bark of laughter far too loud, too raucous. "Whatever you say. But it is never too late to change that. The king will be another hour or two at his feast, if you would like some company."

Her fingers curled into her palms. "No thank you." With Theron as a barrier, she marched by. Masistes would not follow, but his words lodged in her mind.

Did the entire court think her so low? First the prince, now Masistes. Though he had said he did not "realize" it before . . . .

Her breath stalled. Someone must have started the rumor, someone who had always hated her. Someone who had been here to whisper to Darius, someone Masistes would have spoken to as soon as he arrived. She knew exactly who that someone was.

Haman.

Artaynte leaned into the window and sighed. The landscape no longer looked beautiful, the mountain seemed only to snarl at her. Though the rest of the people rejoiced around her to have the king among them again, she cared little. What did it matter?

Mother sat nearby, looking pleased as could be. And why not? Father was home, they would head back to Susa soon, and she insisted all went well with Darius.

But it did not. Perhaps he had paid her attention lately, but Artaynte knew no love lay behind it.

What was it about Kasia? Were her hands the perfect shape for a king's heart? Did she possess some magic that drew those who ruled?

The king entered the chamber again, power undulating from him. Was he not enough for her once-friend? He stood taller than any other in his company, had a chiseled countenance of strong beauty—even his moods drew the people to him. But perhaps Kasia was ambitious and greedy like everyone else. Perhaps she wanted a place in the court of Darius as well.

The king charged toward her, and Artaynte focused her gaze out the window. He may be her uncle, father of the man she loved, but he had always terrified her. She breathed easier when he headed for Mother.

"Good evening, my lord," her mother said. "Are you happy to be back in Sardis?"

"I was happier a moment ago." Yet his voice sounded light, as if he were smiling. Joking.

Artaynte sneaked a glance. He sat close to her mother—too close—and his lips pulled upward. Yet his eyes glinted cold and hard.

Mother frowned. "What is the matter?"

The king lifted a hand, trailed it through Mother's hair. Artaynte's stomach twisted.

"You are a beautiful woman, Parsisa."

Artaynte folded her arms over her stomach. Mother pulled away from his hand, but only slightly. "Hence why your brother values me so highly. You know well I love him."

"And he knows well my wife loves me, but that did not stop him from approaching her moments ago. As he has done before."

Artaynte feared she may lose her dinner, but for some reason the news seemed to calm her mother. "That is what this is about?"

Again, the king's smile belied the look in his eye. "It is high time he learn how it feels to have one's brother attempt to seduce one's wife."

Mother smiled. Actually smiled. "Yet you respect him too much to force matters, and you know well I will not submit to you willingly."

"I do not want you to." He kissed her fingers. "He does not need to know that."

Mother chuckled. "I will play your game to teach him a lesson, my king. So long as you swear to stop at appearances."

"You have my word."

Artaynte crept away, desperate for the sanctuary of her room. This was her world, this place of lust and indulgence, of indiscretion and intrigue. This was the life Mother had groomed her for. This was why she had needed to learn how to show a face that covered her heart. How to speak poison even when she longed for honey.

Apparently one did whatever one must to get one's way.

So be it. She had learned her lessons.

Susa, Persia

Mordecai rubbed a hand over his chest, his eyes locked on the two figures strolling the banks of the Choaspes ahead of him. The discomfort in his heart was not a physical one. Nor was it based on logic. So far as he could discern he ought to be rejoicing with Esther over the progressing relationship with Zechariah.

But the unease would not let up. It had been weighing on him since the day they heard of the victory at Athens, and no matter how much prayer he gave the subject, it would not go away.

He wanted Esther to be happy. And as he watched her walk alongside her beloved, arm looped through his, he knew she was.

Why, then, this mounting fear that Zechariah was not the husband Jehovah intended her for? Why this suspicion that something was not right between them?

His gaze settled on the young man he considered a son. Zech loved Esther. When he looked at her, it was as if his whole soul strained toward her. And at the start of the courtship, Mordecai had been without reservation. Now . . . .

He could not shake the image of chains around Zechariah. They held him captive, though to what Mordecai did not know.

Unless the Lord gave him peace, he could not allow a marriage. Yet how in the world would he ever say no when Zechariah asked for her hand?

He sighed and kept pace far enough behind to let them speak privately, close enough to keep an eye on them. *Dear Jehovah, show me your will.*

If they were outside it, the happiness would not last.

Sardis, Lydia

"Master, your brother approaches. Angrily."

Xerxes turned from his exercise area and wiped the sweat from his brow. He grinned when he spotted Masistes storming his way. It was about time—it had taken nearly a week for the dolt to realize Xerxes spent half the evenings flirting with Parsisa after Kasia retired. "So he is, Zethar. Towel, please."

He cleaned up as best he could in the half-minute it took Masistes to thunder over and stop just short of shoving him.

"You wretch! You think just because you are king you can have my wife?"

Xerxes schooled his features and pulled a fresh tunic over his head. "I think I can have whatever woman I want—do you not agree? You are only a prince, yet you take whomever you please."

Masisted pounded a finger into his shoulder. "You know I love my wife. Yet now half the court is whispering about how *you* have fallen in love with her."

He certainly hoped that gossip had not reached Kasia. "A compliment to the extraordinary beauty of your woman. You ought to be flattered."

His brother sputtered, and for a moment Xerxes thought he might try to strike him. "Flattered? You expect me to feel flattered after watching you try to seduce her?"

Xerxes folded his arms over his chest. "Let me consider it. How did *I* feel two years ago when Mother told me you had threatened to have Kasia's family killed if she did not sleep with you? Not flattered, I suppose."

Masisted paled. "That was ages ago, and the threat was vain. Surely you know that."

"A more recent example then? Very well, how did I feel a week ago, when you approached her again, insulting her virtue and the legitimacy of my child? I was not particularly flattered to overhear that either, I grant you. So I suppose I expect you to feel much like I did. Furious."

Matching his stance, Masistes sucked in a long breath. Some of the rage disappeared from his face. "If you are so sure of her fidelity, you have no reason to grow angry."

"So you think I have a chance of success with Parsisa?"

Masistes pressed his lips together and then tossed his hands up. "You win! Your point is thoroughly proven. I will never again whisper an untoward word to Kasia, if you promise to stop foisting your attention upon Parsisa."

"You have my word." He chuckled—he ought to have done this years ago.

Masistes turned, but Xerxes caught his arm. "While I have you here, there is another matter to discuss. Your daughter."

"Artaynte?" Masistes lifted a brow. "You may have her for a queen, but she will not be another nobody in your harem."

Xerxes winced at the reminder of the task awaiting him in Susa. "She will be queen, but not mine. Darius would have her as his first wife—I spoke to him yesterday."

His brother's eyes lit up. "Ah! A perfect arrangement."

"We can announce the betrothal tomorrow, and they can wed as soon as we get to Susa."

Masistes grinned and clapped a hand to his shoulder. "This was a much better meeting than I thought we would have this morning, brother. I will go share the excellent news with Parsisa and Artaynte, and our men can draw up the legal contracts."

"I will come inside with you." And there part ways. He would inform Kasia, too, that neither his brother nor his son would bother her again . . . and find a way to do so without admitting his tactics. He had a feeling she would be none too pleased to realize his methods of procuring the promise from Masistes.

But it was hard to argue with what worked.

Mesopotamia, en route to Susa

Darius drew in a breath of the warm night air. The longer they traveled, the more temperate the weather became. They were halfway home, a fortnight into the trip, and he longed to be home.

He had not considered, when he set out on campaign, how much he would miss his younger siblings. His mother and grandmother. Now that he knew he would see them so soon, each day dragged against anticipation and seemed twice its normal length.

He glanced around as he entered his tent. A lamp burned within, welcoming and golden. "Themis?"

A woman stepped from behind the screen, but it was not his slave. "I sent her away. She objected, but given that I shall be her mistress in a few weeks, she decided it was wise to obey."

A simmer of excitement heated his blood. Not like if it had been Kasia greeting him in that translucent garment, but he could not help but respond. His future bride may not have the heart he wanted, but no one could find fault with her beauty. "Artaynte, what are you doing here?"

She smiled. She probably meant it to be seductive, but it wobbled around the edges. "I would have thought it obvious."

Pasting incredulity onto his face, he headed for wine. "A new plot of your mother's? I assumed her satisfied, now that you are my betrothed-wife."

"Mother would be furious if she knew I was here."

Her voice shook, but it was the defiance in it that grabbed his attention. He sloshed some wine into a chalice and faced her.

She lifted her chin. "I will follow my own advice now. And yours, when you are my husband." One step toward him, then she stopped. "I have always loved you, Darius. I cannot bear the thought that I have ruined any chance of winning your heart because I listened to my mother."

He took a gulp of the wine then set it down. "And this is how you think to prove your love?"

Whatever determination had brought her here, he watched it lose the battle to her modesty. She grabbed at a shawl and wrapped it around herself as she flew toward the exit. "You are right. It was stupid of me to think—"

"Wait." He jumped into her path and caught her. His grin refused to be tamped down. "I did not say I was disinterested."

She trembled under his hands. "I will give you all that I am, all that I have . . . but I must know that it will not be for nothing."

He knew what she wanted—promises of love, his word that he would give up dreams of the one he could not have and focus his heart on her. He could say the words, but they would be empty.

Too long had he used dreams of Kasia to distract him from frustrations with Artaynte. Now he could not banish her from his mind. He ought to have listened to Artabanas when Kasia first arrived and kept from so much as thinking of her. Perhaps then it would not have been so easy to fall in love.

Climbing back out—was that even possible?

"Darius."

He closed his eyes against the heartbreak in her tone. "It will not be for nothing. We will find a way to make our union strong."

They might as well start now. If fantasies of one woman could have such great effect, perhaps the reality of another could do even more.

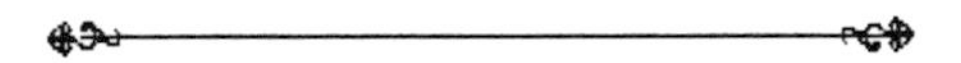

Susa, Persia

Kasia let the emotions crash over her, let the tears well, let her breathing go ragged. Two and a half years since she last set eyes on the golden bronze of home, and now it stretched out before her. Sun-baked and beautiful, long-missed and familiar.

Susa. She stood on the wall of the palace and looked out at the city. Sought and found the market, the temple, Abba and Ima's house. And there, three doors down, Mordecai and Esther. She splayed her hands over the kicking babe within her. Would Abba relent and agree to meet his granddaughter? Let her put the child in Ima's arms, the first of the next generation?

Or was it? Zechariah could be married. The twins probably were. She had missed so much, knew so little of them.

Zechariah, at least, she could see. The liaison between the palace and Abba's shop said he would be by with deliveries in a few weeks. She would speak to him, wrap her arms around him. Ask him to beg Abba to bring Ima to the palace.

Arms closed around her from behind, hands covered hers on her large stomach. Kasia smiled. "It is good to be home."

Xerxes pulled her back against him and rested his cheek on the top of her head. "Indeed. You are thinking of your family. If you would like to go visit them—"

"Not without Abba's leave. But my brother will come to the palace soon, and I will speak with him then. Perhaps he can convince my father to let me come, or to bring Ima here."

"Anything you want. Perhaps your mother could attend you when you labor. That would make you happy, I think."

She knit her fingers through his. "Very."

"Look there." He turned them a bit, toward the river. Figures walked along it;

some too far away to seem anything but specks, a few close enough to make out their costly Persian attire. Apparently the whole city had been in mourning, but rejoicing had taken its place when they saw their king home safe and well. "There is the spot where I first saw you."

A grin tugged on her mouth. "Oh, I have not forgotten."

He chuckled in her ear, and then nipped playfully at it. "It is almost strange to remember that day now, after all we have been through in so short a time."

"Mmm. And yet it is still clear as crystal in my mind. The derision on Haman's face, the intrigue on yours." She rested her head against his shoulder. "All because I enjoyed wading in cold waters. What would you have done had I been drowning?"

Xerxes rubbed the spot where the babe prodded. "Dashed in and hauled you up. And once I had you in my arms and gazed into those eyes, I imagine I would have fallen in love as surely as I did through your conversation. Although had it happened that way, I would not have seen your loyalty and bravery—facing down two of those awful Persians to protect your sister."

Her sister. Only in heart. She ought to have told him long ago that it had been her friend behind her, not one of the twins, but what was the point, now? "She needed protecting from you barbarians—she is a beautiful girl."

"Is she?" He tickled her side. "I confess I could not tell you anything about her, other than that she *was*. You had my total attention." He kissed her on the cheek. "You still do."

"Well, I—" She lost her breath when her stomach tightened.

Xerxes turned her halfway around. "What was that? Was that a contraction?"

"Doubtfully. Not a real one, anyway. My mother often had small contractions in the weeks leading up to a birth. She said it got her body ready."

Her husband frowned, looking far from convinced. "You should be resting. The quick travel has probably taken its toll on you."

"I am fine."

He kissed the tip of her nose. "I will see you safely back to your little speck of a room and into bed, and if these not-real pains continue, one of your servants had better notify me."

She wanted to grin at the renewal of insults for her small room, but her stomach was still so tense—and hard, like a rock. Lying down would be welcome. "I will not argue. But it is nothing."

"If it were nothing, you would argue." He led her away from the wall, down through the garden and into the women's palace.

Her room was at once unfamiliar with all its new furnishings and blessedly recognizable. Her father's touch, Zechariah's. The artistry that must be Joshua's. And, if she were not mistaken, the soft, thin cover on the bed had been woven by her mother's hand.

Though she had spent only a few hours in it this morning, already it was home. She settled onto the bed and gave her husband a smile. "There, resting and docile. Go plan some ridiculous extravagances for your son's wedding and leave me in peace."

After a grin and one long, sweet kiss, he left. Kasia covered the taut muscles of her abdomen with her hands as another preparatory contraction gripped her. In all likelihood, they would taper off as she rested.

Still . . . she wished Ima were here.

Xerxes sighed, his heart giving a twist at the way little Chinara hid behind her mother's legs. What had he expected? That she would remember him, when he had been gone nearly half her life? He would have to either win her affection again or accept this new reality—his favorite daughter no longer knew him.

Still, it could hardly hurt to bribe her. He crouched down and held out the confection he had ordered from the kitchens especially for her. "I brought you something, my little sweet."

The girl regarded him for a long moment, then the impish grin he adored flashed. She grabbed the cake and scampered off with a giggle of delight.

Jasmine rolled her eyes. "Do not let her fool you—she remembers you, and loves you as always. She also remembers that you are generous with your gifts when you think she needs bribed into something."

He straightened and chuckled. "Smart little devil. I shall reward her for it with some trinket she does not need."

"Some things never change." Jasmine glanced around, stepped nearer. "Even some things you intended to. I did as you asked, my husband, and kept my eyes and ears open to the goings-on of the harem."

"And?"

She shook her head. "You will not like it. Amestris has grown more powerful than ever. The women still cower in fear of her, and the palace guard answers to her without question. Everyone calls her the queen again."

Xerxes scrubbed a hand over his face. He should have had her killed after she delivered his child. Mercy was troublesome. "I shall banish her to Persepolis again after my birthday celebration, but I want all my children present for that. I imagine her youngest is still quite attached to her."

"Artaxerxes, yes. Have you met him yet? He is a dear little boy."

"Not yet. Soon." He sighed and surveyed the garden where most of his wives were out, trying to look as though they were not vying for his notice. He would have to get to know them again, divvy out his favor.

There would be time enough for that when Kasia was indisposed after giving birth. For now he would focus on her, on his son's wedding two days hence, and on planning his birthday feast in a few weeks.

He glanced down at Jasmine, still as plump and pleasant as she had been when he left her. A worthy friend. "Kasia would appreciate a visit, I am sure."

The woman smiled. "I saw her briefly this morning, when she returned from your palace. We plan to dine together later."

"Good. See that she is still resting. I worry for her."

"Another thing that has not changed." She settled gentle fingers onto his arm, then withdrew altogether. "I had better chase Chinara down."

He let her go, glanced through the garden again. And froze when he spotted the shadowed figure hovering in the far entryway.

Amestris. She would not dare take another step, not while he was there—she would never enter his presence again. But he knew what look would be on her face, what challenge in her eyes. He could sense the darkness of the god hovering around her.

You shall be undone by the women you think you rule.

Xerxes spun on his heel. Let the god try to bring his curses to reality. He would fail. No one, not even Ahura Mazda, would take Kasia away from him.

Thirty-Five

Artaynte laughed and spun to a halt, clapping with the rest of the guests for the musicians and their magical beat. She wore the finest the world had to offer, soft linen embroidered with gold, fastened with jewels. Her hair flowed in a glossy river, sparkling with gems, and a diadem of precious metals encircled her brow.

All her life she had been the daughter of a prince, but today she was the wife of one, destined to be queen. As she looked out over the sea of faces crowding the palace for the wedding, she saw rejoicing everywhere. Everyone was still so thrilled to have the king and his family back in Susa that spirits already soared. Never had wedding festivities been so rapturous.

Darius gave her one more twirl and then tugged her off the dancing floor, toward the wine. He seemed happy today, genuinely content. Perhaps her plan was working, and that handful of nights they had already spent together helped him warm to her.

Wine in hand, he led her toward the throne where his father sat, Queen Atossa beside him. Xerxes' was the only unsmiling face in the crowd, which she had not looked at him long enough to notice before. Darius obviously had.

"Father. Not enjoying yourself?"

The king offered a tight-lipped smile. "It is a magnificent celebration, and the two of you are a beautiful couple." An unspoken "but" hovered in the air.

Darius frowned and looked around. "Where is Kasia?"

Artaynte forced a swallow. He only asked because her absence would explain his father's mood, surely. But why, then, that dark curiosity in his eyes?

The king drew in a long breath. "In labor."

"So soon? I thought she had several weeks to go." And why did her new husband know when Kasia ought to have been having her child?

"I suspect the journey taxed her. The pains began two days ago, though they did not apparently become 'serious,' as she called it, until this morning."

"Let us know how everything goes with her."

The king narrowed his eyes. "You will not have time to worry with my wife today, Darius—not with your own fetching new bride and all the guests here to celebrate you."

Darius smiled. "She and Artaynte are close friends. It is for my bride I ask."

She barely refrained from snorting. Perhaps the king would believe that explanation, but her bridegroom had some gall to claim it in front of her.

Queen Atossa cleared her throat. The king's gaze burned into her, too discerning. She glanced at him long enough to verify that he had seen her reaction, then focused on the golden vessel in her hand.

A sip of wine did nothing to cool the fire building within her.

Kasia bore down, every fiber of her being concentrated on pushing. She remembered well Ima's labors and births, the easy ones and the difficult. She had thought she knew all she needed to about this process.

It looked different through the cloud of pain. Desma and Leda kept asking her questions, but the words made little sense. She just shook her head—she cared about nothing but getting this child out, healthy and well.

"I can see the head, mistress."

Kasia closed her eyes, drew in a long breath during the uncomfortable calm, then gathered her strength when the tension built again. Pushed. Bit her tongue against a scream when searing pain continued after the contraction abated.

Desma patted her knee. "That has to hurt. The head is halfway out."

The next contraction could not come fast enough. After it did, relief followed quickly.

"One more."

She pushed, then strained forward, hungry for a glimpse of her daughter.

"It is a girl."

She smiled when her maid settled the squalling babe on her chest. "Of course it is. My precious daughter."

Desma cut the cord and took the babe back so Leda could swaddle her and wipe her clean. Another contraction struck, which Kasia had been braced for. Her maid helped her with the afterbirth, then gave the babe back.

She put her to her breast, but she had barely had time to admire the healthy pink skin and matted dark hair of her daughter. Warmth spread where it should not have. "Desma. Something is wrong."

"You are bleeding." Her maid's smile was strained. "It is normal to bleed."

"It does not feel normal. It feels . . . ." It *felt*. The only time Ima had mentioned feeling the blood like this was when she hemorrhaged with Eglah.

Her arms grew heavy, but she worked to keep them around her now-suckling babe. "Desma . . . Desma, you must pray. This is not right. I should . . . I cannot . . . ."

The world tipped.

Mordecai slipped away from the wedding feast, wishing he could have declined the invitation altogether—or convinced Esther to come with him. He had stayed as long as he could tolerate the isolation, but he tired of feeling like the one guest who did not belong. He set a course that would take him through one of the gardens and toward the gate nearest home.

Passing under a palm tree, he halted. Images flashed before his eyes, his spirit shouted within him. *Kasia*.

The need to pray for her had not struck so intensely, so clearly since that time a year ago. He found a quiet spot beside a fountain and fell to his knees.

Xerxes sneaked away at twilight. The celebration would continue long into the night, but the bridal couple had said their farewells. Surely no one would begrudge him a reprieve too.

He headed straight for the house of wives, trying to convince his fingers to relax as he walked. There was no reason to dread what he would find. Kasia would be fine. Their babe would be fine. All would be well. He would hold his daughter, kiss his wife, and go back to the feast.

The moment he stepped into the hall with her chamber, Desma appeared. She sketched a quick bow. "Master."

She looked exhausted, and blood stained her garment. Normal, surely. Surely. Xerxes swallowed. "How does it go?"

"You have a beautiful daughter." The maid smiled, and it looked sincere. "She joined us a few hours ago."

He tried to stop his frown but could not. "Why was I not told immediately?"

The smile faded away, and she glanced over her shoulder. "There were complications with my mistress. She is fine now," she rushed to add. "Resting. She told us not to tell you, but—"

"But you have more sense than that." He planted his fists on his hips. "What happened?"

"She was bleeding. A lot. I have seen such things before—sometimes massaging the stomach is enough to stop it."

"And sometimes it is not. Like with your previous mistress."

The maid nodded. "I was afraid the same would happen with Kasia. The blood would not stop, no matter what we did, and when she lost consciousness . . . ."

He squeezed his eyes shut. She was all right. That was what mattered. But . . . . "Obviously something worked."

"The flow did not stop until we did. Until we dropped to our knees and prayed to Jehovah as she had told us to do at the start. Then it slowed, dried up. She slept for a while, woke up hungry and wanting her babe. They are both sleeping again."

"I will be quiet, but I must see them." He stepped around the maid.

"Master?"

And halted again with a sigh. "What is it?"

The girl drew in a long breath. "Mistress did not want you to know because she is afraid your fear for her will keep you away again."

"No. Never again." But she knew him well—already worry gnawed at him, worry that if it had been so close this time, next time may be worse.

Desma sighed. "I understand your concerns. But Jehovah preserved her."

"He always does."

Desma nodded and motioned him toward the room.

As he entered a soft cry came from the bed, and a moment later the cadence of Kasia's voice, speaking in Hebrew. When the babe hushed, she looked up with a smile. "Xerxes. Come meet your daughter."

After a moment's deliberation, he settled beside her on the bed. Usually he would have taken a chair, let a servant give him the child for a moment, praised mother and babe, then taken his leave. He had no intentions of following his usual pattern today. So he scooted close, where he could see the tiny girl as she nursed.

"She is so small. Are you certain she is well?"

Kasia chuckled and smoothed down a wisp of the girl's black hair. "Very. Smaller than average, but I can detect nothing wrong with her. Is she not beautiful?"

"She is perfect." Despite the threat of the god. He caressed her little ear, then offered his finger for her to grip. A smile possessed his mouth. "And strong. Just like her mother. I will have a message dispatched to your father's house. Perhaps he will let your mother come."

"Speaking of that . . . ." She trailed off, worried her lip. "I would like to call her Zillah, after Ima. Though if you prefer a Persian name—"

"Zillah." He tested it, weighed it, measured it against their daughter. Then nodded. "I like it."

Kasia beamed. "You do not mind that it is Hebrew?"

"Why should I? Yours is too, and there is no sweeter name on the earth." When she rolled her eyes, he chuckled. "Though when we have a son, I may insist on a family name."

The gleam in her eyes said she understood his promise of more children. "That is only fair."

Silence held for a few minutes, until little Zillah fell asleep again and Kasia handed her to him. It felt as though he held a doll rather than a babe, the way she fit in his hands—though no doll could ever snuggle against him and make love expand his chest.

He glanced at Kasia and found her blinking heavily. "You look like you could sleep too."

She hummed. "I am still tired from the birth." And the bleeding, though of course she would not mention that. "But I will stay awake to visit with you. You will have to return to the feast soon."

"I am the king, I can avoid it however long I want." He grinned and kissed her brow. "Right now I want to hold our daughter a little longer."

With a slumberous smile, she stroked his cheek, then trailed her fingers through his beard. Her smile went crooked. "You are wearing jewels in your beard."

"The occasion called for it." He narrowed his eyes playfully. "Why is that so amusing?"

"We used to laugh at stories of such outrageous wealth." Her lashes eased onto her cheeks. "Tell me, my love—what would you do if one fell into your soup?"

He chuckled and traced Zillah's miniature nose. "Have it ground up for its impudence, of course. And then used to season the next night's meal."

She laughed quietly. "Remind me to fast the next day, if ever a jewel goes missing during a feast."

"Well, if it would cause you to go hungry, perhaps I would simply dry it off and reattach it. Though then all the other jewels may think they could get away with such behavior."

How he loved that smile of hers, especially as she curled against him. She kissed their daughter's head, then him. "I love you, Xerxes."

"And I you, lovely Kasia. More than anything. Now—sleep."

He must have slept too, for he jerked awake when the babe in his arms began to fuss and root for nourishment. Smiling, he passed her back to Kasia and stretched. "I suppose I must bid my guests good night. I will visit again in the morning."

Kasia nodded, eyes closing again once Zillah was settled at her breast. "Good night, my love."

He stole another kiss, then left her room. The hall outside was not as quiet as he had expected—two of the other wives walked down it, laughing. Just returning from the celebration, he would guess.

They bowed, their gazes darting from him to Kasia's door. Their contemplation was obvious—never before had he left a feast as important as this one to check on a wife and new child.

Well, let them all learn anew that Kasia was like no other wife. He picked up his pace, the servants who had been waiting for him rushing ahead to open doors. The refreshing evening air breathed over him, scented with jasmine and night-blooming water lilies.

"Father."

He paused, knowing a thunderhead gathered on his face. That particular voice ought to have been nowhere nearby. He turned slowly. "What in the world are you doing here? It is your wedding night—you ought to be with your bride."

Darius smirked. "She is sleeping and satisfied. I thought I would check on Kasia for her."

Every muscle in his body went taut. He stepped close to his eldest son, pitched his voice low. "You think you fool me? Not for a moment. Artaynte does not care so much about Kasia anymore—probably because you care far too much. Leave my wife alone and go tend your own."

The smirk faded away, challenge sprang up. But only for a moment—whether by force or acknowledgment that he would lose this battle, Darius looked contrite. "She is my friend, Father. I only wanted to make sure she was well. I asked a servant for an update, but all he knew was that you had been with her for more than two hours. I feared the worst."

Would that have been enough to lure *him* away from his beautiful bride on their wedding night? He did not think so. But there was little point in arguing it. "She is well, as is our daughter. Now return to your own house before your wife awakes and realizes you are gone."

Charging past Darius and the guilty obstinance on his face, Xerxes returned to the celebration.

Thirty-Six

"This is ridiculous. How many times can one woman flirt with death and still escape it?"

Haman sighed as Amestris paced and muttered. He understood her frustration—since their return a fortnight ago, the king's behavior had been disturbing. Every spare moment, he was with the Jewess. Even when about business of the empire, he seemed all too eager to dispense with it so he could leave the throne room.

All the work Haman had done, all the rumors he had carefully planted . . . perhaps he just needed to tend those sprouts more diligently now that they were home. "It matters little if she lives, lady. There is still much hurt between them, and your husband is more jealous than ever where she is concerned. I can use that."

"See that you do." Amestris shoved a coil of hair off her forehead, though it looked as though it had been placed there deliberately. "It is insufferable. When he was gone, I could do as I pleased, and all knew better than to disagree with me. Now—it is that snake Parsisa leading the women against me. Now that her daughter is married to my son, she thinks the kingdom is hers. Then there are these whispers that the king fell in love with her at Sardis—preposterous!"

Haman studied a mosaic on the wall. "I cannot speak to Parsisa's ambitions, lady, but I can assure you the attention the king paid her was only to make his brother jealous. Masistes had attempted a seduction of the Jewess."

Amestris stopped before his seat and glared. "We agree that the Jews are a menace, one that will only increase in power as long as that witch holds the king's attention. I will do what I can in the harem, but being forbidden from the king's presence . . . ."

"Leave that to me." He stood, dredged up a smile. "I will go speak with him now."

"Good. That frees me to deal with Parsisa. Had she been here all along, she would not dare spout such poisonous words as I have heard from her—about me, her natural superior . . . ."

Haman escaped with a roll of his eyes. He would indeed leave the battles of women to her. It would be effort enough to deal with the men.

The god must be with him—when he finally located Xerxes, he was directing a fierce scowl at Darius's retreating form. Hopefully Haman's smile did not look too victorious. "Good afternoon, my king. Trouble with the younger generation?"

"Tell me, my friend, did I not arrange the most favorable marriage imaginable for my son? Is his new wife not everything a prince could possibly desire?"

Ah, perfect. Haman nodded. "You did indeed, master. Masistes' daughter is everything desirable. What is more, I happen to know she is very much in love with the prince."

"Exactly!" The king spun with a growl, though Haman could not guess at his destination. "Yet when I asked him why I saw his bride in tears this morning, he said she was impossible to please and he had given up trying. Apparently more than two weeks of effort is just too much to ask of him."

Haman pressed his lips together against the observation that Xerxes rarely gave a woman more than a single night to win his affection. To be fair, he had not been so impatient twenty years ago, when he had fewer wives. "Perhaps, master, you ought to let them work things out on their own."

"Stay out of their marriage? That is what my son said I should do." That particular scowl was one that had led to mountains being smitten in the past. The prince ought to know better than to provoke his father . . . though it did play perfectly into Haman's hand. Xerxes' nostrils flared. "Strange he would dare say such a thing to me, when he is doing his best to interfere in mine."

Haman cleared his throat.

The king stopped and glared at him. "You said I ought to speak with them. I did, but neither said anything to explain the fact that Darius cannot keep his eyes off Kasia, and she refuses to look at him at all. I will ask *you*. What went on between them in Sardis?"

Praise the god—this opportunity must be from him. Haman kept his countenance serious. "I am not surprised Darius would tell you nothing—though I expected the Jewess to admit what transpired." True enough—she seemed the type to think she needed total honesty in her relationships.

Honesty had its place, to be sure—a kernel of truth went a long way toward convincing others of whatever you wanted them to believe.

Xerxes' hands fisted. "She said he may have been infatuated, but nothing more. I did not want to push her. But I would know whatever you do."

He nodded and clasped his hands together. "It started innocently enough, I suppose. Parsisa forbade Artaynte to associate with her, after what happened at the start of the campaign, and all the other women followed her lead." Helped along, no doubt, by the rumors he had started about her being sent away because her child was illegitimate. "The prince sought her company solely to ease her solitude."

"Laudable, until I consider the look now in his eyes when he regards her. Tell me it is as simple as a one-sided interest—that he fell in love, she rebuffed him, and hence what I see."

"I cannot." That version of the truth certainly would not help his cause. Haman shook his head. Sadly, he hoped. "I saw them together one afternoon. He sent her servants away, then embraced her."

The king's cheeks went red. "And you did nothing to stop it? Why do you think I sent you to Sardis, Haman?"

He spread his hands before him, palms up. "He was the acting king—if I had dared come against him, I would not be alive to tell you about it."

Xerxes grunted and stomped onward. "So he embraced her. She would have fought him, acting king or not."

"Yes, she did . . . for a moment."

The king's jaw ticked. "What are you saying?"

"Only what I saw. I cannot say whether he convinced her or forced matters—I left at that point—but surely you realize he would not have let her go without getting what he wanted."

His companion shook with rage, and Haman fought back a grin. The king may rant at his son, but he would not harm him. And the Jewess would be damaged in his eyes. The king of kings would have no use for spoiled goods when he had his pick of the most beautiful virgins the world over.

"You did your duty," the king said through clenched teeth. "Now excuse me."

"Certainly, master. I only wish I did not have to report such a truth." He kept his head bowed until Xerxes stomped off. Then he let the smile curl his lips.

His vision blurred. His blood pounded. His muscles bunched and coiled. Xerxes could not remember the last time the rage had come upon him so intensely. When the bridge was destroyed? No, this was worse. This was not about wood and rope, earth and water.

This was about flesh of his flesh, wife of his heart.

How could he? How could his son—his own son, the boy he had spoiled, had taught, had handed the reins of his kingdom to—do this to him? He knew—*knew*—what Kasia meant to him. He could take any other woman—blast it, most any other *wife*— with minimal consequences. But not her.

Not. Her.

Why had he thought it worth the risk? Had she encouraged him in some way? Never—he had no doubt Kasia fought him with all the might she could spare, but she had been weak with the pregnancy and would have feared hurting their child.

Poor Kasia, having to endure such a thing. No wonder she refused to look at the prince, no wonder she changed the subject whenever he came up. What agony must she feel around him? He could not blame her for not telling him. It would hurt too much, and she would fear his reaction. But he knew exactly who to blame.

His son would pay.

He stormed to the palace that had once been his father's personal quarters, the one he had given to his son upon his wedding. Just inside the front columns, he halted and spun to face his servants. "You come no farther."

The furrow in Zethar's brow was deep as a canal. "But master—"

He slashed a hand through the air. "No. This is between me and my son. Stay here."

Knowing they would obey whether they liked it or not, Xerxes strode forward again, through the cavernous entryway, through the empty receiving rooms. Where was he? "Darius!"

He pounded into the bedchamber when all others proved empty, sending the door crashing into the wall. If his son were not here—

A startled cry drew his gaze to the corner of the room. Artaynte stood by one of the low windows, hand clutching her throat.

Xerxes was in no mood for female dramatics. "Where is your husband?"

Her hand fell away, and with it went all expression from her face. She looked as cold as he felt molten. "I do not know. Probably off trying to get a glimpse of your wife."

The blackest of curses tripped off his tongue as his hand sought and found something to send into the wall. Its crash resonated perfectly with the notes of fury within him. "You know."

Artaynte made no reaction to the display of temper. "I would have to be blind not to see the way he looks at her. And deaf not to hear him cry her name when it should be mine."

A roar left his throat raw and aching, like the rest of him. "Do you know what he did in Sardis? Do you know he forced himself upon her?"

"I saw him kiss her and assumed the rest." Her voice was low, but it throbbed. "I thought I could still take back his heart. I was a fool."

"I will not forgive this." But how to punish him?

Artaynte turned her face away. "What good is forgiveness? I would see him humbled."

"Humbled? He is all pride."

And he was his heir. Xerxes could not smite Darius without smiting himself, not if he took any public action.

"Then I shall strip him of his pride." The girl trembled as she spat the words.

"How?" Then again, it had not been a public crime. It had been a private one, an intimate one.

She raised her chin. "The same way he stripped me of mine. I shall give myself to another and let the court laugh at *him*."

He realized his vision had been edged with red only when it went dark. The room felt heavy, shadowed in spite of the afternoon sunlight.

His voice sounded strange to his ears, too cold for the rage slicking through his veins. "Who did you have in mind?"

Something was wrong. Kasia could not put her finger on what, but she could feel it. A discord, a pebble in life's shoe.

She studied her husband as she bounced little Zillah gently against her shoulder. They sat in the gardens, the sun bright and warm, the flora fragrant. But sorrow lurked in the corners of his smile, tension shadowed his eyes. It had been there for weeks, but she could not figure out why.

Xerxes caught her gaze and quirked a brow. "Why do you look at me like that, my love? Have I an epic inscribed on my forehead?"

She refused to smile, though it took some effort. "I will figure it out eventually, you know."

"I have no idea what you mean." Yet the sorrow flickered before he smiled it away. "Unless perhaps that you will figure out what gift you ought to request during my birthday feast?"

She breathed a laugh. "I maintain it is a dangerous practice—granting everyone whatever they want on your birthday, unable to say no . . . ."

"I have to *agree* to grant them something—then I am powerless to deny them. Hence why I only allow a few requests every year." He stroked Zillah's bald head—Kasia was not certain where all that dark hair had gone—and grinned. "And I am eager to extend the right of request to you this year, my love."

"Unnecessary." She kissed his hand, then the babe's head. "I have everything I want already."

"Oh, come now. You could ask for that city you have always wanted. Up to half my kingdom—say the word and it is yours."

Laughter bubbled up and spilled out. "Very likely. Perhaps I shall instead ask that you tell me what troubles you."

His grin faded away. "There is nothing to tell."

"Xerxes."

He sighed and cupped her cheek. "And if there is, and I want to spare you the concern of it, you ought to grant me the indulgence. It is my birthday."

"It is not." But he needed the indulgence. Anything to banish that sadness from his eyes. "Your birthday is next week, and I think it strange you take seven days to celebrate it."

He chuckled. "Perhaps that was how long the empire celebrated when I was born."

"Ha! At the time, you were only another son."

Something flickered across his face when she said *son*. Whatever bothered him was linked to Darius then.

In which case, she would stay out of it. "Very well, I will relent. Consider it the first of my gifts to you."

"You are the only gift I need." His eyes slid closed as he rested his forehead against hers. "Join me at the feasts. I know you have not been purified yet, but I read these Levitical laws. There will be nothing sacred—"

"No, my love. I do not feel up to presenting myself before the court yet. Between nursing and diaper changes and restless nights—"

He pulled away with a hum. "Did I not tell you to ask for a nurse to help during the nights, at least?"

"And in the middle of the night, I am tempted to do so." She offered him a cheeky smile. "But in the morning, I cannot bear the thought of letting another give her life instead of me."

"Stubborn woman."

"I must be, to hold my own against you."

He offered her a crooked smile. "And on that note, I must go." He pushed himself to his feet and helped her to hers. "I love you."

She echoed the sentiment and watched him walk away, his shoulders hunched. A frown tugged at her brows. What could be between him and Darius, to cause such distress? Had he discovered that the prince approached her in Sardis?

No, it could not be that. If he knew, he would not be sad—he would be angry. He would rant and rage, and Zethar would call on her to soothe his temper. He had not.

She would give it some prayer. With a smile for her servants, she headed toward her room.

"Kasia?"

She paused at the semi-familiar female voice. Another wife approached her, one a decade her senior. One who had muttered against her before the war. She had not interacted with her since. "Good morning, Aglea."

The woman gave her a flustered smile. "Good morning. May I walk with you back to your room?"

"Oh . . . of course." She repositioned Zillah and tried not to look too curious. "How have you and your children been?"

"Quite well." Aglea sucked in a breath. "It is my son I wanted to discuss."

Kasia's brows lifted. What advice could Aglea possibly need from her? "I saw him yesterday—he brought his little sister to the garden when I was telling stories."

Aglea smiled. "He said he enjoyed it. That he put a few questions to you and recited a Persian poem that was similiar to the Hebrew psalm you sang."

Her lips tugged up at the memory. "He is a clever boy."

"I know." Aglea stopped, and put a soft hand on Kasia's arm. "That is the thing. When the king left, Damon struggled in his studies, and our husband more or less dismissed him from consideration for future offices. I know the tutors will give him a good report now, but it would . . . he would believe it more readily if you spoke to him. If you told him what a smart young man he has become."

She could only stare, then remind herself to blink. "You want me to speak to the king about your son for you?"

Aglea dropped her gaze. "I know it is much to ask. I have a tapestry I have been working on that I would be happy to give you in exchange—"

"No. No, you need not purchase my goodwill." She patted Aglea's hand. "I already told Xerxes about how well Damon recited, the cleverness of his questions."

"You did?" Tears glimmered in Aglea's eyes. "Thank you. You cannot know what this means to us."

Perhaps not. She was not even certain what it meant to her. Yes, Diona and Lalasa had asked favors of her from time to time, but they were fellow concubines, friends. Aglea was the daughter of a king, a wife of such high rank . . . yet asking her for help.

Desma leaned close as they continued toward her chamber after Aglea dashed away.

"We told you this would happen, did we not?"

"You did." But she was unaccustomed to receiving respect from these women. She felt better capable of handling their derision than this.

Artaynte twisted the bedcover between her fingers. Her heart pounded, but not from passion. Oh, she could forget he was more than a man when he held her, but the moment he eased away, it all crashed down again.

She had taken the king as a lover, and the weight of it may just suffocate her. He was no less terrifying than ever, especially given the look on his face now, as he sat up and stared ahead. Panic curled inside her. He may have offered himself as a conspirator in this plan, but each time he came to her, he seemed a little more on edge, a little more deadly.

He despised her for this. She saw it in the shutter of his eyes, the tension in his arms as he reached for his tunic. It was only a matter of time before he called a halt to it and instructed her to pretend it never happened.

But Darius had not caught on yet, and she would not let this be for nothing. All the terror, the nausea that seized her after each tryst—what was the point of it, if her husband did not even realize what she had done? He could not be humbled if it remained a secret.

And surely the king wanted him to know too. How was it a punishment otherwise?

She cleared her throat and prayed the god would steady her voice. "My lord."

He paused but did not look at her. He never looked at her, except when his eyes were glazed with animal instinct. "Hmm?"

She drew in a deep breath. "I need a boon."

Now his hard gaze rested on her, and she wished it did not. "A boon."

She looked at the bedcover, woven with gold in an intricate pattern. "Yes. Your son does not pay enough attention to me to realize what is going on, but it is pointless unless he does."

The king sighed and rubbed a hand over his face. "What do you want?"

Her gaze fell on the shawl still draped carelessly over a chair. The moment she thought to ask for a favor, she knew exactly what it must be. She nodded at it.

His face twisted. "No. Not that."

"Nothing else will work, my lord. He will know the moment he sees it on me what has happened."

"As will everyone else."

Yes, that was the point. Humility would not be complete if it were private—not when all the court whispered that Darius had no use for his wife. "If you are worried of what Kasia will think, you need not be. No one will speak of it to her."

He gripped the frame of the bed until his knuckles went white. "But what of Amestris? She will not appreciate that I have given the work of her hands to her son's wife."

Amestris—Artaynte had done her best to avoid the former queen all her life, and for good reason. But since the woman could not appear anywhere the king did, she would be safe enough wearing it to the birthday feasts. "I want the shawl."

Even when pleading, he looked fierce. "Would you not rather have a city? Ten cities?"

"The shawl."

He growled and spun away muttering, "No one wants my cities." Whatever that meant. When he faced her again, she knew they were finished. Part of her cried out thanks to the god while another prayed he would relent and come again if need be, and again until Darius opened his eyes.

His shoulders edged back. "Take the shawl. It had better be enough for you, because this is over."

Her limbs trembled. "It is enough."

But what if it were not? Would she have to play the harlot with someone else? She certainly hoped not. There was no other affair that would hurt Darius if this one did not. No, if this did not work, she would be out of options. Out of hope.

Which was why she must succeed now.

Thirty-Seven

Zechariah brushed the shavings from his tunic and craned his head to look into the street. Esther should be by soon. Most of the city was celebrating the king's birth, no one conducting business, but Abba would still expect him to put in a full day in the shop. He would not mind him taking a break when Esther arrived though. Not today.

The addition was finished. He had smoothed the last coat of clay onto the last wall that morning. Had moved in the last of the furniture he had fashioned for it. Today he would show it to Esther, tell her he loved her. Today he would speak with Mordecai and ask for her hand in marriage.

Sweat slicked his palms. He knew she loved him, knew Mordecai would agree. Yet his stomach was in knots.

He stepped out into the warm winter breeze just in time to see Esther exiting the house three doors down. His heart galloped. The knots loosened just enough to release a smile onto his face. "Good morning, Esther."

"Taking a break already?" She grinned as she approached. When he held out a hand, she fit hers into it.

Her fingers were so soft, so small. He squeezed them gently and pulled her into the shop. "It is a special day—a break is allowed."

"Ah yes, the start of the king's birthday celebration."

"Not quite what I was thinking of, no." He led her through the shop, out the back to where the house he had built for her cast its shade. "It is finished. Do you want to see?"

Her breath caught, her eyes widened to enchanting circles. "Yes. Of course."

"I thought you might." With a wink, he pushed open the door.

"Oh . . . ." She turned the word into a happy sigh as she stepped inside and moved in a slow circle. He had not invited her in since he started filling it. Seeing the pleasure on her face as she saw all he had done, he knew it was worth the wait. "Zech. What a beautiful home."

"This is the main living area. Through here are bedchambers for the children."

Her fingers tightened around his. "Room enough for a large family."

"Blessed is the man with a quiver full of children, as Abba always says."

She chuckled and ran a hand over the chair he had worked on day and night, one he had envisioned her sitting in as she soothed his babe to sleep someday. "When did you make all this?"

"Whenever I could. Abba and Joshua helped too. Come. There is more you must see." His heart kicked up again as he led her back through the main part and into the remaining chamber.

The bed took up most of the space, its frame carved into a delicate design. Beauty disguising strength, to match its mistress. He had incorporated the same pattern in the chest, in the vanity, in the table.

"Zech, it is exquisite." She stopped just inside the door.

"Not so exquisite as you." He stepped in front of her and framed her face with his hands. Had he ever been blind to her perfection? Impossible. She filled every crevice of his being now. "I love you, Esther."

She blinked rapidly, but tears still crowded her eyes. "I feel as though I have waited a century to hear you say that. You know I love you, Zechariah."

He eased a little closer. "I know not why Jehovah blessed me so, but I praise him for it. I want you to be my wife, Esther. I want to spend my life beside you, I want us to fill this house with children and laughter."

Her eyes slid shut. "Nothing would make me happier." One eye squinted up at him, and she grinned. "Though you will have to speak to my cousin."

"I will. As soon as he gets home." He leaned down until his lips hovered a breath from hers.

"Mmm. You will have to wait—he will be at the feast into the night, but will be home all day tomorrow."

Disappointment struck, but it could not take hold. Not when she was so close, when he knew that, though unofficially, she was his. Unable to wait another second, he brushed her lips with his.

His blood sang, his heart soared. When her arms came about him, he knew this was the key to paradise. Esther. Only Esther.

He deepened the kiss, ran his hands down her back, pulled her close. Just as he had expected, her response combined the sweet and the eager, the innocent and the confident. How he wanted to lose himself, to be overcome—but no.

Easing away, he drew in a long, shaky breath. "I am hoping that since we had a lengthy courtship, your cousin will agree to a short betrothal."

Her eyes smoldered, her lips curved. "I do not see why he would object."

"Good." He took one more kiss, which stretched longer than he intended, and then stepped away. "Tomorrow? Perhaps I will hunt him down at the palace, demand an answer this very hour."

She chuckled and closed the distance between them again. "You have waited all these months—you can wait one more day." She looped her arms around his neck and pulled him down again.

"Not if you do that much more." He pivoted them so that he could walk her into a safer area. Gave her one more kiss, then propelled her outside. "I am going to be a menace with the tools today—my thoughts will be all on you and none on the blade."

"Well, mind your fingers." She caught both his hands and raised them to kiss a knuckle. "I am fond of them."

He could not hold back the grin. "Away with you, woman, before I forget that there is work to be done."

She gave him a smile, his fingers a squeeze, and scampered through the kitchen into his parents' house.

Zechariah hooked a hand around the burning back of his neck and watched her go. He had known she would like the house. And once they were wed, he would give her something she would love far more—the knowledge that Kasia lived. Perhaps he would even take her to the palace sometime, if it could be arranged.

He smiled as he returned to the wood shop. Abba was nowhere in sight, and the quiet of the room wrapped around him. Humming a quiet psalm, he picked up his awl.

"Excuse me."

The voice struck some distant bell in his memory, but it was not until he looked up that he recognized the man as one of Ruana's servants. His shoulders tensed. "Yes?"

The man stepped inside, glancing all around as if to check for listening ears. Apparently the emptiness did not satisfy him, for he stepped close, leaned closer. "I have a message from my mistress."

Zechariah sighed. Why today of all days? Why must she interfere in his life now? "Deliver it and go."

"She must speak with you. Today, she says."

He snorted and struck the end of the awl with a hammer. "Not a chance."

"She bade me beg on her behalf. It is urgent, or she would not ask it of you. She says if you do not meet her, she will come here."

"No." He tossed the awl down with a clatter and breathed a curse. "Not here. But I will not go to her home again."

The man nodded. "She expected as much and proposes a meeting. Wherever you would like, at whatever time."

A headache pounded to life, and Zechariah pinched at the sudden pressure in his nose. Why was it that wherever Ruana was concerned, he felt as though his hands were bound? He had no choice. But he could at least make sure there would be no temptation, no opportunity—and yet remain unseen. "Beside the bend in the river, at moon rise."

Perhaps if he were in the place he associated with weapons training, he would be quicker to see and avoid any traps.

Amestris straightened her robes, her jewelry, and smiled at her eldest son. "You are certain I will not be breaking any laws?"

Darius chuckled, but his gaze admonished her for the sardonic tone. "Father will not be there until evening."

"Good. I tire of solitude. I can hardly venture from my rooms without some servant barring my way and forbidding me go this direction or that because your father is there." She scowled and corrected the position of one of the roundels on Darius's garment. "Perhaps if he did not spend all his time in my palace with that Jewess . . . ."

"Let us not speak of her." Darius turned away and started for the exit.

Amestris hurried to catch up. She only had a few hours to present herself, to show the world she was still the queen they had known before. A few hours to dazzle them, strike fear into their hearts. She would not waste a moment.

"It is good to have you back, though I did not expect to see you so much. You have been neglecting your bride." She could not stop the smirk. "Do you not like life with Parsisa's mouthpiece?"

"Mother—"

"I warned you years ago to stay away from her. I told you when you arrived to break off the betrothal. When will you learn to listen to me?"

"Perhaps when you offer something other than negatives. Can we not speak of Artaynte? I would like to enjoy the feast."

Amestris huffed and lifted her chin. "Of what shall we speak then?" They mounted the stairs into the spacious garden where the feast had been set up.

"I am sure you will think of something. You never . . . ."

When he let his sentence hang, Amestris glanced at his face. It had washed pale, and his gaze was caught on something across the garden. She scanned the crowd for what might have struck him dumb.

She saw the colors first. Those bright, distinctive colors she had chosen with such care, had dyed over and again until the hues saturated each fiber. They swirled and danced in the pattern she had sweated and cried over, the one so detailed that at times she feared she would go blind trying to focus on it.

Her shawl. The one whose weaving had cramped her hands for months, the one she had presented to her husband with such pride when he became king.

Her shawl—on that empty-headed harlot her son had married. She hissed where she wanted to scream, clenched her hands where she wanted to rip the cloth from the whore's shoulders. "What is she doing with that?"

Darius's nostrils flared. "I think it fairly obvious. He must have given it to her. And there is only one reason he would do that."

A million vile names vied for a place on her tongue. How could he? Was it not enough he had given the Jewish wench the torc she had commissioned for him? Was it not enough he deposed her? Did he now dare to toss her most acclaimed creation—the one thing he still wore that she had given him—so carelessly onto the shoulders of that—that—

Darius's arm shot out like a bolt of lightning and hurled a pedestal and its bowl of fruit into the crowds. After a few shocked screams, silence pounded through the gathering.

Amestris held her rage close while her son's pulsed from him in waves. She watched the wordless accusation fly from his eyes, saw when it pierced his wife. Could hardly believe that the girl dared to raise her chin and meet his burning gaze, even pull the shawl a little closer.

Unbearable. Unacceptable. She had not worked so hard to have her son destroyed by a careless father unable to contain his lust and an insipid wench that never should have been promised his crown.

Darius spun and thundered back the way they had come. The twit had the audacity to smirk when he left.

Amestris turned to her servants. "I want you to go to the king during his feast. Wait until he is merry with wine, and then ask him to grant me a request. Remind him, if you must, that I have obeyed his edicts entirely and do not wish to go against them now. Promise anything, but get him to agree."

Her maid bowed. "As you wish, mistress."

She headed back to her quarters, one thought crystalline in her mind—Artaynte never did anything without her mother first telling her to.

Xerxes set his rhyton of wine upon the table and laughed. "Artabanas, I have missed you."

His uncle smiled and lifted his own cup in toast. "And I you, my nephew. It is with the greatest joy that I welcome another year of your esteemed life. Long live Xerxes, the king of kings!"

A cheer went up around him, echoing throughout the gathering as people surged to their feet. How could a man not smile at that? Not feel the warmth all the way to his core? Xerxes motioned his guests back to their seats. "May this year bring wisdom as well as age, eh?"

Laughter filled the garden, and Xerxes sat back with a sigh. It was a good evening, even if Kasia was not beside him.

"Master."

He looked over his shoulder to where a maid genuflected. "Yes?"

She offered a humble smile. "My mistress would request a favor."

He chuckled. Many had asked for favors already, and it was only the beginning of the feast. "Which wife do you serve?"

"Your first, master."

He nearly groaned. Surely Amestris did not actually expect a favor, did she? But then, she had been better behaved than he had expected since his return six weeks ago. She had remained out of sight and had caused no trouble.

His gaze flicked to the other side of the gathering, where Artaynte pranced around in his shawl. He owed Amestris a favor, whether she realized it or not. "Very well—so long as it does not contradict my former word."

"It does not." The girl's smile lost its humility and gained something far darker. "Her request is simple. She would have Parsisa."

"What?" He must have drunk more than he thought—that made no sense at all.

"Parsisa, master—she requests you deliver Parsisa into her hands."

No, he had obviously not drunk enough—the pleasant haze of celebration burned off and left a scorching reality behind.

She must have seen Artaynte, the shawl. She must have thought Parsisa somehow responsible.

And he could not deny her, not after already agreeing. His eyes slid shut.

"I have the palace guard here already, master." The maid's whisper sounded at his ear. "All you must do is nod to them."

Xerxes opened his eyes again but could only stare straight ahead, unseeing. He did not ask what Amestris intended. He did not need to. "She will pay for this."

"You were the one to grant the favor, master."

Impudent slave—yet she had the right of it. He pushed himself to his feet. One glance showed him the guards waiting just beyond the garden hedge. His head felt weighted with the guilt, pulling down, down.

They spun and marched away.

A shudder coursed through him. "Zethar. Where is Masistes?"

"Inside, master."

He headed that way, though he had no idea what he intended to say to his brother. Language had no words for this. He could try to warn him, but it would be too late—he knew Amestris well enough to realize her plan would be executed quickly.

Perhaps . . . perhaps he could soften it somehow.

"Brother!" Masistes embraced him the moment he stepped inside, grinning like a sot. "A wonderful feast. You are a wonderful brother. A wonderful king."

He grimaced and steered Masistes away from prying ears. "You are a wonderful brother too. I was thinking . . . I want to reward you for your excellent service. I would give you Amytis as wife."

Masistes frowned. "A generous offer, my lord, but your daughter must be a first wife."

"I know. You must . . . divorce Parsisa. Put her away this very night, and tomorrow you can wed the princess." He held his breath.

His brother shook his head. "I thank you, Xerxes, but you know I love my wife. She has been my companion for years, we have grown children together. I cannot just put her away. Worthy as your daughter is, I would keep Parsisa."

Xerxes turned away so that Masistes would not see him wince. "Then I am afraid you shall have neither."

Thirty-Eight

Esther shook her head, but it neither rid her ears of the words her cousin had just spoken nor changed the image of his earnest, sad face. "But Mordecai . . . I do not understand. You know I love him. You know he loves me."

Mordecai eased himself to a seat, his eyes willing her to hear him out—as if he were not speaking utter nonsense. "I know."

"And his intentions have been clear for months." She threw her arms out. "You never discouraged his suit, you never so much as hinted that you would not approve."

He sighed. "Because I did approve. I wish I still did. But my daughter, there is disquiet in my spirit whenever I ponder this. I cannot shake the feeling that he is bound by something we cannot see."

Esther tossed her head back, though no answers were scratched into the ceiling. This was unbelievable. Years she had waited for this day, the day Zechariah confessed his heart and took her into his arms. She had passed through the afternoon on a cloud of bliss, had come home this evening so happy. When Mordecai returned, she had spilled her good news, only to be hit with *this*. "Cousin. I respect you above anyone. I know Jehovah speaks to you. But this makes no sense."

"I realize that." He rested his head on his hand. "I will spend the night in prayer, Esther. Perhaps the Lord will show me what can be done to resolve the issue."

She held her place as Mordecai stood again and shuffled toward his chamber. Was it so easy for him? He would go, he would pray? He would hear, he would obey?

Well, what of her? Would Jehovah really expect her to give up the man she had always loved? Without even a reason?

No. She would not. She had already lost her parents, her only real friend. Asking her to relinquish Zechariah was just too much. She had never disobeyed Mordecai before, but she would fight him on this.

Oh, she could not simply go to sleep and await his decision. She grabbed her shawl and headed out the door, toward the river.

She had not made the trek in moonlight since she first discovered Zechariah's clandestine training, but her feet did not stumble. Each step into the cooling night air cleared her mind and soothed a ragged edge inside her.

At least this was not like the last time she walked this gilded path. Mordecai's words were not as final as Kasia's death. Fear of his decision would not induce nightmares like fearing Zechariah would die by the sword.

Still, the memories flooded her mind, bringing thoughts of losing Kasia to the fore, then of Zechariah's training. He still rose before the dawn, she knew—some mornings she would watch him leave, a large, fluid shadow in the pearly grey light.

A shadow much like the one moving ahead. Exactly like. She nearly called out to him—but he had probably come out here to think and pray before speaking with Mordecai tomorrow, and she did not want to interrupt. Happy to observe him undetected, she found a dark spot to nestle in for a few minutes. She would catch him when he was on his way back, and they could walk home together. Perhaps share another of those heart-racing kisses.

Her eyes slid shut as she relived those minutes in his arms that morning. Soon she would awake each day in that beautiful bed he had carved for her, snuggled against him. He would get up to exercise, and she would rise to tend the baby that would surely join them within a year. Finally, life would be perfect.

"Zechariah." A female voice. Esther's eyes flew open and scanned the moonlit shadows. There, a cloaked woman ran toward Zechariah.

The figure threw herself into Zechariah's arms. He caught her, quickly set her away.

But why would a strange woman think she could greet him that way?

Zechariah glanced over her shoulder. Esther looked too, and saw a few servants a stone's throw away. Whoever she was, she must be wealthy.

His whisper streaked through the night and slithered over Esther as well as their intended recipient. "Ruana, what is so important that you would threaten to come to my home to discuss it? You know this is over."

Esther's heart sputtered. *This?*

"Nice to see you again too, Zech."

"Ruana—"

"I know, I know." The woman's voice . . . it sounded strained, as though she strove for levity to hold back tears. "It was wrong, you are in love with another. You have made yourself clear."

"Have I?" Zechariah spoke lowly, bordering on harsh. "Then why are we here?"

A very good question.

The woman—Ruana, was it?—sighed. "I had to speak with you one last time. To explain . . . and to let you know."

Moonlight caught his jaw as it lifted. "Let me know what?"

Dread slowed Esther's blood.

Ruana's head dipped forward. "I am with child."

Dear Jehovah, no—there was only one reason she would feel she had to tell Zechariah such news . . . .

He sucked in a sharp breath. "It is mine?"

The woman breathed a dry laugh. "There has been no one else since my wedding night, Zech."

Wedding night? She was married, and Zechariah still . . . had . . . .

His hands landed on Ruana's shoulders. Would they be gentle or firm? Even from here, she could hear the quickness of his breath. "Ruana—have you told Asho? Is he angry? If you are in any danger—"

"No, nothing like that."

Perhaps her words brought relief to Zech. But his slicked another layer of desperate incredulity over Esther. If, then what? What would he do to help this woman, his . . . his lover? Steal her away from her husband? Run off with her?

Leave Esther to face a broken future?

Or would he care for her in secret and keep lying to everyone else? Let Esther think she was the only one he wanted, the only one he cared for, then sneak off to see to his bastard child?

Oh, Lord above. How had Mordecai known?

"He is not angry?"

Ruana shook her head. "On the contrary. Zech . . . that was his whole purpose in recommending I take a lover. He said you realized his . . . tastes, when he came to your shop last time. He has no interest in me, not in that way. But he needs an heir."

"So you used me." Would his nostrils flare? Would his grip harden against the woman's shoulders?

"I am explaining *his* motivations, not mine. You know how I feel for you, Zech."

"Do I?" Finally, he stepped back, dropped his hands. Yet it did not help Esther breathe any easier. "It hardly matters. You have your life, Ruana. I am making mine. I do not want to see you again."

"I know. You have said so before."

Zechariah looked at her for a long moment. What did he see? Was she beautiful? Did he want her even now, was he thinking about his babe in her womb?

Oh, why did the earth not open and swallow Esther whole?

He drew in a ragged breath. "You only come now . . . please tell me this did not happen that day, when the victory news reached us."

The day of victory—after he had begun the addition meant for Esther? After he had made his intentions clear?

"I would have let you know earlier otherwise—why does that make a difference?"

Zechariah only shook his head.

Esther wanted to scream. Was this the woman she had seen launch herself at him? The one she had actually chuckled about? Had she . . . had they . . .? And now this? A child, from that day?

That day when he was supposedly in love with *her*?

The woman took a step back. "Asho did not want me to tell you, but it is your child, and you deserve to know."

Zechariah only nodded.

"I . . . do you want me to send a message when the child is born? I expect nothing from you, I will keep my distance. But if you wanted to know whether you have a son or a daughter, I will have a servant bring the news."

Esther squeezed her eyes shut.

He drew in a long breath. "Yes. Let me know."

Pain cut through her middle, leaving a trail of fire in her chest. How could he? How could he do this? She had thought him a good man, strong and courageous. Did he not know the Law of Moses? Were the words of Jehovah not etched on his spirit? So how could he throw away his covenant for a Persian seductress? How could he take a married woman to bed, when he knew the price for such sin was death?

"Farewell, Zech. I will not bother you again, though I will let you know."

"I will pray for you, Ruana."

Pray? To Jehovah? For *her*?

"Pray the babe is a boy. If he does not get his heir, I know not what I will do."

Esther's nails bit into her palms. She would probably come to Zechariah again, that was what. And she obviously had the power to tempt him, so who knew whether he would stand firm or go merrily to her bed.

"I will." His voice was heavy with resignation. "Ruana . . . I do not like this situation with Asho. If he threatens you or the babe, you can come to me. I will find some way to protect you. I owe that much to your brother."

"Bijan would thank you, I am sure." Cynicism and amusement mixed in her tone.

Bijan's sister. As if knowing who she was made any difference.

He breathed a laugh and lifted a hand in farewell. Ruana rejoined her servants, and they melted into the night.

Esther could not move. Could not breathe. Could not think. If only she could not be, as well. Disappear.

She heard his footsteps, but she could not force her eyes up. She did not want to look at him, lest his face show his heart.

She did not want to know his heart. Not anymore.

The current in the air changed, the footsteps halted. "Esther?" Panic in his voice, tinged with disbelief. "What are you doing out here?"

Laughter nearly bubbled up—had he not asked her that same question years ago, when she caught him practicing with Bijan?—but she bit it back. It would have come out hysterical. Still, she remembered her role. "I might ask you the same question."

He touched a finger to her chin. She jerked away. "Do not touch me."

"Esther, please. Let me explain—"

"What explanation can you possibly give? It is bad enough that you would have a lover. But a married one?"

Guilt twisted his face. His conscience was alive then—but apparently in subjection to his lusts. "I know. I do. I never meant to get involved with her."

She snorted and spun away.

"Esther." Voice desperate, he caught her arm. "I am sorry—"

"That is not enough." The tremors started in her stomach and pulsed out to the tips of her fingers. "To think that I would have married you. Would have given you everything

I am, my entire heart, never knowing that you have a bastard child with another woman."

He looked as though his heart tore in two. Good. "I love you, Esther. You, only you."

"What would you have done had her husband been angry with her?"

His agony increased . . . but it was nothing compared to hers. "I do not know."

"Or if we married, then she came to you in a year, in two years, and said the child needed something, needed you? What then?"

He sighed. "You think I have answers? I only know that while I do feel responsible for . . . this, I also love you. I want you to be my wife."

She pulled her arm free. "No."

"Esther." When he reached for her again, she leapt away and spun toward home. He fell in beside her. "I understand you are angry. Hurt. But please, do not give up on me. Surely, if you really love me, we can work this out."

A fire swept through her. "If I love you? What about if you really love me? Like, perhaps, 'if you really loved me, you would not have slept with another woman'? What about *that?*"

"I know." His voice shook. "It was a mistake, one I regret."

"Well, I hope your regret keeps you company. I want nothing to do with you."

"Esther—"

"Just stop!" A sob ripped out, her eyes burned. She clenched her fists against it. Better the anger than the pain. Better to keep her head high than let him see her break. She had broken enough in life. Had let tragedy bend her each time it struck. She was done. "You knew what you were doing, Zechariah."

He reached for her again. She stepped out of his way and shook her head. "I saw you that day. I saw her leap into your arms, and I laughed. I thought it just another crazed Persian. Unimportant. And then that evening, I sat there beside you while you built our house, and you said nothing about it. Nothing about what must have filled your thoughts."

His arm held suspended in the air, frozen in its reach. "I did not want to hurt you."

"Too late." Half hoping he would leap into the river and let it carry him off, she ran the rest of the way home.

THIRTY-NINE

Evil flew through the palace. Kasia could feel the beat of its wings upon her soul. It kicked her heart to a higher speed, made her thoughts race in prayer. Still, fear soaked her.

"Jehovah, help me."

You are safe, my daughter.

The promise did little to ease the anxiety. What of those she loved?

Screams pierced the air. The kind that came from fear, then they shifted, grew into the kind born of the most excruciating pain.

Her mind flashed back to Sardis and the cries of Pythius's son—only these were higher, feminine.

Somehow Zillah slept through it, and Kasia whispered a prayer of thanks for that, added another that the angels would insulate her from whatever chaos set upon them. She looked to Desma. "Stay with her."

"Mistress—"

"I must see what is going on." She sped out the door, knowing her eunuchs followed. She found Jasmine at the end of the corridor, pale-faced. "Jasmine. What is happening?"

Jasmine reached for her hand and gripped it. "Amestris handed Parsisa over to the guards. Her instructions do not bear repeating."

Her stomach cinched tight. "Why?"

Jasmine's eyes filled with tears. "You were not to know. You will not like it."

"What I like is of no consequence right now." She did not mean to snap it, but the cries . . . .

Jasmine's eyes slid shut. "Artaynte arrived at the feast this afternoon wearing the shawl Amestris gave Xerxes at his coronation. Darius flew into a rage, and Amestris requested a favor of the king—Parsisa. She obviously thought the mother behind it."

Behind . . . *it*. She did not want to consider *it*. Did not want to think of why Artaynte would have Xerxes' most prized possession.

Yet even without considering, she knew. Her blood ran cold through her veins, and a chill swept up her spine.

She heard his footsteps, even over the agonizing screams and the shattering of her own insides. In that second before action, she considered running away, back to her chamber. But she had to know. She spun to face her husband.

He must have seen something on her face—his expression shifted from distress to despair. He stretched out a hand, but she took a step backward and whispered, "What have you done?"

"It was not supposed to hurt you. You were never to know."

"Of all the inane—"

"I am sorry. Kasia, I am so sorry."

"Sorry?" She shook her head, stepped away from his reach again. "How many wives do you have, Xerxes? And added to them, you have the right to any slave you desire. Is that not enough? Must you steal your son's wife as well? Your own *niece?*" The thought of that sent a shudder up her spine, even though she knew he would not recognize the connection as incestuous. "I hope you loved her. Hope you enjoyed yourself, that it was worth her mother's life."

Xerxes winced. "It was not . . . I only wanted to punish Darius. For what he did to you in Sardis."

For a long moment she could only stare at him. This was because of *her*? Because he was jealous? "You slept with Artaynte because Darius kissed me?"

He turned his face away, presenting his ticking jaw. "Because of what came after."

"After? You slept with Artaynte because I threatened to kill him if he touched me again?"

He met her gaze again, his strangely soft. "My love, we both know my son would not accept such an answer. I realize the memories must be painful—"

"There *are* no memories! Do you not think I would have told you had it been something more? Do you think I could have hidden my heart from you, and the scars that would have left behind? Have I seemed at all hurt?"

His Adam's apple bobbed. "You avoid him. Avoid the mere mention of him."

"Because he kissed me." A particularly gruesome shriek pierced the air. Kasia squeezed her eyes shut. "I cannot believe we are having this conversation while Parsisa is . . . why do you not stop it?"

"I cannot. I agreed to grant her a request."

The screams came to an abrupt halt. That, even more than the terrible noise, sent a wash of fear through her. Xerxes motioned one of his eunuchs toward the exit.

Kasia shook her head, tried in vain to blink back the tears. "Why would you do something so stupid? Not just the affair, which is awful enough. But you know Amestris's wrath. Why would you give away the shawl? And why, after doing so, would you be so foolish as to grant her a favor?"

Only at the collective gasp behind her did she realize all the other women had come out. She bit her lip. Perhaps she could get away with speaking to him like that in private, but to call the king a fool in front of all his wives?

She might as well offer herself next to the murderous guards.

Xerxes did not seem to notice. He rubbed a hand over his face. "I did not realize she knew already. But I felt guilty for it and thought . . . ."

The eunuch reappeared, his face pale as a specter. "She is yet alive, though I cannot imagine for long. They are taking her home."

"What did they do to her?" Xerxes' voice was dead and even.

"Mutilated her, master, in ways I cannot say in front of the women."

His eyes slid shut. "My brother will not forgive this."

He was not the only one. Vision blurred and rocking, Kasia turned toward her quarters. The sea of wives parted before her.

"Kasia, wait."

Instead she ran, ran until she gained the tremulous sanctuary of her own room, where Zillah still slept peacefully in her cradle.

She ought to have realized Xerxes would follow. His hands curled over her shoulders, and he stood so close his body heat wrapped around her.

She did not want it. Did not want the comfort it would give or the familiarity it exuded. "This is too much, Xerxes. Artaynte is my friend."

His thumbs stroked up her neck. "She used to be. But seeing how Darius loves you, I think her anger eclipsed everything else. As mine did. I did not love her, Kasia. I know the court will say I did, will whisper about how well she must have pleased me for me to give her that shawl, but it was only revenge."

This, then, was why the Lord claimed vengeance for himself. It was too bitter, too terrible for the likes of men to bear. "You have destroyed your family, Xerxes."

His hands tightened, then fell away. "I did not do it alone. Darius was the one who decided lust meant more than blood."

She spun, hands fisted. "Which was wrong. But Darius is little more than a boy, ruled by his emotions and desires. You are a man, Xerxes. A king. You ought to know the price for such things."

Anger kindled in his eyes. Good. Better a battle than the sobs she felt building in her throat. He drew in a long breath. "I know this will mean nothing to you, but it was her idea."

"Nothing at all. You betrayed your son in the worst way imaginable. And then your brother . . . ."

His eyes slid shut. "I know. I did not realize what Amestris would do."

New fury simmered. "And why not? You know venom flows in place of her blood. You know what she tried after you gave me the torc. Yet you have done *nothing* to curb her power since we returned, nothing to remind the world that she is not still the queen."

Eyes flying open, he spat, "I was a little preoccupied with the woman I love nearly dying in labor."

She shot Desma a reproving glance. "It has been nearly a month and a half since then."

"During which I was settling back into rule."

"And seducing your son's wife."

"I did not seduce—" He cut himself off with a curse. "What would you have me do,

Kasia? I cannot undo it, though I wish I could. I cannot save Parsisa. I cannot even punish Amestris, not with the responsibility of it weighing on my shoulders."

"You can name a new queen."

He looked weary and unconvinced. "What would that solve? I cannot name you, but bringing in new young women will take a year."

It stung, even though she would have been the first to agree. "It will convey a message."

"She is right."

She looked beyond her husband, to where his advisers came through her doorway. A sigh gathered in her chest. The last time these men had stepped foot in her chamber, Amestris had ended up deposed. Hard to believe they were here again, again in response to the first wife's atrocities.

Perhaps she should not have stopped him from having her killed years ago.

No, that was anger speaking. Anger and horror, and a dash of guilt mixed in. She should have told Xerxes about Darius when he arrived in Sardis. Should have told him exactly what happened, so that he would have known what did not. Trying to spare his temper had only given it fuel.

The eldest member of the council inclined his white-haired head. "Persia has been too long without a queen, my lord. The women need someone to follow. The harem needs a leader."

"Which you expect they shall find in some fresh-faced virgin?" Xerxes shook his head. "Kasia has assumed leadership. That is enough."

Kasia folded her arms over her chest. "Obviously not."

When these men had come to her chamber a few years before, they had looked at her with skepticism. Now the speaker inclined his head with respect. "My lady does indeed command the respect of all the women. And when we bring in virgins for you, my lord, she can take them under her wing and lend them her wisdom. She can show the one you select how to be a queen worthy of you."

Xerxes met her gaze, held it.

Kasia clenched her teeth. "Do it. Anyone would be better than Amestris."

Still he held her gaze. "I do not need more wives."

She raised her chin. "Your mother told me when I arrived that a king's wealth is measured not only in gold and lands, but in wives and sons. They will be bringing you new virgins until the day you die, Xerxes." Giving him a pointed look, she added, "It is not *your* wives I mind."

"Fine." He sighed, his eyes sliding closed for a moment. "At first light, have the scouts go out into the city."

"The king has made a wise decision."

His first in weeks, though Kasia pressed her lips together against the words. The council retreated from her room, and Xerxes stepped closer. She backed up, which earned her another sigh and a pleading, "Kasia . . . ."

She shook her head. "She was the only friend I had not already your wife, the only one I did not have to share you with. You robbed me of that."

Regret twisted his face—but regret never changed anything. "I was not thinking. When I heard that my son had taken you in his arms, with no signs of stopping . . . I have never felt such rage."

"Then you know how I feel now."

He paced to the window, hands on hips. "You are remarkably measured for being enraged."

True. It was not a flash, it was a throb. More pain than anger. More disappointment than thirst for revenge.

One of Xerxes' lesser eunuchs stepped inside. "Master. Your brother just returned to his house and found his wife. She died in his arms, and he . . . he took off for the stable, shouting that he would rally an army against you in Bactra."

He felt the pain too, she knew. Perhaps saw his empire waver before his eyes. If Masistes succeeded, it would mean civil war. Unrest. Uprisings, assassination plots. The weight of it aged him a decade before her eyes. "You must stop him . . . whatever it takes."

They all knew what it would take.

Kasia sank onto her bed, wondering how many more deaths would stain this night. "Go to your son."

"What?"

"Preserve what family you have left, Xerxes. Go to Darius and Artaynte. Beg their forgiveness, before your kingdom fractures beyond repair."

He stood there a long moment measuring her. Then he dropped a kiss on Zillah's head, kissed Kasia once before she could draw away, and sped from the room.

She closed her eyes and wished for the comfort of her mother's arms. Wished she had fallen in love with someone other than a king who thought he could bend the world to his will. Wished for a simpler life.

Something she would never know. Too weary to hold the tears at bay another moment, she fell onto her bed and let herself cry. Wrapped her fingers around the torc, tugged it down to her wrist, pulled it off. She gripped it, unable to cast it aside as she had done once before, unable to put it back on.

She was trapped. Trapped between love and hate, between loyalty and disgust. There was nowhere to go from here.

Xerxes followed the sound of sobs through his son's palace. So many haunting, taunting reminders of their shame. Pulling, tugging until he felt he would shatter.

It was not supposed to be this way. Perhaps he wanted Darius humble and apologetic. Perhaps he wanted to see in his son's eyes the same pain Xerxes felt.

But not this. He had never wanted Parsisa's gruesome death. And Masistes . . . his throat burned when he thought of his brother. This never should have involved his brother. How had the consequences reached so far, touched so many?

He stepped into the room and saw Artaynte curled into a ball on a chaise, Darius staring blankly out a window. And in the distance between them, in the stony look on his son's face, he saw a million fractures that could splinter, break away, fester. A million ways this could go worse still.

Masistes had promised war. Darius could stage a coup. His empire, his father's empire, could crumble and burn, Xerxes could end up dead at an assassin's hand. Those loyal to him could be killed along with him, or forced into exile.

What a bloody, ugly world hid under the polish and shine. And all for a miscalculated revenge.

Somewhere in the tangle of thorns and fangs, there must be a path to safety. There must be a way that would strengthen rather than break.

For the first time in months, his soul yearned for the guidance of someone larger than himself. He could not return to Ahura Mazda—which left only one option.

Jehovah, God of the Jews. Kasia would say you know me. She would say you concern yourself with me because I am the ruler over your chosen ones. I do not know if you care about the man as well as the king. But if you do, if you would lend me your wisdom, I need it. I want to preserve my empire, preserve the lives within it. More, I want to preserve my family. How do I do that?

He paused, waited. Would he recognize the voice of his wife's God? He did not know.

But he could hear hers. She had said something at Thermopylae, when they argued. Something about humility granting her peace.

Humility and a crown did not go hand in hand. A humble king could not command the respect of nations.

Darius jerked his head around, finally spotting him. Banked fury smoldered in his gaze.

He was not here as a king, he was here as a father. A father who had deliberately hurt the son of his flesh. Perhaps a father could be humble without being weak. Perhaps a father could find strength in granting his son healing.

Darius lifted his chin. "What do you want? To take my wife again? Perhaps parade her around the court so all can see you have made a whore of her?"

Xerxes sucked in a long breath. "I deserve your wrath. And I am sorry."

"Sorry?" Darius sent a flickering lamp to the floor, where its own weight snuffed it out. "Being sorry does not restore my pride, or my wife's honor."

"No. Nor does it return Parsisa her life."

From the chaise, Artaynte groaned. "It is over then? She is dead?"

"She is dead." His voice sounded old and ill-used. "In your father's arms. He sped off to Bactra, claiming he would raise an army."

She groaned again—she would know what that meant.

Xerxes took another step into the room, faced his son. "I cannot undo what happened—would that I could. Haman told me that he saw you embrace Kasia, and he had assumed it went further than it did. I did not stop to ask questions. I judged, I sentenced. I wanted you to hurt as I did." His eyes squeezed shut, and he shook his head. "I am a miserable father and a fool of a man. I could see nothing but my own rage, my own pain. I am sorry, Darius. You are my son, and I treated you like an enemy."

When he opened his eyes again, he saw Darius sink into a chair. "You never take blame, you . . . I wanted to fight you. Now you force me to admit I am as miserable a son as you are a father. I knew you loved her above any other, knew you would not forgive it, and I pursued her anyway."

"I forgive it." The words tumbled out before he knew they had formed, shocking him as much as the two whose gazes flew to his face. "I did not before, but at this moment . . . our blood, our relationship is too important to sever."

Darius plunged a hand into his hair. "Because I am your heir."

"Because you are my son. Because I love you. And yes, because I want to pass to you a united kingdom, not one torn by civil war. I want to give it to you freely, after working to make it strong for you, as my father did. I do not want to help rip it to shreds before you or my brother force it from me, and me from life."

Darius rubbed his eyes. "I wanted to hate you. I was doing an excellent job, but you are making it difficult."

Somehow, a small laugh tickled his throat. "That was my goal. I do not want you to hate me—I saw the price of hatred today, and it is too bitter. If you learn anything from your mother, I hope it is that."

"Mother did this." The words rang with an incredulous resignation. "Had Parsisa killed."

"She would have been angry over the shawl." The next words got stuck, but Xerxes swallowed so he could force them out. "And I imagine she was furious on your behalf. You are her joy."

"No, I am her pride. There is a vast difference." He shoved to his feet, paced, but Xerxes could see that he had a goal in mind. It just took him a moment to work his way there, to his wife's side. The hand he put on her shoulder looked hesitant, as if he feared she may turn and bite him. "My mother killed yours. That, on top of all that has passed between us, must make you despise me. If you want a divorce, I will grant it, and be generous. I will even arrange a marriage to a better man, one who will not treat you this way."

Artaytne lifted her swollen, wet face. "You fool. I never wanted a better man, I wanted you. I thought—I thought if you saw me act as you had, it would make you see how I felt."

He sat beside her, pulled her to his chest. "You succeeded in that."

"At a price beyond reckoning." Even from where he stood, Xerxes saw her shudder. "It cost my mother her life. It will cost my father his."

But they held each other, Darius and Artaytne. Their arms came around each other, their tears mixed.

Something. Small, when one considered all the terrors of the evening. But something good.

He sighed. "I will leave you two to sort through this. Please, both of you—know I am sorry. Know that I crave your forgiveness more than anything."

Artaytne did not look at him, but Darius did. His gaze was absent the rage, absent the fury. The nod he gave was not one of forgiveness itself, Xerxes knew—but it was the promise to try.

It would be enough for now.

He turned, left. And nearly collided with Zethar, whose face bore the stress of the night. "They caught up with your brother, master."

Part of him wished Masistes would have made it home to Bactra, would have raised his army so that he might get his justice. The part that was brother rather than king. "And?"

"He is dead."

Xerxes nodded, strode outside. He felt half dead himself.

FORTY

Esther rose with the dawn after a night filled more with tears and fury than sleep. She washed her face, glanced in the polished brass mirror to see how terrible she looked. And snorted when she realized her eyes were no longer swollen, not even circled with shadows. She looked as though nothing had happened. As if her world had not fallen apart.

The frozen rock where her heart used to be said otherwise.

Zechariah would come by at some point today, try to speak to her again. She had no intention of listening, but she dressed in her finest just to spite him. Carefully arranged her hair, even wore the gold necklace her cousin had given her for her birthday. She did *not* touch the intricate wooden bracelet Zechariah had made for her. Perhaps it was childish, but she did not care—she wanted him to see what he had given up.

She stepped out into the living area, and the walls closed in. There was no sanctuary from the truth within her cousin's home.

"Esther." Mordecai stepped out of his chamber, his face set. "I spent the night in prayer about you and Zechariah—"

"You need not say it. It no longer matters." She should have told him last night, should have saved him the hours on the floor. But she had been too upset to face anyone. "I will not marry him."

Mordecai's brows drew together. "What happened?"

"I saw for myself the chains you felt binding him. They took the form of a lovely, married Persian woman carrying his child."

He drew in a sharp breath and even gripped the doorframe. "I am sorry, my daughter."

Was he? Sorry Zechariah had acted in such a way, yes. But was he sorry she had discovered it, or grateful she had seen it with her own eyes, so that he would not have to insist on what she did not understand?

Esther squeezed her eyes shut. She was unfit for company. "I need to get out for a while, cousin. Just to walk, to think."

Mordecai nodded. "I believe Martha needs some things from the markets, if you wanted to head that way."

"That is fine. I know what she needs, I will take care of it." It would give her feet direction, her hands purpose.

Her mind, though. Her mind spun every which direction as she stepped into the cool morning air. With every footfall, it churned over thoughts of Zechariah, of Ruana, of her own dashed dreams. Of Mordecai, so close to Jehovah that he knew something was wrong. Why, then, had he not found a way to tell her long ago? Why had he let her love so much, so deeply, when he knew he would have to refuse Zechariah's request for her hand?

Why could nothing ever go right? Nothing. Ever. Her parents, Kasia, now this. Oh, for a mother's shoulder to cry on, for Kasia to talk to. She had only Zechariah's mother, and she could hardly turn to her in this.

Tears stung the backs of her eyes, but she blinked them down. So many years she had geared everything, absolutely everything, to gaining Zechariah's attention. And for what? To hope, only to be destroyed?

No. She would not break. Not again.

The market stretched out before her, a cacophony of sounds and scents and sights even at this early hour. She breathed in the smell of spices and fruit ripening in the sun and let herself forget the rest for a moment. She headed for the grain-seller, and a minute later had a bag of it to be milled. Her next stop would be the Egyptian, for some chamomile.

When she turned, she smacked into the steady gaze of a stranger. It felt solid, somehow, as corporeal as if he had tossed a rope around her. For a second it held her immobile. Then she focused her eyes on the ground and hurried across the market to the Egyptian's stall.

"Excuse me."

It was the man, she knew it even before she turned around. Yes, the stranger. He looked at her intently, with eyes narrowed in contemplation. His clothing . . . the clothing of the palace officials.

He gave her a small bow—why would he bow to her?—and smiled. "Forgive me for staring. You are very beautiful."

She straightened her shoulders. Somehow, he made it sound more like fact than compliment, as if he were only commenting on the weather. Did such an observation warrant a thanks?

He did not wait for her to respond before inclining his head. "I am a scout for the king, in search of the most beautiful virgins in Persia. He will choose a queen from among them. Are you married?"

She could only stare. Would the king's men really scour the markets for the next queen? It must be some joke.

But those garments. The sobriety of his gaze. Esther gathered her shawl about her shoulders. "No, I am not married."

Satisfaction, not pleasure, lit his eyes. "Who is your father?"

"I am afraid my father has been dead these eight years, and my mother with him. My guardian—"

"An orphan."The man's face fell. "Then you likely have no dowry. To be a full wife and have a chance for the crown, you must have a dowry."

He assumed too much, assumed she *wanted* a chance at the crown . . . yet pride forced her chin up. "I have a dowry. My father was not poor, and my guardian has preserved what he left for me."

"Ah." Face bright again, the man reached into a bag slung around him and pulled out a tablet. "These are the terms of the marriage. If you and your guardian agree to the contract, you may present yourself and this tablet at the palace in a week. At that point, final candidates will be selected and taken into the house of women for purification and treatments."

She took the tablet—it was easier than arguing. Could even provide an amusing story, proof that the king's officials thought her worthy to be queen, though a certain foolish Jewish man did not value her enough to remain faithful.

Quickly, she purchased the rest of the things Martha needed and hurried home. When she entered and saw Mordecai sitting down to his first meal of the day, she even managed a smile. "You will never guess who I came across in the markets."

Her cousin arched his brows. "Who?"

"A scout for the king." She slid the tablet onto the table. "They have apparently begun the search for a new queen."

"High time." Mordecai picked up the tablet. His face shifted as he read, though she had no name for the emotions she saw. He looked up at her again. "Esther. This is a marriage contract."

"The man gave it to me to consider—quite a compliment, is it not? I needed that this morning."

"Esther," he said again, placing the tablet carefully on the table. "It is more than a compliment. These scouts are discerning men. They will send no more than twenty to the palace from all of Susa and the surrounding areas. They will select no more than a dozen to go into preparation for the king. Esther, you could be the next queen."

A tickle danced up her spine. "Nonsense, cousin. I am a Jewess."

"Do they know that?"

She frowned. "I suppose not. I did not mention it, nor your name."

He closed his eyes and drew in a long breath. She knew he was praying. What she did not know was why her pulse kicked up, why her palms went damp. "Cousin?"

"When I prayed last night, I felt clearly what I have suspected for years—trials lie ahead for the Jews in Persia. Too many of the powerful voices in the court are against us. But if the new queen could offer moderate and well-informed opinions to the king on the subjects that concern us . . . ."

Her stomach quivered. "Let us be reasonable. Even if I took this contract to the palace, even if they added me to the harem, that would not guarantee I be queen. It would not even guarantee the king *like* me, much less listen to my opinions."

"No, there are never guarantees. But there are promises." His eyes shone bright, but not with excitement. With . . . knowledge. Faith. "You are destined for great things, my daughter. This is the path for you."

Gooseflesh prickled her arms. But what greatness could she have inside? It felt like the only thing hiding within her was fear. Fear and sorrow. "Would it not mean lying about my heritage, about my connection to you?"

"It would mean not mentioning it. And yes, that would be difficult. But we would find a way to stay in touch." He stood and rested his hands on her arms. "I will not decide this for you, but this is the marriage to which I give my blessing today. Not to Zechariah, but to Xerxes."

The door banged open, and Zechariah stepped into the room with horror in his eyes. "You will *what?*"

For a moment they only looked at him, as if he were some stranger barging in uninvited. Zechariah fisted his hands and tried to slow his breathing back to normal. He must have misheard. Must have caught only the tail end of the conversation, out of context.

Because there was no way on Jehovah's bronze earth that he would lose Esther to Xerxes as he had lost his sister. His God would not be so cruel. And Mordecai—his friend, his neighbor—would surely never give his ward to the gentile king instead of the Jewish man who loved her.

Esther blinked, raised her chin, and glared at him. "Why did you come?"

He must still be dreaming, caught in the nightmares that had plagued him all night. "I wanted to talk to you. To both of you."

"I have nothing left to say to you."

"Esther—"

"Zech." Mordecai turned to him, his countenance determined yet gentle. "It is good you have come. I know you intended to ask for Esther's hand."

"I still do." He cast a pleading glance her way. "I know she is hurt and angry, and I imagine she has told you why. I deserve her disregard. But I love her. I will be a good husband."

Mordecai shook his head. "No, my son. I have felt for a while that there was something holding you back from giving your whole heart to her. I suspect it is this other woman."

"There is nothing holding me back, she *has* my whole heart." Every crevice. The part of him that Ruana appealed to . . . that was not his heart, not love.

Esther folded her arms over her chest. Gold winked at her neck, her finest dress draped her frame so perfectly that a lump formed in his throat. One long day ago, this vision of perfection had been his, in his arms. How could she now stand there as if the whole world were between them?

"You may have a better chance convincing me of that," she said, "had I not seen you with her last night. Had I not heard in your voice that you would do whatever you must to protect her."

"Never at cost to you."

She snorted and averted her face. "It does not matter anyway. My cousin told me before I saw you with her that he would not approve. Which is just as well. I am going to marry the king, perhaps be the next queen."

For a moment he could only stare as those incredible words sank in. Countless thoughts boiled. He knew not which would find the way to his tongue until he heard himself say, "You are angry with me for involvement with another woman so will marry a king and join his *harem*? That makes sense to you?"

Mordecai put a steadying hand on her shoulder. "He does not claim to be a faithful Jew. He does not lie to her heart of hearts."

"But what *does* he do? Have you considered that? He takes whomever he pleases." Like his sister, with no warning and no choice. "This morning I heard he even took his son's wife. Is that better than me?"

Esther spun on him, looking angry enough to spit. "Yes! It is better to marry an adulterous king who has no power over my heart than to have it broken by you!"

Mordecai pulled her back, stepped in front of her. Sighed. "She has a good chance of becoming queen, Zech. Can you not see what that would mean for all our people? Can you not wish such honor for her?"

Queen? Honor? He cared nothing about such things when it meant losing her. Losing yet another of his favorite people to the palace . . . .

He sucked in a breath and straightened his spine. Kasia was there. Kasia would find her, they would be able to embrace again, to whisper and laugh and finish each other's sentences.

Looking from Mordecai to Esther, he was not sure he was strong enough, selfless enough to let her go for the sake of giving her back another she had lost. But really, what choice did he have? He could yell, he could beg, he could toss himself into the river—nothing would change her mind. That was clear.

He could be furious and hurt—and he was both—but when those cooled, he could find some comfort in the knowledge that a reunion would await her.

At the moment, that promise was meager indeed.

Darius paused to take a breath that did nothing to fortify him. His limbs still felt like lead, his soul like an empty vessel. But his hands were steady, at least. His steps were sure.

They took him through the house of wives, into his mother's chambers. His brother was there, quietly at his schoolwork, only darting a glance at him when he entered. A glance that said more than he cared to interpret.

His sisters were there too. Amytis, nearest him in age, her eyes on the ground even as her fingers flew over the loom. Perhaps she had heard their father offered her to Masistes last night to try to lessen the blow of Parsisa's death. Rhodogune sat beside her.

They had obviously heard enough to know that nothing was the same this morning.

His mother exited her bedchamber and smiled. Oblivious, even victorious. He felt heavier than ever. "My son," she said in greeting. "I was wondering when you would come by to thank me."

What world did she live in, that she could think her actions so simple, so . . . acceptable? "I cannot thank you. You mutilated my wife's mother."

Amestris waved that off. "You know as well as I that you did not want her ruling you through Artaynte. Now that she is gone, and now that your harlot of a wife's true nature is known, you can put her aside."

"I will not." Even after swallowing, his throat felt dry. "Artaynte and I have decided to forgive past wrongs and try to build a true marriage."

She stared, then her lips curled back. "Fool! Why would you forgive her? She made a laughingstock of you."

"And of you?"

"Yes, and of me. She and your father both—he cannot treat us this way, then shove the blame onto another. To kill his own brother when Masistes dared stand against him, to—"

"He can, Mother. He is king. He is never to blame when someone rebels against him." She would never accept that, he knew. Odd, since she thought that very rule applied to her. He sighed. "Moreover, he apologized. He came as a father, not as a king, and begged me to forgive him."

She spat out a few curses and spun to the window, to the table, back to him. "He betrayed you!"

"Yes. But I would have betrayed him first, had his wife not been of stronger morals than mine."

"The Jewess?" Her voice ran as cold as the snow-fed Choaspes. "I ought to have known. With your father, everything goes back to the Jewess."

"At the moment, it all goes back to you, and what you did." He had asked Father to let him do this. To let him draw the line. "You will be sent away, Mother. You may go to whichever capital you please, but never again will you be near us."

Her eyes narrowed on his face. "'We'? You align yourself with your father? Even after he stole your wife?"

"He is capable of atrocities. You both are. The difference is that he always regrets them and does not make the same mistake again. You revel in them and find new, bigger ways to horrify the world."

"No, the difference is that he acts only for himself and his Jewish witch. All I do, all I am is for my children."

"I could do without your actions." He took a step back. Not in retreat, but in symbolism. "When I am king, I will echo my father's edict and keep you apart. You are a threat to your family and the empire. If not for the swift action of my father's men, the kingdom would be falling into war even now."

"It would have served him right."

"And it would have served me right to have to deal with a fractured empire. Yet I daresay you did not think of that." He drew in a breath. "You will leave tomorrow."

She stood still as a statue, but for the sparks flying from her eyes. "Do not align yourself against me, Darius. I have more power than you can know, more even than your father in the ways that matter."

"You will be stripped of it. Even now the scouts are out in search of young women, one of which will be the next queen."

She sneered. "You think it will be so easy? As long as I have breath, I will have might. I warn you now—stand with him instead of me, and you will fall with him. I have other sons. I will raise one of them up instead of you, one that will give me the honor I am due."

He heard the rustle behind him, felt the movement of his brother. Hystaspes stood just behind him, at his right elbow.

He glanced at his sisters. Amytis rose, grabbed Rhodogune's hand, and dashed behind the cover of her brothers.

Their mother shook. But no fear, no uncertainty showed on her face. "Will you steal my babe from me too?"

He and Father had already discussed that. "Artaxerxes will stay with you half the year, in the summer. He will winter here with us. Beginning next year, once he is weaned."

Perhaps, had tears filled her eyes or pain tinged the anger, he would have felt some pity. But she only snarled. "You will all regret this. If my youngest is the only one I have left, then in my youngest will I put all my efforts. My youngest I will see on the throne. And do you know why? Because you are too weak to kill your own mother—but your mother is not too weak to kill her own sons."

"Goodbye, Mother." Turning, he guided the flock of his siblings out the door.

FORTY-ONE

Mordecai nearly jumped when the king spoke his name. Never in his life had he been so jittery as these past three days, since Esther had been admitted into the house of women. He was not accustomed to hiding anything, especially something as soul-deep as his love for his adopted daughter. Still, he knew she must keep her heritage, and hence their relation, secret. Much as he liked Xerxes, the king would never give the crown to a Jewess.

Now, Jehovah willing, he could face his king without letting on that his daughter was one of the new brides. "My lord."

"You are coming from a meeting with a few of my lesser officials, are you not?"

Mordecai inclined his head and met the king's gaze. Nowhere in it did he see an accusation ready to strike. "Handling what we can without your involvement, my lord, yes."

The king smiled. "Are you in a hurry to get home?"

As if there were anything to go home to now. "Not particularly."

"Then you can walk with me. I have been meaning to speak with you since I returned to Susa, but time has not allowed it."

"The king has been busy." Given that he had ears, he had heard the rumors as to how he had been occupied. Given that he had logic, he knew most of those rumors would be false.

The father in him would have liked to know which parts held the kernels of truth.

Xerxes chuckled and led him into the gardens, but discomfort filled his eyes. "When we last spoke, you said I would see the power of Jehovah for myself."

Enough small talk then. Mordecai nodded. "Perhaps you did, while at war?"

"More than once. Still, it took me nearly a year to admit there was something about him that my god lacked. Something he lacked that my god unfortunately did not."

Yet still he called him his god. Mordecai nodded. "It is difficult to change one's views on such things."

"Yes, but I cannot deny the power of your God. He saved my wife more than once. Saved me and my army, according to her. She says other Jews were praying with her, though I know not how they could have known to."

Mordecai drifted to a halt, hoping the king did not misinterpret his frown. Usually only the queen would be called "wife" with a stranger, but he obviously did not mean Amestris. It sounded, rather, like he had a Jewish wife. A faithful one.

But who? He knew all the Jewish families in Susa, and none had given a daughter to the king. Perhaps one from another of the capitals?

Irrelevant. "There were indeed times I felt a strong urge to pray for the army. One time in particular, it was strong enough that I roused all my people to pray for you as well. I later learned it was during the battle at Thermopylae."

The king's breath leaked out. "Just as she said. Amazing. And interesting. I see her pray daily, yet I am always surprised when I see what results from it."

The curiosity was too great. "She must be a woman of strong faith. I confess I did not realize the king had a Jewish wife."

"No?" The king's lips curved, his eyes lit. More love saturated his face than Mordecai had ever expected to see from the ruler of nations. "I thought I mentioned her when last we spoke, but perhaps not. She is my heart." The love flickered into pain. "Though not very pleased with me right now. You have heard the rumors."

"All of Persia has, my lord. As a rule, I do not believe them."

"You are a wise man. Suffice it to say enough is true that my favorite wife is rightly angry." He shook his head, erased the emotion from his face. "It has been a long while since she has spoken to another of her people. I think she would enjoy a few moments to exchange these stories with you."

Mordecai chuckled and nodded. "I would be honored to meet your wife. And if that regains you a bit of favor in her eyes, all the better."

Xerxes laughed. "You obviously know how one thinks when trying to sweeten a woman's mood."

"My wife and I had our share of squabbles before she passed away."

"This goes beyond a squabble, but I will not bore you with it." Instead, he led him through a maze of paths, beyond hedges, and into the heart of the gardens. Here children's laughter rang out along with feminine voices. He saw none, though, as he followed Xerxes to a secluded little nook surrounded by trees, shrubs, and myriad blooms.

Several figures occupied the space. He saw first the servants, two maids and two eunuchs. They stood in a protective circle, but upon spotting the king, they broke apart.

Mordecai halted. He was not so sure his heart did not stop too. Even before she looked up, he knew her. Knew the cascade of her hair, the slope of her shoulder. Knew the hum that reached his ear the moment he entered this sanctuary. Knew the spirit that pulsed from her.

"Kasia." He could only pray no more came out in the word than should have. None of the love, none of the loss, none of the wonder and worry.

He had never expected to see her again, never expected to watch her eyes go wide with shocked recognition, her mouth curve into that brilliant smile. Never expected to be told she was the favorite wife of the king.

She sprang up, at which point he noticed the babe in her arms. "Mordecai!"

"You know each other." The king sounded pleased.

He cleared his throat. "I know all the Jewish families in Susa, my lord."

"Especially those only a few doors away." Kasia reached out her free hand. Mordecai took it, bowed over it. Made himself let go. Still she smiled. "Mordecai and my father are good friends. I have known him all my life."

"Perfect. He can update you on your family. I will give you time to catch up." The king cupped her cheek. A blind man could have seen the tenderness, the devotion. He could take comfort in that. Just as he could in the complex response he saw in Kasia's eyes. On the surface was only polite acceptance, which barely covered the apathy beneath. But Mordecai knew such apathy was only a bandage for hurt—the kind inflicted when one loved.

Xerxes sighed and brushed the lightest of kisses over her lips. Then he lifted the babe from her arms. "Zillah and I shall go make a few laws while you gossip of mutual friends and share stories of how your God outshone mine in the war."

Warmth flooded Mordecai's heart. "You named her after your mother." And the king had allowed it.

But . . . if Kasia were his favorite, she would have sway. Why, then, had he felt so strongly that Esther needed to accept the marriage? Had he forced his daughter into something needlessly?

No. He could not believe that. He may not understand, but he had faith.

Kasia relinquished her daughter to her husband, a bit of feeling sparking through the apathy. "She should not be hungry for another hour."

"I will return her to your room then. Come, princess. Let us go awe my court with your beauty."

The babe yawned and nestled comfortably into the king's chest. This must not be an unusual occurrence, for her to be so content in his arms.

Mordecai smiled as Xerxes nodded at him and then left. "She is indeed beautiful. How old?"

"Two months next week." Sadness pervaded her smile. "You thought me dead."

"Not for long." He sat down on a bench when she motioned him to it. "Jehovah had me pray for you many times. I could not think he would have, had you been dead. Though I confess, I did not imagine this."

She sat beside him, hummed out a breath.

Poor Kasia. How much of the rumors would have to be true to explain her pain? "He loves you very much."

"Too much, I have begun to think." She squeezed her eyes shut, her hands balled in her chiton. "His brother is dead, his brother's wife, because of his love for me. His empire could have crumbled. His son could have led a coup. All because of his jealousy."

Warning noted. He took a moment to praise the Lord that his love for her had deepened to something beyond the desire to make her his wife. Then he drew in a breath. "Did you by chance go into labor during the wedding?"

She looked over at him, lifted her brows. "I did."

"That accounts for that time of prayer, then. What of the first, two weeks or so after your supposed death? That one took me by surprise."

Her lips twitched. "That would have been when Amestris first tried to kill me."

He felt his face tighten, each and every muscle. "What of the worst one, the day the army was set to leave Sardis for Abydus? Were you with them when you fell down the cliff?"

She stared at him, mouth agape. "How could you have known that?"

His eyes slid shut as the echo of sensation filled his memory. "The Spirit came upon me, impressed the need to pray. I felt your pain—at first, I think, just to let me see how urgent the need was. But as I felt it, I knew you could not survive that as well as the injuries themselves. As I prayed for healing, I prayed also that I might take the pain for you."

"I . . . I know not what to say. Your prayers saved my life, then. I was pushed from the wall of the palace, down the mountainside. When the darkness fell . . . ."

"Who?" He looked at her again. "Who would push you?"

She shook her head. "At this point, I assume we will never know."

"Disconcerting. But you lived."

"Miraculously. The next morning, my wounds were all healed. All but one." She turned her face away and gripped the bench. "I lost a son that day. He was stillborn."

"Kasia, I am sorry." He covered her hand with his. "I should have done more. Prayed more."

"It does not sound like you could have." She dug up a smile. "Enough of me. Tell me of those here in Susa. My family?"

"All are well. The twins married last year, both are now with child. Your parents are well. They have had much work from the palace . . . which suddenly makes sense."

Her smile flashed and faded. "What of Esther?"

She had spoken in a hush, and he could not help but glance around in search of prying eyes, listening ears. The only others present were her servants, and he had a feeling they could be trusted. "She is here, Kasia. She was one of the twelve admitted to the house of women for a chance to become the queen."

"What?" Excitement, disbelief, caution warred in her eyes. "But a Jewess—"

"They do not know." He pitched his voice still lower, leaned close. "They did not ask who her guardian was, did not seem to care—she has grown so beautiful, Kasia. I told her to keep her heritage a secret. It is the only way she will have a chance at the crown."

"She is here? There?" She motioned at a roof, which he presumed belonged to the house of women.

"Wait." His stomach churned, twisted. "You have probably spoken of her. I obviously had not considered that her secret could be undone so easily."

"No. No, I never have. I thought it was because I wanted to hold that friendship close, but I think Jehovah must have stopped my mouth all these years. To preserve her chances. Mordecai." She took his hand, squeezed it, and met his gaze. "She will be queen. You have my word."

Hope quickened inside him, but reason still nudged it aside. "She will at least have her chance."

"She will have more than that. I will see to it." She straightened her shoulders, drew in a breath. And looked regal herself. "Never in my years here have I played at intrigue, but in this I will. I have been charged with instructing the new brides. My word will have much sway over the king."

"You would do that for her?"

"I would do anything for her. She is as much a sister to me as my blood, the dearest friend I ever knew. And I can then 'introduce' you to her, Mordecai, so you might still see each other once in a while."

He let his eyes shut, let the gratitude swell. "Praise the Lord. He has orchestrated all of this down to the last detail. And you will have each other here."

She patted his hand, then stood. He looked up at her and saw that her gaze was on that roof again. "I must move with care, make it appear that we have only just met but have taken to one another." She glanced over her shoulder at her servants.

One of the maids offered a smile. "You know we will do anything to assist you, mistress."

She nodded, lifted the hair from her brow. "I cannot quite grasp it. I had hoped she and Zechariah . . . ."

"Nearly. You will have ample time to speak to her of that, I suspect. And for that matter, your brother will be by the palace next week with deliveries." He sent her a pointed look. "You ought to speak with him of it too. And perhaps give him a good wallop for the behavior that led to their break."

"Oh dear." Her hands moved to her cheeks, then fell. "I have missed so much of their lives."

"And we of yours. Do your parents know you are home? That you have a daughter?"

"A message was sent, but I have heard nothing back."

He nodded. He would speak to Kish as soon as he got home, do his best to convince his friend to relent. He pushed to his feet. "I ought to go. Seeing you are well . . . it is the best gift I have received in many years."

"Now that it will not mean breaking my father's trust, I will seek you out. Update you."

He nodded, turned. And grinned. "I think someone will have to lead me out of here."

"I will." One of the eunuchs stepped forward, though it earned a strange look from Kasia. She waved them on, though, and headed the opposite way.

The eunuch waited until they were out of her hearing range before saying, "I usually refuse to leave her side—whenever I must, I regret it. But I wanted to speak to you."

"Of course. You serve her out of love."

He drew in a deep breath and motioned Mordecai down a path to his right, near the fountains. "Many love her—more hate her, and the influence she has over the king. Threats hide everywhere."

"And you want to be sure I am not another."

His companion smiled. "I can see you are not. More than once I heard her beseeching Jehovah to rally other Jews to prayer. You seem to be the one those requests started with."

He was useful, then. "It warms me to realize that."

"She has never spoken of this Esther to us—your daughter?"

"My cousin. I raised her as a daughter. She and Kasia were the closest of friends, though your mistress is four years the elder."

"Desma spoke for us all. We will serve her, and hence you and your daughter, in this. You have my word on top of theirs."

"I thank you for it." And he could not help but smile. Perhaps this was not the way he had imagined their lives, but Jehovah obviously had it planned out.

Jehovah would see them through.

This was not the way life should be. His best friend dead, his queen and conspirator banished. Haman stood on the wall with arms crossed and looked out over Susa. Swarming everywhere were those worthless Jews, constant reminders of all he had lost. All his world had been whittled down to.

It was Kasia's fault. Had she not sunk her claws into the king, then into his son, none of this would have happened. Amestris would not have gotten herself deposed and sent away. Masistes would still be alive.

Before she left for Persepolis, Amestris had told him to get rid of the witch and her people, no matter how long it took.

And so he would. He would be patient, he would be sly. He would send that harlot into the bosom of her precious Abraham and all her family and neighbors with her.

"Haman."

He turned to face his king. Xerxes approached with a babe asleep in his arms. No need to wonder which wife it belonged to. He forced a smile, forced a warm tone. "Your newest daughter grows lovelier by the day."

Let her grow lovely. Let her be the loveliest thing in the land—perhaps it would protect her when she was motherless.

"That she does." Xerxes grinned, though it faded fast. "Haman, I have wanted to speak with you. My brother was your closest friend—you must be angry with me."

Only an idiot would be angry with the king. Better to accept reality as it was . . . and change it when one could. "You did only what you must, master. He was always rash, always walked the line between pleasing you and provoking you—it was only a matter of time before he stumbled into a situation he could not grapple out of again."

"True things—but fact never changes how we feel. If you wish for a position somewhere else, where you do not have to face me, you may have your pick. A satrapy, a governorship—"

"If it pleases the king, I would rather stay close to your side. You, too, have always been my friend. And I know you grieve as well."The fault did not belong to Xerxes—Xerxes had done only what he must.

It was Kasia. It was all the Jews. And he would never find a way to rid Persia of them without Xerxes' power behind him.

The king nodded, his face relieved. "I am glad. You were always a loyal friend. I hope, since you wish to stay, you will stay at my right hand."

Haman did not have to force the smile this time. "There is no place I would rather be, my king."

FORTY-TWO

Thanks to his fussing daughter, Xerxes had the rare opportunity to observe Kasia unnoticed. He watched her dash over to the cradle and pick up the baby, only to hurry back to the vanity when Desma scolded her with a smile. He saw the naked affection on her face when she soothed Zillah, the friendly, sheepish laugh she gave her maid.

Would she ever look at him with such love again? This past fortnight, she had been a ghost. Present but not—untouchable. It was not like those months after the stillbirth, when grief and loneliness overcame her. Not like that at all—she was her same vibrant self now with everyone else. The same bright woman, full of passion and life.

Just not for him. Oh, she would put on a show when it was called for—she would smile, laugh, place her hand on his arm. But it was empty.

His gaze fell on the tell-tale torc. On her table, not her arm. She would put it on again before she left the room, he knew. But the second she regained this sanctuary, off it would come.

He was down to his last few ideas on how to stir her heart again. If he failed . . . he could not contemplate it. Could not imagine a life without her love.

He cleared his throat and took another step into her room. "You look stunning, my love."

Her smile went tense, her shoulders square. "Thank you. I appreciate the new garments, though they were unnecessary."

"And a small enough gesture." He drew in a long breath and regarded her reflection, since she would not look at him. "Hegai tells me you will introduce yourself to the new brides this morning."

"That was the council's will, was it not? Though if you would prefer—"

"I am glad you are going. Though if you did not want to . . . ." He winced. Had they resorted to this?

A month ago, that tight smile would have been a grin. "If one of these girls is going to rule me, I would just as soon know her beforehand, and offer my opinion of which of them it should be."

"You could choose entirely, for all I care."

"Xerxes."

Well, reproach was better than indifference. "You are the only one I want, Kasia."

She turned even her reflected gaze away.

He looked to her servants, then his own behind him. "Give us a moment." Once they filed out, he crouched down before her. "Tell me why that upsets you. Is it that you do not believe me, or that you fear it is too true?"

At least she looked at him, showed him the churning of her mind, the uncertainty in her heart. "Both, if that is possible."

He sighed and took her hand, though her fingers did not curl around his. "I am not a temperate man. You know that, and I dared to hope you loved me for it, not just in spite of it."

"That is unfair, Xerxes. This is not a rope or a river or even a single man you sentenced to death. This could have destroyed all of your family . . . even all of mine, had Masistes succeeded in an uprising."

"I know that. I can only try to do better, which is far more likely if you are beside me." He squeezed her unresponsive fingers and stood. "As for my devotion—all I can do is prove it. You underwent your purification yesterday, did you not?"

His heart twisted when her face hardened. She nodded, but rebellion gleamed in her eyes. He could call her, and she would come . . . but only because she must.

Must was not good enough. He kissed her fingers and then released them. "I will not force you to my bed out of duty. But I will call no other until you have come to me freely."

And there, disbelief. "Be realistic, Xerxes. There have been times enough when you would not or could not touch me—you never had difficulty finding your pleasure elsewhere."

A reality he suddenly wished he could spare her. "This time is different. This time our love is at stake, where it never was before. We are going through the fire now, Kasia, and I do not want us to melt away or burn up. I want us to emerge the stronger."

She lowered the lids over her lovely eyes, but it only forced the tears in them onto her cheeks. "I feel as though I have already been consumed."

"Impossible. Only impurities are consumed, and that is not you. Me, perhaps."

Earning that smile, tiny but true, made his day worthwhile. She sniffed and shifted Zillah so she could dash at her eyes. "And what if it takes me too long, and you lose patience?"

"I will not. You are worth waiting for, my love."

"We shall see." She sobered into weariness and patted the baby's back. "Hegai will come for me soon."

"Dismissed, am I?" Hoping for one more smile, he tapped her on the nose. "And some people think *I* am the one in charge."

She offered no return tease, but for a moment laughter lit her eyes.

For now, it would do.

Dear Jehovah, what was she doing here? Esther smoothed nervous fingers down the length of her fine chiton and tried to banish the doubt, the fear.

She was not like these other young women. Their jokes never struck her as funny, their gossip concerned figures she was not familiar with. She did not care who had received the better length of cloth, whose necklace weighed heavier with gold. She took no pleasure in pecking at the others' vanity, though they did little but peck at hers.

It would be a lonely year. Quite possibly a lonely life.

"Lovely, all of you."

At the voice of the custodian, all the girls straightened, beamed. Esther could barely dig up a smile. She liked Hegai, and, if she were not mistaken, he liked her a bit more than the others. Hopefully that counted for something.

He smiled at the line of them. "This morning you will have a couple visitors."

Whispers sprang up—did they not realize how that would make annoyance flicker over Hegai's face? Esther held her tongue as the others speculated as to whether it might be the king. And hoped against hope it was not. She felt nowhere near ready to meet . . . could he really be her husband? This man who tread over nations, whom she had never even glimpsed? It felt unreal.

"Ladies." Hegai waited for them to quiet again. "I already told you the king will not see any of you until it is your turn with him. But this morning two very special women have come to talk to you. First, the Queen Mother, to tell you what is expected of the next queen. She will be coming every few weeks to share her wealth of knowledge."

The most outspoken of the brides laughed. "All well and good, but who will tell us how to win the title?"

Hegai gave the girl a tight smile. "That falls to our other guest—the king's favorite wife. Since she joined the harem three years ago, the king's heart has belonged to none but her. If anyone in the world understands him and knows how to please him, it is her."

The girl raised her chin. "Then why is *she* not the new queen?"

"Because she is only a concubine. But make no mistake—you may join the harem as queen, but you will still answer to her. All of you. So watch what you say, do not try to fool her with duplicity, and be grateful for the help she is offering you. Now if I can trust you to behave yourselves and refrain from giggling for half an hour . . . ."

He led them into another room, where couches and cushions and chairs dominated. Esther chose one tucked into the corner, well behind the other girls, and settled in with a sigh. The tittering kept up for another minute, until Hegai shushed them and the door opened again to a slew of servants.

Perhaps she should have chosen a closer seat. She could barely see anything, first through the other brides and then the mass of servants. They spread throughout the room, one maid ending up so close Esther had to crane around her to try to get a glimpse of the queen mother and wife.

The maid leaned toward her, face intent. "You are Esther?"

Her voice was barely a breath, but it shot an arrow through her. She nodded.

The maid sent her a look filled with . . . warning? "Watch your reaction."

"What?"

The girl stepped aside, and Esther sucked in a sharp breath. The woman that stood in the center of the room—more beautiful, a bit older, but . . . Kasia? It could not be. Kasia was dead, Kasia had been sucked away by the monsoon-swollen river—yet . . . .

The maid blocked her view again and gave the slightest shake of her head.

Esther drew in a calming breath. It did not quiet the race of her heart, but she schooled her features.

Kasia.

To the others, Kasia would seem casually deliberate as she looked at each of them in turn, gave each a smile. But the others did not know her as Esther did. Did not realize that she looked at each of them only so that she could meet Esther's gaze and smile without it seeming strange.

Esther knew. She had to blink back tears, and she knew her smile was shaky. But no one else would see. Only Kasia, whose gaze held all their past, all their secrets, and a whole future of promises.

Who cared if she became the queen? Esther had her sister back.

The Queen Mother stepped forward, her face absent a welcoming smile. "Women come into this palace all the time, but the twelve of you are special. One of you will be queen. With that title comes immense responsibility. You will think it also comes with power, and to an extent that is true. But as your predecessor can attest to, power can be taken away. My son is a fair man and a wise man, but he is done tolerating insubordination from his women." She angled a grin at Kasia. "With, perhaps, one exception."

Kasia chuckled. "When I was brought to the palace nearly three years ago, I felt overwhelmed and confused about what would be expected of me. I was blessed to have Queen Atossa take me under her wing. Shortly thereafter I left with the king for the war, and since we returned, I have been a bit occupied with a new baby. But I have been looking forward to extending to others the same advice and welcome I was given."

Nearly three years . . . then she had come here from the start—but of course, Kish would not have liked that. He must have come up with the other story.

But how had she then gone with the king? Should she not have still been in her preparation when he left?

So many questions.

"Kasia will be speaking with each of you individually over the course of the next few weeks, answering questions and sharing her insight into my son." The queen mother put a friendly hand on Kasia's arm.

Kasia grinned. "I will meet with one of you each morning, as Hegai sends you to me. After our initial talk, you may decide whether you want to spend more time with me or if your time would be better spent in other pursuits."

Esther gripped her skirt. How many meetings could she reasonably ask for without raising suspicions? Perhaps if she made a point of bumbling, she would need instruction each and every day.

As if reading her mind, Kasia glanced her way and seemed to fight down a grin. "And now I shall retire to the back and let the queen mother dispense her wisdom. Afterward, the first of you shall meet with me."

Oh, praise Jehovah. There was no telling when Hegai would send her, but it hardly mattered. He would at some point.

"Do you mind if I sit here?" Kasia asked quietly, eyes twinkling as she took the chair beside Esther's.

"Not at all. It is . . ." What was it safe to say, to speak of? " . . . kind of you to come speak with us."

"Ah, well." She nodded to the front, where Atossa launched into an account of the Achamenid kings. "Had the queen mother not extended the same favor to me, I would have been lost. I only had a week's preparation, you see."

"A week?" She figured that would shock any of them. "But why?"

"It is a rather romantic story." Kasia moved her chair a little closer, leaned in. "You see, I was at the river one day with my . . . little sister. We met two Persian men, one of whom gave me a torc. I did not know it then, but it was the king."

Her stomach flipped. "It was?"

"Mm. He sent his men to my father a few days later, and I was brought here. He knew he would be leaving soon, though, and did not wish to wait until he returned. So after one short week, I went to him."

"Very romantic." And terrifying. Would he recognize her? Take one look at her and realize she was Kasia's "sister"? If so . . . what did the king do to those who lied to his delegates?

But if Kasia feared that, she would not be protecting her identity. She had obviously known Esther was here, perhaps had spoken to Mordecai. For now she would trust. She smiled. "And you just had a baby?"

"A little girl." Pure contentment flooded her friend's face.

"Your first?"

Pain shot through the contentment. "The first to make it to term. A story for another day." She nodded toward the queen. "I ought to stop distracting you. Dull as the history of kings can be, you will need to know it. You may be the next queen."

The way she said it, so sure, so simple. Esther's stomach did another cartwheel. It had never occurred to her that she would have an ally, one who apparently had the king's ear.

Then again, it had never occurred to her that she would have to share a husband with her dearest friend. Somehow, that felt different than sharing him with all these other women.

When had life gotten so complicated?

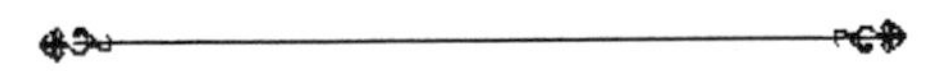

"So you were a peasant." The beautiful young thing across from Kasia blinked her doe-eyes in innocence and gave her a sickeningly sweet smile. "What a change it must have been for you, then. Of course, my father is cousin to the king."

Naturally that meant Xerxes would drop the crown onto her brow and kiss her feet for good measure. Kasia tried to push her cynicism away, tried to smile at the girl.

What a gem she was. Sweet as nectar . . . left to ferment in the sun. Always knew the right thing to say . . . to belittle whomever she spoke to.

Definitely a daughter of royalty.

Kasia saw no point in prolonging this. Not when she ached to return to little Zillah, who would need fed. "You will have no trouble adjusting to palace life, then. If you have any questions about the king—"

"Oh, I have known him all my life." She batted those wide eyes of hers. "I suppose that means longer than you have, now that I think of it."

"Then I shall not bore you with what you already know." Kasia stood and gave her a tight smile. "Though if you have questions later, I will be happy to answer them."

"I do hate to bother you, what with that new baby. A daughter, you said?"

Kasia gritted her teeth at the tone. "Indeed. It was a pleasure to meet you."

She saved the roll of her eyes until she had left the chamber. Hegai grinned and took her arm. "I figured you would want to get that one out of the way, mistress."

"You could have warned me." But she chuckled. Largely because she caught a glimpse of Esther, and the joy . . . it was nearly like when she returned to Zillah after time away. That feeling of family, of home. She nodded her way. "The young lady I sat beside seemed very sweet."

"Esther—my favorite already. You will like her."

"I am sure. You have excellent taste."

"Liking you straightaway as I did, you mean?" The custodian chuckled and led her out of the house of women, toward the house of wives. "It is good, what you are doing, mistress. Many of them will not heed your council, just as they do not heed mine. But we will know the ones who will, and it is they who have the potential to be the kind of queen Persia needs."

Her servants fell in around her, and Kasia nodded. "You are right about that. Perhaps you could sprinkle in a few of the receptive ones early on? I am not overly fond of bashing my head into a wall day after day."

Hegai gave a hearty laugh. Kasia grinned, but her mirth was cut short. Artaynte stood planted in the path.

Kasia patted Hegai's arm. "I shall have to ask you to give me a minute, my friend."

The custodian covered her fingers, gave them an encouraging squeeze. "I shall speak to you later, then."

He headed off on another path. Kasia continued on hers until she was an arm's span from Artaynte. Her once-friend looked uncomfortable at the best—and that built on the shadowed eyes, the sloped shoulders. Sympathy stirred, but she ignored it.

Artaynte shifted her gaze to the ground. "You look well. I see your figure has returned."

Kasia blinked. "A year and a half since we last spoke, and that is the first thing you say to me?"

Tears welled in the girl's eyes. The fact that she made no move to clear them gave Kasia the impression that the brine was a constant companion. "I had no choice in the distance, at first."

"You always had a choice. I respect obedience, Artaynte, but you must still think for yourself."

She tucked her chin to her chest. "I tried that with Darius. We all know how that turned out."

Accusations tripped over one another for a place on her tongue. Kasia held them down. They would accomplish nothing. "I wanted to thank you for tending my son's grave. For planting the flowers. That meant the world to me."

A few tears dripped onto Artaynte's cheeks. "I thought . . . I thought you had already been unfaithful to the king. That was the rumor. I doubted it at first, but then I saw the way Darius paid you attention, and jealousy . . . I began to think, 'Why would she *not* give herself to him?' Everyone else thought the same."

The words burned. "Everyone else did not know me as you did. Everyone else had not spent hours in my wagon with me, chatting and dreaming. You *knew* how I loved Xerxes." She pressed her hands to her eyes and willed herself to calm down.

Artaynte edged closer. "Please tell me I have not ruined that too. Please. I have already caused so much damage."

"It can never be the same." Kasia took a step back. "I know now what you would both stoop to for your jealousy and pride. When I look at either of you, all I see is someone who took deliberate action that you knew would be destructive. Took it *because* it would be destructive. And I want nothing to do with such a person."

When she tried to step around her, Artaynte latched hold of her arm. "Kasia, please. Can you not see our sides too? His, at least. The king thought Darius had forced himself on you. He thought you had been hurt."

Kasia drew in a quavering breath. How long had she staved off jealousy? But it still snapped at her, threatened her. Still whispered in her ear that Artaynte taking Xerxes' part meant things were not as over as they should have been. She breathed a silent plea for help.

Then realization creased her brow. "You still call him 'the king.' I have never heard you use his name."

Artaynte wrapped her arms around her stomach. "He always terrified me."

"Even now?"

"Especially now." She offered a weak smile. "You are the only one who calls him by name consistently, Kasia."

Because she had always thought herself in love with the man, not the king. She had to wonder, now, if she had been wrong to draw a distinction. But that was not to the point in this moment.

After another silent prayer, Kasia gripped Artaynte's hand. "I appreciate that you want to help relationships heal. You do realize now that nothing ever happened between me and Darius, do you not?"

She nodded. "He explained his feelings, told me what happened that day I saw him kiss you. I explained my heart, my hurt. We are going to try to put everything else aside and build a marriage."

"Good. That is good." But as she led Artaynte along the path, she felt certain that some things would always remain rooted between them all. Between husbands and wives, between father and son. Between friends.

She could try to forgive. But it would not change facts.

FORTY-THREE

Zechariah paced the confines of the small receiving chamber and refused to be intimidated by its wealth. How long had he been waiting for Kasia? It felt like half of forever, but probably only a few minutes.

He had to talk to her. See if she had seen Esther, make sure she was well.

Hurried footsteps sounded seconds before the door swung open. When Kasia stepped in along with a passel of servants, a smile won over his mouth, and he put thoughts of Esther aside for a few minutes. "Kasia."

"Zech." She flew through the room and into his arms, but he still had time enough to note how little she had changed. Her face had a few more angles, her hair seemed a little different. Certainly, she wore finer clothing than she ever had at home, and a simple gold rope around her neck. But none of the audacity of the rest of the palace.

He swung her around and gave her a mighty squeeze. "I missed you, little sister."

"I missed you too, big brother. And I mean *big*." She laughed and rested her hands against his biceps. "You are huge. Did you get taller?"

"Or else you shrank."

She gave him a playful punch, then another squeeze of a hug. "Did Mordecai talk to Abba?"

"He tried, but you know Abba. I promised Ima I would sneak her over if it came down to it, though. She wants to meet this granddaughter of hers. When Mordecai said you named her after her . . . ."

"Let me introduce you." She turned to one of the maids and took a sleeping baby from her arms. "Your niece, Zillah."

Zechariah smoothed a hand over her downy head. "Are you going to let me hold her, or is there some law forbidding commoners to touch the children of a king?"

Kasia laughed and eased the girl into his arms. "There may be, but I pay little attention to such things."

His smile strained. "You still have no fear, I see."

What was that that flickered across her face? She shrugged. "One of the benefits of being the king's favorite."

"I cannot believe my sister holds that title."

Her breath of a laugh did not sound amused. "Sometimes I cannot either." Not-amused hardened into sober. "I also could not believe that Esther accepted a marriage contract. Mordecai said the two of you were nearly betrothed."

Cradling his niece close, Zechariah drew in a long breath. "I fell in love with her. Is that so hard to believe?"

"That part? No. So what happened?"

Not a conversation for a reunion. "Have you seen her yet? Is she well?"

"She is fine, I will speak with her in private soon—and in the meantime, I am speaking to you. What happened?"

He sighed. "I wooed her as I built our house. It was finished, I declared myself, was going to speak to Mordecai the next day . . . and then Esther overheard something."

Her eyes narrowed. "What kind of something?"

"I . . . that . . . ." No matter how he phrased it, it would sound terrible. Was terrible. "That I had been involved with Bijan's sister."

Far too quickly, her eyes widened. "Zechariah son of Kish! Bijan said his sister is married."

She was not the only one who could narrow her eyes in that look stolen from Ima. "When were you chatting with Bijan?"

"On the way to Sardis from Thermopylae, which is irrelevant. Define 'involved.'"

He pitched his voice to a bare murmur. "She carries my child."

Her fist connected with his arm hard enough to make him wince. She never had pulled her punches, and her eyes spat genuine fury at him. "Idiot! How could you do that? To Esther, first of all, but—Zech. Adultery?"

As if he did not know how sinful he was? "Must you say it like that? Like I am the worst kind of man?"

"Not so far off."

"Oh, look in your own house, Kasia. From what I hear, your husband is no paragon of virtue, stealing his own son's wife."

"Thank you for that reminder." Her face a stone mask, she took the baby back. "Tell Ima I miss her."

"Kas, wait." Gusting out a breath, he caught her as she spun away. "I am sorry. I have never even seen this man, yet first he stole my sister, then the woman I would have married."

"For which you ought to praise God." She jerked her arm free but did not try to run away again. "There are those who are not pleased with how much power I have over him, Zech. And unfortunately, one of them is now at his right hand. When Esther is queen—"

"You mean if."

"I mean when. When she is queen, she will be able to do much for the Jews without earning the obvious contempt of Haman and his like."

Zech shoved frustrated fingers through his hair. "I have lost her to *politics*?"

"You have lost her to your own stupidity, and do not forget it." She jerked her chin up. Her nostrils flared. "Three years apart, and still we squabble like—"

"Siblings." He forced a grin and tugged on a lock of her hair. "I have missed your squabbling. The others do not squabble like you do."

She laughed, then sighed. "I have missed you, Zech. I am sorry things did not work out as you wished, but this is all in Jehovah's plan. I know it, here." She splayed a hand over her heart.

"You sound like Mordecai."

Her lips quirked up. "We have apparently shared many prayers over these past three years."

For a moment, he could only stare. Kasia had always struck him as an average Jew—she knew the Law, certainly she believed in Jehovah. Like him. But now . . . she did not just sound like Mordecai, now that he thought on it. She . . . *seemed* like him, too. "You were never one for much prayer at home."

Her eyes went soft, yet intense. "It became far more necessary here. I would be dead several times over had Jehovah not protected me."

Like that day Mordecai had writhed in pain for her. He nodded.

"Mistress." The eunuch at the door sent her a warning glance. "The king comes."

Zechariah bit back a curse. "I should go."

"No. He will want to meet you, or he would not come."

And what of what Zechariah wanted? Because it was certainly not to face Esther's husband. The very words made everything within him clench up. But there was no other exit to the room, and he would probably run directly into him if he tried to leave the way he had come.

A swarm of men entered, but there was no mistaking the king. He was taller than Zechariah had expected, every bit as tall as Mordecai, and broad. Well-muscled, especially for a man who did nothing but sit on a throne all day—and seduce other men's women.

He wanted to dislike him on sight, and on principle. But then Xerxes looked at Kasia with the same expression Abba always had when he glanced Ima's way. How was Zechariah supposed to hate a man who loved—genuinely *loved*—his sister?

"I hope I am not interrupting, but I wanted to meet some of your family, my love."

Kasia repositioned the babe and shot her husband a glance half amused and half frustrated. "Allow me to make introductions, then. Zech, this is Xerxes, the king of kings and self-proclaimed master of creation, who thinks he can bend all of nature to his whim. Xerxes, my stubborn, idiotic brother Zechariah who understands consequences about as well as you do. You two have much in common. Enjoy each other's company."

With that, she left. Actually left him there, standing in the room with no one but the king and his servants.

Xerxes stepped to his side, his gaze on Kasia's retreating back. "She is the only person in the world who would dare speak to me like that."

A laugh surprised its way out of his mouth. "She has always been outspoken."

"I learned that within moments of meeting her—and fell for her that quickly." He flashed his smile Zechariah's way and extended a hand. "It is good to meet you, Zechariah. Kasia has told me much about you, though she never mentioned we share vices."

Zechariah clasped the king's wrist, and marveled. He may resent the man, but still. He was king. "I suppose some things are common to men no matter their station."

"And those things will never fail to anger their women." His gaze swung to the door again. "I do not suppose you know any secrets to earning their forgiveness. I have tried all I can think of."

Zechariah breathed a laugh. "Had I such divine wisdom, I would have used it on a young lady a few weeks ago. Perhaps then she would not be married to another instead of me."

The king winced and clapped a hand to his shoulder. "My sympathies. It is bad enough fearing I have lost Kasia's heart—I still have the knowledge that she is my wife, which guarantees time to work through things."

Zechariah deflated, like a wineskin emptied of its last drop. He could not hate the king. Could not even dislike him. He may be able to maintain some resentment, but mostly he ached—and not only for himself.

The king loved Zechariah's sister with all his heart. What would be left for Esther?

Xerxes sighed. "I could order this husband killed for you, but the women would probably hate us more."

He could not help but grin. "I suspect so. I appreciate the thought, though."

"Well if there is anything else I can do, please ask. You are family now."

A strange and terrible thought.

Kasia kept her smile casually welcoming until the door closed. Then she flew through the room to fold Esther into a hug. "Finally! Had I not feared giving you away, I would have demanded Hegai bring you in far sooner. This week has been torture."

Esther laughed—that same sweet, beautiful sound Kasia remembered—and gave her a mighty squeeze. "You cannot know how I felt to see you! I had thought . . . ."

"Abba."

"I know. But to see you, not only well but wed to your Persian . . . ."

Kasia pulled back enough to smile. "I begged them to tell you."

Esther grinned. "It does not matter now. You are alive, and you are here."

"And *you* are here." She still had to shake her head at that. "I cannot believe it. Which is to say, I can, when I see you. You are stunning, little Esther."

"Not so much as you." Her smile was still innocence and freshness—sorrow still lurked in her eyes. "Oh, I must hug you again."

Kasia obliged with a laugh. Then she steered her friend over to a couch and pulled her down alongside her. "Mordecai told me the plan. And I spoke to Zechariah last week."

Pain coated with anger washed over her face. "Did he tell you?"

"I hit him for it." She gripped Esther's hands and smiled. "It hurts. Trust me, I know—you have no doubt heard the rumors about Xerxes and Artaynte. But this is the will of Jehovah. I am sorry you had to go through what you did, but I cannot regret your presence."

Esther studied her for a long moment, contemplation in her eyes. "You have changed. Deepened. The same Kasia, but more."

"I have been through much in these three years." She returned the even regard, noted the flawless face, perfect figure. The spirit within that had emerged from the coals of sorrow stronger than it had been before. "So have you. We were girls together, Esther, and now we get to be women together. I prayed for you every day."

Tears filled Esther's eyes. "I missed you every day, but I did not know to pray. I am sorry for that."

"It is all right. My parents and Zech knew to, and Jehovah apparently whispered it in Mordecai's ear in my darkest moments."

Realization streaked across her countenance. "That was you! He would instruct me to pray without giving me names."

Kasia grinned. "See there, you *did* pray for me. Jehovah knew."

"And Zech did too?" Her expression hardened again.

"He would not have gone against Abba, Esther, though I know he wanted to." Though why he would obey Abba in *that* and not the Lord in instructions on purity . . . .

Esther shook it off and forced a smile. "Enough of him."

"Indeed. You are a married woman now."

She had said it in a tease, but Esther's face fell. "I did not mean to marry your husband, Kasia. Had I known—"

She laughed. She could not help it. "Sweet one, countless women are married to my husband."

"But you love him." Esther gripped her fingers and looked into one eye, then the other. "He is your Persian, and you are his favorite wife. How can you abide the thought of others?"

"It is not always easy. To share him, or to love him." She cast her gaze toward the window, needing the view of a world larger than the harem. Open skies, endless desert. The sun slanted in, on its way to its nightly rest. Zillah had been fussy today, and she had not been able to get away earlier.

Esther sighed. "I do not know what I imagined when I agreed to this—other than it would get me away from Zech—but now that I am here . . . the other women are awful."

"I know. It is no better in the house of wives. Amestris tried to kill me when I first arrived." She smiled into Esther's horrified gasp. "Things have changed for me since I returned from the war, though. Shocking as it is, the others seem to look up to me now. Only because they know I have the king's ear, but . . . ."

"And his heart, if Hegai is right." Esther moistened her lips. "But then—the stories. They make him sound . . . ."

"Awful." Her own reaction to Atossa's description of him shifted into her recollection.

"The deaths he has caused, the marriages he has destroyed."

Esther shuddered. "How can you love him?"

It felt as though her whole being thudded, and shadows blurred her vision. All she could see was the horror on Pythius's face, the shattered soul within Artaynte's eyes. The thousands upon thousands dead in the war while he sat on his throne and watched them die. How had she loved him through all that?

Is that your husband? The words whispered through her, cool and sweet as the Choaspes.

More images, blinding in their beauty. The tear on Xerxes' cheek that gleamed with all the brilliance of a diamond. The haunting fear in his eyes when he considered losing her. Those precious creases that fanned his mouth when he smiled at his children's antics. The laughter so quick to replace anger in his eyes when she jested him out of a temper.

Yes, sometimes greater concerns made him hard, even cruel. Yes, sometimes his temper got the best of him, and the world shook in consequence. But he who raged like no other loved like no other.

She could hold tight to the pain to protect herself from more. But who, then, would show Xerxes the Lord? And Esther—Esther's heart was too precious to stay closed, but how could Kasia urge her to open it, if she kept her own locked tight?

She must let herself love. Not for the sake of her own happiness—that would hardly be worth the risk—but for their sakes.

She drew in a long, soothing breath, and felt Jehovah's peace bloom inside her. "The heart of a king is a strange, wonderful thing, Esther. There are so many expectations and demands he must balance. And because he is a man of passion, there are many times when he reacts before he thinks. I will make no excuses for that—more than once, he has hurt those he loves because of his temper. But his love . . . ." She let her eyes slide shut and shook her head. "There is nothing in the world like his love."

She opened her eyes and saw tears in Esther's. "I do not want to love him, Kasia. He is yours, first of all, and my heart has endured enough."

"I want you to." She wrapped an arm around the curve of her friend's shoulder. "It will not be like it was with Zech—you can only have one first love—but you do not want to close off your heart for the rest of your life. Perhaps you could survive, but you would not really live."

Esther turned her face into Kasia's shoulder. "He will not care for me. I am not you."

"Perfect." She chuckled and rubbed a hand over Esther's arm. "He could not handle another of me. What you are, sweet sister, is a woman of depth and solidity. A woman who can stand firm and peaceful through whatever chaos is tossed at you—and there will be plenty in the palace."

"You are a better woman than I. I could not possibly want another to love the man I do, I could not want him to love her."

Was that what she wanted? Her dearest friend to sigh over Xerxes, to send her secret smiles his way? Did she want her husband to desire Esther above any other?

Above *her?*

The peace wavered. How could the Lord expect her to love again, only to watch it be rent in two? And yet she wanted Esther to be happy, to pass a life that was more than an echo. She wanted her to find her place—which would never be secure without Xerxes' regard.

Sweet, steady Esther who did not realize her own worth. He would love her. How could he not? And perhaps she could temper him. He needed that, needed someone who, rather than jesting him from fury to passion, could soothe the savage edges of his soul.

But where would that leave her? The best friend of the queen, the once-favorite of the king. She would still have a night with him now and then. They would still laugh together. She would still have Zillah, and perhaps another child or two down the road.

If that was her lot, it would have to be enough. Even if it was never quite enough.

She would do it. She would love them both—and in so doing, she would prepare their hearts for each other. It would hurt, but she would savor this year, the time with each of them before they met. And then she would accept whatever Jehovah gave her.

"Mistress, Hegai returns."

She nodded to Theron, and gave Esther one last hug. "We will talk again soon. Only one other girl has requested a second meeting with me, and I have but two more new ones."

Esther grinned. "I shall endeavor to be as backwards as possible, so that I have an excuse to need your tutelage."

Chuckling, Kasia drew away. "Only necessary for a while, after which we can let it be known we have become friends."

Esther nodded, then composed herself just before the door opened. Hegai stepped in with a smile. "Did my two favorites have a good visit?"

"Excellent," Kasia replied.

"I look forward to meeting with her again." Esther gave her a warm smile and stood. "I am honored by your attention, lady."

"Come, Esther, you are due for your next session in myrrh." Hegai winked at Kasia. "I am to tell you the king is in his palace, if you are inclined to see him yet."

For the first time in weeks, her heart leapt at the thought. She hurried back to her own room to eat and feed Zillah, put her down for the evening. Then rushed toward the king's palace. She had not the time to waste on anger and uncertainty. Better to give that pain over to Jehovah and ask him to pour new life into their marriage. Life enough to pulse even after his attention went mostly elsewhere.

She found him at a table, studying his scrolls with a frown. "Put it anywhere, Zethar. I am not hungry yet."

Her lips tugged up. "You know, when you call for one of your wives, it is rude to be unprepared for her."

"Kasia." The scroll fell to the table as he vaulted from his seat. Pleasure lit his eyes, though it was underscored with caution. "I did not think you would come."

She took a single step toward him. "Life is too short to waste it on unforgiveness."

Caution gave way to joy. And teasing. "But I have only had a week to prove my steadfast devotion."

She pressed her lips down on the grin and took another step. "Was it a long, torturous week?"

Xerxes sidled toward her. "The longest, most torturous in history. Made the longer and more torturous because it came after two months without you."

She sped across the room and threw herself into his arms. He held her close, then closer, and buried his face in her hair. "You have really forgiven me?"

"I will not lie, Xerxes. Things will never be the same. But that does not mean they cannot be different, even better." She pressed her lips to his neck and breathed in the scent of him, incense and myrrh. "I could have given up my love for you—but what, then, would be the point to life?"

He left a trail of kisses along her jaw, ending on her lips in one both sweet and fiery. "Whatever made you realize that, I am grateful."

She felt a nudge within her spirit and dragged in a fortifying breath. "It was one of the new brides. Esther. She has known much sorrow in her life—but as I encouraged her to open her heart to you, I realized I must do the same."

"I have never met her, and already I am in her debt."

"You will like her. I think she and I will be great friends."

His lips moved along the other side of her jaw. "Mmm. Good. You have arranged a nurse for Zillah tonight?"

"Yes, though if I stay all night, I will get very uncomfortable."

His hands slid down her back, anchored on her hips. "Then when you must go, I shall go with you. You are mine tonight, my love." He pulled away enough to grin. "Though I suppose I shall share you with our princess."

"Very generous of you." She tugged his head down so she could kiss him again. Soon enough she would have to share him too—but not tonight.

Kasia spotted them before any servant found her in the gardens to tell her they were there. They moved with trepidation, uncertainty screaming from the curl of their shoulders and the way they gripped each other's hands.

Hers shook. They had come. Abba and Ima had come. Zech stood behind them, satisfaction tugging up his mouth. Her joy was too consuming to leave room for satisfaction.

Kasia handed Zillah to Xerxes and took off at a run. "Abba! Ima!"

Her mother moved first, leaping away from husband and son to meet her halfway. When their arms closed around each other, Kasia finally felt as though she had come home. "Oh Ima, how I missed you."

"Kasia, my baby." Ima squeezed her tighter—her tears dripped onto Kasia's shoulder. "You have never left my thoughts."

"Nor you, mine. Especially lately, now that I am an ima too."

"Your next time I will be here."

"Yes, next time." She buried her head into the crook of Ima's neck and smiled.

"Daughter."

She pulled back and turned toward Abba. He had stopped a few steps away. His face bore a few more lines, his hair a few more grays than she remembered. But it was still Abba. The stubborn jaw, the strong build. Regret and longing colored his brown eyes.

Instead of flying, she moved to him with slow, measured steps. He held out his arms as his jaw quivered. Caught up in his embrace a moment later, such contentment rushed through her that it took her a moment to notice Xerxes had joined them. He greeted Ima as if she were his own mother, jested with Zechariah.

"I have missed you, my daughter," Abba murmured into her hair. "I hope you know that each piece of furniture we made for you, we crafted with love as much as hammer and chisel."

"I know, Abba." But it did not escape her notice that none of her other siblings had come along.

She may be Abba's daughter once again, but still he would not let her be a sister. In spite of all that had changed, some things had not.

Forty-Four

One year later, in the seventh year of the reign of Xerxes

Xerxes laughed as Zillah wobbled on her chubby legs and then plopped onto Chinara's lap. The elder of his daughters grinned and tickled the baby, who squealed with delight. Was there anything better than a stolen hour with his two favorite girls?

Their mothers swayed into view, and Kasia cast him a warm smile.

Perhaps there was one thing better. "Are you two back already?"

Jasmine chuckled and held out a hand to Chinara. "Afraid so. My parents will be joining us for the meal. Come, Chinara."

The seven-year-old made no objections. Perhaps because she knew her grandparents always arrived with presents.

"Goodnight, Father." She pranced over to give him a kiss and a squeeze, then dashed to her mother.

"Goodnight, Chinara. Goodnight, Jasmine."

Kasia bade them farewell too and scooped up Zillah. Pressing a kiss to the girl's cheek, she came to settle beside Xerxes on his couch. "And you are still dining with us?"

"I am." When Zillah wiggled back down to the floor, he slid an arm around Kasia and pulled her to his side. "And then I shall hide myself away here for the night so that I might not have to deal with anymore of this Greek business."

She smiled but shook her head. "You certainly will not. Another of your potential queens will come to you tonight, as you know very well."

Xerxes groaned and let his head fall onto the back of the couch. "I have surely already dealt with twenty of them."

"You have met ten."

Ten of the most ambitious young women he had ever beheld. They were beautiful, they were well trained. But Hegai and Kasia could not give them the proper spirit. "I am not in the mood. I shall tell Hegai—"

She gave him a playful punch. "You will not. Tonight is Esther's turn."

"Ah. Your friend."

"My friend. You will like her, Xerxes. Not only is she more beautiful than the others, she is sweet and loving, obedient yet strong. She will be perfect."

"Well, if you want me to be fair to her, you had better improve my mood." He wiggled his brows and dug a finger into her side to make her squeal.

She obliged, jerked away, even jumped up so he could chase her. He tackled her onto her bed with a laugh and pulled the giggling Zillah into the heap as well. Yes, this was what he needed. A reminder that life continued after Mardonius's army returned defeated from Europe. He held wife and daughter close and took a moment to savor the simplicity of life with them.

The longer he ruled, the more lands he owned, the smaller the world he cared about. He cared no longer about Europe, about satrapies or provinces. His family was enough. Yet still he must rule and rule well. He must secure a legacy for that family.

Haman understood, though he was the only one. The only one who would quietly take care of the business of the empire that Xerxes did not want to be bothered with. The only one who encouraged him to slip away now and then for a rejuvenating hour with Kasia and Zillah.

He enjoyed his hour with them now, the simple food Kasia ordered, the babe's attempts to wrap her little tongue around "Father." Kasia laughed and encouraged her to say "Abba" instead, but he must put his foot down somewhere. "Try as you might to make me one, lovely Kasia, I am not a Jewish man. I cannot answer to a Jewish name."

She grinned and whispered, "Say 'Abba'" into Zillah's ear again.

Xerxed chuckled and stood. "I shall have a talk with yours next time he visits to ask him where he went wrong in teaching you obedience."

"He will be as clueless on the subject as you." Kasia stood, Zillah on her hip, and tilted her face up for a kiss. "For which you ought to be grateful. Had I obeyed my father, we never would have met."

"A world I cannot imagine. Well, I suppose I must go receive this friend of yours. Though if you have changed your mind and want me to stay with you instead . . . ."

She gave him a little push toward the door. "You are ever determined to make the other women resent me, staying with me when you have promised them time."

"It makes them respect you. And let it be noted that you are literally pushing me into another woman's arms."

She laughed and wrapped her free arm around his waist. Rested her mouth against his shoulder. "I love you."

He turned to give her a proper farewell. "I will see you in the morning. I love you both."

As he exited, she handed Zillah to Desma and turned to her prayer rug. He smiled and shook his head.

The evening was warm and sweet-smelling, pleasant enough to tempt him to linger outside. But he could hear Kasia in his head, admonishing him for keeping a nervous bride waiting. He headed for his palace and only paused for a moment outside the door. Only dragged in one long breath. Only took a single minute to pray to Kasia's

God that this one be better than the last ten.

Zethar gave him half a grin and opened the door.

Usually his brides set a scene for him, arranged cushions and placed themselves just so upon them. A few fell asleep when he kept them waiting too long, occasionally he found one in a chair, once or twice weeping. But Kasia had, until now, been the only one he found at the window, looking out at the rest of the world.

From the back, he could note her excellent figure, the long sweep of unadorned hair. As she turned, he could suck in a breath of appreciation over the beauty of her features.

But they had all been beautiful.

Her smile, though, held no pride. He stepped inside. "You are Esther?"

She genuflected. "My lord."

Her gaze sought the ground before she seemed to remind herself to look up at him. He smiled. "Kasia tells me I will like you."

Her smile changed, went from polite to warm, and it transformed her face from beautiful to something far more. "She tells me I will like you too."

Kasia's regard was mutual, then. That relieved an unnamed worry. "She was certainly right about your beauty—she assured me you surpassed the others in that regard."

The girl blushed and looked at the ground again. "Thank you, my lord. If I may confess, I forgot what a handsome man you are. I glimpsed you once, when I was a girl." She shook herself, moistened her lips, and stepped forward with hands extended. Folded fabric rested upon them. "Hegai said we should all make you something. Kasia recommended this—she said you were in need of a new one."

He moved forward, slowly enough not to intimidate her. Accepting the gift, he opened it up and grinned. "A shawl. Yes, I am afraid my favorite has been lost to me." And leave it to Kasia to recommend this. She could have made him a new one herself, but no. She would prefer the symbolism of having her choice of his next queen replace the garment from his previous one. "You are a talented weaver."

"Thank you." Her voice shook.

He touched a finger to her chin to urge her face up. "Are you scared, Esther?"

"A bit nervous." She smiled again, but it was not so bright as when she spoke of her friend.

"And sad." The sorrow deepened her eyes, as if providing a portal to the secrets of her heart.

"Not sad, exactly, but . . . do you know what she thinks? Kasia? She thinks we will fall in love and she will have to step aside." She blinked back tears and shook her head. "Yet still she has done all she can to mold me into the wife you will want, and I know she has told you only the good things about me."

She thought that? Foolish, selfless woman. He dropped his hand and arched his brows. "What do you think?"

Esther focused her gaze somewhere around his throat. "You are my husband. And given all she has told me about you, I know I will care for you. I hope and pray you will care for me too—but I will never hurt her. I give you what I am, my lord. But I think everyone but her realizes that will never compete with what she is."

Compassionate, considerate . . . yet she clearly understood that no one would ever replace Kasia—even if Kasia did not. He took her hand. "About her, you have the right of it. No one can be Kasia—but no one else has to be." He lifted her hand, kissed it, and smiled. "I think you and I shall get along quite nicely, that we will enrich each other's lives and expand each other's hearts."

Peace gleamed in the eyes she lifted to him. "I think we shall."

Kasia had been a fool if she really thought anyone, even as sweet a girl as Esther, could take his heart from her. But she had also been right. He had found his next queen.

Esther pulled her robes tighter and rested her elbows on the bottom of the window. The first strokes of dawn painted fire on the horizon. Her first day as a wife, not just a faceless bride. Her first day of freedom in the palace.

Kasia had promised to "introduce" her to Mordecai now, and joy surged through her at the thought. She had missed him beyond words. Missed his quiet wisdom, the sound of his unintelligible prayers. She had missed the short walks to Kish and Zillah's house, the chaos of all their children. And yes, Zechariah. She had missed him too.

Her gaze moved to the river for the tenth time in two minutes. She could just make out the figures doing mock-battle in the soft morning light. There must be twenty now, though their shapes blurred in the distance. Which figure was his?

The anger had faded months ago, leaving in its place a pervasive resignation when she thought of him. She would always love him. How could she help it, when he was one of her oldest friends, the only man she had ever dreamed of until she married the king? But he was not hers. He had never been hers. And now she was no longer his.

Large hands enveloped her shoulders. Esther started, then grinned. "Good morning."

Xerxes hummed sleepily and pressed a kiss to the top of her head. Her insides reacted with a strange little flip. This was her husband, this man she barely knew. Already she liked him. She had enjoyed the long, languid night with him. She looked forward to getting to know him better.

But Kasia was right—he could never be her first love. That part of her heart would forever reside there on the banks of the Choaspes, caught between sword thrusts and hurtling spears.

"It is Kasia's brother out there," Xerxes murmured, apparently following her gaze. "Zechariah. I have watched him many a morning from this window, and he has the skill of the best Immortal."

A shudder coursed through her before she could stop it. "I have no heart for conflict."

He chuckled and rubbed at the tension in her neck. "Her brother was born for it. He has mustered quite the little army of Jews, which drives my friend Haman to insanity. He keeps begging me to put a stop to these daily drills, but I have forbidden anyone from interfering. Poor Zech is working off a broken heart. If this were taken away from him . . . ."

She forced her breathing to stay measured, even as his words struck her like a whip. Kasia had mentioned that Zechariah and—finally—her parents had visited several times, but she had not realized Xerxes and Zechariah actually knew each other.

Her feet were on a thin line. Pray Jehovah she could keep her balance.

"Well." He slid his hands down her arms. "The servants will be in soon, and we must get ready. You will move into the queen's quarters now, and the ceremony will take place this afternoon. I will declare a holiday tomorrow in your honor."

She spun, knowing her eyes were round as the full moon. "What?"

His lips smiled. His eyes laughed. "Do you not think 'Queen Esther' has a pleasant sound?"

Mordecai had said he had faith . . . Kasia had said it would be so . . . but deep inside she had never believed either of them, not really. She could hardly wrap her mind around his words.

Her. Esther. *Queen*. "I . . . know not what to say. Is this simply because Kasia recommended it?"

"Would you refuse the crown if it were?" But he chuckled and shook his head. "Rather, my dear, she recommended it because she knew exactly what I needed in my next queen. A woman of beauty to stun the masses, yes. But also one of a sweet and caring spirit, who will be able to guide the harem with quiet wisdom. One who will put her own ambitions aside for the sake of her position and her kingdom. You are that woman."

There must be something wrong with her, that the very thing she had set out to achieve now terrified her when it was given her. "You have not even met the last girl yet . . . ."

"I do not need to. I called Hegai in last night while you slept—my last new bride is no better suited to the crown than the first ten. Only you, Esther."

If he really wanted a queen who was opposite Amestris, then she could see that. She nodded and drew in a long breath. "I am honored beyond words, my husband."

So long as she did not think of the deception. Of the ambitions that indeed hid within her . . . though really, those were vague, were they not? She only wanted to be in a position to help if necessary, which would never happen with the king so determined to support Kasia's people. And the deception was really no more than silence for the sake of safety.

She closed her eyes and praised Jehovah that she had been such a recluse in recent years. The only people who would recognize her were her own, and none of them would ever come to the palace. No Jew did but Mordecai.

Her secret would be safe, and she would be queen.

"Ah, there are the servants. Come, let us dress. We will tell Kasia before I make the announcement to the court."

She only cast one last look out the window before she obeyed.

"What happened to practicing at night?"

Zechariah jerked around, nearly dropping his spear at the once-familiar voice. A smile split his face. "Bijan! I did not know you were home."

"Just yesterday." His friend came over and clapped him into a one-armed embrace. "I thought to catch you last night, but no one was out here. Luckily, a few questions in the right ears told me 'that band of trouble-making Jews' now gathered each morning for their mischief."

Zechariah laughed and set the spear down. "We would have been forbidden from it long ago, had the king not given his approval."

"I suppose it helps to have a sister in the harem." Bijan quirked a brow and folded his arms over his chest. "Did she tell you I was in the party that accompanied her back to Sardis? I could hardly believe it."

"She told me. It is so good to see you, Bijan. I kept you in my prayers." And there had been many of them, under Mordecai's tutelage.

Bijan aged before his eyes. "Perhaps that is what kept me safe when all my fellows died around me. This last year was horrible, Zech. Have you heard that my father was killed?"

He nodded, though he did not trust himself to speak. The news had come in the same message from Ruana that informed him he had a son. After swallowing he managed a tight, "I am so sorry."

"Thank you." Bijan looked out over the river and huffed out a breath. "It is good to be home. I have never been so happy as when Susa came into sight. And I had the added pleasure of meeting my nephew last night—she named him after our father—and hugging my sister again."

Silence would strike his friend as odd. He forced a smile, and the question. "I have not seen her for some time. Is she well? And the baby?"

"Both well and healthy. Although I must ask what you did to her, Zech."

Had it not been for the teasing in his voice, Zechariah would have snapped into a defensive position, ready to battle off an enraged brother. "Ah . . . pardon?"

Bijan chuckled. "She found, of all things, a Jewess to serve as little Navid's nurse. Now she prattles on about the different Jewish laws and customs as if they are the most interesting topics in the world."

He shook his head and tried to ignore the swell of feeling within him. A Jewess? She allowed a Jewess to nurse his son, to talk of the ways of Jehovah? "You cannot lay that at my door, Bijan—I do not recall ever mentioning the Law to her."

"Asho is none too pleased about it, but she refuses to dismiss Rachel." Bijan shrugged and motioned that they should walk. "I must go to the palace. Word came just before I left in search of you that the king has selected a new queen."

Thank Jehovah he had been bending down to pick up his weapons so that his friend could not see his face. He hoped it returned to neutral when he straightened again. "Oh?"

"Mm. Some girl of no family—orphaned, I believe—who is supposedly so beautiful the sun pauses in awe when it passes over her." Bijan grinned and wiggled his brows. "I cannot miss the chance to glimpse her, so I will go to the ceremony. I believe her name is Esther."

Esther. Zechariah swallowed and told himself his heart did not thud, his soul did not howl. Told himself he had been prepared for this—and that it made no difference. Queen or not, she belonged to Xerxes. Not to him. "Beautiful as she may be, I do not envy you the afternoon at the palace."

"I was hoping I could convince you to come—surely your sister can get you an invitation."

Zechariah grimaced. "My sister may be the king's wife, but I am still a man of profession, and that order for a new throne will not fill itself."

Bijan's eyes bulged. "You are crafting a new throne?"

"Alongside a goldsmith, with whom I will be spending this afternoon and many others in the near future."

Not to mention it was a far better excuse than that he was not ready to see her again, to realize anew that she had slipped right through his arms.

As Mordecai had taught him, he turned his mind to prayer until the throb of it faded to an ache.

FORTY-FIVE

The ceremony was solemn, beautiful. Kasia felt the hush of awe down to her core as Xerxes lifted the circle of gold to catch the sun. A shaft of light reflected through the hall.

Esther knelt before him, her face down but her spine straight. Exquisite multi-colored robes flowed over her shoulders and spilled out behind her. Kasia could not have been more proud had it been her daughter evoking such gasps of appreciation. Could not have been more pleased had Xerxes tossed expectation to the wind and given the crown to her instead. She did not want it, would not have known what to do with it. But Esther. Esther had the soul for this.

Mordecai drew in a long breath at Kasia's side. "I fear I am dreaming," he murmured, so quietly she barely heard.

"I know." Kasia smiled. She nearly laughed when she saw the way Esther's fingers gripped the edge of her robe, then slowly released it. No one else would notice. No one else would realize that even now, she doubted herself. Kasia knew—and knew too that she would soon come into her own.

Xerxes slowly lowered the crown. When the gold found its perfect fit around Esther's gleaming hair, Kasia sensed light drape her friend along with the diadem. A shiver of recognition swept over her.

All her life she had heard stories of the prophets. Of their mantles, their commissions. Esther had just been give hers—not by the king of the kings, but by the Lord of lords. Would she feel it? Know it? Perhaps not in full, not yet, but Kasia saw the subtle change come over her face.

Peace. Always she had exuded a measure of it, but before it had been her own. This, though. . . this was the Lord's, lent to her. Her countenance shone with it.

Kasia blinked back tears. Proud ones and joyous ones. And perhaps one or two that came from realizing her own purpose must now be fulfilled. She had given her husband the wife he needed most, had given Persia its perfect queen. No longer was she the sole ambassador of the Lord to the palace.

She would still have to pray, relentlessly and diligently, especially since Esther would not have that freedom. But she would do that from the comfort of her rooms, where she would tend her family. No longer from Xerxes' side when he stood as king before the nations.

So be it.

A roar of approval sounded from the crowd as her husband helped Esther to her feet and turned her to face them. She gave the masses a sweet smile.

Xerxes lifted a hand to silence the gathering. "Let the word go out that we shall feast to honor Queen Esther!"

More shouts and whoops, claps and cheers. Musicians took their cue to lift their instruments. Kasia lost sight of Esther as the crowd swarmed forward to meet her.

"A day of rejoicing in Persia." Mordecai loosed a contented sigh. "You did well."

She nodded. Part of her wanted to slip away unnoticed, but she would not. "We should find couches."

"I shall get us drinks."

More than wine, she suspected he wanted a moment with his own thoughts. Kasia smiled and turned away. When Haman stepped into her path, she wished she had stayed with Mordecai instead.

"Lady." Though his lips turned up, his eyes glinted cold and hard.

Kasia sighed. "Haman. It was a lovely ceremony, was it not?"

He leaned closer. His cloying scent clawed at her, making her head spin with . . . what? She backed up a step. Haman sneered. "Your star is setting, Jewess. You think yourself clever, recommending a bride you think a friend? Your song will change when the king falls in love with her and she forgets you. Your spell will finally be broken."

Forcing a swallow, Kasia lifted her chin. "If that is Jehovah's will, I shall praise him for it."

Haman snorted and spun away. Kasia stood where he left her for a long moment, until a familiar arm slipped around her waist. Xerxes pressed a kiss to her temple. "I thought you would be pleased, my love. Why do you look so stricken?"

"It is only Haman. There is something about him . . . ."

Her husband chuckled and turned her toward the couches. "A centuries-old feud, nothing more." He turned her around and gazed long into her eyes. "I love you entirely. You know that, right? Perfect as she may be for my queen, your young friend will never replace you in my heart. It is impossible."

The truth of that shone from his eyes. And when Esther headed their way, she aimed her smile at Kasia rather than Xerxes.

Realization settled over Kasia. For now at least, she was the thread that held them together.

Will you follow me even here? Will you lend your strength to their marriage?

She drew in an uncertain breath. She loved them both—but did she really have strength enough to sustain not only her own relationships with each of them, but also theirs? And even if she did . . . .

Esther joined them, gripped her hand, and smiled. That new peace in her eyes brushed over Kasia like Ima's loving touch.

Yes, Lord. I will.

Persepolis, Persia

Amestris hurled the wooden tablet against the wall. Some low-born nobody now sat on *her* throne, wore *her* crown. Well, the new, beautiful, *young* Queen Esther would soon wake up from her dream-come-true and realize she held no power in Persia. Nor would she ever—not if Amestris had anything to say about it.

She would not strike against the girl herself—what would be the point? Xerxes would just put the crown on some other harlot's head. No, *he* was the problem. Better to be ruled by her weak-willed son than her despotic husband. Darius would not hold out long against her. And if he did . . . well, she could bide her time until she could either woo her other son back or Artaxerxes could grow up.

"You." She motioned her head eunuch closer. "Find a trusted servant and send him to Bigthan in Susa. Have him find those who grumble against the king and feed the flames of their discontent. I want Xerxes dead—and when he is, tell Bigthan he will move out of the gates and into high esteem. He has my word on it."

The eunuch bowed. "It will be done."

Yes, it would. But it could not be done soon enough.

Susa, Persia

Mordecai rose from his usual seat in the gate, stretched, and indulged in a smile. Tonight he would dine with the queen. Everyone may think his excitement came from her title, even the beauty that was already legendary. He and Jehovah knew that had nothing to do with it. He started through the gate.

He could still barely believe his little girl wore the crown. She got to spend her days with Kasia again, and he had seen them together enough these last months to know both of them glowed with it. They had been given back their sisterhood.

So much he owed Kasia now. Not only had she used her influence for Esther, she had paved the way for an easy life in the harem. From all he could see, Esther was settling in well, winning the other wives over with her calm way, her gentle touch.

His only sorrow was in knowing she would not be in Susa much longer this year. Another few weeks and she would travel with the rest of the royal house to Persepolis. He sighed, paused, and leaned into an alcove to say a quick prayer for her.

"I can tolerate no more."

Mordecai perked up at the harsh tone, even as he slid deeper into the shadows. A familiar presence settled over him, held him immobile. *Yes, Jehovah. I am listening.*

"Teresh, quiet. Your anger will get you killed."

Teresh . . . the doorkeeper?

"Then so be it—I have had enough. Do you know how many of my brothers died in his pointless war, Bigthan? Four. All four dead, and me castrated to serve at his blasted *door*. My father's name will die now."

"Lower your voice. You must be reasonable."

"I just watched the youngest die, after suffering from those festering wounds for six months. And yet the king does not care that so many of his men died, are *still* dying for his pride. He is too concerned with his wives, with his affairs. If I were the prince I would have killed him months ago."

The second—Bigthan? Another doorkeeper, then—loosed a low chuckle that sent a shiver of warning up Mordecai's spine. "We do not need the prince to step in. We can manage it ourselves."

A beat of silence, then Teresh whispered, "What are you saying? Surely you do not think we could get away with anything."

"I have a plan."

Mordecai listened, nausea churning in his stomach as the two eunuchs unfolded and perfected their plan to assassinate the king, step by quiet step. At some point he closed his eyes, focused entirely on their words, and on the steadying presence still holding him.

Only after the voices moved off, after their footsteps had faded, did he feel the comforting weight lift from his spirit. And into his mind came a simple command: *Go!*

Esther ran down the hall, through the garden, into the king's palace. Fear snagged in her throat and made her breath go ragged. What if they had already put the plan into action? What if there were more conspirators that Mordecai had not heard about, or if they got through the guard Xerxes would post?

Her servants sprinted ahead of her to open doors, clear hallways. She could barely catch enough breath to speak when she finally burst into the king's chambers.

He looked up at the noise and frowned. Not with anger, though—with concern. Letting a scroll fall to his table, he stood. "Esther, what is wrong?"

A measure of relief, scanty but precious, poured over her. Thus far he was still well. Still alive. "There is a plot. Assassination."

He motioned a scribe forward even as he came her way, took her arm. She let him guide her to a seat and dragged in a long breath. He sat beside her. "Tell me."

"I was dining this evening with Kasia and Mordecai, the Jew."

Xerxes nodded and cradled her hand. "I know. I visited her this afternoon."

Yes, of course. He always found a sliver of time for Kasia and Zillah. "Mordecai overheard something at the gate today. Two of the doorkeepers, Teresh and Bigthan—they are planning to kill you."

She gasped and heaved her way through what Mordecai had told her. At some points in the tale, he squeezed her hand, then at the end he patted it and looked to Zethar. "I want this matter investigated."

"Yes, master." Zethar charged from the room.

Xerxes eyed the scribe. "Did you write all that down?"

"Yes, master."

"Good. You may leave, then." He turned back to Esther and gave her an encouraging smile. "They will take care of it. Thank you."

"Of course." How could he handle it so calmly? She still shook, and her dinner felt uncertain in her stomach. This was an aspect of marriage to the king she had not considered—that he garnered enemies that plotted against him, that at any moment he could be killed.

She squeezed her eyes shut.

Xerxes slid an arm around her. "It will be well, Esther. Do not let it upset you so."

Shaking her head, she prayed the sob would stay in her throat where it belonged. "I am sorry. I have lost so many people who mattered to me . . . ."

He hummed and rubbed a hand up her arm. "I understand the fear. I was trying to ignore my own version when you came in. Did Kasia tell you?"

She blinked away the tears. "Tell me what?"

"She is with child again." With a sigh, Xerxes pinched the bridge of his nose. "I told her I was overjoyed. I am—but she nearly died giving birth to Zillah. What if . . . ?"

Her throat tightened. Kasia had not told her of any difficulties with Zillah, and she had not yet shared her news about another babe—she would have wanted to inform Xerxes first, and she had left dinner early, saying she felt ill.

Which made sense now.

She could not lose Kasia. Jehovah had protected her through every travail thus far. Just as he had put Mordecai in place to overhear this plot. Her God would protect them. And if he chose not to, then he would sustain her.

Panic still gnawed, but she forced it back, forced her mind to dwell on the provisions of the Lord. Her husband was safe. Her cousin would probably be rewarded. Her best friend would be in a state of bliss over her growing family.

Her hand was steady when she rested it on Xerxes' knee. "She will be well. Her God will watch over her."

"I know." He smiled, but the worry still lurked in his eyes. Not over the would-be assassins, she knew. Only for Kasia. "Still, I will fret. It is my prerogative."

She laughed and stood. "I cannot argue with that."

He stood too, grinning. "I will get back to my distractions. They will not work, but I have begun them now and ought to finish."

Had she been Kasia, he would have invited her to stay, would have put the scrolls aside. He did not, and she did not mind. She was content with the warm embrace he gave her, with the gentle kiss. She was content with the affection in his eyes as he sent her on her way.

She would not want any more—she would not have been able to return it. But this was a fine arrangement.

"Esther?"

She paused in the threshold and looked over her shoulder.

He sat at his table again. "When we arrive in Persepolis, Amestris will relinquish Artaxerxes to me. I would like you to take charge of him."

Yes, she was content with what she had. His regard, his trust. She smiled. "I would be honored, my husband."

"I thought you would be." His grin faded as his gaze fell to his work.

She left him to it and continued down the hallway. The evening air soothed her as she spotted Kasia on the stairs.

Her friend's brow creased upon spotting her. "Is everything all right? I heard you rush out."

"Mordecai overheard an assassination plot. I had to let him know."

Fear flashed across Kasia's face but subsided quickly. "Praise Jehovah Mordecai was there to hear it."

"Yes." They met at the top of the steps. "Are you feeling any better?"

"Much. It is nothing to worry about. In fact . . . ."

"I know, he told me." Esther rested her hand on Kasia's arm. "Kasia, why did *you* not tell me you nearly died with Zillah?"

Kasia sighed, but her expression held a tease. "So you could worry too?"

Esther grinned. "It is my prerogative. You are my dearest friend." When that dearest friend glanced toward the palace, Esther nodded. "He is worried about you."

"I knew he would be. But Jehovah will take care of me."

"As I told him." She leaned over, kissed her sister's cheek. "But you must take care of yourself, too. We would all be lost without you."

The gleam in Kasia's eye was more than contentment, more than satisfaction with her place. "I have no intentions of leaving, so rest assured I will take care of myself." She glanced toward the palace again. "I will check on him."

"Good idea." Esther would go back to her elegant rooms, where she had the luxury of praying with no prying eyes to discover her. She would lift up Kasia and Xerxes both to Jehovah until the last of the fear released her.

She had a feeling she would not get much sleep tonight.

Persepolis, Persia

Amestris cursed, cursed again. Better anger than despair. Better vile words than hot tears. Failure again. A loyal servant dead instead of a faithless husband. And saved by whom? The hand of a Jew.

She spun, then seethed to a halt and looked out into the gardens where Artaxerxes frolicked. Patience was called for. Patience and perseverance. She would wait for Haman to thrust the Jews from the king's favor. She would bide her time, woo the right men. The ones who could succeed where Bigthan failed.

Then Ahura Mazda would finally rule. Through her chosen son . . . and through her.

FORTY-SIX

Five years later, in the first month of the twelfth year of the reign of Xerxes

Esther scanned the gardens for her daughter and tamped down a grin when she saw Zillah urging her into the fountain. Her Amani—could she possibly be three already?—dipped one toe in the water and shrieked. Six-year-old Zillah laughed and plunged in until the water reached her knees.

So like Kasia and her, only these two truly were sisters. Whoever would have guessed at such a future?

Kasia settled at Esther's side with a moan, one hand on her swollen stomach. Child number four would join them any day. Any hour, if Esther correctly interpreted the tension that crossed Kasia's face. Her friend grimaced and rubbed at her side. "I feel as though one wrong move and I will rip in two."

Esther chuckled. "I recall that feeling." She had hoped to experience it again by now, but Xerxes called her so rarely lately . . . not surprising. Whenever Kasia grew large, he could think of no one else. Perhaps it was because his worry overwhelmed him. Or perhaps it was because that was when Kasia was too tired to insist he pay attention to the rest of them.

She suspected the latter.

Esther touched her shoulder to Kasia's. "You look exhausted. Nightmares again?"

Kasia shuddered. "I know not why they plague me in my last weeks of pregnancy. Every time I sleep, I am back on the wall at Sardis, watching the darkness descend. Hearing the scream behind me, smelling that blasted scent, feeling the push."

Esther could only shake her head as Kasia craned around to note where her sons scampered. The elder of the boys, Artarius, led two-year-old Arsames in a game of chase. "Do you have any idea who . . . ?"

Kasia's mouth tightened. "None that Xerxes will entertain. But I have my suspicions." She looked up at the wall.

Esther followed her gaze. A chill swept her spine when she spotted their husband's closest friend. It was no secret Haman was an enemy of the Jews. But exactly how far would that hatred take him? She could only hope the king was right to believe him trustworthy.

Doubt eclipsed the hope every time she saw him.

Haman clasped his hands behind his back and looked out over Susa. The morning sun bathed him in light. Each degree it crept higher, each increase in heat made the secrets of his heart burn hotter.

It was time. He had waited so long, patient and polite. Done the king's bidding, carried out his wishes even before he could ask him. Finally, finally he had been given his due. Elevated even above the princes. A week ago he had dined at a feast in his honor. Everywhere he went, the palace servants bowed to him.

All except one. Haman glanced toward the gate where the Jew always sat. Obstinate and rebellious. He knew the king had a fondness for the swine, but he was done waiting for the affection to fail.

It was time to force matters. And he knew exactly where to start—the Jewess witch. From there, it would be easy enough to obliterate her entire people.

The very thought made him smile.

There ought to have been pain. Kasia felt every muscle coil, every ounce of strength focus on the next push. She could feel the pressure, the way the babe within her inched closer to life.

Why was there no pain? There had been pain with Zillah. With Artarius and Arsames. Even with each child she lost in the first years of her marriage.

But this . . . it was too like the time in Sardis. The time when Mordecai had prayed her agony onto himself so that she might survive it. The time when her child had been born lifeless and she had nearly joined him in the bosom of Abraham.

Sardis. Why did everything remind her of Sardis?

Something was wrong, and fear of it shook her, from sweat-soaked brow to curled toes. "Pray." The command croaked out, rasped, but she knew Desma heard. Not just the word, but the desperation.

Her maid's brow furrowed. "Mistress, what is it? Everything is well."

"No. No, it is not. I cannot . . . there is no . . . ." More tension, more pressure. She squeezed her eyes shut. Why did Jehovah take the sensation from her again? She was not injured, not weak. She could handle it. She could . . . .

The tension eased. Leda caught the babe, shouted, "A girl! Another beautiful daughter, mistress. Two of each now."

She wanted to smile, she wanted to laugh, she wanted to cry. She wanted to reach for this newest wonder and put her to her breast.

A single arrow of pain shot through her like lightning. And she could not move.

could neither lift an arm nor open her mouth. Her bent knees fell flat, and the rest of her went lax.

No! No, no, no. She must move, she must regain control. The babe—Leah, they were going to name her after Ima's mother—would need nursed. Zillah and the boys would be in soon.

"Mistress?" Desma squeezed her hand, shook her leg. She could feel it. She could hear, she could see. But . . . . "Mistress, what is wrong? Mistress? Mistress!"

Oh to be able to soothe her, to calm the fear that she saw rock her trusted friend. A stream of tears tickled her cheek, and she could not even sniff, could not wipe them away.

Chaotic shouting clanged in her ears, but she saw them fall to their knees, all her loyal servants. She saw precious Esther come in, saw the horror in her eyes. Heard her wail as she knelt beside Kasia's bed.

Sweet friend. Dear sister. She would take care of the children, Kasia knew. But Xerxes—if she died, he could fly into a rage that would shake the world. Or crumble, which would rock it. How could the nations stand firm when their foundation gave way?

Jehovah, sustain him. Comfort Esther. Knit them together with something other than me. Put your arms around my children. Oh Jehovah, why? Why is this happening?

Warmth on her left side, as if someone sat beside her. Yet the mattress did not sink, no sound filled her ears. She could blink, she could move her eyes. But she was not sure what she saw. An edge of light, so white it nearly hurt. An outline of a man, of broad shoulders and . . . wings?

Comfort. Peace. Familiarity. A shimmering, half-visible arm lifted, and warm fingers touched her cheek. *Rest, child. This is the only way.*

Kasia closed her eyes and sank.

Xerxes could only stare at Esther, unaware his knees had buckled until he felt the cushion of a chair beneath him. "She what?"

His queen trembled, and tears rushed down her cheeks in a swollen river. "I do not even know what to call it. She cannot move, cannot speak. We called in the physicians, but they have never seen the like, not exactly. Apoplexy is their best guess."

"Stroke?" He pushed to his feet so he could pace, raked a hand through his hair. "No. She is only twenty-five."

"They have seen it strike women in labor before, though it does not match the symptoms exactly." Esther raised her hands, let them fall. "Perhaps she will come out of it."

"She must. She *must*." His arms swung out, swept an urn from a shelf.

Esther jumped when it clamored against the stone of the floor. His queen had never learned how to deal with his temper—of course, she rarely saw it.

He lunged toward the door, a million thoughts battling in his mind. Kasia could not die—he would not allow it. He would do whatever he must, bring in the best physicians from the world over. Anything, so long as she lived.

Esther ran after him, but he spun and halted her with a raised hand. "No. I will go alone." He needed to see Kasia, see his love, without any other company.

"But . . . ." Hurt filled her eyes, but that only kindled his fear-soaked anger.

"Will you argue with me? Disobey me?"

Gaze on the ground, she took a step back. He ignored the tears on her cheeks and sped away.

The palace grounds passed in a blur, light and shadow merging. Until he stepped into her room. In there he saw the light and, at its slicing edge, hovering darkness. His knees struck the floor beside her bed.

Perhaps she only slept. How could it be otherwise? She looked perfect, her hair flowing over the pillow, her face peaceful.

Yet she was never so still, even in slumber. Her chest barely rose, scarcely fell. When he wove his fingers through hers, they did not tighten in response.

A sob ripped up through his chest and lodged in his throat.

"Father?" Zillah crept close and leaned into him. His precious girl. "What is wrong with Ima?"

"I do not know, princess." He pulled her into his lap and held her tight. He motioned the boys over too and wrapped an arm around them. "She is sick. We will get the best physicians to care for her."

"And Savta."

Yes, she would want her mother. "You are a smart girl." He kissed her head, then glanced toward the servants. "See that a message is sent to her family. Tell them to come straightaway."

Squalling filled the room, and Xerxes started. He had forgotten to ask about the babe.

As if reading his thoughts, Desma picked up the squirming bundle and swayed his way. "A daughter, master."

"Leah, then." He gave the three older children each a kiss and reached for the newest addition. The sob threatened to tear loose. She looked so much like Kasia. "My love, you must wake up. You must meet little Leah."

Surely she could not resist that.

Her eyes opened. Then slid closed again.

He swallowed against the pain. Leah's cries subsided for a moment, then her face screwed up once more. She needed her mother. They all needed her mother.

Desma took her back. "I will deliver her to the nurse to be fed. Come, children, give your father a moment with your ima."

He took her hand again as the room emptied. "Kasia, you must not leave me. If you do not open your eyes and speak to me, there is no telling what I might do. You do not want to unleash me on the unsuspecting world, do you?"

He could hold the tears back no longer. He rested his head against her hand, clasped between his.

Her sleeve slid up her arm, revealing the heavy torc she still wore. Proof of her love. Their love. "Please, lovely Kasia. Do not give up." If she did, he did not know how he would keep from doing the same.

Perhaps he would refuse to move until she did. It was only a matter of time before someone demanded something of him, but he had no idea what he could give. He felt suspended along with Kasia. Useless.

The world would just have to understand.

Haman stared at the servant. "What happened?"

"Apoplexy, as best as they can guess. She is unresponsive. Immobile."

Unbelievable. He had not even had to raise a hand against her. Did he need any more proof that the god was for him? Ahura Mazda had struck down the witch himself, and the king was no doubt too grief-stricken to care for anything else.

Perfect. Utterly perfect. "Quickly, bring the Pur."

His man dashed off, returned a minute later with the lots. As Haman watched, his servant let loose the two small discs. The first slid to a halt over the symbol for the twelfth month. The second over the marker for the thirteenth day.

Nearly a year away—he must need that much time to prepare. To rouse the anger of the world against the Jews.

So be it. He strode from his home, toward the palace, and deliberately chose the gate where the witch's friend would be seated.

His servants went ahead of him, insisting all nearby bow in deference to the favored of the king. Satisfaction swelled in his chest. Until, of course, they reached the Jew.

"Why do you transgress the king's demand?" his head eunuch demanded.

The swine looked past them, to Haman. Recognition of an enemy flickered in his eyes. "I will bow the knee to no man, especially a man such as him. I worship only the one God, Jehovah."

Hatred boiled up as Haman strode past. Yes, he worshiped only Jehovah, just like the witch. Now he and all his people would die because of it.

He headed toward the quarters of the royal family and found the king in the Jewess's chambers. Hunched beside the bed, looking as lifeless as the figure on it. "Master?"

Xerxes lifted his head. "Haman. I am glad you have come. She is . . . ."

"I received the message. Master, you are over-wrought. Yet there is business to be done. Even now I have learned of a people dispersed throughout your kingdom that refuse to keep the king's laws—and the last thing you need right now is an uprising. If it pleases you, let a decree be written to destroy them. I will pay ten thousand talents of silver into the hands of those who do the work, and have the plunder from their homes and businesses brought into your treasury."

The king did not even look at him. "Do whatever you deem necessary, Haman. Here." He covered one hand with the other, tugged.

Haman nearly shook when he saw the signet ring.

"Act in my stead, my brother. Do as I would do."

Better, he would do as the king *should*. He took the ring, slid it onto his own finger. Was it his imagination, or did power pulse from his hand? "You will not want to be disturbed, master. Let us also make a decree that none are to enter your presence without being called, or they shall be put to death unless you hold your scepter out to them."

"A wise thought."The king rubbed his face. "I shall have to return to court for a few hours each day. To keep up appearances."

"Of course. But I will take care of everything in your time of need, master."

"Thank you." His voice broke, and Xerxes rested his head on his hand. "I do not know what I would do without you."

"You need never find out. I arranged for some wine for you, master—you must keep up your strength. Go, refresh yourself for a moment."

Xerxes sighed, but he stood and shuffled from the room. The Jewess's eunuch immediately entered, but Haman ignored him. He sat in the king's seat and leaned close, so close his breath would have tickled her ear had she any ability to sense it. "You are lucky the god struck you before I could, witch—I would have cast the blame on your precious people. But it is no matter. No matter at all. Die now, as you should have done in Sardis, or die later. It makes no difference to me."

Did her face pale? Was there a twitch in her cheek? He could not be sure, but it hardly mattered. Whether or not she knew who caused her undoing, the point remained she would be destroyed. Finally.

Chest full of satisfaction, he left the room with its glowering but oblivious eunuch and headed for the inner court. His place of honor. He summoned a scribe and smiled when the servant stood with tablets at the ready. "Take this down. 'To every satrap, governor, and officials of all the people under Xerxes, the king of kings over all Persia and Media. That on the thirteenth day of the twelfth month, the month of Adar, every Jew shall be annihilated. Young and old, children and women, and their possessions shall be taken and added to the king's treasury.' Let the word go out to all the land and be read in every public place."

Chuckling in delight, he took his seat beside the throne. His gaze fell on the signet circling his finger. With its seal, he created law. And no Persian law could ever be undone—even by the king himself.

FORTY-SEVEN

When his parents fled, weeping, Zechariah took their spot beside his sister. Poor Kasia. To look at her, one would think she only slept. Her hair was neatly arranged around her, no pain on her face. But her cheeks were pale, and even at Ima's urging, at Abba's begging, Kasia made no response.

Zechariah took her hand and sighed over it. Closed his eyes. "Dear Jehovah, whatever your purpose here, I ask that you minister to us. Kasia needs your strength and, if she can still hear, will grow frustrated. Soothe her spirit as you heal her body. And the rest of us need you too. Need your support and peace."

"Amen." The sweet, soft voice flowed into the room like a brook.

He jerked up, spun around. His breath snagged. Esther. All these years, he had managed to avoid her whenever he visited his sister. He had never felt up to facing her, seeing her exactly as she was now—regally dressed, elegant and beautiful. He never could have given her the things that suited her so well.

He inclined his head. "My queen."

Her lips twitched up. "No need to stand on formalities. You are my dearest friend's brother, after all." She stepped into the room, one hand behind her. Behind her skirts he spotted a little girl with an adorable mess of dark curls.

He smiled at the little one and crouched down. "You must be Amani. Kasia and Zillah have told me all about you."

The girl buried her grin in her mother's leg. Esther turned to her servants. "I would like a few moments to speak to Kasia's family. Please take my daughter with you."

One of the maidservants scooped up the girl with a tickle, then the mass of them bowed out and closed the door behind them. Esther released a pent-up breath. "How have you been, Zech?"

Throat suddenly too tight to answer, he could only stand up again and nod.

She moved to the bed. The resignation on her face confirmed that Kasia had looked exactly like this for the past two days. "I believe that was the first time I ever heard you pray."

That observation earned a breath of a laugh. "Mordecai and I have spent much time together these past years. He has taught me how to pray from the heart, and how to listen."

"Your sister has taught me the same. It is necessary, if one wants to remain faithful in this faithless place." She blinked rapidly and wiped at her eyes. "The physicians can tell us nothing. But I have hope."Yet her voice broke on the word.

"There is always hope. Jehovah has performed bigger miracles for her than this would require." He took Esther's hand, but only so that he could urge her into the chair. And perhaps to test himself.

Not so many tingles anymore. Not so much regret. It had been a long, busy five years since she took the crown.

"I know." She settled into the seat and wrapped her arms around her middle. "I will make sure someone tells the king you and your parents came. He will let no one but their children stay while he is here. I tried to speak with him yesterday. That did not go over so well." She nodded to a large pottery jug on the table, missing one of its handles.

He nodded, well able to imagine the king's temper. But one thing he had not yet convinced his mind to picture was the king and queen together. Every time he had seen Xerxes over the years, it had been as Kasia's husband. Not Esther's.

She drew in a shaky breath. "I have met her, you know. Quite a number of times now."

He blinked, then sighed. "Ruana?"

"Mmm hmm. The first time was at one of my banquets for the wives of the court. I let myself feel superior when I realized who she was, even toyed with the idea of snubbing her so that others would have to do the same." Her lips turned up into a self-deprecating smile. "But then she sat down beside Kasia and began asking her questions about Judaism. I think, were it not for her husband, she would have converted by now."

Bijan told the same tale. He never knew what to make of it. "Bijan has mentioned that the queen always has a smile for her."

"And for her son." Her gaze fell to her lap. "He is a beautiful boy. Looks much like his father."

Navid. He prayed for the boy every morning, every night.

His fingers curled into his palm. So many times in the past five years he had started toward Asho's house with his cart of carvings, fully intending to deliver them himself so that he might catch a glimpse of his child.

But then as he drew near, as the shame and guilt of memory crashed over him, he realized he would cause turmoil for the boy if he showed up. And he turned away.

Esther forced a smile. "I hear Joshua is to marry next month. Kasia tells me he has been busy building a home for his bride."

"With a foolish grin upon his face every moment." He had encouraged Joshua to use the addition already finished and furnished, but his brother had refused.

He probably feared it would curse his match.

"And what of you?" She met his gaze again, held it. "When will you marry, Zech? It has been six years."

She had forgiven him. Kasia said so, and he could see it for himself now. But forgiving himself . . . he was not sure he could ever accomplish that. What he had done to Esther—the way he had treated Ruana. He shook his head. "I have nothing left to give a wife."

"I cannot believe that. Please, Zech, try to be happy."

"I am. Or content, anyway. I have my family, a passel of nieces and nephews to keep me entertained, with more sure to come after Joshua weds."

"And your little Jewish army." She grinned, eyes gleaming. "I sometimes rise with the sun so I might watch the lot of you practicing. Your numbers keep growing."

She watched him, from her home in the palace? He shook that thought off. "We have broken into several groups, actually. And it is not only Jews. Bijan and many of his friends join us too, to keep their reflexes sharp."

A knock sounded at the door, and Zethar poked his head in. "Excuse me, mistress. Zech. The king is coming, and he would like some time alone with her."

"Of course." Esther stood, moved to the door.

Zechariah fell in behind her. Out in the hall, they both paused. He hesitated, then figured he might as well ask. In an undertone, so no one else would hear. "Are you happy? I want to think you are, but I am never certain. Your husband is so in love with my sister . . . ."

She gave him a smile he knew well. At peace with who she was, where she was, even if no one else understood that. Even if they thought she ought to reach for something more. "I am content."

How odd, that only now did he fully understand that. He nodded and watched her walk away, then turned toward the exit.

He found Abba and Ima at the gate, which was curiously absent of Mordecai. They held each other, rocked to the rhythm of Ima's keening. He gathered them up and urged them home.

Mordecai rent his garment and fell to the floor with a guttural cry. He had known Haman hated Kasia, hated him, hated all the Jews—but he had never thought it would come to this. Had never thought he would hear such a decree in the streets.

"Jehovah! He has set a day for destruction. A day to wipe your children from the face of the earth. First Kasia, but now *this*?"

A whisper moved over him, through him. *Mourn for my people. Take your lamentations into the streets.*

He trembled and curled his arms over his head. "I will mourn, Jehovah. I will mourn, and I will trust in your deliverance."

Dragging in a breath, he moved to the trunk in the corner of his room. On the bottom rested the sackcloth he had not worn since Keturah died so many years ago. He drew it out, ran a hand over the scratchy, irritating cloth.

The time for the Lord's purpose had come—and the first step was reminding the people of Susa that the Jews were their neighbors, their friends.

He slipped the sackcloth over his head, then strode out to the kitchen. Martha dropped her spoon when she spotted him, but he did not speak. Not yet. He plunged a hand into the ash bin and rubbed it over his face. Down his arms and legs. Across the back of his neck.

Then he headed for the streets. He would mourn until the whole of Susa mourned with him. So loudly the king would hear even through the cloud of his grief.

Ima's hand shook as she ladled soup into Abba's bowl. Abba stared blindly at it. The younger children all glanced at one another, at their parents, then to Zechariah.

He sighed and dropped his hand onto the table. "Enough of this. You must tell them what is going on, Abba. She needs all the prayers we can muster."

Abba raised weary eyes to him. So long he had fought this, clinging to his stubborn pride. He looked devoid of strength to fight any longer. He sighed and waved a hand. Ima pressed a hand to her mouth and sank to her seat.

Zechariah looked at his younger siblings. "It is Kasia. She did not die nine years ago, she was merely taken to the palace to wed the king."

Joshua's cup splashed as he dropped it to the table. "What?"

Sarai frowned—did she even remember her eldest sister? The younger boys surely did not.

"She has been with the king ever since." He met each of their gazes, held them to be sure they believed him. "She went with him to war, she came back six years ago. But now she is ill. She just had her fourth child, and something came upon her. Apoplexy, it seems. She lies even now caught between life and death, and you all must pray. Every one of you. We should fall to our knees and fast until she revives."

Joshua muttered a curse, and Ima was so beset she did not even chide him for it. Eglah pushed away her still-empty bowl, Sarai blinked back tears. "I still remember that last day with her," she murmured. "The way she tickled me when she realized I had Esther's bracelet. That is the only image I have of her, that smile on her face when she tickled me."

"Place that memory at the footstool of Jehovah, Sarai, and beg him to intercede on her behalf. Come, let us—"

A pounding at the door interrupted him. He glanced at Abba, who made no move to get up. It came again, harder and more frantic. "Coming!" Zechariah wove through the crowd of siblings and over to the door.

When he opened it, Bijan gusted in with a mountainous cloak in his arms and a whole contingent behind him.

"Bijan. What—"

"We need your help." Bijan uncovered the bundle is his arms, revealing a boy. About five years old. Zechariah's throat went dry.

His son. His son was here, in his home.

Bijan turned and handed Navid to . . . Ruana, he saw when the hood of her cloak fell. Her hands shook as she reached for him, her face white as the moon.

Her brother's side oozed red. Zechariah reached to support him when he wobbled. "You are injured. Ima, we need help! What happened, Bijan?"

His friend winced in pain. "I was visiting them when the announcement reached the house about the Jews."

Ima rushed up, a bowl of water and rags in hand. Zechariah eased Bijan to a seat. "What announcement?"

"You have not heard?" Bijan blinked, then shook his head. "Haman has been given control, and he issued a proclamation that all Jews are to be killed on the thirteenth day of the twelfth month."

The bowl of water crashed to the floor, shattered and splashed. Silence pulsed through the room, then an explosion of voices. Some angry, some confused, some incredulous.

Zechariah met his friend's gaze. "How did Haman get authority to do this?"

"The king gave him his signet." Bijan shifted, hissed out a breath. "When the proclamation reached our ears, Asho went wild. Said something like, 'Why wait until then?' and lunged at the nurse, shouting that he would rid his house of the Jews before they stole his family."

Zechariah darted a glance at where Ruana huddled in a corner with her son. She met his gaze, things in her eyes he never thought he would see. Things that added depth, maturity . . . and with them beauty beyond what he had found so tempting six years ago.

Ima crouched down to pick up the pieces of broken pottery, even as Eglah rushed over with another bowl of water. His mother looked around. "Where is the nurse? Is she injured too?"

Bijan clenched his teeth, nostrils flaring. "She was dead before I could get across the room. Then Ruana was shouting that her heart was already Jehovah's, and he came after her." His eyes went unfocused. "Navid was right there, watching, yet Asho flew at her with the same dagger . . . ."

"You stopped him." Eglah's hand shook as she dipped a rag into the water. "I need to see the wound, Bijan."

"I stopped him." He pulled his arms out of the tunic and secured it at his waist. The angry gash in his side still oozed blood. "I had to kill him to do so."

Ruana shifted the child in her arms and stepped forward. "Now Mother is furious and has disowned us both for casting our allegiance with the Jews. And Asho's family that was there . . . they would kill us. They threatened to take Navid away."

"I could think of nowhere else to bring them." Bijan gasped when the wet cloth touched his wound.

Abba stepped into the circle and surveyed first Bijan, then Ruana, and finally the collection of servants they had brought. "You have proven yourself a true friend to my son, Bijan. And that you would risk your life like this . . . you and yours are welcome here. There is no room for all of you in the main house, but I imagine Zechariah will let you stay in his."

"Of course. High time it get some use."

Ima dropped the broken bowl into the refuse bin and spun away. "I will air it out and give it a quick cleaning."

Two of Ruana's maidservants scurried after her.

When Ruana shifted again under the weight of Navid, Zechariah gave in to the urging and went to her. Led her to a couch, where she could sit and settle his son against her. Navid's eyes were closed, but Zechariah could not tell if he slept or merely tried to hold out the world.

Esther had been right. He was a beautiful boy. Pride swelled before he could remind himself that so far as anyone else knew, this was Asho's son.

Ruana smoothed a hand over Navid's hair and rested her cheek against his head. "He should not have had to see what he did today. It is no wonder he is exhausted."

Zechariah folded his hands together to keep from reaching out to him. "You will be able to put him to bed soon."

"Will you sit?" Her eyes begged. And how could he refuse, given all she had been through this afternoon? Her own husband trying to kill her . . . Zechariah sat beside her. She loosed a shaky sigh. "I am sorry for bringing this trouble to your door, Zech. I tried to think of somewhere else we would be safe—"

"You are welcome here." Their gazes met, knitted together. "You know that. I will not let anything happen to you."

Ruana blinked back the moisture in her eyes and turned her gaze on her brother. "He is close, as well. To putting his full faith in Jehovah." A wisp of a smile flew over her mouth. "Perhaps if he takes the final step, he will have the courage to ask for Eglah's hand."

Zechariah jerked his head around to watch his little sister tend his friend. Bijan had never mentioned anything . . . but was that pleasure underscoring the pain? And Eglah—she had certainly never tended any of Zechariah's wounds with that much care. Did she love him? Was that why she begged her way out of all the matches Abba tried to arrange?

He breathed a laugh. "I am blind."

That line of conversation halted when Abba folded his arms over his chest and measured Bijan. "This proclamation—as soon as the king realizes what has been done, he will stop it."

Zech shook his head. "Not if it was sealed with his signet. He cannot undo a law."

Abba muttered a curse. "Do they really expect us to accept it? To let them obliterate us?"

"They expect you to be overwhelmed by your neighbors, who they have promised to pay for killing you." Bijan looked over to Zechariah. "We will not make it so easy for them."

"No. We will not."

Abba relaxed again and turned to him. "Of course. You will finally have your war, Zech. And you will fight for the children of God."

A warm weight settled into place over his shoulders. Purpose. He nodded, then glanced at Ruana. Her eyes squeezed shut tightly, and her arms held Navid close against her. More violence was probably the last thing she wanted to hear about, but they must plan.

Best to get her out of the room first. "Come, Ruana, let me show you and your son where you will stay. Shall I . . . carry him for you?"

Perhaps she was too tired to do so herself—or perhaps she realized how desperate he was to hold his son. She smiled and held the sleeping child out to him. "Thank you."

He would have to thank *her*, but not with an audience. He eased Navid to a rest against his shoulder and stood. The boy draped himself over him, even looped an arm around his neck.

Love shafted through him, so fierce it left him breathless. He spun toward the back entrance before anyone could see it on his face and led the way to his never-used home.

Ruana stayed close to his side. "This is the house you built for your bride. Bijan said she married another instead."

"She overheard us. That night."

"Oh, Zech." Ruana paused just outside the door. "I never intended to ruin anything."

He debated, decided. She was one of them now, would be in their house for the foreseeable future. She would soon learn the truth anyway. "You have met her."

"I have?" She frowned.

Half his mouth quirked up. "Many times, apparently. Her name is Esther."

"Esther." Her eyes went wide, the last of the color leeched from her cheeks. "Surely you do not mean—"

"The queen."

"But . . . you were going to marry a Persian? Surely your father—"

"She is Jewish." He gave her a moment to let that sink in. "No one at the palace knows."

Instead of surprise or frustration, relief settled over her face. "Then between her and your sister, surely they can convince the king—"

"Kasia is near death. If something happens to her, I am unsure what the king may do."

Her shoulders edged back. "We will pray for her. And for the king and queen. Jehovah will prevail."

"He will. Come." He stepped through the open door. Ima and the maids had lit several lamps, and he could hear them working in the bedchambers.

"Where should I put Navid?" Ruana asked. When he nodded to his left, she headed that way. "I will see how they are coming along."

Ima emerged from the room that would have been his and Esther's. Would Ruana sleep with their son tonight, or in there? And why did the question not make anger or regret churn within him?

His mother smiled. "They ought to be comfortable enough for now. We will do a more thorough cleaning tomorrow, after . . . ." Her smile faded, her eyes darted from him to Navid. Studied the boy, studied Zechariah with wide eyes.

He sucked in a breath. She would see the resemblance—such things never slipped past Ima.

She stepped close, gaze on Navid. "He is the image of you. The very image. Zechariah, what have you done? Is this how we raised you? How could you treat her that way, then let her marry a monster?"

Had he thought all these conversations over years ago? He sighed. "She was already married, Ima."

He expected that to set off a new storm. But she only drew in a sharp breath. "She is not now. Make this right, Zech."

She hurried toward the other room, from which Ruana emerged. Gathered her into an embrace and whispered something. He thought he caught, "You are ours now." Then, with one last pointed glare his way, she left.

Who could ever comprehend how a woman would react? Shaking his head, he carried his son into the room he had designed for his children. These last six years, he had never dared think one might actually sleep in it.

The maids had set up a pallet, and he bent down so he could settle Navid onto it. The boy went lax, one arm flopped above his head, the other over his belly. He certainly had the look of their family.

Ruana sniffled behind him. He turned his head and found her with a hand pressed to her mouth, tears streaming. Not surprising, given the day she barely survived.

That warm purpose surged again. Zechariah straightened and went to her, gathered her close. In spite of the years, in spite of the guilt that colored the memories, his arms still remembered her. And this time, it felt right to hold her. "Shh. It is all right, Ruana. You and Navid are safe."

"I know." She clung to him, buried her face in his chest. "It is just—I never thought to see you with him."

"I never thought to see him. So many times I wanted to, but I could not disturb the life you had set up for him. Tell me Asho was a good father to him. Please."

"Most of the time." Her eyes closed with a sigh. "Unless he would say something about Jehovah, or the Law. He did not like *me* learning it, much less Navid. But I wanted him to know where he came from."

No words existed to thank her for that, so he just buried a hand in her hair. "And you? Bijan told me Asho's affection for you had faded, but . . . ."

"Suffice it to say I will not mourn him." A shiver ran through her.

He pulled back just enough to look into her face. He could not love her before, not with the guilt, then not given Esther. But now . . . he could, so easily. The mother of his son, who had risked her life to teach the boy the ways of his people. "I want to be a father to him, Ruana. I want to be a husband to you."

She rested a hand against his cheek. "I have always loved you, Zech. Even when I jested it away, I loved you."

His lips found hers, familiar yet long-forgotten. Old flames fanned to life, but it was different now. Tempered by time and growth, heated by promise instead of the forbidden. They could build a life together, a family. One worth fighting for.

"I would ask if I have to kill you too, Zech, were I not so confused. You two have not even spoken since I returned from Europe."

Zechariah broke the kiss but did not release her as he looked to where Bijan and Eglah stood in the doorway. He smiled. "There was good reason for that."

Still frowning, Bijan studied them. "Apparently, as that did not look like your first kiss. Do I need to thrash you after my side heals?"

"You would have reason, but I would prefer you give me your blessing to marry her."

Bijan looked long at his sister, then sighed. "I expect someone to tell me what I missed while at war. But yes. Of course you have my blessing." He glanced past them, to the pallet. "You do not mind raising another man's son?"

Ruana's eyes verified his thoughts—the truth would not stay hidden once they saw Navid beside Zechariah's family. He cleared his throat. "He is my son, Bijan, not Asho's."

"*What?*"

"It was my doing, do not get angry with Zech." Ruana's spine went rigid under his hands. "And was Asho's idea, actually."

Her brother scowled. "That makes no sense."

Her eyes slid shut. "He touched me only on our wedding night, to consummate the marriage. But he did not . . . like women. He preferred men. And—well, boys."

Bijan cursed. "You will waste no time mourning him. Marry Zech as soon as his rabbi agrees, and let us all forget such a man ever ruled you."

Ruana snuggled in and loosed a long breath. "Gladly."

FORTY-EIGHT

"Mistress?"

Esther turned from Kasia's bed to where her maid stood in the doorway, face perplexed. "What is it, Calisto?"

The girl's frown deepened as she stepped inside. "It is Mordecai the Jew, mistress. When I went out to the markets for you, I saw him before the gate, in sackcloth and ashes."

Esther stood. "Surely not over Kasia—he would not mourn while she yet lives, would he?" Unless he knew something the rest of them did not. Had Jehovah told him she would not . . . ?

"No, I cannot think so. The square was filled with Jews, all weeping and wailing."

Not Kasia then—their whole people would not know to mourn for her. So what in the world . . . ? "Ask him to come and tell me what is happening."

"He cannot enter the gates dressed like that, mistress."

"Then take fresh garments to him first."

Calisto bent her knee then dashed off.

Esther rested a hand on her forehead and turned back to Kasia. Dread curled in her stomach.

Something was wrong. She had felt the scratch of its claws when she stepped from her room this morning but assumed it the same worry that had dogged her for days.

Her knees ached to join Kasia's servants in their supplication to Jehovah. She prayed silently as she sat beside her friend, but it did not feel enough. The weight of need pushed down on her shoulders, doubling as her mind turned over possible explanations for Mordecai's lamenting.

Something was very, very wrong.

Calisto returned a few minutes later. "He refused the garments, mistress."

The dread cinched tight. "Hathach!"

Her head eunuch stepped in from his post in the hall. "Mistress?"

Fear mounted upon dread and shook her from the inside out. "Hathach, go find Mordecai. Ask him why he mourns."

Though she tried to sit patiently beside Kasia while he was gone, she ended up pacing the chamber, her soul crying silently to Jehovah. Yearning forward, upward, anywhere answers may lie. Answers for her friend, for her cousin. Answers, any answers to be had.

She jumped when the door opened and Hathach stepped in again.

His face was grim. "Your husband gave his signet to Haman, mistress, who immediately made it law that the Jews are to be destroyed, and their murderers rewarded for it. It is set for the last month of the year—the proclamation is being read in every town, every province. Here. A copy of it."

Esther reached with trembling hand for the tablet, the news not even allowing relief that Mordecai's mourning was not over Kasia. Her eyes blurred too much for her to read it. "I cannot believe it."

"Mordecai asks . . . ." He paused, swallowed, and gave her a strange look. "He commands you go before the king in supplication and plead for your people."

Esther sank onto the chaise behind her. So, then. Her cousin thought this her purpose.

Hathach knelt before her, dipping his head so he could look her in the face. "Mistress, why did you never tell me? You know how we love you, you know you could trust us. Why did you not tell us he is your cousin?"

"I have no answer for that, Hathach. I could trust no one in the beginning, and afterward . . . ." She shook her head and placed the tablet beside her. "I cannot go before him without being called—it would mean death."

"Unless he holds out the scepter. Which he will surely do for you, mistress."

"Will he?" Tears scalded her eyes, burned behind her nose. "I am not so sure. He has not called me for a month—"

"But you are his queen, Kasia's dearest friend. You have gone to him before without being called."

She turned her face away, which put Kasia in her line of sight again. Motionless, like nothing more than a doll. "But the last time was to tell him that his greatest love was struck down. When I tried to speak to him days ago, he lashed out. I have never been able to predict him like she can, Hathach. Perhaps he hates me for bearing the news. Perhaps he hates Jehovah for not sparing her this. And if I admit I lied about my heritage . . . ."

He reached out and gripped her hand. "Mordecai said you ought not think in your heart you will escape any more than the rest of the Jews. If you do not stand for the Lord's people, then another will be raised up and you and your father's house shall perish."

Her shoulders slumped. Mordecai had always understood her, had always encouraged her—yet now, when she most needed his support, he sent her a message of doom and refused to speak with her himself?

It felt as though the summer sun beat upon her, drying her up and scorching her flesh. She had never been the brave one, the risk-taker. She had never been the one to charge in and fight off the enemy. That was Kasia's part, Zechariah's. Never had she been suited for anything more than dwelling behind them. "If Kasia were awake—"

"She is not," Hathach snapped, more angrily than he had ever dared speak to her. "But if she does not die now, she will by year's end—as will your cousin, your neighbors. As will *you*, if you do not take a chance. Mistress." He squeezed her hand, lowered his voice again. "Who is to say you did not come here for such a time as this? If Haman succeeds in his plans, your people will be wiped out in all of Persia, even those who have returned to Israel."

A cool breeze blew across her soul, soothed the fire. It moved through her veins, along each nerve, until even her roiling mind felt the breath of peace.

All her life she had feared losing those she loved. Feared violence, disease, disaster. Afraid, always afraid someone else would be snatched from her—and now that possibility taunted her. They could all be taken, all of them in one fell swoop.

She was no longer a child, to cower in the shadows of her father's house until a stranger came to rescue her. No longer a girl, to beg someone stronger to take care of her.

If she must die, better to do it fighting for others than while running like a coward in eleven months. Better to draw the king's anger onto her for her deception than let it destroy her entire people.

She stood up, rolled her shoulders back. "Give this message to Mordecai: Go, gather all the Jews in Susa and have them fast for me for three days. They should neither drink nor eat, only pray. My servants and I will do the same here, and on the third day, I will break the law and go to the king. If I perish . . . well then, I perish."

Hathach stood too, and nodded. Pride gleamed in his eyes.

Mordecai surveyed the empty streets, listened to the pulse of countless voices murmuring to Jehovah in the sanctuary of their homes. Below it, an undertone that set his pulse to dancing. It was not mankind alone that gathered tonight. He sensed the hedge around them, wings stretched wide until tip touched tip. Outside it, the shadows dipped and dove.

But his people would not be bothered these next three days, while they prayed for deliverance—first for their queen, and so for themselves.

Sending Esther such a harsh message had not been easy, but he had known it would make her stand tall, take her rightful place as leader of their people. His lips tugged up as he recalled all the surprise from neighbors who never realized his reclusive cousin had left his house and gone to the king's. But then hope had lit every single set of despairing eyes.

He strode past his empty home and to Kish's. His friends had been praying for Kasia before he brought them Esther's request, but they had redoubled their efforts. Even the Persians now among them—an irony he hoped was not lost on Kish—joined in the prayers to the one God.

He let himself in, found his place on the floor beside Zechariah. On the young man's other side lay his betrothed, prostrate before the Almighty. Only the youngest of the children were absent, out in Zechariah's house with Sarai. He could hear her voice from here, lifted up in a psalm.

Jehovah would prevail. Their weeping had already turned to prayer—soon enough it would turn to singing.

Xerxes sat on his throne and wished he were in Kasia's room, her hand in his and their children fighting for a place in his lap. Wished she would open her eyes and look at him with more than that leashed emotion. Wished she would sit up, admonish him for his worry with one of her witty rebukes, and demand he hand her the babe.

A week. A week she had lain there without moving, her body shrinking before his eyes. His lovely Kasia. His heart and soul.

He tried to pray. He did. But Jehovah never spoke to him but through her, and now that her lips were silenced . . . .

A headache pounded. He lifted a hand, rubbed at his neck. One more meeting today, then he could leave. At least the court was quiet. All but empty.

Except for that movement at the perimeter of his inner court. He frowned and waited to see who dared disturb him.

Sunlight angled off the polished columns and glimmered against gold at head, neck, wrists, waist. Shimmered in the fabric as she moved.

He sighed and even managed a smile. Esther. Had he really yelled at her the other day? Kasia would have chided him endlessly for his behavior.

Esther's company would do him good. He should have seen that a week ago. She would share his concerns, share his grief. He lowered the scepter in his hands and let his smile grow as she walked forward, all the way to the throne.

Grinning, she reached out and touched the top of the scepter. "I have a petition, my husband."

Peace filled her eyes. He knew not how it was possible, but it was a balm on his soul. For the first time in a week, hope surged. "What do you wish, my queen? A city? Ten? I will give you up to half the kingdom."

She laughed at the joke she had long shared with him and Kasia. "I have prepared a banquet. Will you and Haman join me?"

That was obviously not her petition, but a thoughtful gesture. Haman had been working nonstop for him this past week, always so busy that Xerxes had scarcely seen him. He deserved a break—and Xerxes needed one too. An hour or two in her calming company, yet still near Kasia.

"Zethar, fetch Haman and let the general know I will talk to him tomorrow instead of this afternoon."

Zethar sped away, and Xerxes stood, stepped down. He offered his arm to Esther and smiled when she tucked her slender fingers into his elbow. "I must apologize."

She smiled up at him. "There is no need. I understand that you want time alone with her."

Yes, she always understood. Was there a sweeter, more serene woman in all the kingdom? He had never met one. "Still, I should have sought you out. Artaxerxes wishes to winter with us next year."

"I would love to have him, you know that. Amani would love it too—she adores him."

He nodded, then searched his mind for another topic. Only one presented itself, but what could they say about Kasia? He contented himself with basking in Esther's soothing silence. Smiled when he saw the beautiful table she had set up in the outer chamber of her rooms.

Haman arrived a minute behind them, and they all took their seats. His friend beamed with pleasure—had he ever been invited to one of Esther's banquets before? He did not think so.

Well, then, let him enjoy it for a while. Xerxes did his best to keep his smile in place as servants brought out the first course and filled their cups. But with each degree the sun sank, he had to fend off the urge to end the meal and go check on Kasia.

When his first cup of wine sat empty, he gave in and turned to Esther. "What is your request, my queen? It shall be granted to you, whatever it is."

Esther met his gaze, searched his eyes for a moment. "You are eager to see Kasia. If it pleases you to grant my petition, come with Haman to another banquet tomorrow, and I will present it to you."

Xerxes smiled. "We will be here." And he would be sure to visit Kasia first, so that he might better give Esther his attention.

Haman nearly danced his way out of the gate—until he found himself face to face with that insubordinate Jew, Mordecai. He stood in the middle of the street, arms wide and face toward the heavens. What in the world was he doing? Haman stepped forward. "Out of the way, swine."

The Jew's arms lowered, as did his face. But his expression was pure defiance. "You have done your best to remove us permanently, have you not? It will not be as easy for you as you think."

Haman smirked as his guards took a menacing step toward the wretch. "It will be even easier. Now that your precious friend is lying on her deathbed, the king cares for nothing else. Get used to the feel of my heel, swine—it will crush you until you die in a few short months."

"Kasia is in Jehovah's hand—and I have no fear of your heel." The swine stepped to the side and gave him a mocking smile. "You may want to watch your step, though. It is a rickety bridge you attempt to build your empire on."

Haman stormed past and forced himself to remember all that went well. When he entered his house, he greeted his wife with a kiss.

Zeresh pushed him away, but amusement sparked in her eyes. "What has gotten into you? And where have you been? You send word to gather everyone together, then do not show up for more than an hour."

He pulled her into the hall and grinned when he saw all his sons and their families, his daughters and their husbands. His neighbors, his friends. Rickety—never. "The god has blessed me beyond measure, my friends. This evening I dined with the king and queen. No one else, just the three of us. And I am invited again tomorrow."

They gushed, they congratulated, Zeresh even slid an arm around his waist. But his smile would not hold. "Still, when I see the arrogance of the swine—when I left the palace that Jew was in the gate, mocking me."

Zeresh shook her head and patted his stomach. "What is that to you? Soon enough his whole people will be killed."

"Not soon enough. Not for him."

"Then let a gallows be made." His eldest son lifted his cup of wine, a hateful smile curling his lips. "You are second only to the king—ask him in the morning to put the man to death for the grief he has caused you, then go merrily with him to the banquet."

Did he dare? The king had always liked Mordecai. But then, he need not name him. He would define him by his actions, just as he had done before.

Yes, he would do it. At first light, he would put it to the king. Then he would watch the first of his enemies die.

He spun to his eunuchs. "Do as my son suggests. Build a gallows, fifty cubits high."

His friends cheered him as the servants left to do his bidding.

Forty-Nine

Would he ever sleep again? Really sleep, without jerking awake in a panic? Xerxes had his doubts. For the third night in a row he gave up while the moon stood at its highest point in the heavens and dragged himself to his table.

History. Nothing would tire a man like the chronicles. He had Zethar bring it over.

"Here you are, master."

"Thank you." He unsealed the scroll and nudged it so it would unroll to whatever spot it willed.

Six years ago, when he returned from the war. He read through it, barely seeing the cuneiform script.

Still he did not think he could sleep.

Five years ago. Esther's first year with him, and when Kasia had Artarius. Mardonius's army had just returned, emaciated and near-starving. His hands had been full with so many things tied to that. Then—what was this? He frowned and reread. The assassination plot, the doorkeepers. They had verified the truth of it, had them put to death. But no other notes finished the story. "Zethar, what honor was given Mordecai for this?"

Zethar glanced down, read the spot on the parchment that he indicated. "Nothing, master."

"Nothing?"

His eunuch's lips twitched up. "It was the same day you learned Kasia carried Artarius, master. You were . . . distracted."

He grunted and glanced toward the window. Nearly dawn. "Is anyone in the court yet?"

Zethar jogged out, returned a moment later. "Haman just arrived, master."

Perfect. "Call him in."

When his friend entered, Xerxes smiled. Haman would have excellent advice on this matter. "What shall be done for the man I would delight to honor?"

Haman's brows lifted in thought for a moment, then he grinned. "For such a man, a royal robe ought to be brought which the king himself has worn, and it ought to be put on the man's shoulders. Then he ought to sit upon one of the king's own horses, a royal crest upon its head, and the reins should be given to one of the king's most noble princes, that he may lead this man through the city and proclaim before him, 'Thus shall it be done to the man whom the king delights to honor!'"

Well, Haman certainly lacked no imagination. "Let it be done for Mordecai the Jew, exactly as you said. And you yourself should guide him, since I hold you in higher esteem than any of my sons."

Haman's face froze. "The Jew."

"I know you are not fond of his people, but I never rewarded him for saving my life five years ago. See to it immediately, Haman. I would start the day without this unpaid deed over my head." Feeling a bit of energy for the first time in days, Xerxes stood and turned toward his bedchamber.

While it was done, he would visit Kasia. Perhaps, if Jehovah saw him honoring one of his chosen, he would show some mercy.

Haman shook as he plodded to his home. His family and friends were still gathered, most dozing on their couches after the night of feasting. His servants returned even now from the gallows they had built overnight.

He felt diseased. Three hours he had trudged through the city, each word of praise forced from his tongue tasting of wormwood.

How could the king make him do that? For the Jew, of all people? Walk the streets with that swine lording over him, mocking in his silence?

And the people—most had cheered, some had looked confused when they realized he was honoring a man whose death he had so recently ordained. Turmoil would ensue. Probably reach the palace.

Then the king would realize what he had done. Inevitable, yes, but he had hoped the witch would die first, so that Haman could use it to point to the power of Ahura Mazda, the inferiority of her God.

Now what was he to do? His original plan to kill her would not work now, with her confined to her bed under guard constantly.

Where was the god? Where was his might, his power? Why did he not fill him now, as he had in Sardis all those years ago?

"My husband, what is wrong?"

Haman shook his head and walked past Zeresh. "The king just honored Mordecai the Jew—by my hand."

Zeresh sucked in a breath. "Why would he do that, when they are all to be killed in a few short months?"

He covered his head, wished he had the luxury to weep. "He does not know. I told him there were troublemakers, but I did not tell him who."

"Haman." His wife hissed, then took a step away from him. "You are crumbling before this Jew, and it will not stop until he towers over you. Worse, you will drag your family down with you. What have you brought on our heads?"

Before he could answer, the king's eunuchs entered. Bowed. "The queen requests your presence at her banquet now, my lord."

Ahura Mazda, where are you?

Esther expected her hand to shake. Jehovah steadied her. She expected nerves to sour her stomach. She ate and drank without problem. She expected her tongue to twist when her husband looked over at her and asked, "What is this petition of yours, Esther? It shall be granted to you, up to half my kingdom."

Peace infused her, and she could look from Haman to the king without a qualm. Perhaps her life would be forfeit, but her people would be saved. She knew that. When he realized what Haman had done, he would find a path of mercy for the Jews. He would do it for Kasia's sake, for her family and friends.

As for Esther . . . who knew how angry he may be to learn she had lied to him all this time? He would spare her people, but the price could very well be her head.

She drew in a calm breath and set her cup upon the table. "If I have found favor in your sight—if it pleases you, my king—then I ask for my life."

Xerxes frowned and set his cup down with a splash. "Your life is in no danger."

"On the contrary, my husband, my life and the lives of all my people have been sold for destruction. Had we been sold as slaves, I would not speak, though the enemy never would have been able to compensate for the loss it would mean for you. But the wicked man who did this would have us all killed. Man, woman, even our children."

His frown deepened. "What enemy? Who?" He sat up straight, that infamous temper kindling in his eyes. "Who would dare devise such a thing?"

She had always retreated in the face of his anger, left Kasia to handle it. But tonight it brought strength to her spine. She whispered a mental prayer, inclined her heart to Jehovah.

The lights grew brighter, the shadows darkened. Esther nearly gasped. Was this what Kasia had told her about? The clear presence of the Lord, and the enemies held at bay? Was that warmth at the base of her neck the touch of an angel? And the emptiness that tried to suck the life from the room, that seemed to crouch behind Haman, was that what her friend had to battle every time she looked at him?

The Spirit settled over her. The breath she drew in expanded her lungs, her shoulders seemed to grow and harden. And the man before her shrank into a shriveling shadow.

"Him." She held her arm out straight, level with Haman. Though it trembled a little, she felt no fear. No, only indignation, and fierce determination. "The adversary and enemy is Haman."

Haman sprang to his feet, face devoid of color. "My queen, I do not know what you mean. Your people—I do not even know who your people are."

Letting her arm lower, she raised her chin. "Perhaps you ought to have inquired before you sent out a proclamation of death against all the Jews."

"You are a Jewess?" Panic and disgust did battle across his countenance. The panic won. "Please, my queen. My king. I did not know. I did not—"

"Silence!" Xerxes surged to his feet, knocking over the table before him. "How dare you use my authority for such a grotesque task? After I trusted you with my kingdom, after I called you brother? I could . . . ."

He clenched a fist, took a step. But when Haman cowered, Xerxes only spat a curse and charged through the door to the gardens.

Haman fell to his knees, weeping. "Please, my queen. Please, spare my life. Spare my family."

The darkness came off him in waves, a foul odor in her nostrils. How could anyone embrace it as he had? How could he not see that it did not fill him but rather left him a hollow shell? "You would have spared none of mine."

"Please!" He crawled over to her, gripped her feet in supplication.

She fought the urge to recoil, to kick at him. His touch may be despicable, but it was only that of a defeated man.

The darkness could not reach her.

Xerxes sent an urn of flowers into the fountain and gripped his hair at the roots. Haman. What had that devil done? What had Xerxes allowed him to do? He would really sell the Jews to their deaths? All of them?

Why? Why did he hate them so? Yes, he was an Agagite. Yes, centuries ago the Jews had all but destroyed his people. What did that have to do with *now*, with the people who made Susa flourish, who had prayed them through war and disaster?

What did that have to do with his wife—his wives, apparently—and their families?

He seethed to a halt at the bolt of realization. Haman had always disliked the Jews, but it had been of little import before he wed Kasia and took an interest in them for her sake. He had watered the seed of hatred as he poured favor upon her and hers.

He should have paid attention. Should have realized it was not merely disdain. Why had he not listened to Kasia's grumbles about that?

Because he had been guilty—guilty of killing Masistes, Haman's closest friend.

It was his own fault. He had brought this upon them. And now he would have to figure out a way to save the Jews. To save Kasia, if she lived long enough to be saved.

And Esther.

He turned, stared at the window to her rooms. He still needed a few answers from Esther.

He strode back through the gardens, back into her banquet, then came to a halt when he saw Haman across her lap and horror on her face. Familiar red tinged his vision. "Will he also assault the queen?"

Haman jolted up, tear-streaked and shattered. Terror consumed his countenance—and well it should. Xerxes charged across the chamber and plowed a fist into his face, satisfied when the beast sprawled on the floor.

One of Esther's eunuchs stepped forward with a smirk. He pointed to the window that overlooked Susa. "Look, master. Even now in Haman's house are gallows, fifty cubits high—he had them built for Mordecai."

He stared at the man he had called brother. Nothing but reviling filled him. He leaned down long enough to rip his signet from the wretch's finger. "Hang him on it."

The servants smiled as they grabbed him and dragged him screaming from the room.

When the racket died down, Xerxes turned to Esther. "And you. How can you call yourself my wife, my queen, yet hide who you are from me?"

She folded her hands peacefully in her lap, as if nothing in the world could disturb her. And blast it if that peace did not try to curl into him too, to soothe the ragged edges of his soul.

He pushed it away and folded his arms across his chest.

Esther drew in an easy breath. "Had my heritage been known, I would not *be* your wife and queen."

"You wanted the crown so badly that you lied to get it? You, who I always thought above such ambitions?"

Hurt flashed in her eyes, but the calm smothered it. "It had nothing to do with ambition, only with obeying the will of Jehovah. Do you think he did not know all along it would come to this? Haman would have executed his plan regardless of who your queen was. If it were not me, who then would have spoken to you?"

He spun away, plunged a hand into his hair. Her questions did not bear considering—the answers were all too apparent. Had Esther not spoken, he would have remained in his cloud of oblivion until the guard arrived to hack Kasia to pieces.

He shuddered and faced her again. "Even so. You could have told me at some point, after you were queen."

Her lips curved up. "My husband, if I were going to risk your wrath, it was going to be for a purpose."

He opened his mouth to rebut that, but movement in his periphery captured his attention. He turned—and his words died on his lips.

Kasia gripped the post of the door. "If you are going to be angry, my love, be angry with *me*. I am as guilty of this deception as Esther is."

Xerxes could only stare.

Kasia willed strength into her stiff limbs and motioned her servants to stay back. If she must face her husband on this, she would not do it leaning on Desma or Theron. Jehovah would be support enough.

The screams had jarred her from her stupor, screams she knew well—Haman's. The same screams that had sounded before the mountainside rushed at her in Sardis. And as they rent the air, the gentle shackles holding her down released.

She had all but flown here on her unsteady legs.

"Kasia." Xerxes breathed it as if uncertain of what his eyes beheld.

Unable to ignore the desperation in his voice, she took a step inside. Her knees protested, and she wobbled. In the next moment, her husband's arms were around her.

"My love." His voice shook, as did the hand that stroked her hair. "I feared you would never wake again."

"As did I, at first. But it was the work of Jehovah, Xerxes. He held me protected in his embrace to spare me Haman's scheme."

He shuddered and pulled her closer still. "To think I could have lost you to one of my own decrees . . . ."

She tilted her face to him for the brief, intense brush of his lips. "Jehovah had a plan in place." She pulled away enough to look past him, to where Esther had taken to her feet. "I am proud of you, my sister."

Esther inclined her head. Humble, even in perfect confidence. "I did only what you would have done."

"You did what I could not. Had the Lord not held me immobile, Haman would have killed me and blamed it on the Jews to rouse the king's anger against them."

Xerxes stiffened. "Impossible."

"He confessed it to me, that first day. I could hear, even if I could not respond. You have proven before how far you will go to avenge me." She searched his gaze, praying he would finally believe her. "And he tried before. In Sardis. He is the one who pushed me from that wall, I am sure of it."

"I have no reason to doubt you now." He sighed and led her over to Esther's couch. "Sit before you fall."

She obliged. When Esther sat beside her, she gripped her friend's hand.

Xerxes eyed them warily. "So then. You knew all along she was a Jew."

Esther smiled. "We were neighbors. Best of friends."

"She was told I was dead. Neither of us knew what became of the other until she arrived here."

Each muscle of Xerxes' face hardened. "And instead of letting me rejoice with you over reuniting with this dearest friend, you shut me out. You lied to me, both of you."

Esther's fingers squeezed hers. Kasia drew in a long breath. "Yes. We did."

He leveled an accusing finger at her. "You—you swore you would never play at intrigue. But you manipulated me for your own purposes."

A dozen defenses sprang to her tongue—that he had told her to pick the next queen, and she had chosen wisely. That he had done far worse to her, and she had forgiven him. Every time, she had forgiven him.

But if he were to forgive her, it could not be because he owed it to her.

She bit back all but one truth. "Not for my own purposes, my love. For the Lord's."

"She only went along with what Mordecai and I decided." Esther squared her shoulders and intercepted their husband's gaze. Quiet strength pulsed from her.

Xerxes frowned. "What does Mordecai have to do with this?"

"He is my cousin—my guardian."

He turned his back on them, mumbling something Kasia could not make out as he paced the length of the room. When he stomped back, his face was set in a rare emotionless mask. "And you will not even apologize?"

Esther lifted her chin. "I am sorry, my husband. Sorry this was necessary. Sorry I had to deceive you to assure the safety of my people. Sorry if it hurt you."

"But not sorry you did it." He turned his gaze on Kasia. "And you?"

Tears stung her eyes. "You have known all along I will obey Jehovah above you—even when that comes between us. But I hope you will forgive me. And Esther, especially—she made the decision before she knew you. I am the one who did it knowing full well how it would hurt you."

He blinked rapidly, drew in a hard breath.

"Master," Zethar said from the doorway, "Mordecai the Jew is here. Shall I show him in?"

Xerxes muttered a mild oath. "Why not? It seems he played quite a role in this as well."

A second later, Mordecai entered. "I saw them drag Haman toward the gallows he—Kasia. You are well." Relief saturated his tone, but no surprise.

She offered a tight smile. "I imagine you prayed for me, as you always do. Thank you."

Her husband's jaw ticked. "You are more concerned for her health than whether your *daughter* has been forgiven? It begs a question I have done my best to ignore all these years—why it is always our friend Mordecai that Jehovah asks to pray for Kasia?"

Kasia drew in a deep breath.

Mordecai smiled. Whatever his answer, he seemed at peace with it. "Perhaps because I love her. Or perhaps I love her so that I could pray her through these years with dedication. Either way, there is no need to be jealous—Jehovah also ordained that she be yours. I never held her heart."

"It is true." Esther grinned and patted Kasia's hand. "From the moment we first saw you at the river, you were the only one she loved."

Xerxes' eyes went wide. "*We?* You were the one with her?" He hissed out a breath and folded his arms again. "It seems the bunch of you are one tightly knit lot. Bound together against me."

"Not against you." Kasia stood, silently praising the Lord when her legs carried her to him without argument. "We were bound together *for* you, my love, to strengthen you." She reached out and laced her fingers through his. "Still. Punish me if you must."

He held her gaze for a long moment—so much passed between them, hard times and perfect moments both. All the pain, all the betrayal. All the faith and love. His face softened as he lifted her hand to his lips. "You know I cannot. I might as well rip my own heart out."

Adoration sang through her at the feel of his mouth on her fingers. "Then I ask you again to choose to forgive me. To forgive us."

He gazed long into her eyes, and then turned his face to Esther. He motioned toward his servants. "Let it be written that on this day, the king gives the house of Haman over to Queen Esther."

Esther blinked back tears. "Thank you. I will put my cousin in charge of it. But . . . it is not enough."

Xerxes lifted a brow. "Not enough? Will you finally ask for a city to go along with it?"

Instead of seizing the jest, Esther fell to her knees at his feet. Tears streamed onto her cheeks. "Hanging Haman, giving me his belongings will not undo the damage he has done. He sealed the decree against my people with your signet. Please—please, find a way to undo the evil he devised."

Kasia's gaze fell onto the scepter sitting on the table beside her. She picked it up and handed it to Xerxes.

A decision that would save a nation called for ceremony.

He gave her a lopsided smile in exchange for the length of gold and held it out above Esther. "Rise, my queen."

She stood and wiped the moisture from her eyes. "If it pleases you, let a new law be written to counteract the letter of Haman. Otherwise, forgiving me means nothing."

Xerxes nodded and glanced over his shoulder. "Mordecai. Come forward."

Kasia turned to watch her old friend obey his king.

What could he intend? Mordecai pushed the question, the doubt from his mind and moved to stand beside Esther. The king had forgiven her deception—as for whether he had forgiven the fact that Mordecai loved his favorite wife . . . .

He did not look angry as he slid an arm around Kasia, though. Satisfied and determined, but no longer angry.

Mordecai drew in a long breath and bowed his head. "Your humble servant, my lord."

"Yes, I know. For years you have sat faithfully in the gates to hear the complaints of your people for me. For years, you have prayed for me, for my empire, for my family. Your daughter is right. The house of Haman is not sufficient." The king tugged something from his finger. He offered it in an outstretched palm.

Mordecai stared at the signet. "My lord?"

"Write the decree, Mordecai, concerning the Jews. Sign it in my name and seal it with my ring."

Was he serious? Mordecai studied Xerxes' familiar face, Kasia's smile, Esther's shoulders, straight and strong under the burden of their people.

When the Lord asked him to represent the Jews, to take in his uncle's child, to open his eyes to his neighbor's daughter, he had never expected it would lead him here.

But Jehovah had known.

He reached out and slowly took the ring. "I will use the authority you give me wisely, my king. We shall send out a decree that the Jews are permitted to protect themselves against their enemies on the day intended for destruction. When the people realize the king is on our side, few will dare stand against us. And those who do will have to face Zechariah and his men. I do not envy them that."

"Nor do I. Let it be so." Xerxes angled a smile to Kasia. "And now that we have the pressing business resolved, I suspect someone would like to meet her newest daughter."

Kasia grinned. "Yes, my arms yearn for her."

They moved toward the door together, and Mordecai slid an arm around Esther's shoulders. "I am so proud of you, my daughter. When we needed you, you stood tall for the Lord."

"Only by his strength." She loosed a sigh. "I still cannot believe it came to this. But Jehovah knew it would. It is certainly a good thing you did not let me marry Zech."

"Zech?" The king halted in the doorway and spun around. "*You* were the one . . . I offered to have *myself* killed for him?"

With a bright laugh, Kasia tugged him from the room.

Mordecai kissed the side of Esther's head. "You will be remembered for this. Our people will sing songs in your honor for centuries to come. Your bravery preserved our entire nation."

Esther shook her head and moved toward the side door that he knew connected to the nursery. She would want to check on Amani after all this. "I do not care about being remembered. Only that there will be a people left to do the remembering."

He could think of only one thing to say to that. "Amen."

EPILOGUE

The thirteenth day of the twelfth month of the twelfth year of the reign of Xerxes

Zechariah gripped his spear in one hand, his sword in the other. The straps of his shield encircled his forearm, and the breastplate hung sure and straight over his torso.

He planted his feet and waited for morning to spill over the horizon.

Bijan took position on his right. "Adam's group is ready along the southern wall. The city is covered. If they dare come out, they will be slain."

"They will come. Not many, but some. There have always been those who hate us."

His friend snorted a laugh. "I have learned that for myself."

"I know." He glanced behind him to check his ranks. Hundreds of his friends and relatives stood in position, ready to fight for their lives, for their families. "If we die today, Bijan, know you are my brother by more than marriage."

"We will not die." His words were easy, certain. "If Jehovah protected me against the Spartans, he will have no trouble with these lazy Persians. Besides—you promised Ruana you would be there for the birth of your babe this time."

His lips pulled up. She had not let him leave the house until he swore it, his hand upon her rounded abdomen. "And I am a man of my word. I trust you made similar promises to Eglah."

"Demanding woman." Bijan grinned and looked out over the city. "I am proud to be one of you. Proud so many of my friends have decided to convert as well."

"The truth makes itself known." Zechariah turned his gaze toward the bowl of golden light rising above the bronze earth. Then a few degrees off, to the walls of the palace. "They are watching. I feel their prayers."

"As do I."

The first arrow of sunlight crested the hill, and Zechariah raised his sword to send it on.

Kasia drew in a breath when the slice of golden light reflected off her brother's sword by the river. The day had come. There he stood, his army of would-be Immortals behind him. So many. So many had come to him these eleven months to learn.

Their enemies did not stand a chance. Not against spirits such as her people had. People who fought for a Law the world could not understand.

Xerxes slid an arm around her waist. "All the other armies in the other cities should be ready too. Pythius's sons will lead the efforts in Sardis."

"The Lord is with us. Can you feel him, my love?"

He breathed a laugh into her ear. "Have you still not given up on converting me?"

"Never."

"Ahura Mazda swore he would destroy me through my wives, that he would take you from me. Jehovah prevailed, as I knew he would. Prevails still." He kissed her cheek. "Yes, I feel him. I trust him. The king of Persia can never be a Jew—but you know I love the living God."

"Ima, she is getting heavy."

Kasia smiled down at Zillah and took Leah from her arms. The boys chased each other around the wall, and she bit back a rebuke. Let them run. Let them laugh. There would be fighting enough today.

Esther glided their way, Amani gripping a hand and Artaxerxes at her side. The boy stuck close to her. Ten years with Amestris had made him wary of Kasia, but he loved Esther. Even now, when the world knew of her heritage.

But when Darius and Artaynte took their place beside Xerxes, Artaxerxes turned his face away from them.

Some hurts, some wrongs were still unforgiven. Even in the heart of a boy who could not remember them, who only heard of them from his mother's lips.

Xerxes tensed, shifted. "The city is waking. People are coming out of their homes."

"Perhaps they are only going to the markets," Zillah murmured.

"No one will go to the markets today, my sweet." Her father rested a hand on her shoulder. "If people leave their homes, it is in search of violence."

"I did not think any would dare." Esther sighed. "Come, children. I will take you all inside. We will pray."

Artaxerxes stepped forward instead of back, his eyes trained on the shadows slinking through the streets, toward the Jewish section of the city. "Why do they do it, when they know the consequences?"

"Hatred fuels many a bad decision, my son. Remember that."

The boy shook his head at his father's words. "Do you not worry the Jews will be hurt?"

"No," Kasia said, smiling when he met her gaze. She shifted Leah on her hip and nodded toward the river.

Morning light bathed her brother's army in promise while the enemy crept through darkness. "Our salvation is at hand."

Author's Note

Nothing inspires me like history—but in the past, actual historical events have only played limited (if crucial) roles in my novels. In *Jewel of Persia*, nearly every major plot point revolved around a recorded event. The dreams Xerxes had of his god, the deposing of Amestris (Vashti), the day of darkness at Sardis, the battles of Thermopylae and Salamis, the ill-fated affair between Xerxes and Artaynte and its consequences, and of course the events in the book of Esther. All these things are described either in the Bible or Herodotus's *Histories*. Kasia is my own creation, along with the rest of her family and servants. Most other characters come from history.

There's some debate among scholars whether Xerxes I is really the king mentioned in the book of Esther—primarily because Amestris reigned as queen mother during Artaxerxes' rule. Most read the book of Esther as saying Vashti was put to death, and therefore assume she couldn't have been Amestris. But Esther only says she was deposed and thrust from the king's presence, and when you put the time lines of Esther and Herodotus together, things click into place beautifully. I feel mine is a safe way to read the biblical account.

Some will be surprised that I took a book of the Bible that never once mentions God and created a story of vivid spirituality. I didn't really plan to, but that was how it came to me as I debated how to integrate the odd events the Persians experienced during the war. Most of my spiritual references were taken from the book of Daniel, which would have taken place about 60-100 years before Esther, in another city of the same empire. That Mordecai was a descendent of one of the three thrown into the fiery furnace is a product of my imagination.

Xerxes I, a man of passion and temper who was loved like a god by his people, was assassinated in the twentieth year of his reign, eight years after the events of Esther, in 465 B.C. He was 54 years old. The killer was the head of the palace guards, but it's said that the conspiracy originated in the harem. I read that as "it was all Amestris's idea." Not shocking—history paints her as a cruel, power-hungry woman. What *was* shocking was when I realized it was the youngest of her sons who took the crown. Figuring out why she would cast her loyalty with her youngest son instead of her eldest provided me with much of my characterization.

Artaxerxes I was around 17 when he became king, and he's credited with killing his two older brothers. I find it interesting to note that most of the information we have on him is in the Bible, when he helped the Jews rebuild the walls of Jerusalem. Who's to say he wasn't softened toward them because of his affection for a certain Jewish queen that would have ruled when he was a boy?

I hope you enjoyed seeing some of the most beloved, familiar events of the Bible woven into obscure, oft-forgotten history brought to us by the Ancient Greeks. I had so much fun putting the stories together.

For more information on the history, characters, and just some fun facts I came across, please visit my website at www.RoseannaMWhite.com.

Discussion Questions

1.) Kasia's chance encounter at the beginning of the book leaves her with what Esther calls "a romantic story." How would you have reacted if in that romantic story? Have you ever had an "at first sight" moment, whether it be love, infatuation, or instant connection with a friend?

2.) Have you ever paused to consider what Esther would have been like as a girl? Did anything about this fictional approach to her surprise you?

3.) Is Mordecai what you expected him to be?

4.) Do you like Xerxes? Why or why not?

5.) What would you do if you found yourself part of harem life?

6.) Prayer plays a crucial part in the lives of Kasia and Mordecai. Have you ever seen the Lord respond to prayer like they did?

7.) Is Amestris justified in her response to Kasia and the situation with the torc?

8.) Is there a special object that has great meaning to you and your spouse? Or perhaps an heirloom in your family with a story attached?

9.) Kasia's headstrong outspokenness is both a blessing and a curse. What character trait do you have that leads you both into trouble and out of it?

10.) Do bursts of temper and passion amuse you or appall you?

11.) If you were Xerxes, how would you have reacted to the events during the Day of Darkness in Sardis?

12.) Which deity the characters put their faith in plays a big role in how they interpret the events that transpire. Do you believe things like this can still happen today? And if they did, would you attribute them to God or another power?

13.) As part of the New Testament church, we have certain views and understandings of the Holy Spirit. How did this portrayal of the Old Testament Spirit challenge or line up with your beliefs?

14.) Have you ever chosen not to pray for someone? What happened?

15.) Zechariah makes a series of poor decisions that nevertheless play into the plan of God. How has the Lord turned your mistakes into victories for His cause?

16.) Is your faith stronger when all is going well, or when the storms are raging around you?

17.) The affair that rips apart the royal family is a documented fact of Persian history, though the motivation is fictional. Why do you think Xerxes would have done such a thing? How far-reaching do you think the consequences would have been?

18.) How has Esther grown throughout the book? By the time she joins the harem, is she the Esther you expect from the Bible? Does she grow more while there?

19.) Kasia makes a decision to forgive for the sakes of Esther and Xerxes. Could you have done the same in that situation?

20.) Though before the time of Christ, salvation plays a key role in the theme of this book. How do the ideas of it differ from or strengthen the New Testament realization of salvation?

CPSIA information can be obtained at www.ICGtesting.com
Printed in the USA
LVOW11s0245300615

444378LV00002B/198/P